W9-CXN-409

"Golden Fire is a sensational reading experience from a new author destined to be a bestseller."

—Virginia Henley

Susan Grace dishes up a passionate and suspenseful historical adventure, a magical story tinted with the true colors of exotic India and England.

—*Romantic Times*

A TOUCH OF FIRE

Randy's eyes filled with tears at James's jibe. She turned away from him, but not before he saw how badly his words had affected her. In two quick strides, he pulled her into his arms.

"Why is it that I'm always apologizing to you?" He held her close and sighed. "Forgive me for frightening you to the point of tears, Randy. I only wanted you to be aware of what could happen if you aren't careful."

Randy pressed her face against his shoulder, enjoying for a moment the comfort of his embrace. How could she tell him that the only thing she feared was his learning about her empathic ability? If she earned his disdain because he doubted her talent, it could destroy her more surely than any assassin. She had to get away from him for a while so she could think.

James was surprised when she suddenly pulled away from him. She wasn't crying. Her mouth bowed in a small smile.

"I appreciate your concern, Captain, and in the future I won't take any unnecessary risks, I promise." Standing on tiptoe, she placed a quick kiss on his lips.

"What was that?" James asked, grabbing her arms before she could escape.

"That was a kiss to seal my promise."

"No, Randy. That wasn't a kiss. This is. . . ."

BOOK YOUR PLACE ON OUR WEBSITE AND MAKE THE READING CONNECTION!

We've created a customized website just for our very special readers, where you can get the inside scoop on everything that's going on with Zebra, Pinnacle and Kensington books.

When you come online, you'll have the exciting opportunity to:

- View covers of upcoming books
- Read sample chapters
- Learn about our future publishing schedule (listed by publication month *and author*)
- Find out when your favorite authors will be visiting a city near you
- Search for and order backlist books from our online catalog
- Check out author bios and background information
- Send e-mail to your favorite authors
- Meet the Kensington staff online
- Join us in weekly chats with authors, readers and other guests
- Get writing guidelines
- AND MUCH MORE!

**Visit our website at
http://www.zebrabooks.com**

GOLDEN FIRE

Susan Grace

Zebra Books
Kensington Publishing Corp.

http://www.zebrabooks.com

ZEBRA BOOKS are published by

Kensington Publishing Corp.
850 Third Avenue
New York, NY 10022

First Printing: October, 1999
10 9 8 7 6 5 4 3 2 1

Printed in the United States of America

I dedicate this book to those who helped me achieve my dream:

To my moms, Lois, who supported my decision to follow my muse, and to Emma, who never doubted for a moment I would succeed. To my daughter, Suzanne, who took an active role in helping my writing career and kept up with me, and to my son, John, who knew when I needed a hug.

To "Hearts of Palm," the best critique group in the world. Thanks to Linda, Anna Mae, Bob, and Judi my work was polished to near perfection.

To my literary soul sisters, Bertrice Small, Virginia Henley, Marilyn Campbell, and Kathryn Falk, who didn't let me give up and told me I was going to "do it." Even though it took me nine years to become an overnight success.

To Karen Thomas, who fell in love with Sidra and gave me a chance.

And to the real hero in my life, John H. Koski—the best friend, lover, and husband a woman could ever have, the man who taught me about romance and gave me the confidence to be all that I can be.

Prologue

Calicut, India
September 5, 1831

The scent of danger hung heavily in the air. Not even the cloying fragrance of jasmine, drifting through the open windows, could mask its foul stench. Rising from her sleeping pallet, Sidra sensed the impending threat and knew that she would do whatever was necessary to protect her mistress.

On the bed, surrounded by netting, her beautiful lady was sound asleep. Her long auburn hair, released from its plait, lay loose against the pillow. Clutching her blanket like a child, she slept unaware of the menacing evil that had invaded her home.

Sidra, the vigilant guardian, crossed the room and crouched beside the door. Ever alert to the sounds of the night, she knew that the silence was too perfect, too unbroken. She waited for the intruder to appear.

The door quietly opened. A tall, robed man passed over the threshold, approached the bed, and pushed the net curtains aside. He held a knotted scarf toward his intended victim, meaning to capture her throat in its deadly silken embrace. He wasn't aware of the sentry at his back.

Sidra pounced on the would-be assassin and grabbed his arm. Biting his hand as they struggled, she dragged him from the bed. A howl erupted from the villain's lips. Splayed across his chest, she held him to the floor and clawed his face.

Startled by the man's screams, the girl awoke. "Sidra, what's happening?"

Sidra withdrew from the man, but not before ripping the tattered scarf from his hand. The man scurried to his feet and fled through the open window. Picking up the scarf, Sidra placed it on the blanket beside her mistress.

The commotion the intruder had caused brought the servants rushing into the room. The household steward, Abu Nazir, carrying a pistol and a lantern, issued orders to the staff.

"Sanjay, take three men and scour the grounds. Jai, wake Sahib Collins and ask him to come here. Mahmud and the rest of you, search the house."

With his black hair askew and his gaze dark with concern, Abu reverently bowed to his young mistress. "A thousand pardons, Missy Collins. I should have anticipated an attack such as this. Are you injured, Memsahib?"

"I am fine, Abu. Sidra protected me and took this from that man."

Abu held the lantern over the bed to view the length of stained white fabric that she picked up from the bed. A pale object dropped from within its knotted folds. Recognizing what it was, the girl screamed.

A man's small finger lay upon her lap, ragged and bloody.

Sidra looked proudly at her trophy and knew that someday she would destroy the rest of this man as well. No one would ever harm her charge. Contented and pleased with herself, she sat silently beside her mistress.

The frightened girl gazed into Sidra's clear amber eyes. "Thank you for saving me, Sidra. No one has a better friend or protector than I."

Sidra looked at Abu with an air of smug satisfaction. A smile seemed to curve the corners of her wide mouth.

Abu scratched his pointed beard and shook his head. "It is not possible. Tigers do not smile."

Twitching her tail, Sidra turned from him and caught sight of blood on her front paws. As her large, rough tongue washed the stains from the orange fur, she thought to herself, *I will not forget . . .*

Chapter 1

A pair of richly garbed riders galloped across the green valley into a grove thick with trees. One rode a silvery gray stallion, while the other had a mount the color of a starless night. Their escort of a dozen imperial guards armed with razor-honed scimitars and jezails tried to keep up with their rigorous pace, but failed miserably. Veiled by the forest, the smaller of the two riders looked back and laughed.

"See, Akbar! I told you it would be easy to lose them. Follow me to Mirror Lake and we'll rest until they find us."

"Randy, this is crazy. The guards are for our protection. Why can't you accept that fact and stop playing games?"

"No! I've been shut up in my house for a month and I won't give up my freedom just yet. Come, my brother, or they shall be upon us too quickly."

Akbar shrugged and continued to follow the path through the trees. "I am a crown prince, playing games of children. If word gets back to my *zenana* of this, Randy, I will never be able to face my women again."

His companion's turbaned head bobbed with laughter. "Then

wear a veil, my brother, for I don't think the ladies of your harem would miss your handsome face as much as they would miss your other fine attributes.''

"Randy, someday I am going to grab you and—''

"But you'll have to catch me first!''

Akbar accepted the challenge and raced to their destination. Arriving at the lake's edge first, he dismounted his gray steed and rushed to carry out his threat. In the blink of an eye, Akbar had captured his companion around the waist. His strong fingers began to tickle the slim waist beneath his grasp. Even through the thickness of the linen tunic and trousers, his victim couldn't evade his teasing grip.

"I yield, Akbar! Cease torturing me so I may apologize.''

The *Rajkumar* smiled triumphantly and lowered his opponent beside him. Before Akbar could step away, his former prey hooked a foot behind his knee and sent him crashing to the ground. Yet the prince was undaunted. With a flick of his wrist, he pulled his friend down and the two of them wrestled like children, staining their white trousers on the grass. Within moments, Akbar, the larger and more muscular of the pair, had his companion imprisoned under him.

"You are quite good at fighting, *chhota behin,* but you forget we shared the same teacher. Nazir taught me every move you know, so you cannot defeat me,'' Akbar boasted. Suddenly, warm sensual feelings stirred in his body. Gone were the laughter and smiles; a need for fulfillment now ruled his actions. His lips dipped down to claim a kiss from his captive's unsuspecting mouth. A second later, he jerked back in pain.

"How dare you, Akbar! You call me your *little sister* and then you try to seduce me. Let me up this instant or I'll do far more damage than biting your lip!''

Randy pushed Akbar aside and smacked at his offending hands. In the midst of the tussle, the white turban that had hidden her hair came off. Her auburn braid swayed against the back of her tunic as she turned to confront him.

"Randy, please listen to me. I meant no disrespect. You

have always been my *chhota behin,* but now I want much more than that. Do not judge me harshly for falling in love with you, my *nagina.*''

When Akbar tried to kiss her again, Randy's arm shot out to stop him. With the heel of her hand, she caught the sensitive cartilage under his nose. The painful effect was instantaneous, causing the over-amorous prince to roll away from her. Freed at last, Randy stood up and glared down at him.

"Your *nagina?* Your jewel? I can't believe you would call me that! You might be able to sweet-talk the ladies of your *zenana* in this fashion, but never me, old friend. Never me!''

Seeing the anger in her golden eyes, he was immediately contrite. *''Maf kijiye,* Randy. Please forgive me,'' he implored as he struggled to sit up. ''Regrettably, I am but a man, and as such, am prone to make mistakes. Your friendship means too much to me to risk losing it after all these years.''

When blood began trickling from his nose, Randy knelt beside him and wiped his injured face with the handkerchief she kept in her tunic. Though she tried to remain stoic, she found herself smiling at his woeful expression. Despite his attempt at seduction, she knew she could never remain angry with him.

"All right, Akbar, I will forgive you. But be warned, if you try this again, I won't be held accountable for my actions.''

"It's partially your fault,'' he replied while she ministered to him. ''When my father sent me to live in your home, I was only a boy of seven and you a tiny scrap of a girl, barely four. Who would have imagined that the scrawny child would grow to be such a beauty? With skin like satin, hair of flame, and the gold eyes of a cat, you have become an enchantress. How could I ignore such loveliness? Your voice is melodious. The gods should deafen me rather than torment me with your dulcet tones. Your—''

Randy shoved him away and stood up. ''Someone should remove your tongue so I wouldn't be subjected to your stupid flattery. Do me a favor and just leave me alone.'' She began walking along the shore of Mirror Lake, deep in thought about the past.

Akbar was her dearest friend and the heir to the Maharajah of Mysore. To convince the British of his desire for peace, Javid Surat Kahn had sent his eldest son to live in the household of a man he trusted above all others, Jonathan Collins.

Randy loved Akbar like a brother. When her mother died on her eighth birthday, he had helped her through her grief.

Several times a year, when Akbar journeyed to his home in Mysore, he always insisted on bringing her with him.

During one visit, Javid Surat Kahn considered having ten-year-old Randy betrothed to his son and had his court astrologer, Gopal, draw up a chart for her. A few days later, Gopal brought his opinion to the maharajah while he and Randy were playing backgammon in his private salon.

"Randy is a child born of the Lion. She is forceful and tends to be quick-tempered. The shades of her aura are flame, orange, and gold. There will be sadness and danger in the future for this one, but she will survive. For in her pain, this girl will discover a gift from the gods that will change her life.

"Find another for Akbar. The one meant for Randy has already been chosen. With eyes like lapis and hair touched by the sun, he shall come from the west seeking her. Born under the sign of the Virgin, he is protected by God and will risk his life three times to snatch her from the clutches of death. At his side, she will fulfill her destiny far from here."

Randy noticed the look of sadness on the maharajah's face. "What's the matter, Papa Javid? Is something wrong?"

"Well, little one, I know you love Akbar and I had thought you could have married him someday."

"Me, marry Akbar? Never!" she replied heatedly. "He will be a great ruler, but I would never be content in a *zenana*. I have a dreadful temper and can be the most wretched of creatures if

I do not get my own way. I am also selfish and could never share my husband with anyone. Even if he was the king."

Handing Randy the chart Gopal had prepared, the maharajah explained its implications on her life. When she scoffed at it, Javid laughed and hugged her close. "Honesty and spirit such as yours cannot be overlooked. I decree that you shall be addressed as *Sona Ag,* my golden fire. As my honorary daughter, Sona Ag, I will love you and protect your ever-shining flame."

He sent for the two servants who had accompanied Randy to his palace. "Abu Nazir and Jarita, before the birth of this child, I conveyed you into the household of Jonathan Collins, until such time as he no longer required you. But now I amend my orders. From this moment, your lives and allegiance belong to Randy. In your hearts always remember that she is the Sona Ag of Javid Surat Kahn. Guard her and revere her as you would me."

The maharajah nodded to Randy. "Abu and Jarita belong to you, Sona Ag. They will see to all your needs."

Randy looked at the pair who bowed at her feet. "But they have always taken care of me. Abu teaches me my lessons, and Jarita has been my nurse since I was born."

"Yes, but now they belong to you. These slaves are my gift to you, Sona Ag."

Not wanting to insult her host, Randy smiled weakly and thanked him for his generosity. "My goodness," she thought to herself, "however will I tell Papa about this? I don't think it is at all proper for an English girl to own slaves. I will let Akbar tell Papa. I can always depend on him to help me."

The following year, Akbar moved into a house of his own. With his staff of guards, slaves, and advisors, the young *Rajku-mar* took up residence in a marble palace on the outskirts of Calicut. An ornate residence with majestic towers and gardens, the Opal Court had been built especially for the future monarch.

Randy missed Akbar. Hoping to assuage her loneliness, she

began taking long rides across the countryside with Abu.
Dressed in the garb of a native boy to allow her the freedom
of riding astride, she hid her hair beneath a turban and went
exploring. But no matter how far they rode or what path they
traveled, they rarely came back alone.

On one trek, Randy found an abandoned nest of parakeets.
She removed her turban and placed the three chirping baby
birds inside it. At home, she nursed the tiny birds, feeding them
a mixture of honey, bread, and goat's milk ten times a day.
When they were well enough to be set free, the brightly feath-
ered trio refused to go, preferring to remain in a cage in her
bedroom.

A langur monkey named Hanuman, a mongoose called
Babar, and a falcon, El Rashid, joined the ever-increasing
menagerie. Each creature had been injured and afraid, but came
trustfully into her hands. She sensed their pain and healed
them with her care. Two unusual acquisitions changed her life
forever.

One morning, while riding through the bazaar with Abu,
Randy's attention was drawn to the slave market. Something
about the young man being dragged to the block by the dealer
and his two assistants troubled her. With his hands and feet
held in iron manacles, the man stood heads above his captors,
yet he cowered in fear from them and the whips they held.
Wearing only a filthy loincloth, his broad chest and back were
covered with scars, the evidence of years of abuse. When the
lash struck his sore flesh, he didn't speak, but cried out like an
animal.

"Abu, make them stop beating that man," she demanded.

"Missy Collins, it is not our place to interfere with such
matters. Perhaps beating is the only way the dealer can gain
control of this slave."

Randy sensed the slave's anguish as he cried out, his eyes
darting constantly around him. She could see no madness in
his dark gaze, only fear and confusion. Suddenly, she knew

what had to be done. "Abu, when the bidding starts, buy him for me."

Abu's brow rose in surprise. "But the man is big and uncontrollable and more likely than not insane, Missy Collins."

"Don't fight me on this, Abu. Although I look like a boy and wear Akbar's clothes, I am only twelve and my voice is unmistakably female. So I need you to bid for me."

"What will your father say when you bring this one home? This man is too big for one of your cages and too wild to work—"

"Please, Abu. You have taught me to follow my intuition, and I know what I ask is right."

Moments later, the bidding was completed and Abu paid the dealer for the man. After winning an argument over removing the manacles from the slave's swollen wrists and ankles, Randy looked up into the man's dirty face and found him staring at her. His gaze was questioning, fraught with distrust. Stepping toward him, she touched his cheek and smiled at him. With great effort, an answering smile creased the tall man's solemn face.

Randy turned to Abu. "This man is not crazy; he's deaf. Without having heard spoken words, he cannot talk. He has never known kindness, only pain and fear. But no more. Now he will be a part of our family."

"Missy Collins, how do you know such things are true?"

She shrugged. "How can I explain what I don't understand myself, Abu? But when I touched his cheek, a flood of emotions coursed through me. I felt his pain, his distrust, and most surprising of all, I felt the hope that filled his heart. It was as if I touched his soul. Come, Abu. Let's take Xavier home."

"How did you learn his name?"

Randy smiled wryly. "I don't know his real name, but I think Xavier is a good choice. It means 'bright,' and I believe he is. Because he cannot hear doesn't mean that he's stupid."

Only days later, Xavier was communicating with hand signals. As she had predicted, he was smart and eager to learn.

With good food and kind treatment, Xavier's tall, thin figure filled out and his muscles became firm and strong. When it was discovered that he had a way with animals, he began working in the stables. The horses thrived under his care.

Randy was frightened by her growing empathic abilities. Abu taught her to leash her mystical talent through meditation. If left unguarded, her abilities could constantly disturb her life.

One morning, while riding through the jungles north of town, Randy and Abu heard bellowing roars just ahead of them. Curious to find their source, Randy tethered her mount to a tree and made her way on foot through the entwining bushes. Abu slung a rifle over his shoulder and followed close behind her.

In a wide clearing, two tigers were engaged in battle. Their fur was mottled with dirt and blood as they fought and tore into each other. The brutality of the fight sickened Randy, but a glimpse of a tiny cub hiding beneath a bush near the combatants kept her from leaving the horrible scene.

The battle was soon over, leaving one of the large beasts dead. In shocked amazement, Randy watched the tiger cub rush out into the clearing to nuzzle the animal lying motionless in the grass. Without warning, the cub turned toward the male tiger that had killed its dam and attacked.

Randy cried out as the grown tiger tore into the courageous baby. "Please, Abu. We must stop him before it's too late."

Abu fired at the larger cat, grazing its head with the shot. The tiger ran into the jungle and left the wounded cub behind.

With Abu at her side, Randy rushed to the clearing and knelt beside the battered female cub. Its soft, tawny fur glistened with blood as it struggled to breathe. Her hand trembled when she touched the gaping wounds on its chest, neck, and belly.

"Oh, you poor little thing. Why did you attack that big beast? There was no way for you to win."

The tiny cub looked up at Randy. Her rough pink tongue reached out to touch the hand that stroked the fur on her neck.

"Don't worry, baby," Randy crooned. "I won't let you die."

"But Missy Collins, this creature is a wild animal. If she survives her wounds, you would not be able to keep her as a pet."

Randy cuddled the cub in her arms. "I know that, Abu. Once she's healed, I will set her free. I promise."

A month later, her promise was forgotten when she discovered that the damage to the cub's throat had left it virtually mute. She knew that without a roar to intimidate its enemies, the young tiger she had named Sidra wouldn't have a chance of surviving in the jungles on her own. After getting Abu and Xavier to agree to help her with the animal's care, she told her father about the newest pet in their household.

Jonathan Collins was known to be a fair man, yet he refused to listen to her pleas and demanded that she get rid of the beast by the following morning.

Randy ran from his library and sought the solace of the gardens behind their home. It was there that her father found her, sitting on a marble bench crying.

Sitting beside her, he gathered her into his arms. "Please don't cry, Mira," he implored her. "I love you and I want you to be happy. If that means keeping your Sidra, then so be it. But, you must make me a few promises, Mira."

Randy wiped her tears. "I'll do whatever you ask, Papa."

"I would have you hear my terms first, Mira. So listen carefully. First, you will not bring any other animals into this house. Your main concern will be Sidra's care. Be warned— if that cub harms you in any way, I will kill the beast myself. Do you understand?"

Hearing his concern and his use of his special name for her made Randy smile. "Yes, Papa. Is there anything else?"

"As a matter of fact, there is," he admitted with a grin. "Starting tomorrow, you and I are going to spend more time together. You have a good hand and a way with words, Mira, and I could use your help with my personal correspondence. I also need your aid in getting to know this area. As governor, I rarely get away from my desk to see what needs to be done for the people. We could ride together and you can show me the district.''

During those next few years, she and her father shared a very special relationship. Her empathic gift amazed him, yet he never allowed her to feel awkward because of her ability. Rather than discourage her from using her talent, he suggested that she use it to help others.

Several days a week, Randy did volunteer work at the mission hospital in the ghetto area of Calicut. With her gift, she could touch the sick and injured and tell the physicians what the symptoms were and where exactly the pain was located. Babies, children, any who could not speak for themselves, were given proper care because of her ability. The gift that had helped her treat animals was used for helping people—but only the Indian people.

Randy led two separate lives. At the mission, she dressed like a native woman and was called Sona Ag. She colored her skin with cosmetics and covered her hair with a *dupetta*. With Xavier at her side, they appeared to be a young Indian couple helping the less fortunate in Calicut.

Yet just as easily, Randy could be the epitome of a proper English lady. Gowned in the latest European styles, she attended official functions with her father and charmed everyone with her wit and intelligence. She acted as her father's hostess and arranged parties in their home that set standards that the wives of the other diplomats and military officers found difficult to meet.

By her eighteenth birthday, British men, officers, and civilians alike were vying for her attentions. Her most ardent admirer was Major Brandon Spencer, a young military officer on her father's staff, but she refused to consider his suit. While dining at home one evening, her father admitted that Spencer had asked him to intercede on his behalf.

"Brandon Spencer is quite taken with you, Mira. Why do you spurn his attentions? Has he offended you in some way?"

Randy sighed. "How could Brandon offend me, Papa? He's a perfect gentleman, always proper with his grand manners and his oh-so-blue blood." She added with mocking cynicism, "The pompous jackanapes bores me!"

Her father laughed. "Spencer can be a bit of a prig. But he has told me that he's in love with you."

"Oh, Papa, how can he be in love with me? He doesn't even know me. All he's ever seen of me is my ladylike performance as your hostess." Leaning forward, she cocked her eyebrow. "Tell me, Papa, what do you think Brandon would say if he ever met Sona Ag, who cares for patients at the paupers' clinic and speaks Hindi and Urdu like a native and has a grown tiger as a house pet?"

Jonathan chuckled. "He would probably die of apoplexy."

"So you see, Papa, I won't marry Brandon or anyone like him. I love my freedom, and if it means never getting married to keep it, then I will remain a spinster."

"I will never press you into marriage, Mira, but I hope in the future you'll change your mind. You are far too lovely and giving to spend your life alone."

Randy rose from the table and walked to the archway that led to the gardens. "I may not have a choice, Papa. What man would want to marry a woman who collects animals, can ride a horse like a lancer, and has an odd talent for feeling the pain in others?"

"A very special man, Mira, and someday, when you least expect it, you will find him." Jonathan joined her at the door and hugged her close. "But until the day this paragon comes along, you will continue to be my very precious girl, Mira."

"No matter what, Papa, I swear I will always be your girl," she explained, sealing her promise with a kiss on his cheek. "Always yours, Papa. For ever and ever."

* * *

Standing on the shore of Mirror Lake again for the first time since that terrible September night, tears coursed down Randy's cheeks. "Oh, Papa, who would have known that forever was only a year away? What am I to do without you?"

Akbar's strong hands clutched her trembling shoulders and turned her into his embrace. "He is gone, my sister, but you will go on. Papa Jonathan would have had it no other way."

"But how, Akbar, and more important, where? Because I am not of legal age, I cannot live on my own. The laws of my people say that my mother's brother is now my guardian. Uncle Richard was jealous of my mother, despised my father, and has always treated my grandmother with disrespect. He would force me to go to England, and I don't want to leave India. I must stay and find the man who murdered my father. I must avenge Papa's death."

Akbar held Randy away from him and shook her. "You will stay out of it, Randy! Must I remind you that if it wasn't for that beast of yours, you would be dead as well? My father and I have men searching for the one who murdered Papa Jonathan. A man missing a finger and recovering from a mauling by a tiger should not be too difficult to find. Until then, you must be careful. The guards we have placed around you are for your protection. You must not try to evade them. Do I have your promise?"

Akbar's handsome face was stern with angry determination. Randy knew that arguing with him was futile. "All right, you have my word. I will be careful and I won't sneak away from the guards again. But know this, my brother. I will not rest easy until the murderer of my father has been found and punished."

"Nor shall I, my sister, nor shall I."

The two friends embraced, unaware of the cold, menacing eyes that spied on them from a nearby copse of trees.

Pushing aside a low-hanging bough, the man raised a rifle to his shoulder and tried to take aim in spite of the pain in his mangled hand. Sounds of approaching riders filled the air, and he was forced to take cover or risk being seen by the guards.

"You've been lucky thus far you damn pampered little witch!" he snarled. "But not for much longer. I'll see you dead and buried before you can escape me and leave India, Miranda Collins. I swear to God, I will see you dead first!"

Chapter 2

"Land ho, Captain!" the sailor shouted from the crow's nest. "Calicut's in our sights."

Raising a telescope to his eye, James Grayson got his first view of the ancient city. His thick brown hair, streaked golden by the sun, stirred in the breeze as he studied the shoreline.

The city of Calicut was on the southwest coast of India. For forty years the port city had enriched the coffers of the East India Company with its exports, and now the young English captain wanted to increase his own profits as well.

"By God, Jamie, you said this ship would make the trip in record time, and you've done it!"

James turned to face the man beside him. Three years younger than his own twenty-eight years, Stephen Morgan was his best friend. With dark hair and a hint of laughter in his hazel eyes, Stephen took great joy in teasing him. James had never liked nicknames, but refused to be goaded from his good humor. Rolling his blue eyes toward the sky, he handed the spyglass to Stephen.

"Aye, my friend. I told you this new clipper schooner would

make a difference. It's faster than anything in my family's fleet. The sailing time was reduced by nearly one third. A full hold and the right winds could shave that down even further.''

"You seem very pleased with yourself, Jamie.''

"Why shouldn't I be?'' James stroked the polished railing beneath his hand. "This ship, the *Diana,* was my dream. It cost me every cent of the inheritance I received from my grandfather, but it was well worth the price. With the profits I intend to make on shipping rubber, tea, and spices, the *Diana* is going to be the first of many ships in my own fleet.''

"Did your father help you arrange all this?''

James shook his head. "No, my father doesn't have a thing to do with this venture. If he had his way, I'd be working for his firm and preparing myself to be the next Earl of Foxwood.''

"You sound like being the heir to an earldom is a crime.''

"Not a crime, Stephen, it's just not the way I want to live my life. Call it pride or stupidity, but I want to make my own fortune, as my father and grandfathers did.''

"But you've already got one title and the lands that go along with it. The money earned by the Ryland estates in Sheringham makes you a wealthy man.''

"Yes, I'm Viscount Ryland, but any profit made on the estate goes back into its coffers, not into my pockets.'' James turned and looked up proudly at the three masts of his ship. "If I'm to succeed, it is going to be with the help of this lady.''

"But why come to Calicut? Why not Bombay or Madras? They are bigger ports and far richer than this city.''

Leaning forward on the rail, James gazed at the approaching shore. "I have several reasons. Not the least of which is a letter of introduction to the district governor, Sir Jonathan Collins. With his aid, we will go home with a full hold and contracts for future shipments, too.''

"How did you accomplish that?''

"I got help from the Dowager Duchess of Maidstone.''

Stephen laughed. "Why is Miranda Wentworth helping you?

I remember, when we were children how she would rail at us for racing our horses across her pasture.''

"Jonathan Collins is her son-in-law. When she heard I was going to India, she offered to help me if I would deliver a letter to Collins and a doll to her little granddaughter.''

"So the tyke gets a present from grandmama and you gain the help of the governor. Very clever, Jamie. I can already see my investment in this voyage is going to do very well.'' Chuckling to himself, Stephen sauntered back toward his cabin.

Alone with his thoughts, James recalled the Sunday afternoon he had answered the summons to visit the Dowager Duchess of Maidstone. Though her family's estate bordered his own, he hadn't seen Miranda since she was widowed several years past.

A part of him dreaded his task.

When her stepson, Richard, became the new duke, she had been forced to give up her palatial home. It saddened James to think of the once regal lady reduced to living in the small widow's cottage on the west side of the family estate.

But the dower cottage had been replaced by a large, three-story house that was painted a pristine white. A marble fountain adorned with cherubs spewed streams of water into its pool in the center of the wide circular drive. Lush green lawns and flowering gardens surrounded the house. Well-maintained barns for the livestock stood nearby.

As James turned his horse over to a footman at the door, he couldn't help being amused. Miranda had always been known for her great style and independence. How could he have imagined that getting older or becoming a widow would have changed her?

James awaited the dowager in a magnificently appointed salon. His attention was drawn to the familiar painting hanging on the silk-covered wall over the fireplace. It was the wedding portrait of Miranda Wentworth.

The daughter of a wealthy merchant, Miranda had captured the heart of widower Matthew Wentworth at their first meeting. With her strawberry-blond hair, a pretty face, and an intelligence far beyond the norm, it was easy to understand why the Duke of Maidstone wanted her for his second wife. He courted her in lavish style, and three months later they were married. The generosity of his wedding gifts was proudly displayed in the painting of his bride.

The "Crystal Tears" was a famous set of diamonds that had been made for a princess of the Ottoman Empire when she became *Kadin* to the mighty sultan, Suleiman. In the portrait, Miranda Wentworth wore the entire collection of a necklace, a bracelet, a ring, earbobs, and a brooch set in gold. The gems were cut in teardrop shapes, with the brooch as the centerpiece.

The flawless forty-carat diamond was edged with smaller stones. Unlike the other gems, the center diamond was a deep ruby red. Known as the "Bloody Tear of Allah," its brilliant color made it the rarest of its kind in the world. Legend claimed that the owner of this particular jewel would be blessed with great fortune and would be invincible against all enemies.

Studying the portrait, James heard his hostess speaking from behind him. "I was quite the rage back then. All that red hair and a temper to match. Who would have guessed that the Duke of Maidstone would have fallen in love with such a termagant?"

James turned and smiled at his old friend. "The duke was a lucky man to have found you, your grace."

The dowager laughed affectionately. "You've certainly become quite the charmer, James Grayson. So tall and handsome. If I were forty years younger, you wouldn't stand a chance of getting away from me."

The passing years had been kind to Miranda. Her red hair was now a soft apricot color. Tiny lines creased her pale skin, but her smile was as bright as the green of her eyes.

"Come, sit down and talk to this old lady, James. Tell me about your life and family. How's your friend Stephen? And Diana? You must tell me about your twin sister, Diana."

James kissed her cheek, then sat beside her on the brocade sofa. "My lady, you still issue questions and orders faster than anyone I know." His teasing tone ended when he took her hand in his. "I am so sorry I haven't come to see you before this, your grace. I wanted to, but . . ."

"Oh, fiddlesticks! There's no need to apologize, James. You are here now, and that's what is important. And why all the formality? I've been Nana to you for over twenty years. Tell me about your life, James, and that new ship of yours."

After he described his vessel and his plans for the future, he spoke of the ship's namesake, his sister, Diana.

"Diana's doing well in Virginia. She and Jared are awaiting the birth of their third child. With two sons, they're hoping for a daughter this time." James laughed. "It would serve Diana right if she has a little girl just like herself. Then she'll know how she drove the rest of us to distraction."

"Diana must be happy with her Jared, but what of you, James? Is there no special lady in your life? With your fine looks and noble background, I'm surprised you're still a free man," Miranda teased him. "Has no fair damsel caught your eye?"

"Caught my eye?" James smirked. "London's social whirl is like a cattle auction, Nana. Each mother pushing and parading her daughter about like a merchant hawking his wares."

Patting his hand, the dowager changed the subject. "Your little sister and brothers. What's become of them?"

"Trelane is at the university studying to be a solicitor and Catlin has gone off on an adventure in South America. Only Sarah is at home. She's a cheery bundle of blond curls who keeps Mama and Papa too busy to miss the rest of us."

The elderly lady sighed. "I envy your mama. Not only is Catherine a beautiful and talented woman, but she's mother to such wonderful children. With the others grown, I can imagine the joy she finds in Sarah." She brushed the tears from her eyes and smiled at James. "Perhaps I, too, will find happiness."

Puzzled by her remark, James waited for her to say more.

"Before you arrived today, I knew about your forthcoming trip to India, James—your plans to secure shipments and trade for the future growth of your business. I am in a position to help you, and my price in return will be very small."

Informing James of her son-in-law's position in Calicut and the worth of his assistance through her, she removed a small portrait from the pocket of her gown and placed it in his hand.

The painting was of a little girl with long auburn hair and delicate features. She appeared to be about ten years old, the same age as James's sister Sarah. But unlike his happy sibling, this pretty child was solemn. An aura of sadness seemed to emanate from her large, pale-green eyes.

"This is my granddaughter and namesake, Miranda Juliet. When my daughter, Lenore, died ten years ago, she left her only babe behind. For years I have longed to have my granddaughter join me here in England, but Jonathan refuses to be parted from his little girl. He's been most accommodating, sending me a painting once a year, and he has encouraged the child to write to me. The consolation was small, but I accepted his decision. However, all of this may be changing."

Smiling, she continued. "Next year, my son-in-law will be retiring from government service. If he will come to England, I plan to turn over control of my holdings to him. He's far too proud to accept a gift, so I must convince him that I need his assistance. If Jonathan agrees, I shall give him my town house in London, a generous salary, and a large portion of my profits. I will name him and Miranda as my only heirs. The deed to this house and the surrounding lands are already in her name."

"But isn't this a part of Richard's estate?" James asked.

"I should say not!" she told him sharply. "My stepson never accepted me. So years back I asked my husband to sell this section of land to me. He refused to accept payment for it, but asked that our grandchild be the recipient of this new estate. It will be a gift from us both. Matthew called it Mirage, and the two of us planned it all for our little Miranda."

"Surely Richard will try to reclaim this land as his own."

"Richard would if he could, but thanks to the best solicitors in Europe, my stepson can't touch it."

The dowager leaned back in her chair and sighed. "Richard was twelve years old when I married his father, but he never wanted me as his stepmother. When I gave birth to Lenore a year later, his jealousy was evident to everyone. Matthew tried to reassure his son of his importance to our family, but nothing helped. Richard demanded that he be sent away to school.

"Richard is a spiteful man, whose only redeeming grace is his wife, Amelia. Since Matthew's death three years ago, Amelia has been my only source of comfort." The dowager shook her head. "But it's not enough. I want Jonathan and Miranda here with me."

The old woman walked to a walnut cabinet and removed two sealed letters and a large box. Taking her seat beside him, she handed him the envelopes.

"These are for Jonathan. One is a letter of introduction for you and my request for his aid with your endeavors. The other is a missive that relays my need for his help and the offer of a position as my business manager. By giving him a home and making him my heir, how can he deny my request? My dream of having my little granddaughter in England will at last come true. I will no longer be alone."

The tears glistening in her eyes belied her hopeful smile as she opened the box on her lap. The dowager pushed aside the tissue paper and revealed a lovely doll. Dressed in a gown of yellow velvet, the doll had auburn curls and light green eyes. The fragile porcelain face was beautifully sculpted and seemed oddly familiar to James.

"Nana, this doll is the image of your granddaughter!"

Miranda smiled at his surprise. "I wanted to send her a very special present. I had this doll made for her in Paris. Besides being a thing of beauty, it holds a piece of my heart. In the letter I've enclosed in this box, I've tried to convey my love and hopes for her future." She touched his hand. "James, you are the son I always wanted, but never had. I trust no one but you to deliver my gift to my little granddaughter. Grant Nana this favor—say you will go to Calicut.''

James put his arm around her thin shoulders and kissed her cheek. ''All right, Nana, I'll go to Calicut, visit Jonathan, and deliver your present to Miranda. Perhaps when Jonathan retires next year, they will return with me to England. It would give me great pleasure to see your dreams come true, Nana.''

A glint sparkled in the dowager's eyes. ''If only you knew the extent of this old lady's dreams. . . .''

Standing on the deck of the *Diana* as it neared the port of Calicut, warmed by the memory of Miranda's laughter, James prayed he would succeed in his task to make her happy.

''If all goes well, Nana will have her granddaughter, and my sister Sarah will become friends with her. I pray that little Miranda isn't easily led or she'll soon be a wild hoyden like my baby sister. If that happens, God help us all!''

Chapter 3

"Two hours! Can you believe this, James? We've sailed halfway around the world to spend our first day on dry land waiting two hours in this bloody bureaucrat's anteroom for an audience!"

James watched Stephen pace the length of the waiting room outside the governor's office, more intrigued than annoyed by the delay they had been subjected to. A lieutenant had warmly greeted them on their arrival until he learned that they wished to see Jonathan Collins on personal business. The officer's face had paled as he went in search of his superior.

" 'Tis all your fault," Stephen insisted. "You should have told that pup that you were Viscount Ryland, and I the Duc du Laurent. We might have gotten quicker action had he known we were nobility and not just sea captains."

James laughed. "Why is it you only rely on your title when you want to impress someone? You haven't taken a real interest in your holdings in France in years. And far be it from me to remind you that I am the only sea captain here. I don't believe you could navigate a ship if your life depended on it."

"That's right, take your frustrations out on me," Stephen replied. "You hate sitting around doing nothing more than I, so why aren't you pacing the floor with me?"

Dressed in a dark blue coat, fawn britches and an ivory lawn shirt, James strummed his long fingers on top of the box he held on his lap. "Something is wrong, Stephen. I can feel it in my bones, and I'm going to find out exactly what it is right now." As he stood up, the double doors to the governor's office opened and the lieutenant stepped out.

"Please come in. Major Spencer will see you now."

"But we are not here to see Spencer, we're to see—" Stephen's words halted as James shook his head, and the two of them walked inside the office.

"Welcome to Calicut, gentlemen. Please accept my apologies for the delay in greeting you." With his right arm resting in a sling across his chest, Brandon Spencer shook their hands with his left before directing them to chairs in front of the massive desk. "Please excuse the improper use of my hand. Took a nasty fall a few weeks back, breaking my wrist and two fingers. If you will be seated, I will send my adjutant for tea."

It wasn't the bandaged hand that James noticed, but the officer himself. Attired in a regimental scarlet tunic with gold braid, he was a striking figure, though a bit young to have risen to the rank of major, James thought. He wondered if Spencer had gained promotions through valor, wealth, or family connections.

"The lieutenant informs me that you are here to see Jonathan Collins on a personal matter. Gentleman, it grieves me to be the bearer of tragic news, but our lord governor died nearly a month ago. Were either of you acquainted with him?" Spencer asked.

"I met him in England when I was a boy," James replied. "His late wife's family and mine have been friends for years. Was Sir Jonathan taken ill or was his death accidental?"

"I wish it had been as simple as that, but the bitter truth is, the governor was murdered by an Indian assassin."

"Murdered by an Indian?" Stephen gasped. "Have we come all this way only to witness some kind of revolution?"

Spencer shook his head. "Revolution? Certainly not! This was the act of a group of assassins known as Thugees. These men worship a Hindu goddess, Kali. To appease their heathen deity, Thugees offer her sacrifices by strangling their victims with long scarves. A single man entered the governor's home and murdered him in his sleep. One death is hardly a revolution, sir. I assure you both, everything here is well under control."

James wasn't appeased by the major. "But why was Collins singled out? Did he do something that angered the Indians?"

"For the most part, the native people had always liked Sir Jonathan. His closest friend was the Maharajah of Mysore, Javid Surat Kahn. The locals knew this and they admired him as well. But the governor made the Thugees his enemy when he upheld a movement to abolish their murderous sect after they attacked a squad of British soldiers last year. Because of his attempt to rid the country of this scourge, Collins was murdered by them."

"And his little girl, Miranda—was she harmed?" James asked.

When Spencer didn't reply and merely looked at him with a puzzled mien on his face, James's uncertainty grew. "Major, I asked you a question. Was Collins's daughter injured? Is the child all right?" James demanded.

"Why, ah—certainly, little Miranda is fine." Spencer gave him a solicitous smile. "Word has already been sent to her family in England regarding the circumstances of Sir Jonathan's death. When the arrangements are confirmed, I will see that the child is safely sent on to her guardians. So you need not worry or concern yourself with her welfare."

Something in the officer's overly conciliatory manner put James on his guard. "Thank you, Major. I'm sure that her family will be grateful for your efforts, but I must see Miranda.

Her grandmother has sent this gift and I promised to deliver it.''

"If you're concerned with that, Captain Grayson, I could bring it to her myself. As a matter of fact, I insist on it. I can't allow you to disturb the child with your well-meaning, but unexpected visit. I won't permit you to interfere with her—''

"Allow? Interfere? I was sent here by the Dowager Duchess of Maidstone, and I fully intend to see her granddaughter today."

"Maybe you don't understand me, Captain, but I'm ordering you to stay away from Miranda Collins. As the acting governor, the girl's welfare is my responsibility." Standing up, Spencer glared at James. "With my authority, I could have your ship impounded and press charges against you. So don't cross me, Captain, or you'll regret your actions, I promise you."

Leaning back in his chair, James smiled. "Major, it appears that you are the one who doesn't understand. Besides being captain of the *Diana*, I am also Viscount Ryland and heir to the Earl of Foxwood. My grandfather is the Duke of Chatham, a major stockholder in the British East India Company. Get in my way, and your illustrious career in the company, the military, and the government will be destroyed.

"Now, Major Spencer," he continued, his voice tempered with disdain, "if you will direct us to the Collins residence in the compound, we will go see Miranda."

"Please forgive my tirade, my lord," Spencer offered with a meek smile. "With the search for Sir Jonathan's killer and my new duties, I tend to forget myself. Of course you can visit Miranda, but she doesn't live in the British sector. The Collins family have their own home on the eastern perimeter of the city. My adjutant, Lieutenant Chad Gerard, will take you there. Allow me to provide you with horses while you are visiting the city. If you require anything else, feel free to let me know."

After James and the others left his office, Brandon Spencer grabbed his riding crop and helmet. He sent for his horse and was soon making his way across the city.

* * *

The ornate gold clock in the salon was chiming four when Randy entered her home. Removing her turban, she shook out her hair and started toward her suite. The thought of a lingering bath hastened her steps until Abu's voice halted her progress.

"Forgive the intrusion, miss, but I thought you might want to know about the irate visitor you had this afternoon."

Turning to face him, Randy leaned against the wall. "I bet it was Brandon Spencer. Doesn't he ever give up? The night Papa died, he proposed to me for the fourth time. When I said no again, the fool went crazy. I've ignored him, returned his gifts, refused his letters, and now he's taken to visiting in person. So tell me, Abu, how did you get rid of him?"

"I told the major that you were with the maharajah and would not return for several days. At first, he was angered, but then he looked pleased. He warned me that a man from England was on his way to see you and your being away was a blessing."

"A blessing? For him or me? Did he say anything else?"

"He *ordered* me to send the man on his way and not to tell him where you had gone," Abu replied in caustic tones. "Under no circumstances was I to let this man see you."

Randy frowned. "I don't know what the major is up to now, but I won't allow him to dictate to me. Abu, when this visitor arrives, we must offer him our most gracious hospitality. Have Kira prepare a feast sure to please the palate. I want the guest wing made ready as well. Perhaps we can convince him to spend a few days with us. By then, I should have my answers."

Seeing the question in Abu's eyes, Randy explained. "For some reason, the major doesn't want this man near me and I want to know why. If that means bringing a stranger into our home, then so be it. Before you object, I won't be in danger. Between you, Xavier, and the guards, I am well protected. But I don't want our visitor to know about Sidra. Her presence saved my life once; perhaps it will again."

"It will be as you ordered," Abu answered with a bow.

"While you make things ready for our guest, I will prepare myself. A soothing bath, a change of clothes, and Miss Miranda Juliet Collins will appear to charm and amuse the mystery man from England. Have no fear, Abu—all will be well."

The sun was low in the sky when the three riders arrived at the Collins home. But the dead governor's residence was like nothing James had ever seen before. Resembling a small palace, the marble edifice had tall, carved pillars, wide archways, and domed towers. The high walls around the residence were topped with brass spires, protecting the privacy of those within. The wrought-iron gates were guarded by three massive men dressed in colorful Indian livery.

"This place must belong to an Indian noble," James quipped. "Tell me, Lieutenant, have you made another wrong turn?"

"I've only been here a month and I'll admit my directions have been faulty, but this is the home of our late governor," Chad replied. "Collins purchased this place from his friend, the Maharajah of Mysore, years ago. Due to their close relationship, Javid Kahn and his son have been personally seeing to the care and safety of Sir Jonathan's daughter, Miranda, since his death."

"Isn't that a bit out of the ordinary?" Stephen asked. "A young English girl shouldn't be guarded by foreigners."

Chad's brow shot up. "Need I remind you, sir, that here in India, *we* are the foreigners? We must constantly strive to keep peace with the locals, especially when they are as wealthy and powerful as the Maharajah of Mysore. Perhaps that's why the major hasn't tried to interfere in this matter."

After entering the impressive home, they were greeted by an older man dressed in a knee-length tunic and white trousers. His waist was wrapped in a wide crimson sash, and a turban covered his hair. Though short in stature and mature in years, he exuded a quiet strength.

His gaze lit upon James. "Welcome to the Collins home,

Huzur,'' he announced with a bow, using the highly formal term reserved for only the most honored guest. "I am Abu Nazir, the steward of this fine home. What has brought you to our door?"

"I am Captain James Grayson. I have come to see Miranda and to bring her a present from her grandmother in England."

"Have you known the dowager a long time, *Huzur?''*

"I've known her grace all of my life. Knowing I was coming to India, she asked me to deliver her gift. When I learned of Sir Jonathan's death, I became concerned about his little girl, Miranda. On my return to England, I'd like to assure the dowager that her granddaughter is fine. May I see the child now?"

Abu continued his own questions. "These other gentlemen— have they come with you on your journey as well?"

James was annoyed by the servant's clever evasion of his request, but introduced his companions. "This is my friend, Stephen Morgan, and Chad Gerard, adjutant to Major Spencer. I'd like to see little Miranda as soon as possible, so the lieutenant can lead us back to the compound and return to his duties."

"That will be no problem, *Huzur.* The lieutenant is free to go. One of the grooms can take you back. Perhaps I could impose upon you and your friend to remain for dinner? With all Missy Collins has been through, your presence will bring joy to her."

James recalled the portrait he had seen of little Miranda. The pretty child with a haunting sadness in her pale green eyes had been in his thoughts for weeks. Staying for dinner wouldn't be an arduous task for him. He liked children, and if his being there would lift her spirits, then it would be time well spent.

"All right, Nazir, we will accept your kind offer and remain for dinner." Turning to Chad, James shook his hand. "Thank you for your assistance. In spite of the confusion in our travels, I did enjoy the tour of the city."

Abu summoned a footman to show the lieutenant out. He led James and Stephen to a large formal salon that overlooked the gardens. "Please make yourselves comfortable, while I see to the arrangements for dinner. Missy Collins will be joining you soon." With a bow, Abu left them alone.

Stephen looked around and shook his head. "My God, James, this house is magnificent! Look at these furnishings. Jonathan Collins certainly knew how to live." He walked to the open archway to gaze at the vast array of flowers, trees, and shrubs.

"Jamie, if my mother saw this garden, she would think she had died and gone to heaven. Look at the variety of flowers they have. Those trees are full of fruit. I recognize the oranges and plums, but what are those large red and yellow fruits?"

Placing his package on a table, James followed Stephen out to the tree he had pointed at. He plucked one of the fruits from it and rubbed his hands against its sweet-smelling, waxy skin.

"This is a mango," James informed him. "When I was in the West Indies years ago, I became very fond of mangoes. They only grow in the tropics, so I seldom get to enjoy them." Looking at the abundance of nature around them, he smiled. "Surely the Garden of Eden must have looked like this. All we need is an Eve to make that old story come to life."

A female voice laughed behind them. "Well, if this is Eden, then I must be Eve. Now, which of you fine gentlemen is going to portray Adam in our reenactment?"

James dropped the mango and turned to see if the woman was as lovely as her voice. He was far from disappointed.

She stood on the portico bathed in the fiery glow of the setting sun. A tall, elegant lady with a face that could only be described as exquisite came toward them. Her dark auburn tresses were arranged in a coronet of braids, with wispy tendrils framing her perfect features. Her stylish gown was made of lavender lace with a full skirt and a modestly scooped neckline that enhanced the lush feminine curves beneath it.

The color of her eyes astounded James the most. Fringed by thick dark lashes, they were a sparkling amber gold.

Stephen stepped forward and kissed her hand. "I would be honored to be Adam in our little drama, ma'am. I am Stephen Morgan, and I put myself completely at your disposal."

She smiled. "You would certainly make a handsome Adam, sir, but I sense you might be better suited to portray the serpent."

Stephen was stunned. "Do I remind you of a snake?"

"Oh, no, that's not at all what I meant," she assured him, laughing over his surprise. "The serpent represented temptation, not an ugly, slithering reptile. I feel you are more a charming rogue than a man who gives his heart to just one lady."

James chuckled at her accurate observation of his friend. "It appears that even in India you can't escape that well-earned notoriety you've acquired, Stephen." Not to be outdone by his companion, James deftly took the lady's hand and placed a kiss on the pulse of her wrist. Her skin was soft, lightly scented with roses. Gazing into her eyes, he smiled.

"Lovely lady, I am James Grayson, Captain of the ship *Diana* and newly arrived in India. Pray tell, who are you? The child's governess or another dinner guest, perhaps?"

Before Randy could respond, Abu rushed out. "A thousand pardons, Memsahib. I should have been here to make the proper introductions." Stepping before James and Stephen, he continued. "Most honored sirs, may I present Miss Miranda Juliet Collins."

James dropped her hand. His look of shock startled Randy. Stephen's laughter caused James to glare at him.

"Jamie, you thought . . . the dowager said . . . this is priceless!" Stephen's words, clipped by his laughter, confused Randy.

"Will someone kindly tell me what's going on here? Captain Grayson, if I have offended you with my teasing banter, please forgive me." When he didn't reply, she turned to Abu.

"Meri samajh men nahin aya."

Randy's Hindi words, indicating that she did not understand what she had done wrong, brought a smile to Abu's face. "You have done nothing, but I fear someone else has. It appears that the good captain has been told that you were a *bacha, a chhota larki.*"

"A child? A little girl? Who would do that?"

With an air of rancor, James answered her. "Major Spencer and your grandmother led me to believe that you were a child."

"Nana knows that I turned nineteen months ago. Mayhap it was a silly jest on her part. As for Spencer, this may have been his way of trying to protect me. I'm sorry you were deceived, Captain." Hoping to soothe his injured pride, Randy put her hand on his arm. "Maybe I should ask for your forgiveness after all," she admitted with a droll smile.

Her admission piqued his curiosity. "For what reason?"

"For disappointing you. Perhaps if I were an eleven-year-old girl, you might still be smiling, Captain Grayson."

James covered her hand with his own, and a rush of warmth coursed through him. "If I am to be honest, ma'am, I would have been far more disappointed if you were eleven. Finding you as you are is a very pleasant surprise. But when I return home, I'm going to scold Nana for not telling me more about you."

"You appear to know my grandmother quite well, Captain. We've exchanged letters for years and she seems to be a wonderful lady. While you're here, I hope you will tell me about her."

"Most certainly, Miss Collins."

Randy frowned ruefully. "Miss Collins seems so formal and ancient, Captain. I wish you would call me Randy."

Her face was radiant, and James found himself unexpectedly drawn to the beguiling young woman. Her golden eyes captivated him. It was only Stephen's timely interruption that broke through his momentary trance.

"But Randy sounds like a boy's name. Though only an idiot could mistake such a lovely creature as you for a lad."

"Fie on you," Randy scolded. "I'm not as sophisticated as the ladies in England, far more a rustic raised in the provinces, but such talk merely shows me that I was right about you."

Stephen's cheeks flushed a deep pink. "I—um, never meant to offend you, Miran—I mean Randy."

"Don't you dare apologize to me," Randy told him with an

easy laugh. "I only wanted to tease you. Thank you for calling me Randy. Though Miranda is a fine name, I've never been at ease with it. Papa always calls me—"

Her words caught in her throat. When she spoke again, her voice was soft and low. "I sometimes forget that Papa is dead. It's hard to believe that he is gone from my life."

"Major Spencer told us of his death," James explained. "You have my heartfelt sympathies on his passing. If there is anything you require, ma'am . . ."

Randy gave him a pleasant smile. "Thank you, Captain. You are most kind, but everything has been taken care of. If you gentlemen will excuse me for a moment, I'll see how dinner is coming along." Before they replied, she hurried into the house.

"Now that was a relief." Stephen sighed. "Usually females are all teary-eyed, sobbing over such things. I've never seen a woman so composed and unemotional. Don't you agree?"

Giving Stephen a shake of his head, James went after her.

Alone in the salon, Randy used her handkerchief to dash away the tears that escaped her eyes. She had to be brave. She could not let her visitors see her like this. James Grayson said he knew her grandmother, but she didn't know the man at all.

"You need not run away to cry, Randy."

Her heart lurched at the sound of his voice. The captain's voice. He had followed her into the salon.

"I didn't run away to cry, Captain," she said, brushing the last tear from her eye before turning to face him. "My father insisted that I not wear black or mourn for him when he died. But I was not prepared to lose him this soon."

Randy settled on the divan, and James sat next to her. "I am sure your father would be very proud of you."

"Do you really think so, Captain?" Randy looked up, lost for a moment in the depths of his sea-blue eyes.

James took the handkerchief from her hand and began dabbing her cheeks dry. "Of course your father would be proud of you. I am sure of it."

A shiver of warm excitement ran through Randy. No one had ever affected her quite like this man. Almost as if he knew what she was thinking, his hand dipped beneath her chin and tilted her face upward. She was powerless to stop him when he bent to kiss her. His lips were gentle, caressing her mouth with his. When he backed away, she sat motionless, her lips moist and quivering, wanting him to continue.

"Forgive my intrusion, Missy Collins," Abu announced from across the room, "but Kira has a question regarding dinner."

At the sound of Abu's voice, Randy's demeanor quickly altered. Coming to her feet, she faced him. No longer sad and weepy, she was poised and calm, every inch a lady.

"Abu, while I attend to the problem, please show the captain and his friend to the guest wing. After their ride, they might like to freshen up before dinner." Smiling, she gave James a nod. "Captain, I leave you in Abu's capable hands."

Her abrupt change of mood so stunned James that Randy was halfway to the kitchen before he could stand up or speak. He shook his head. "Well, I'll be—I've never met anyone like her."

"Nor shall you ever again, *Huzur,*" Abu replied.

"I meant no disrespect to your lady," James explained, "but in the past half hour, I've seen several sides of her personality that totally contradict one another. One moment she's witty and confident, the next vulnerable, almost childlike. You came in and suddenly Randy became a thoughtful, capable hostess. I wonder which side is really her."

"Missy Collins is like a rare jewel with many facets, each unique, adding to her beauty and worth. Do not question how they were formed; rather enjoy the loveliness they have created."

Randy was all that a lady should be, yet something about her puzzled James. He wasn't sure what it was and throughout dinner, he watched and listened to her, hoping to solve the mystery.

The meal was a combination of English and native Indian foods. Roast lamb with mint sauce was served with baked potatoes, peas, and crusty rolls. But it was the fragrant chicken and rice dish that garnered Stephen's attention.

"Curried chicken is very hot and spicy," Randy warned him.

"Nonsense. You're eating it, so how bad can it be?" Stephen put a heaping forkful into his mouth. In a matter of seconds, he was nearly choking. His eyes watered and his face turned crimson. He swallowed the food, then drank the goblet of water, hoping to douse the burn. It didn't help.

He was gasping for air when Randy left her seat at the head of the table to assist him. She picked up a bowl and spooned some of its creamy contents into his mouth.

"This is yoghurt, Stephen. Milk curd mixed with papaya and mango. It will relieve the burning. Try a bit more. I promise it will make you feel better."

Obediently, Stephen allowed her to feed him.

"Are you feeling better now?" she asked after a moment.

"A little," he answered in a pitiful voice. "The sweetness of the fruit and the smooth texture of the yoghurt seem to help. Perhaps if I had some more, it would cure me entirely."

"Then feed yourself," James demanded, standing on the other side of him. "The lady warned you, but you ate the curry anyway. You deserve whatever discomfort it brought, Stephen, so stop looking for sympathy."

"Don't be harsh with me, Jamie boy. You know I've always been a bit of an adventurer. Having such a beautiful nurse makes the pain worth suffering."

Randy looked at the two men. James was obviously annoyed by his friend's attempts at flirtation. As she allowed the captain to help her back into her seat, she couldn't figure out why he was so angry. She didn't need protection from Stephen. No, the one she really needed protection from was herself. From herself and her reaction to James Grayson's kiss.

James intrigued her. For the first time in her life, she found herself attracted to a man. When he held her in his arms, she had felt the depth of his emotions and the strength of his character within herself. In a weak moment, she had allowed him to see her pain. A dangerous thing to do. Until she knew exactly why he had come to Calicut, to her home, she had to be wary around him.

"Gentlemen, we will be having tea and dessert in the salon," Randy announced as Abu pulled out her chair. "While we are waiting for it to be served, Captain, perhaps you will tell me what brings you to India. Are you a man who travels for pleasure, or is this business?"

James offered his arm and led her from the dining room into the salon. "My journey is for business, but I do not want to bore you with the dreary details of such things."

"Nonsense, Captain, I'm eager to hear all about it."

"Very well, if you insist." James sat beside Randy on the divan and talked about his plans for setting up trade in India. When he mentioned the dowager's letter of introduction, he remembered the package she had sent to her granddaughter.

He retrieved the parcel from the console table and gave it to Randy. "Nana asked that I give this to you. There's a letter from her inside the box."

Randy untied the cord and opened the box. Wrapped in many layers of tissue paper, she found the delicate porcelain doll.

"This doll looks like me," she exclaimed. "Not now, of course, but when I was a little girl."

"Nana called it a portrait doll. She gave the artist a miniature painting of you that your father had sent to England." James studied her closely. "There is one thing that puzzles me, Randy. The miniature and the doll have green eyes and light auburn hair. I can understand hair getting darker, but has your eye color changed as well?"

Laughing, Randy shook her head. "No, my eyes have always

been gold. On occasion, my eyes reflect some of the colors I wear, but that's not what happened in this case. You see, the artists here in India are very good, but highly superstitious. They have never seen eyes the color of mine and thought I had some sort of mystical powers. Rather than duplicate a color they think magic, they painted all my portraits with green eyes.''

She placed the doll back into the box. ''Thank you for delivering Nana's present to me. Before I retire tonight, I'll read her missive and begin one of my own for you to return to her. I believe you mentioned another letter from Nana?''

''Yes, I did. Actually there are two. One was a letter of introduction asking your father to assist me in my business negotiations and the other is a very important message to him from Nana.'' He removed the packet from his coat and gave it to her. ''By rights, both letters now belong to you.''

Randy stared at the sealed envelope. It was addressed to her father in a familiar hand. After listening to James talk about Nana and seeing the doll, she wanted to believe that he was telling the truth and was not a part of some scheme orchestrated by Brandon Spencer. With another piece of evidence in her hand, she was anxious to see what it contained.

''If you gentlemen will excuse me, I will read this alone in the library. Abu will serve you tea and dessert while I'm gone.'' Not waiting for a reply, Randy quit the room.

Sitting down in an upholstered side chair, Stephen stirred sugar into the cup of tea Abu handed to him. ''I certainly hope the letter isn't bad news.''

James walked toward the mantel, deep in thought. ''According to that letter, Randy is destined to be a very rich woman. Now that her father is gone, she is Miranda Wentworth's sole heir.''

''What about the dowager's stepson?''

''Richard inherited his father's titles, lands, and holdings. This fortune is strictly the dowager's. She is one of the wealthiest women in Europe.''

"Then why are you so distracted? Telling a person she will be coming into a great deal of money should be good news."

James nodded. "I know, but the dowager has asked that her granddaughter come to England. Under the circumstances, it would be for the best. I would gladly take her back on my ship, but something tells me Randy will not be eager to go."

Randy dropped the letter on the desk. "Oh, Nana, I am sorry, but I just can't do it. I would never be able to fit into your world. I would be an embarrassment to you. Here in India, they accept my strange abilities and I can use my skill to do good. I have work at the mission, friends, and my pets. Besides, I have a debt to repay."

Sitting behind her father's desk, she stared at his portrait hanging on the far wall. "Someday, Papa, the person who murdered you will be found and severely punished. And if justice is lax in its duties, I shall see it done myself."

She put the letter in the desk and returned to her guests.

"Tell me, Captain, did Nana reveal to you what was in that letter?" Randy asked when James stood to greet her.

"Yes, she did. If your father was reluctant to accept her offer, Nana wanted me to champion her cause. To that end, I now ask you to consider her plight. She is widowed and alone, living for the day that her only grandchild will join her in England. It would be an honor if you traveled on my ship and let me be a part of making Nana's greatest dream come true."

Randy governed her reaction to his gently spoken words. "Thank you for your generous offer, but the answer is no. As much as I would like to help Nana, I cannot leave India. Not now, nor any time in the future."

"Why not?" Her cool reply rankled James. "You are alone here and you need your family."

"You know nothing about me or my needs, Captain. I have obligations here that you could never begin to understand."

"England is your home. Your true home."

"India is my home." Randy folded her arms across her chest and glared defiantly at him. "I was born in this house, and this is where I intend to stay."

James's voice rose with irritation. "Without a doubt, Randy, you are the most obstinate woman I have ever met."

"And I'm sure there have been plenty of women in your life to compare me with!" Randy quickly realized what she had said and was embarrassed by her words. She began to laugh.

The music of her laughter was contagious and served as a balm to James's irritation. His deep laughter joined hers.

"Oh," she said with a giggle, "I'm so very sorry."

James shook his head. "No, I'm the one who should apologize. I don't know what came over me."

The effect Randy had on him surprised James. And distressed him somewhat. With all he had yet to do, he knew he should distance himself from this beautiful young woman or risk losing everything—his control, his plans for the future, and his heart.

Stephen heaved a sigh as he came to stand beside them. "I'm glad that confrontation is over. For a moment, I was afraid you two would come to blows." He chuckled when James scowled at him.

"I hope you will let me make amends for my behavior, James," Randy offered brightly, "and allow me to help you with your business contacts. I am acquainted with my father's associates and I could ask—"

"That won't be necessary," James replied, his tone cool and impersonal. "If I can't handle these meetings on my own, then I should not be in business."

"But if I spoke to these gentlemen on your behalf, it would make your task a bit easier."

"Thank you, but the answer is still no."

"You were willing to accept my father's assistance."

James nodded. "That was different. I could never ask a lady to sully her hands in my business. Chad Gerard offered to show me around Calicut in the morning so I can meet the merchants and plantation owners on my own.''

"Fine, try it your way," she replied tersely, "but don't be surprised if you find doors closed to you. The local vendors are a tightly knit group who trust no one. Even the native growers shirk from dealing with strangers, especially stubborn foreigners who refuse to understand their place here.''

James was noticeably incensed. He was a wealthy man with his own ship, a large estate in England, and numerous successful investments. How could this young chit deem to tell him how to conduct business? With her genteel manners, she was far better suited to tending a garden or pouring tea in a drawing room. Arranging flowers and sewing embroidery were probably the most difficult things Randy had ever done.

"As I said before, ma'am, I won't be needing your assistance, but I thank you just the same.''

It was after ten o'clock when James and Stephen left the Collins home with one of the footmen. The native servant led the way to the port as the two friends discussed the outcome of their evening.

"I really can't believe that you turned her down," Stephen complained. "You may enjoy sleeping in the oversized bed in your cabin, but my bunk leaves a lot to be desired. After six weeks of sleeping on something akin to an inquisitor's rack, I would have loved to spend a night or two in a big feather bed. Hot baths, good food, beautiful company—and you said no!''

"Stop grousing," James told him. "If you're tired of living on my ship, why don't you spend some of your money and stay in a hotel? I am sure there must be a suitable inn near the British compound that could accommodate even you, your lordship.''

"Don't be angry, James. I just don't understand why you refused the lady's invitation to stay in her home. She was very disappointed when you declined her offer.''

"Not that I owe you an explanation, but there are several good reasons why I said no to Miranda Collins," James replied. "For one, she's a young lady, single and gently bred. Imagine how it would appear if two men stayed in her house without the benefit of a parent or guardian. Second, I don't want to interfere with her life."

Stephen shook his head. "But she assured you none of that was a problem. Between the servants, guards, and groundskeepers, there must be fifty people with her. And that doesn't include her nurse and Abu. They are adequate chaperons."

"I really don't care. I'm sure the lady only made the offer because she was grateful for receiving the gift and letter from her grandmother."

"That's absurd, James. She wanted us to stay. Randy is—"

"Stop calling her that!" James demanded sharply. "Miss Collins is not one of your tarts, to be seduced with honeyed words and pet names. Stay away from her or you'll deal with me."

"Sorry, Jamie. I didn't know you wanted the lady for yourself," Stephen taunted.

"Your overactive imagination is going to get you in trouble. Miranda Collins is a lovely young woman, but she's not the sort to get involved with unless one wants to get married. I'm not looking for a wife, nor will I pursue a relationship with her. Besides, the lady made it abundantly clear that she doesn't want to leave India, and I will never give up my home in England. So you see, Stephen, other than her being Nana's granddaughter, I have no interest in Miranda Collins."

Stephen laughed. "Say what you will, Jamie boy, but I don't believe a word of it. I'll wager a thousand pounds that you'll be married to Randy within the year. And you know I've never made a bet that I didn't win."

"Then this will be a first, my friend. By the way, I will take my winnings in gold," James called out as he rode to catch up with their guide.

Clenching the reins in his hands, James fought to quell his

irritation. Stephen was far too perceptive for his liking. How could he explain the growing feelings he held for Miranda Collins when he didn't understand them himself? Only once before in his life had he been drawn to a woman so quickly. And that little escapade had nearly cost him his life.

Her name was Caroline Sutcliffe. With a pretty face, silvery blond hair, and violet eyes, she was the eldest daughter of Viscount Hedley. At twenty-one, James thought he had found the woman of his dreams in his sweet Caroline. On their second meeting, he declared his love to her and made plans to offer for her hand in marriage.

Yet a sense of uneasiness had swept over him when she encouraged his attentions and swore that she loved him too. He wondered whether she was telling the truth or being coy. Caroline was a lady, he admonished himself; it would be wrong to doubt her word. A few days later, he knew believing her had been a mistake.

"I was a fool to follow my heart, but never again," James muttered under his breath. "Not ever again."

Chapter 4

Dressed in a nightgown, Randy sat on her bed playing with a small, chattering monkey while Jarita drew a brush through her thick hair. Like the motherly bird she was named for, the ayah was vigilant in caring for her charge. The tiny woman with dark eyes and graying hair loved the girl she had raised and took great pride in all of her accomplishments.

"So, my baby, tell me more about the visitors you entertained tonight. They were tall, English, and pleasing to the eyes, but was there nothing special about them?"

"The one named Stephen was quite funny," Randy admitted, a note of laughter in her voice. "He tried to impress me with his boyish charm. But the other . . ." Her smile faded as she searched for the proper words. "Something about him frightened me."

The hand holding the brush stopped in midair. "You think the *Angrezi* would harm you, my lamb?"

Hearing the fear in the older woman's voice, Randy rushed to reassure her. "No, Jarita, that's not what I mean. Though I've just met him, I know James Grayson would never hurt me."

"Then how does he frighten you?"

Randy rubbed her cheek against the soft fur of the tiny monkey in her hand. "James is like no man I have ever met. When he became angry, I could see into his soul. When I touched him, I felt as though I had known him forever. In the past, he must have been hurt by someone, and now he has little faith in others. His pain became mine; I wanted to hold him and give him comfort. Oh, Jarita, I wanted to protect his heart."

Jarita nodded. "It is your nature to care. Your gift gives you the ability to see these things, my baby."

Randy got up and placed her pet in his brass cage. "No, this was different, Jarita. Until now, I've only been able to use my gift on animals, children, and people too ill or unable to speak for themselves. But James is strong and able to fend for himself. Why was I able to see through him? When he kissed me—"

"He kissed you!" Jarita exclaimed, running to her side. "That *dacoit* dared to touch you?"

"James is not a bandit, Jarita. It was innocent enough. He was only trying to offer me comfort." She placed her arm around Jarita's thin shoulders and walked toward her bed. "Though I must admit his kiss was quite exciting. I have never experienced anything like it."

The dreamy tone of her voice made Jarita smile. "Has my baby at last found a man to love? Is that what frightens you?"

"I am not frightened of James, only my reaction to him. I would sooner love a porcupine than that man!"

Angered by her memories, Randy dropped onto her bed and punched her pillows. "He's the most stubborn man I have ever had the misfortune of meeting!"

Jarita rolled her eyes. "After but one meeting you can say this? What has he done to anger you so?"

"The brute insulted me! When I realized that James had been sent by Nana, I offered to help him set up trade in Calicut, by introducing him to Papa's friends. And do you know what he said? He said no! And do you know why? Because I am a woman!"

By the time Randy finished her declaration, she was shouting. She crossed her arms over her chest and fell back against her pillows in a fitful huff.

"Hai-mai!" the ayah exclaimed, shaking her head. "Such a temper for a lady. I pray you did not blister the *Huzur's* ear with such anger."

"Well . . . just for a moment or two," Randy confessed, "though I did try to make amends for my behavior. Like any gracious hostess, I offered them the use of my home during their stay in Calicut, but the captain chose to decline this as well." Turning over, she sighed. "Perhaps it was all for the best."

Without warning, Randy sat up in bed and looked around the room. "Where is she? Has Sidra been in tonight?"

"Ai-yee! That one has as little patience as you, my baby." Jarita held up her hands. "She was here earlier, but departed when she found that you were gone."

"Sidra probably went hunting in the jungle beyond the grounds. She never stays around when strangers visit the house." Randy pulled the covers over herself and eased back onto her pillows. "Leave the terrace doors open. Sidra will come in when she's ready. Good night, Jarita. Pleasant dreams."

The ayah began to douse the oil lamps in the room. Her dark eyes darted toward the open doors. "Perhaps I should remain with you tonight, my baby."

Randy understood the woman's apprehension and was warmed by her concern. "I shall be fine, Jarita. Akbar's men are patrolling the grounds and Sidra will be back soon. Since the day I found her in the jungle, she has slept in this room with me. So find your bed and do not worry."

"A dog to protect you, I understand, but a tiger . . ." Jarita muttered as she shuffled out the door. "It would be wiser to ask a python for a hug."

Randy stared at the netted canopy over her bed. Only the light from a small lamp on the side table illuminated the room.

Since the night of her father's murder, she couldn't sleep in the dark. Her words to Jarita had been spiked with bravado, meant to reassure the older woman, but did little to relieve her tension.

She suddenly recalled the gift from her grandmother and the note she had yet to read inside its box. Getting up, she brought the parcel to the bed and opened it. As she knelt on the bed, Randy read the letter aloud.

Dear Miranda,

I love you, and someday everything I have will be yours. Rather than wait for my death, please accept this small token with the knowledge that a piece of my heart goes with it. May its magical powers bring you happiness and keep you safe. Above all, may it bring you love. Remember never to take things at face value; look below the surface and a treasure will be yours.

All my love,
Nana

"Now, what does that mean?" Randy took the doll from the box. Her finger grazed the delicate porcelain features. "This gift is quite extraordinary, but magical powers? Nana, your imagination is as fanciful as mine." She put the doll on the bed beside her while she reread the cryptic note.

A shiver ran up her spine. She wasn't alone. A knowing smile came to Randy's lips.

"Shame on you, Sidra. How dare you lurk in the dark and scare me like that! Come over here and stop this foolishness." Though Randy tried to remain stern, she couldn't disguise the amusement in her voice.

The large orange-and-black striped beast silently stepped from the shadows. With a graceful leap, Sidra jumped on the bed and took her place beside her mistress. Looking to be stroked, she placed her head on Randy's lap. The amber glow of her eyes settled on the doll lying nearby on the bed.

"You're really very spoiled, aren't you, Sidra?" Randy rubbed the cat's brightly colored fur. "You stay out all evening and now you want me to spend the rest of the night petting you."

The tiger's long tail whipped rhythmically against the bedding while she enjoyed the gentle touch of her mistress's hand. Her eyes narrowed to wary slits; then, without warning, one of her front paws reached out and knocked the doll to the floor.

"Honestly, I'm getting quite annoyed with your tantrums." Randy leaned down and retrieved the doll. "Yesterday you frightened my new monkey, and tonight you're attacking toys. See, it's only a doll." As she shook the doll in front of the tiger's nose, Randy felt something move inside its body.

"Now you've done it. Your little show of temper has broken my gift from Nana." Setting the doll on the bed, Randy lifted its gown and petticoats to survey the damage. Under a flap of material, she discovered a hidden compartment built into the torso of the doll. She reached inside the hollow body and found something cold and metallic resting in the cotton batting. After pricking her finger on a sharp point, she deftly removed the mysterious object.

Randy was awestruck as the lamplight touched the stones of the brooch. The sparkling white diamonds were only outshone by the fiery glow of the massive red gem that was set in the center of the magnificent piece of jewelry.

"Oh, Nana, how can you describe this as a small token? With all his wealth, the Maharajah of Mysore has nothing to compare to this. Why have you sent it to me?" Randy held the brooch in her hand. Recalling her grandmother's note, she laughed and shook her head. "It isn't possible. There's no such thing as magical powers. Maybe James knows about this. When I see him, I'll ask him. Whenever that will be." She sighed. "After this evening, I doubt I will ever see him again."

Randy was jarred from her sad thoughts when Sidra hissed at her. Due to the damage in her throat, the tiger could only growl when provoked or angered, or purr like an oversized

kitten when she was content. The hissing sound was how Sidra
gained attention. Dropping the brooch on the coverlet, Randy
cupped the tiger's head in her hands, her golden eyes meeting
the animal's warm amber gaze.

"You feel my sadness, don't you, Sidra? I could easily love
James, but I must not let this happen. He would never be able
to accept me as I really am. I can't read all of his thoughts,
only those fraught with anger. With his deeply held convictions,
he would probably consider my gift a betrayal. So you see, my
friend, it will be for the best if I never see him again."

A deep loneliness encompassed her heart. Tears welled in
her eyes, escaping to trickle down her heated cheeks.

As if sensing her mistress's pain, Sidra leaned forward and
rubbed her furred jaw against Randy's face, coaxing and comforting her with its silky touch. Randy hugged Sidra tightly
around the neck while she cried.

"But I won't ever forget him, Sidra. While James held me
in his arms, my troubles disappeared like the morning mist on
a summer's day. His lips touched mine with tenderness, and
for the briefest of moments I saw a glimpse of what love could
be. But not with him. No, never with him. . . ."

Chapter 5

The large bazaar in the center of town was bustling with activity. Vendors loudly hawked their wares, selling brightly colored fabrics, livestock, wool rugs, spices, fish, jewelry, and produce. People crowded the open stalls, bartering for goods as their ancestors had done for hundreds of years.

The strange sights and smells attacked the senses of the newly arrived visitors. James and Stephen were struck by the contrast of wealth and poverty that was found in the marketplace. People dressed in silks and jewels rushed by beggars wearing rags, begging for alms. The thin children of the poor played in the dusty street, while the well-fed offspring of the wealthy were toted about by their ayahs and servants.

Making their way through the crowd, James's attention was drawn to a horse trader's barn that was set back from the street. In its fenced corral stood an animal he wanted for his own.

The magnificent horse was a spirited Arabian. The muscular line and build were proof of its breed, but the stallion was the largest Arabian James had ever seen. Besides its size, the horse's coloring was unique. Its coat was a burnished gold, while its mane and tail were long, silky, and silvery white.

Stephen and the lieutenant rode with James to the horse trader's barn. The spirited animal pranced nervously inside the corral when they dismounted and walked toward the fence.

"Have you ever seen anything like him, Stephen? Look at that color, and the size of him! I must have him. Chad, go tell the dealer that I want to buy this horse."

In less than a minute, Chad returned with his news. "Sorry, James, but the animal isn't for sale. According to the old man, this horse has already been sold."

James wasn't easily put off. "Tell the man that I will double his price. I like this horse and I mean to have him."

When Chad returned with the same reply, James became more determined to possess the golden stallion and tripled his offer. Before the lieutenant could turn around, the horse dealer himself called out to James in English.

"Forgive me, sahib, but as I told the officer, this beast is not for sale. Not to you or anyone."

James regarded the small, dark-turbaned man. "Perhaps the one who purchased the stallion would be interested in making a profit on this animal. Only a fool would turn down the chance to triple his money."

The old dealer grinned with yellowed teeth. "Or perhaps a very wealthy man who has no need for making a profit, sahib?" He chuckled and explained. "The one who purchased this horse is the *Rajkumar* Akbar. I have searched two years for one such as this for him. The prince is making it a gift to his friend, sahib."

Stephen poked James in the ribs with his elbow to tease him. "Some friend you turned out to be! You never bought me a horse like this one. Come to think of it, what have you ever done for me, Jamie boy?"

"Leave off, Stephen, or I'll abandon you here in India when I sail home and you can see how much you can do on your own," James replied with a grin. Returning his attention to the dealer, he asked the man to make his offer to the prince. If Akbar accepted, James promised the old man a substantial fee for his efforts.

"I will make the offer, sahib, but should he decline, you may be the better for it. The stallion is remarkable in looks, but mean in spirit. No one has been able to mount him, and he injured three of my men as they groomed him. I told the prince, but he is not concerned. He claims the one who is to receive him will be able to tame him." Shaking his grizzled head, the old man grumbled as he walked away. "May Allah preserve us all from the wisdom of such fools."

"I think we should be on our way, my lord," Chad suggested. "I don't know the city well, and I would like to get back to the compound before dark."

They had just mounted their horses when a large contingent of riders arrived at the horse dealer's barn. In the midst of the heavily armed royal guards were two richly dressed native men. Though some distance away, James and Stephen could easily view the activity near the fenced corral.

"Let's wait and see if the prince's friend is capable of handling his new present," James proposed. After seeing Akbar assist the smaller rider from his mount, James laughed out loud. "If that's the one who's meant to tame that beast, I may be able to buy that stallion for a bargain price after all. I hope that little fellow doesn't get killed for his efforts."

"What do you think of your surprise, Randy?"

Randy shook her turbaned head in awe. "Akbar, he is magnificent. But why did you buy him for me?"

"I wanted a golden horse for you, Sona Ag. The golden fire of the house of Javid Surat Kahn deserves no less. What will you call him?"

Leaning against the fence, Randy studied the noble beast. "I will call him Garuda. Like the god Vishnu's mythical mount, he is all golden with a touch of white."

"But Garuda had the wings of an eagle and the body and limbs of a man."

"I know, Akbar, but I don't care. My Garuda's limbs are better than any man's and with me on his back, he shall run like the wind."

Suddenly, a man called out from behind them. "Excuse me, your highness. May I have a word with you?"

Recognizing James's voice, Randy kept herself partially hidden by Akbar when she turned to steal a peek at him.

James was dressed in fine European clothes. His head was bare, revealing his tousled light brown hair. Randy thought he was quite handsome, but the arrogance he exuded made her ill at ease. As he approached Akbar, he seemed totally unconcerned by the guards that surrounded him. When the prince waved off his men, James smiled and held out his hand in greeting.

"Prince Akbar, I am Captain James Grayson. I spoke to the dealer about this horse and he informed me that you had already purchased him."

Akbar shook his hand and placed himself between Randy and the smiling captain. "Yes, I purchased the stallion, and before you ask, I am not interested in selling him. Only a moment ago, I gave the horse to my friend."

James nodded toward the slight figure standing behind Akbar, looking into the corral. "No offense, your highness, but I doubt that your friend there can handle this horse. The dealer told me the stallion is extremely wild and mean. Are you willing to risk your friend's life with such an animal?"

Akbar grinned. "There will be no risk involved, Captain. I have never come upon an animal my friend could not handle."

"We are discussing a stallion, your highness. Not a kitten or a dog. This horse could very well kill your friend. If you think about it, I'm sure you will see that I am correct."

It took all of Randy's control not to answer James herself. Though she wasn't looking at him, she would have wagered her mother's strand of pink pearls that James was smiling over the victory he was anticipating. He wanted her horse, but she wasn't about to let him win it.

Lowering the tone of her voice so it sounded more like a young man whispering, she spoke in Hindi to Akbar.

The Prince nodded and turned back to James with a cocky grin on his face. "Captain, if you will step back a few paces, my friend will show you the error in your thinking."

Randy climbed over the fence. The stallion backed up several steps and nervously eyed her as she came toward him. Whipping his head from side to side, he snorted a warning before he reared up on his hind legs.

"No, no, my handsome Garuda," she crooned in a low voice. "You must not fear me. I would never hurt you, my heart. There are no weapons in my hands, and I won't let anyone harm you. Come to me, Garuda." With her arms held out to the horse, she quietly waited for him to approach her.

At first, the stallion charged at her, but Randy never moved a muscle. Stopping abruptly before her, he viciously pawed the ground in a threatening manner. He then began to run around the corral, circling her as she remained motionless in the center of the yard. The circles became smaller and smaller, and soon the horse was brushing against her as he passed. Intrigued by the smell of her, his curiosity to get closer to her seemed too difficult to resist. His velvety nose touched her outstretched hand, inviting her caress. With her fingertips, Randy lightly stroked his jaw and began speaking to him.

"Yes, Garuda, that's right. I will not harm you. All will be well, my handsome friend. You can trust me."

Rubbing her cheek along his snout, she blew into the horse's nostril and let him become accustomed to her scent. From her tunic, she removed a handkerchief, and after allowing him to sniff it, she used it to brush against his clenched jaw and neck. As she continued to stroke his golden coat, Randy's voice soothed his fears. When the cloth came in contact with his right foreleg, she felt the large animal recoil.

"Poor Garuda. You are in pain. Allow me to help you."

Kneeling on the ground, she ran her hands down his long, muscular leg. As she reached the hoof, the stallion jerked back from her touch. His dark eyes watched when she took his hoof into her hands and studied the bottom of it. A jagged stone was imbedded in the frog of the horse's hoof. Taking the dagger from the sheath she wore in the sash around her waist, Randy carefully dug out the pointed rock.

"When we get home, Garuda, I will soak your injury and apply an ointment that will ease your pain and help you heal quickly."

The stallion cocked his head to the side and gazed at her as though he understood her words. When Randy walked back to the fence, the large, imposing animal was at her side.

"Randy, you are amazing." Akbar opened the gate for her. "You have made this wild stallion behave like a trained pup. I knew you could do it!"

She looked around the corral. "Where is Captain Grayson?"

Akbar chuckled. "The *Angrezi* rode off with his companions in quite a state of temper. I suppose he saw enough to convince him that you weren't going to get killed by Garuda after all."

With a rueful smile, Randy shook her head. "I would never admit this to anyone but you, Akbar, but for a moment, I wasn't sure myself. When Garuda first charged at me, I wondered if I had finally found an animal too wild or too hurt to be helped."

"Ah, little sister, I doubt there is a beast in the world who would not fall victim to your charms. Even two-legged ones like me are not immune to your beauty, grace, and—*ooooph!*"

"Behave yourself, brother," Randy warned in a low voice, "or next time I won't punch your stomach. I will select a far more sensitive target for your punishment."

Akbar held up his hands. "Randy, I cannot help but tease you. Even though you want to be angry with me, I know there is a smile meant just for me hidden in that grimace of yours."

Randy couldn't hold back her grin. "You do know me well, Akbar, and our friendship means a great deal to me."

Akbar found himself staring at her mouth and shook his

head. "Come, Randy, let's take your new pet home before I taste your lips again and earn myself another penalty."

"Not only that, my brother, but how will you explain why you were seen kissing another young man in the middle of the bazaar? Such behavior would totally destroy your reputation as the great lover of Calicut."

Akbar's eyes regarded her appearance as they mounted their horses. "You may be dressed as a boy, Randy, but with a face of an angel, one would have to be . . ." Seeing her brow rise, he changed the subject. "Perhaps on the way to your home, you can tell me of this reputation I have acquired. Am I really called the great lover of Calicut?"

"Dear Lord, save me from vain men with overdeveloped egos," Randy called out toward the sky. Suddenly, she felt Garuda nipping at her tunic sleeve. Stroking his nose, she smiled. "But never from you, my handsome one. I think I prefer my males with four legs. They have no vanity, they don't torment me, and best of all, they can outrun the two-legged breed without even trying. Come on, Garuda! Let's go home."

With Garuda beside her, Randy steered her mount through the crowded marketplace. Akbar and his guards followed, leaving a billowing cloud of dust in their wake from the sunbaked street.

"Well, Stephen, for once in your life, you were correct. I should have chosen a larger port to set up trade," James stated bitterly as they made their way along the crowded docks to his ship's berth. "Between the distrust of the locals and Spencer's lack of support, this entire venture has come to naught."

Stephen mopped his brow with his handkerchief. "But Spencer didn't say he wouldn't help you. Chad said the major was called away on an urgent matter and would return within a week."

"Are you really so gullible, Stephen? Spencer knew I would come to him for an explanation of the lies he told me about

Randy. Rather than face me, he found an excuse to leave the city. I wouldn't be surprised to find that he is holed up in his quarters at the compound, waiting for me to leave Calicut.''

"If that's the case, then what are we going to do now? Do you want to wait a few days and see if he appears?''

James shook his head. "I'm not going to waste any more time in Calicut. If I work on my charts this evening we'll be able to sail on the morning tide.''

"Tomorrow? You want to leave tomorrow? But what about Miranda Collins? We can't leave without saying farewell.''

"I have a great deal of work to do tonight, Stephen. If you're so concerned about the lady, why don't you pen her a note and have one of the men take it over to the governor's office. I don't care one way or another.''

Though his words sounded calm, his disinterest was a sham. Since he left Randy the night before, she had been constantly on his mind. He had lain awake for hours, recalling her lovely face. The kiss he had placed on her lips left him yearning for more. But what would happen if he extended his visit? What if he became addicted to Randy's kisses? Leaving her behind when he returned to England would be an impossible task.

Staying away from her was his only recourse.

Deep in thought, James climbed the gangplank to his ship and was greeted by his first mate, Emmet O'Donald. The lanky Irish seaman had worked for his family for many years, eventually becoming the captain of one of their ships. When he learned of the plans James had made for the clipper and his intention to sail to India, Emmet had offered his services aboard the new vessel. James had known the older man all his life, so he eagerly accepted his offer to help.

"Captain, you've a guest waitin' in your cabin,'' Emmet called, his brogue as thick as his copper-red hair and mustache.

James smiled expectantly. "A guest? Is it a lady?''

"No, sir, a man. He said 'twas most important that he talk to you as soon as possible. He's waitin' below with your cabin boy, Harry.'' Seeing the crestfallen look on James's face,

Emmet asked, "Have I done somethin' wrong, sir? Shall I send him on his way, Captain?"

"No, Emmet. I'll go down and see what the man wants."

As James walked away, Emmet shook his head. "If naught is wrong, then why is the lad frownin' so?"

Grinning, Stephen patted Emmet on the back. "You're not the cause of his distress. In spite of his denials, I think James is a bit disappointed that his visitor wasn't a lovely auburn-haired minx with golden eyes."

James entered his cabin to find Harry staring at the bearded man sitting beside the dining table. Wearing a turban and gold earrings, Abu Nazir had garnered the unabashed curiosity of the twelve-year-old boy from Liverpool.

"Nazir, why are you here? Has something happened to Randy—I mean Miss Collins?"

Abu came to his feet and bowed respectfully. "Missy Collins is quite well at present, Captain. It is my concern for her future that brings me here today."

"Then if she is well, did Randy send you to me, Nazir?" James considered the possibility. A slim smile crossed his lips.

"She knows nothing of my visit, *Huzur*. I have come on my own. Although we have just met, I know you can be trusted with the information I am about to impart. May we sit?"

With some reluctance, James nodded in agreement. "Fine, Nazir, I'll listen to what you have to say, but first allow me a few minutes' respite. This heat is plaguing me." He removed his coat and washed his face over the basin of tepid water that Harry had prepared.

After sending his cabin boy for refreshments, James took the seat across from Abu at the table. "I don't know why you have come to me, Nazir. But I'm hot and tired. It's only because of my concern for the dowager that I've agreed to listen to you."

"You must take Missy Collins to England. If she remains in India, she will die."

Abu's ominous pronouncement caught James totally unprepared. He couldn't believe that he'd heard the man correctly. "Randy will die? What's the matter with her, Nazir? Is she ill?"

"My lady is quite healthy, *Huzur*. Her only affliction is that someone has been trying to murder her. There have been at least three attempts on her life thus far." Seeing the disbelief on James's face, Abu continued.

"Several weeks ago, a basket of peaches arrived at the house. The bearer claimed that Prince Akbar had sent them to my mistress. Peaches are her favorite, and because the prince often sends such gifts, no one questioned the man, and the basket was placed in her suite. Among the family pets was a langur monkey who constantly got into mischief. Drawn by the sweet fragrance of the fruit, he got out of his cage in my mistress's sitting room and took a peach. After eating several bites, the monkey fell dead. The fruit had been poisoned.

"Missy Collins was still upset over her father's death, and rather than alarm her, I decided not to tell her of the incident. By the time she came home that afternoon, the dead animal and the tainted fruit had been disposed of. She was told that her monkey had escaped to the gardens."

James was perplexed. "Was keeping it from Randy a wise thing to do, Nazir?"

"At the time, it seemed to be. But when the snake was found in her room that night—"

"A snake? In her room?"

Abu nodded. "Snakes often seek shelter in our homes here in India, but this serpent was carried in. Most likely in the basket of peaches."

"If snakes are such a common thing, then what makes you suspect this was an act of treachery?"

"Because the snake found in her bedchamber was not a native creature, but a spitting cobra from Egypt," Abu informed him. "This cobra can spit venom into the eyes of its victim, causing blindness and extreme pain. That is when the viper goes in for the kill. But thanks be to the gods and my mistress's quick reflexes, a tragedy was averted. She saw the snake hiding along the wall. The guards captured the cobra and killed it."

Running his fingers through his hair, James shook his head. "Thank heaven Randy saw it. But didn't you say that there were three attempts on her life? Tell me about the other."

"When Sir Jonathan was murdered, he was not the only intended victim. The infidel dog tried to kill Missy Collins in the same wretched manner. If not for Sidra's intervention, he would have succeeded."

"Who is Sidra? A servant or a guard?"

Abu stroked his beard. "Sidra is a companion to my lady. Ever watchful of our mistress, she sleeps on a pallet in her room. When the villain tried to harm Missy Collins, Sidra knocked him to the floor and stopped him. The screams from the suite woke everyone in the house. Guards rushed in, a struggle ensued, but during the melee, the intruder escaped."

"Damn that Major Spencer!" James snapped, slamming his fist on the tabletop. "He told me Jonathan had been murdered by a worshipper of some cult in retaliation for his work to dispose of them. Spencer never mentioned that Randy had been attacked."

"If he had done so, *Huzur*, it would have condemned him. Other than the maharajah and Akbar, no one outside the household knows of the attempts on her life," Abu told him simply.

His impassive tone enraged James. "Damn it, why keep it a secret? Why didn't you report these incidents to the British authorities? Where are your loyalties! Are you going to wait until some fanatic succeeds and Randy is dead? Obviously some native faction has set the Collins family as a target."

"Or so it would seem. I have my doubts. Until I am convinced otherwise, no one, especially anyone at the British compound, will learn of the attempts on her life," Abu announced, angrily coming to his feet. "And never, Captain, are you to question my loyalties. I have pledged my life to keeping my mistress safe. On the day she was born, Miranda Collins was placed in my care. If she were my own child, I could not love her more than I do. I would gladly die for her.''

The vehemence in Abu's voice calmed James. ''I am sorry, Nazir. Please accept my apology.'' James stood and offered Abu his hand. ''Sit down, my friend. Share your doubts and fears with me. Help me to understand.''

Taking his seat again, Abu started to speak.

''It is true that Sir Jonathan was strangled in his bed. The killer crept into Randy's room for the same purpose. He was dressed in native garb and carried a knotted scarf to complete his deed, just as the followers of Kali, the black goddess, have done for hundreds of years. But the man was not an Indian, nor was he a devotee of the evil deity.

''Thugees are an ancient secret cult who murder to appease Kali, but they are not a mindless rabble. As assassins they have strict rules about how victims are chosen, where the killings are done, and exactly how they are to carry out their deeds. The faithful use yellow scarves called *ramaals,* while the leaders have *ramaals* that are black, red, or green. But never white silk, such as our intruder used.

''Thugees attack travelers on the road. They would not enter a man's home, nor do they act alone. But our intruder's most telling error was trying to kill Randy. Because Kali is a goddess, the murder of a woman is strictly forbidden. To harm a female would bring dishonor and invite the wrath of Kali.''

''If this is a secret sect, then how do you know so much about them?'' James asked. ''Are you one of their number, Abu?''

''No, *Huzur,* but I nearly was.'' Abu's gaze became distant and remote. ''When I was a boy of five, I accompanied my father to Jaipur. He was a gem merchant who made such journeys several times a year. One night, Thugees attacked our camp and killed everyone except me. The leader, who had lost his son to illness, took me and taught me their ways, but I wanted no part of him or his group of murderers. Two years passed before I escaped. Yet where was I to go? I was a small boy alone in the jungle with no knowledge of my real home. I prayed for assistance.

"The gods must have been listening, because a hunting party led by the old Maharajah of Mysore, Niranjan, found me on the sixth day. After nearly a week alone in the wilderness, I was grateful to be alive and told Niranjan that I would rather be a slave cleaning his stables than to be returned to the leader of the Thugees. But Niranjan recognized my intelligence. He had me educated with his sons, saying I might one day be a help to him in his court. Not only did I learn the subjects taught to the princes, but I also studied with the priests, the physicians, and the scholars who visited Mysore. I served Niranjan and his son, Javid, as scribe and advisor. When Jonathan Collins received his appointment in Calicut, I was sent to assist him. I have been with the Collins family ever since."

"So, you're not a Thugee," James conceded, "but what makes you think that the man who murdered Collins wasn't an Indian? The Thugees aren't the only ones angered by the British government."

"During the struggle in my mistress's room, the infidel was hurt and left something behind," Abu replied.

"Well, what was it? A weapon? An article of clothing?"

Abu smiled coldly. "No, *Huzur,* nothing so mundane as that. What we found can only belong to this one man. You see, during the fight, he was wounded and lost a part of himself. The small finger of his right hand, to be exact. It was clean, without callous, and unmistakably from a white man. Find a man with the missing appendage and you have found the murderer."

In spite of the heat in the room, an icy chill ran through James. A myriad of recollections crowded his mind. When Harry delivered the pitcher of orange juice he had ordered, James was oblivious to his presence. It was only after the boy had served the drinks and left the cabin that James began to speak.

"Tell me about Brandon Spencer. The major did his utmost to keep me away from Randy, and I want to know why."

"The major claims to be in love with her, but Missy Collins has declined his many proposals of marriage. Even after Sir Jonathan's death, he did not relent in his quest of her. She tried to keep it from me, but I know Spencer threatened to send word to her uncle in England of her father's passing if she did not agree to marry him. She may think he is bluffing, but I am not so sure. Spencer appears to be a very desperate man."

Crossing his arms over his chest, James nodded. "I agree, but is he desperate enough to commit murder? Collins's death gave the major an excuse to take over his position and left Randy vulnerable. Maybe the intruder only meant to frighten her. But the lady was well guarded and the intruder found himself injured. If Spencer was responsible for Jonathan's murder, a missing finger would prove his guilt. Was his blackmail a way of forcing Randy into running? When she didn't flee, did he try to have her killed? And if so, was Spencer working alone or is someone else involved in his plot?"

Abu cocked his brow. "So, *Huzur,* you now see why I have kept the truth from the authorities. A word to the wrong person could prove disastrous. Keeping my mistress safe is most important to me. But Missy Collins has sworn to avenge her father's death, regardless of any danger to herself. Akbar, the maharajah, and I have done all we can to protect her, but with each passing day it becomes more difficult. That is why I am asking you to take her to England with you. She will be safe there, *Huzur.*"

James gulped down his glass of juice and chuckled. "You may ask and I may agree, but convincing Randy to go is another issue entirely. Your mistress has made it quite clear that she has no intention of leaving India."

"That is true, *Huzur,* but together, you and I should be able to convince her that going to England will be for the best.

Leaving India at this time is all a part of her destiny. Even your arrival was preordained.''

"Preordained? By whom?"

Abu carefully regarded James and then told him about the court astrologer's prediction and the description of Randy's savior.

"Gopal's words have been with me for eleven years. You are the one, Captain:

> *With eyes like lapis and hair touched by the sun, he shall come from the West seeking her. Born under the sign of the Virgin, he is protected by God and will risk his life, not once, but three times to snatch her from the clutches of death. . . .''*

James scoffed at his words. "This is ludicrous! Many men have my coloring, and blue eyes are quite common in Europe. And the rest of what you said makes no sense to me. Sign of the virgin? Protected by God? Next you'll hand me a brass lamp and tell me that a magic jinni is going to grant me three wishes."

Abu ignored his glib attitude and explained the astrologer's words. "The date of your birth falls between the twenty-second day of August and the twenty-second of September, does it not?"

"Yes," James admitted, "I was born on September the first."

"You are a Virgo, hence referred to as a child born under the sign of the Virgin. As such, you are intelligent, discreet, hard-working, and demand honesty above all things."

James suddenly felt restless. He left his seat and began to pace the room. Abu's words were striking a chord in him.

"*Huzur,* do you know the meaning of your given name?"

James stopped to look at him. "Yes, I do. My aunt keeps a journal of name definitions. It's a hobby of hers. She told me James comes from the Hebrew and means the 'supplanter.' "

"Then perhaps you should inform her that your name in Arabic also means 'protected by God.' So you see, the old astrologer was correct on all counts. Accept your destiny. It is karma that you were sent here to save Missy Collins's life."

"I was sent here by her grandmother to deliver a doll and a couple of letters. Nothing more, nothing less," James snapped. "I will only help because I know how upset the dowager would be if anything happened to Randy. It has nothing to do with some fool soothsayer and his whimsical predictions! Shall we start working on a plan to save your mistress, or would you rather wait until this assassin tries again to carry out his deadly deed?"

"As you wish, *Huzur,*" Abu replied. "Before we proceed, there are things you should know about my mistress. Hurt by losses in her life, she conceals her pain. She is independent, with an education more befitting a man." He stroked his bearded chin. "Tell her you have reconsidered her offer and have decided to accept her help. Gain her trust, and Missy Collins will listen to you. Once you accomplish this, we will tell her about the other attempts on her life and then persuade her to leave India."

James shook his head. "That would take too long. After our confrontation last night, Randy may take a month to forgive me, let alone trust me. She should be told about the attempts on her life right away. Ignorance may be bliss, but in this instance, it could prove deadly." He nodded confidently. "Yes, when we explain the jeopardy she is in, I'm sure Randy will agree to go."

"*Huzur,* Missy Collins is not going to be easy to convince. She is most determined to find her father's murderer. I fear her stubborn nature will prove to be the downfall of our plan."

"Then the lady has met her match," James boasted. "I am just as hard-headed. If reasoning won't move her, I'm not above using physical persuasion to achieve my goals." A sardonic laugh rumbled from his chest. "Perhaps I should haul Randy over my shoulder and carry her onto my ship. I'll warrant she'd scream and claw me like an a cat, but at least she would be safe.''

"You must not attempt this, *Huzur*. To use force could prove painful to—"

"Don't worry, Abu, I would never hurt your mistress."

"No, *Huzur,* you do not understand. I fear you will be—"

James interrupted him again. "All right, Nazir, I promise I won't use force on Randy. She's a fragile young lady and deserves civil treatment. It may take a few days to convince her, but I'm willing to try. Before I gather my things, I'll tell Stephen of our plans."

As the door shut behind James, Abu laughed. "I hope you remember your pledge, *Huzur*. The consequences could prove most embarrassing for you and extremely painful, I fear."

"Ali, you bad boy! How did you get out here to the garden?" Randy lifted the fluffy gray kitten from her lap to scold him. "Until your paw is healed and that bandage removed, you're not to be out. Can't I meditate without your interference?"

In response to her reprimand, the kitten licked her cheek. Randy laughed and nuzzled her nose against his fur. "You win, Ali. If you behave, I'll let you stay here with me."

She placed the kitten in her lap, stroking his silky coat. When Ali had settled into the folds of her saffron gown, she closed her eyes. Sitting on the bench beneath the rose arbor, she inhaled deeply, letting the heady fragrance of the blossoms fill her lungs. Sunbeams filtered through her shuttered lids and warmed her already flushed cheeks. She willed herself to relax, hoping to force all conscious thought from her mind.

Randy had always prided herself on her ability to control her mind, but now her discipline was shattered. No matter how hard she tried, she couldn't stop the haunting images of the previous night from flooding her memory.

James, the handsome English captain with the sparkling blue eyes and a smile that could coax the birds to sing. James, the compassionate man who tried to help her deal with her pain. James, the honorable and thoroughly aggravating gentleman, who refused to accept help from a lady.

"I must stop thinking about him," Randy muttered to herself. "Besides, he's gone and that's all there is to it." Taking a deep, cleansing breath, she cleared her mind. Peace was finally at hand—but not for long.

The flesh on her arms began to tingle. Without warning, Ali jumped from her lap and scurried into the bushes.

"Ali, come back here. You're not supposed to be running about yet." Randy knelt on the ground and searched for the kitten amongst the thick lower branches of the flowering bushes. "When I find you, I have half a mind to lock you up in a cage until your paw heals."

Randy spotted the striped kitten hiding beneath the leafy boughs. She leaned forward, but as her fingertips touched his silky hair, Ali playfully scampered out of reach. It was only when she tried to back away from the bush that Randy discovered that her coronet of plaited hair was snarled in the thorny branches. When she tried to free her braid, thorns pierced the flesh of her hand.

"Ouch!" Randy shook her hand to relieve the pain. Spots of blood erupted on her fingers and palm. The harder she tried to release her hair, the more impossible the task became.

"Ali, when I find you, you're going to make amends for this," she muttered in frustration. "So help me, I'm going to—"

"Randy, what are you doing down there?"

Even without turning around, Randy recognized the identity of her visitor. She was thrilled that James had returned, but humiliated by the position he had found her in. But pain quickly overcame her embarrassment.

"Captain, could I ask you for assistance? I was searching for my kitten and I—well, I've snagged my hair on this bush."

James knelt on the ground beside her. "This shouldn't take

long, Randy. Just sit still for a few moments, and I will get
you out of this,'' he assured her.

Randy felt James carefully finding the pins that held her hair
in place. One by one, he removed them and eased the stinging
in her scalp. She would have sighed with relief, but warm
tremors of excitement coursed through her as his touch turned
the pain into soothing caresses. Randy was so caught up in the
welcome sensation his hands were affording her, she barely
heard what he was saying.

"So, you were hunting for your kitten. I always wanted a
cat, but they made Diana sneeze. I didn't know that until I
brought one home as a gift for her. It was a tiny white kitten.
Poor Diana adored the little thing, but within moments of holding it, she started sneezing and her eyes watered like a flood.''

"Who is Diana?" Randy asked softly.

"Beg pardon—did you say something?''

Randy imagined this Diana he spoke of must be someone
very dear to him. No doubt she was the lady he had named his
ship for. Not wanting to appear too curious about the woman,
she asked a safer question.

"It must have been awful for Diana. Did other animals affect
her as well?''

"No, only cats. But with all the horses and dogs we had
about, I don't think she minded very much,'' James replied.

He gently massaged her tortured scalp and allowed his fingers
to stroke the length of her hair. The wavy locks hung down to
her waist. Like a kitten, she was wooed by his soothing touch.
Randy was so caught up in his tender ministrations, she leaned
back against him and sighed.

Suddenly, she was shaken from her reverie when James
noticed her bloodied hand resting in her lap.

"Dear Lord, what have you done to your hand?''

James lifted her in his arms and carried her to the bench.
Using his handkerchief, he carefully dabbed the blood. Their
foreheads touched when he bent to inspect her injuries.

"It's nothing serious. I pricked myself on the thorns. If you will wrap your handkerchief around my hand, it will suffice until I can find my kitten. I can't leave him in the garden."

James completed his task and raised his eyes to look at her. "You sound very concerned about this cat. You must care for him a great deal."

"Of course I care. I love all my pets, but right now Ali needs me more than the others. I have to find him—"

James suddenly pressed his finger to her lips and halted her words. Grinning, he leaned forward to whisper near her ear.

"Your missing kitten is peeking out from beneath the shrub behind you. If we pretend to ignore him, I think he will come out on his own. What do you think of that idea?"

Randy turned to face him. The finger he had placed on her lips now rested on her cheek. James stroked her skin with the back of his knuckle. She watched him with nervous fascination and felt the warmth of his breath on her face as he brought his mouth closer to hers.

Her eyes closed as James kissed her. She savored the moist, delicate touch of his lips pursed against hers. Her heart was pounding with anticipation when she felt his tongue tracing the edge of her mouth. Just as she was about to return the favor, James suddenly pulled himself away from her.

"What in the devil?" James scowled at the kitten perched on his lap. "Your little friend just climbed my leg like a tree. I must have dozens of claw marks on my thigh alone." Not hiding his annoyance, he lifted the kitten by the scruff of the neck. "Madam, I believe this belongs to you."

Still dazed by their kiss, it took Randy several seconds to gather her wits. When she saw Ali dangling from James's fingers, she snatched the kitten from him and cuddled it to her breast.

"Don't be so rough with him, Captain. Ali didn't know he was doing anything wrong. After what happened to him, it's amazing that he is so playful."

James scratched Ali's head. "I didn't hurt him. He's fine.

But what happened to the little fellow?'' James pointed at the bandaged paw. "Did he have an accident?"

"No," Randy replied with a sigh. "Someone at the British compound tried to cut off one of his claws." Turning the kitten on her lap, she showed James the other paw. "As you can see, Ali was born with extra claws on his front feet. It looks like a human hand with a thumb."

James agreed. The small white paw resembled a hand enclosed in a fuzzy glove. "But why would someone want to cut off his extra claw? It is unusual, but it doesn't seem to bother him."

Randy gazed down at the kitten and stroked his uninjured leg. "People don't like things that are different. Rather than accept Ali and his oddity, some fool tried to cut it off. They would destroy what was special about him, even if it killed him in the process. Those in your civilized world would deem him a freak, while the so-called unenlightened natives of this country readily accept his differences. Some even believe that it is lucky to own such a special cat."

James cupped his hand beneath her chin and made her look up at him. "I think Ali was lucky to find someone like you to take care of him. If I'm ever hurt and in need of help, I pray that God delivers me to one such as you."

His comforting words only added to Randy's apprehension. If James knew of her mental abilities, she wondered what he would do. Would he be appalled by her gift or fully accept it? Would he glory in the knowledge or be repelled by her claims? Either way, the risk of knowing was too great, the cost too high. She decided that the secret would remain her own.

She pulled away from his touch. "So, Captain, what has brought you here today? Have you come to bid me farewell or are you man enough to accept the help of a lady now?"

James was again surprised by the sudden change in her. The forlorn concern for her pet had vanished. A cool smile graced her face; a daring glint sparkled in her eyes. Even the tone of her voice was challenging and abrupt. Only his concern for her safety halted the angry retort that was quivering on his lips.

"It's not my problems that I'm here to discuss, my lady, but rather your own. You are in grave danger, and I want to help you. If you'll allow me a few minutes, I will explain it to you."

Her curiosity piqued, Randy nodded her acceptance.

"This afternoon when I returned to my ship, I found a visitor waiting to see me . . ." Sitting at her side, James related what he had learned from Abu that day. Though he didn't accuse Brandon Spencer by name, he did tell her of his suspicions that someone at the British compound was involved in her father's death and the attempts on her life as well.

"But why didn't Abu and Akbar tell me any of this?" she asked when he finished. "I have the right to know if someone is trying to kill me."

"I agree, but I can also understand why they kept it from you, Randy. They care for you deeply and only meant to protect you. Once Abu was assured of who I was, he asked for my help. He wants me to take you to England."

Randy shook her head and gazed down at the kitten cuddled in her lap. "I thank you for your generous offer, Captain, but I can't go. India is my home and this is where I intend to stay."

"Your friends have been trying to find the man responsible for these crimes for many weeks, but to no avail. Should you remain here in India, it could mean your death."

"There are worse fates than death," she answered simply. "I refuse to be run off. Everything I know and love is here."

"That's very noble of you, but what about Nana? Have you any idea what your death would do to her?"

Randy's head snapped around, and James could see the pained confusion in her eyes. Perhaps he could use her concern for her grandmother as a ploy to get her to leave India.

"Nana is not a young woman, and she has suffered many losses in her life. The hope of seeing you is keeping her alive. I'm afraid the knowledge of your death would kill her. Please,

Randy, for her sake as well as your own, think about coming to England with me. You don't have to stay forever, just until the man who murdered your father has been captured.''

''But what about my Uncle Richard? I could never live under his domination.''

''Perhaps we can find a way of getting around him. Your grandmother's wealth is far greater than Richard Wentworth's. With her money and powerful connections, Nana could petition the court and be appointed your guardian.''

Getting to her feet, Randy walked to the end of the arbor to survey her gardens. ''You think I'm selfish by refusing to go, but there are many things to consider. For example, I could never go without my servants.''

''Randy, you have a staff of at least fifty running this house. They could remain here until you return.''

She smiled. ''I wouldn't take them all. But Abu, Jarita, and three others belong to me. They're my responsibility.''

''Belong to you?'' James asked as he approached her. ''Are they your slaves?''

Randy nodded, then quickly shook her head. ''Yes . . . and no. You see, it's a bit complicated. The maharajah gave Abu and Jarita to me as a gift when I was a child. Rather than risk insulting him, I accepted his generosity. I gave them their freedom, but they refused to consider it. They say their place is with me. If I abandon them, they will be dishonored.''

''You said there were three others. Were they gifts also?''

''No, I . . . um . . . bought them at the slave market at various times over the past few years. They were being beaten or abused by the dealers. I couldn't abide such cruelty, so I bought them, treated their wounds, and gave them a place in our home. But like Abu and Jarita, they refused their freedom. All of them are a part of my family now. Do you understand?''

''Fine. They can come with you,'' James agreed with a nod. ''There are only a few cabins on my ship, but it can be done.''

Randy nervously gnawed on her lower lip. ''But my pets— I can't leave them either.''

James reached over and stroked the kitten she held in her arms. "I suppose we can make room for them as well."

Turning away from James, Randy searched her mind for another excuse she could use to thwart his insistence that she go to England with him. She couldn't very well tell him the truth about herself—that she was like her kitten, a freak among her own kind. If he wasn't so kind and caring, she might have been able to devise a reason he would accept. Convincing him to leave her behind was going to take time and trust. First she would get one and then she would gain the other.

Randy turned to face him. "Captain, you have given me a great deal to think about and I will need a few days to make my decision. Until then, I wish you would reconsider my offer to help you with your business contacts. I know it's unconventional for ladies to be involved in such things, but I . . ." Gazing at his smiling face, Randy recalled the harsh words she had used the night before.

"Last evening, I'm afraid that I behaved in a very rude, unladylike manner, Captain, and I am heartily sorry if I offended you. Is there anything I can do to gain your forgiveness?"

James cocked his head. "Well, there are a few things I can think of. Would you allow Stephen and I to stay in your home until we set sail? Knowing what danger you're in, I would feel better if I were here to help protect you."

"Of course, Captain. Perhaps during your visit, you will let me show you around the area. I'd like you to see why I love India so much. Maybe you'll come to understand why leaving will be so difficult for me. Is there anything else?"

James lightly grazed his cheek with her hand. "Randy, I would deem it an honor if you would help me with my business contacts. My ego isn't so fragile that I can't admit to needing your assistance."

"I promise you won't regret this, Captain. Papa's friends were merchants and plantation owners. I will only introduce you to them, and I won't interfere in any otherway . . . unless you really want me to."

James laughed at her teasing and shook his head. "There's only one more thing I want from you, Randy. Your promise to call me James."

"Well, that should be the easiest promise of all to keep, James." Taking his arm, Randy directed him down the path. "If we hurry, we can get you and Stephen settled in before dinner. Who knows? Before this adventure is over, maybe we can all be good friends."

Chapter 6

After spending two nights as a guest in Randy's home, James realized that he was far from his goal of convincing her to leave India. As a new day dawned, he found himself lying awake in bed wondering what had gone wrong with his plan.

Following their talk in the garden, Randy had welcomed him and Stephen into her home and had personally shown them to their suites. Ever the efficient hostess, she then took them on a tour of the house. She smiled and laughed, and even blushed prettily when Stephen teased her about the big tub in the bathing chamber being large enough for six people.

But within hours of their arrival, Randy's demeanor had undergone a drastic change. No longer friendly, she became cool and removed. What had caused it? James wondered.

Dinner had started out pleasantly enough. There was a festive mood in the air. The meal was a mixture of European and native fare, each dish superbly prepared. Randy took great joy in teasing Stephen about his introduction to Indian food.

"You mustn't feel badly about curry. I know your pride is a little battered by your reaction to it, but being a man has nothing to do with eating spicy foods. I love curried dishes, but then again, I have eaten them all my life.''

James chuckled. ''What the lady is trying to do is warn you, my friend. Unless you want to make a fool of yourself again, you should ignore that platter of curried shrimp sitting in front of you.''

Stephen scowled at James and spooned a small portion of the shrimp onto his plate. ''I'll do as I damn well please, Captain.''

Randy seemed discomfited by the tension between the two men and changed the subject. ''I know James owns a ship, but you are a mystery, Stephen. Are you a businessman or an adventurer?''

''I'm neither, ma'am,'' he replied in a voice colored with a hefty dose of self-importance. ''You see, I am Etienne Michel Charles Morgan-Bouchard, the Duc du Laurent.''

''A French nobleman? But I thought you were English.''

''My father is English and my mother is French. My maternal grandfather was killed during the Revolution, but thanks to some clever negotiations between my parents and the government of France, I inherited his title and estate. I've been the Duc de Laurent since I was born, but I prefer living in England.''

''By residing in England and traveling as you do, aren't you shirking your responsibilities?'' Randy asked coolly.

Stephen didn't seem to notice her disdain. ''Not in the least. I have a fine property manager to oversee my estate for me. It's a fairly common practice in Europe. Why, James has two managers, a solicitor, and a staff of thirty for his estate—''

''Stephen,'' James warned, ''that will be enough.''

''Don't be bashful, Jamie. This lovely lady might like to know that her guests are of the nobility,'' he boasted. Before James could stop him, Stephen continued. ''My lady, may I present Viscount Ryland, heir to the Earl of Foxwood and second in line to the Duke of Chatham—James Garret Grayson.''

For several moments, Randy stared at James. Something akin

to anger flashed in her eye, but quickly disappeared, making him doubt what he had seen. A mysterious smile curved her lips.

"Well, this certainly has been a day of surprises," Randy declared as her gaze found Abu standing in the entrance of the dining room. "First, my reluctant guests return to protect me from a killer who, unbeknownst to me, still means to have me dead. Then lo and behold, I discover that I am playing hostess to not one, but two noblemen at my table. I can only imagine what new surprises tomorrow will bring."

But the following morning, James was the one surprised. Eager to gain Randy's friendship, he had planned to spend the entire day with her. At breakfast, Abu informed him that she had gone out and wasn't expected to return until late afternoon.

"Missy Collins left the house an hour ago, *Huzur.* Several days a week she works in the clinic at the Christian mission."

James glared at Abu. "I don't believe this. Yesterday you said you feared for her life, and yet you allow her to roam free."

"My lady is well protected and has nothing to fear from the people at the mission. I have tried to dissuade her, but the only joy in her life now comes from her time working there."

"And what am I supposed to do? Just sit here and patiently await her return?"

Abu shook his head. "No, *Huzur.* My lady has sent out several letters of introduction for you and has made a few appointments on your behalf with some local merchants. We are due at the rug weavers within the hour."

"Did you say *we,* Nazir?"

"Of course, *Huzur.* Your success is most important to Missy Collins. She would trust no one other than myself to escort you. If you prefer, I could send word and postpone—"

"No, we shall keep the appointments, but the moment we return, I intend to have it out with her. Randy must be made aware of the peril she's in."

Abu bowed and sighed. "As you wish, *Huzur.*"

Abu's sigh should have warned James of the folly of his plan. Not only was she still out when they returned, but according to Jarita, Randy wasn't expected back until dinner.

"She has sent word of a delay, *Huzur* Captain," the petite woman informed him. "A young mother was brought to the mission heavy with child, and my lady stayed on to assist in the birth of her baby."

"That could take all night!" James felt his temper building. "Doesn't your mistress realize the danger she is in? There's a man out there bent on killing her!"

Jarita placed a consoling hand on his arm. "My baby does what she must. Not even the threat of death can stop her. Be patient, my son, and someday she will explain it all to you."

The old woman's cryptic remarks and Stephen's attempts at lifting his spirits while they waited for Randy to return only irritated James more. Escaping their watchful eyes, he took a walk alone in the gardens. The sun had dropped below the horizon when he saw an Indian woman running toward him on the path near the house. With her head held low and covered in a shawl of gauzy orange fabric, she ran right into him. It was only the strong hold he had on her arms that kept her from crashing to the ground. After righting herself, she suddenly jerked away from him and bowed respectfully.

"I'm sorry if I frightened you," James said, "but you should watch where you are going. Are you all right?"

The woman nodded, her eyes averted from his. Dressed like the other female servants, she waited silently to be dismissed.

"You'd better get back to the house. Your mistress will be home soon and may require your help with dinner."

James watched her go into the house. From his tour of the house, he knew she had entered Randy's suite. Perhaps this was the servant Abu called Sidra, he thought. The one who saved Randy. She seemed taller than the other Indian women in the household, but was she large enough to stop an assassin set on killing her mistress? He shrugged and continued his walk.

Returning to the salon moments later, he learned that Randy had come home. As soon as he saw her, he intended to reprimand her for being so careless. But when she arrived in the salon, the words died in his throat.

Randy was radiant. Her face looked pink and freshly scrubbed. Her shiny auburn hair was tied with a ribbon at the nape of her neck and hung down her back in thick waves. Garbed in a gown of rose silk, she rushed into the salon bubbling over with the excitement of her day.

"The birth of a baby is truly incredible. It has to be God's greatest miracle," she proclaimed. "When I held that tiny boy in my arms, I felt my heart beating with such joy. At first, we had been worried about the mother. She comes from a village far from here and is little more than a child herself. There seemed to be one problem after another . . ."

In vivid detail, Randy related the events that led up to the birth of the baby. It wasn't until she had nearly completed her telling of the difficult delivery that she noticed the fiery blush on Stephen's face.

"Stephen, have you taken ill?" She rushed to where he was sitting on the settee and put her hand against his forehead. "You are a bit warm, but I don't think you have a fever. This is strange. You've actually broken out in a cold sweat."

Stephen nervously pulled at his perfectly knotted cravat and loosened it. "I'm fine, truly I am. It's just that . . . well, I tend to get a bit squeamish about certain things."

"He faints at the sight of blood," James added with a wry laugh as he came to stand beside Randy.

"I do not," Stephen countered. "Well, maybe that one time I did, but it was all Diana's fault."

"Don't blame Diana. It was your own doing. You were half in love with her. For the longest time, you followed her about like a puppy. When she wanted to witness the birth of her mare's foal, you insisted on going along. Before the colt had made his way into the world, you had crumbled to the stable floor in a faint."

"But it wasn't only the blood, James. The foal was born breech. I thought the mare was going to die. If Diana had mentioned that this had happened to her horse before, I wouldn't have been so affected by it."

"Diana wasn't responsible for your weakness, so don't blame her because you disgraced yourself."

Stephen shook his head and chuckled. "Damn, I don't believe this. Even after all this time, you're still defending her."

"Gentlemen," Randy interrupted, "please stop bickering and tell me what this is all about. A few seconds ago, Stephen looked quite ill, and I want to know why."

When Stephen refused to answer, the task of explaining fell to James. "It was the topic of your conversation that bothered him. Childbirth, though a wondrous marvel, isn't considered appropriate for drawing-room chitchat. In proper society, such things are never discussed in mixed company, if at all."

The warmth in her eyes faded. "I do humbly beg your pardon, my lords. Being a gauche colonial, I rarely have to worry about doing what's acceptable in proper society. In the future, I will keep this in mind and will not embarrass you with my idle talk about the work I do at the clinic. If you will excuse me, I must see how dinner is coming along."

As Randy tried to walk around James, he caught her wrist and stopped her. Though he wanted to soothe her battered pride, the words he had bottled up all day came rushing out.

"There will be no more working at the mission, Randy. It's much too dangerous. Until we leave for England, you shall remain here in the house or I will accompany you where you wish to go. If anything happened to you, Nana would never forgive me."

Randy stared at the hand holding her wrist. "If you value the use of your arm, my lord captain, I would strongly advise you to unhand me this instant."

Her voice was low, barely more than a whisper. It wasn't her words that caused him to release her, but the cold, assured way she issued her warning. After crossing the room, Randy turned around to face him.

"You are not my father, my jailer, or my God, Captain Grayson. Unlike the members of your crew or the tenants who reside on your noble estate, I do not take orders from you. Because you are a friend of my grandmother, I invited you to be a guest in my home. Until I decide whether or not to accept your offer of passage to England, I will continue to live my life as I see fit. If you cannot accept that, or if you feel that I'm not 'proper' enough for your exalted company, you can pack your bags and be out of here by morning, you sanctimonious prig!"

In a flourish of rose silk, Randy turned on her heel and walked toward the hallway that led to her suite of rooms. James ran to catch her, but was halted in his steps when Abu suddenly stepped out in front of him.

"No, *Huzur,* it would not be wise to speak with her at this time."

"But Abu, I must apologize. I didn't mean to upset her. I was only worried about her taking such risks with her life."

"Her ire will only deafen her to your words. My mistress's temper is like a summer storm, fast and furious, but quickly spent. Have dinner with your friend, *Huzur,* get a good night's rest, and see her in the morning."

Reluctantly, James had accepted Abu's suggestion and spent the night tossing and turning in his bed, trying to devise a way of apologizing to Randy.

"I must be gentle with her. If I push her, she will rebel and pull further away from me," James told himself. "I must allow her to lead the way. I'll ask her to show me this land that means so much to her. By seeing it through her eyes, I may be able to understand what keeps her here. And why she is willing to risk her own life to stay."

His mind made up, James quickly washed and dressed. If

he was to catch Randy before she left the house, he knew there was little time to spare. On his way to her rooms, he got an idea.

"I'll bring a flower. No lady can resist a peace offering."

Rushing to the garden, he selected a perfect white gardenia. Surrounded by dark green leaves, it was fully blossomed, its fragrance intoxicating.

James was at the end of the garden path when he spied a young Indian man leaving the house. Attired in rich clothes, fine leather riding boots, and a turban adorned with a gold medallion, the native man leisurely strolled off across the grounds. James became enraged when he realized that the man had come out of Randy's suite.

"Damn her, she's no different than the rest!" James crushed the gardenia in his fist and threw it down. "I was such a bloody fool. It's not India that Randy would miss, but the nights spent with her lover."

Fueled by emotions he couldn't define, James followed the olive-skinned man to the stables. He intended to beat the man senseless, then confront Randy with the bloodied evidence of her secret affair. He'd teach this would-be saint of a woman a lesson she would never forget!

When the Indian man stopped inside the entrance of the stables to pull on a pair of doeskin gloves, James came in behind him and barred the door.

"Who the hell are you," James demanded, "and how long have you been involved with Miranda Collins?" He savagely grabbed the shoulder of his smaller opponent and spun him about. One look at the startled golden eyes glaring back at him told James all he needed to know.

"Randy, I'm sorry. I had no idea—"

The words of his apology were trapped in his throat. James felt a strangling grip around his neck and waist as he was lifted high above the floor. He didn't see his attacker, but he could hear a beastly growl below his ear.

"Xavier, put him down," Randy commanded with words

and hand signals. "He did not hurt me. Put him down immediately!"

James suddenly found himself being propelled through the
air. His breath was knocked out of him when he landed on a
pile of hay in a nearby stall. Struggling to sit up, he saw Randy
scolding the biggest man he had ever seen. Not only was he
tall, but the mountain of a man had muscles that resembled
sculpted marble. Dressed only in white trousers, the giant stood
silently watching Randy as she spoke to him in slow, distinct
English.

"I know you meant well, Xavier, but I did not need your
help. The captain is my friend. He would not harm me."

Xavier looked over at James. His eyes were as black as the
wild mane of hair that fell to his shoulders. After a moment,
he turned to Randy and made several movements with his
hands.

Randy giggled. "The captain did not know me. He thought
I was a man."

James got to his feet, brushing the straw from his clothes as
he witnessed the strange, one-sided conversation. When Randy
began laughing again, his curiosity got the better of him.

"Will someone tell me what's so funny? After being thrown
around like a sack of oats, I could use a reason to laugh."

"Xavier wants to know if your vision is impaired," Randy
told him with a wide grin. "In spite of my best efforts, he
claims only a blind man would be fooled by this disguise."

James kept a wary eye on Xavier as he approached Randy.
"Your large friend has a lot to say, but can you explain why
I've yet to hear a single word from his lips? Has it something
to do with the hand signals that you're both using?"

Randy glanced up at Xavier. During the past few years, she
had taught him many things. Besides the sign language, he
could also read lips. But Xavier wasn't the only one who had
learned from the time they had spent together. On occasion,
she was able to read his thoughts.

The previous summer was the first time it had occurred.

While riding past the slave auction with her and Abu, Xavier became very excited. He tried to use sign language to convey a message to his mistress, but in his anxiety he couldn't recall the proper signals. Seeing his distress, Randy grabbed his arm and suddenly realized that she was touching his thoughts.

"Abu, there is a young woman wearing yellow on the slaver's stand that I must purchase. Before you scold me, you should know that she is Xavier's friend. When they were children, she tried to protect him."

Kira joined the Collins household that day, and like the other slaves who were given their freedom, she refused to accept it. The young woman was an excellent cook and was soon running the kitchens. She and Xavier were married a month later.

Looking at James Grayson, Randy's decision was made. Her psychic talents were a gift from God, but had no place in the world James came from.

"You are correct, Captain. Xavier is deaf and must use sign language to convey his thoughts. I reply in kind, though it's really not necessary. If you face him and speak slowly, Xavier can usually read lips." Randy turned to her servant. "Bring Garuda to me. I want to see how well his hoof is healing."

While Xavier went to do her bidding, she returned her attention to James. "Captain, may I ask what you are doing here this morning? Do you often follow ladies about in this manner?"

"Only when they're dressed as men," James admitted with a sheepish grin. "I was on my way to apologize to you for my behavior last night when I saw what appeared to be a man coming out of your suite. I went a bit crazy and decided to have it out with him."

"Have it out with him? I saw the look in your eyes, James. You meant to kill him! Why, one would think that you—" The thought that James had been jealous of her seeing another man caused her to be thrilled and yet alarmed. Rather than deal with these feelings, she changed the subject.

"Well, I am pleased to know that my disguise fooled you, James. Even if it was only for a little while. Between staining my skin with cosmetics, binding myself, wearing men's clothing, and pinning up my hair beneath a turban, I work very hard at keeping my identity a secret.''

"But why do you do it, Randy?"

The question brought a one-word reply. "Freedom."

Seeing his disgruntled expression, she explained. "Freedom means a great deal to me. Dressed as a man, I can come and go as I see fit. I'm not bound by conventional standards that apply to women. For example, I am properly schooled in riding sidesaddle, but prefer to ride astride. It's far more comfortable and a darn sight safer than the alternative.''

Randy became indignant when James laughed. "How dare you mock me! I tell you what's in my heart and you think it's funny.''

James shook his head. "I laughed because what you said about riding was all too familiar. My mother's been preaching the same thing for years. She says sidesaddles should be considered lethal weapons.''

Randy smiled. "Your mother must be an extraordinary woman.''

"That's putting it mildly. I could tell you things about Mama that would positively amaze you. Not only does she ride astride, but she can outshoot anyone. Last year, the family went hunting in . . .''

Over Randy's shoulder, James saw Xavier leading a horse toward them. He immediately recognized the golden Arabian stallion as the one he had tried to purchase earlier that week.

She followed his gaze and saw the reason for his distraction. After sending Xavier to prepare her other mount, she rubbed her hand on the horse's snout. "Garuda is a magnificent creature, don't you agree, Captain? Though it seems wrong to tame such a noble beast, I'm glad that he belongs to me.''

"You own this stallion? When I tried to buy him from Prince Akbar the other day, he had just given this horse to his friend—''

A light of understanding flared in his eyes.

"By God, it was you in the corral with this beast! Are you insane or do you always take such risks with your life? This animal could have killed you."

The anger she saw on James's face pricked her own temper. Like a mother protecting her child, Randy came to Garuda's defense. "He was injured and the pain made him act that way. Garuda would never hurt me. He knows I would never harm him."

"And just how could you know that? With all your vast accomplishments, are you a mind reader as well?"

James had no idea how true his jibe was. His sarcastic words struck Randy speechless. Her eyes welled with tears. She turned away from him, but not before he saw how badly his words had affected her. In two quick strides, he pulled her into his arms.

"Why is it that I'm always apologizing to you? If we're not shouting at each other, I'm searching for ways to make amends." He held her close and sighed. "Forgive me for frightening you to the point of tears, Randy. I only wanted you to be aware of what could happen if you weren't careful."

Randy pressed her face against his shoulder, enjoying for a moment the comfort of his embrace. How could she tell him that the only thing she feared was his learning about her empathic abilities? She didn't want to care for this man, but it was too late. If she earned his disdain because he doubted her talents, it could destroy her. She had to get away from him for a while so she could think.

James was surprised when Randy suddenly pulled away from him. She wasn't crying. Her mouth bowed in a small smile.

"I appreciate your concern, Captain, and in the future I won't take any more unnecessary risks, I promise." Standing on tiptoe, Randy placed a quick kiss on his lips.

"What was that?" James asked, grabbing her arms before she could escape.

"That was a kiss to seal my promise."

"No, Randy. That wasn't a kiss—this is."

Randy knew she should have pushed him away, but as James pulled her close and kissed her, all thoughts of escaping fled her mind. His lips felt like warm satin against hers, coaxing her into responding to his lead. Tremors of excitement shot through her when his tongue parted her lips to explore her mouth.

What had started as a gentle caress turned into a heated duel as her tongue countered his movements with seductive motions of its own. James tasted like sunshine, spice, and all-consuming passion. He groaned with disappointment when she slowly eased away from him.

"If you'll . . . ah, excuse me," Randy stammered, taking a step back from him, "I must return . . . ah, Garuda to his stall and . . . apply some ointment to his hoof before I leave."

The glow of desire in her eyes pleased James. He wondered if he would ever get used to Randy's erratic moods and smiled to himself. Recalling her last words as she led the horse to the rear of the stable, he frowned.

"What do you mean, before you leave?" he called out to her. "Where do you think you're going?"

"Randy is going riding with me, Captain. Have you any objections?"

James turned to the entrance of the stables and found Akbar leaning against the door frame with his arms crossed, grinning at him. Dressed in an outfit similar to Randy's, the prince was a handsome figure of a man.

"Eavesdropping is a breach of etiquette where I come from, Prince Akbar. Tell me, how long have you been standing there?"

"Long enough to know that you care a great deal for my Randy," Akbar replied simply.

The prince's knowing smile and the easy way he had said "my Randy" bothered James more than he wanted to admit. Clenching his fists at his sides, he tried to mask his feelings. "Of course I care. If anything happened to her, her grandmother would be devastated."

Akbar raised a cynical brow. "So you protect her for the dowager and not yourself, *sahib*. How truly gallant of you."

Laughing, the prince moved away from the door and offered James his hand. "Captain Grayson, forgive my ill-placed humor and accept my friendship. If we hope to convince Randy that leaving India is the best thing for her, we must work together."

James shook his hand and nodded. "So, you agree with Nazir. You believe that she would be better off in England."

"Randy is my dearest friend, Captain. When she leaves, a large portion of my heart will go with her. But I love her far too much to allow her obstinate ways to destroy her."

Before they could continue, Randy came out leading her ebony mare, Ratri. She walked directly to the prince and stood before him, shaking her fist in his face.

"Akbar Xerxes Surat Kahn, you should get down on your knees and thank all the gods that I was born with a forgiving nature. You lied, kept secrets from me, and conspired with your father and Abu to keep me ignorant of the threats on my life."

"But Randy," Akbar injected, "we did it because—"

"You wanted to protect me. But if I had been told from the start, I would have been better prepared to take care of myself."

"*Chhota behin*, my lovely Randy, we only meant to spare you—"

"Now you've involved Captain Grayson in this plot," she went on without pausing. "He's a titled nobleman and the grandson of a very powerful duke. If anything happens to him, you will have the wrath of the British Empire on your head!"

"We never meant to cause him problems, Randy. Besides, he wants to help you. You will be safer in England—"

"I am not a helpless child, Akbar, and I resent being treated like one. Furthermore, I won't be bullied into leaving India by you, him, or anyone!" she announced, poking his chest with each word. "Do you understand? It's my decision!"

James couldn't help but smile over Randy and Akbar's spat. They were sparring like a brother and sister, reminding him of the many sibling battles he had shared with Diana. He was caught up in his memories when he realized Randy was talking to him.

". . . and I'm going for a ride with Akbar. We won't be long. If it would ease your mind, you're welcome to join us."

He looked at Randy and Akbar. The prince had his arm draped over her shoulder. James understood their special friendship and found himself envying the closeness they shared. To impose on their time together would be wrong.

"As much as I would like to accept your offer, I cannot. I'm due at the Bentley plantation this morning to negotiate the shipping of next year's crop of tea. Another time, perhaps?"

After Randy agreed, James shook Akbar's hand. "It was a pleasure meeting you again, your highness."

"For me as well, Captain. I am hosting a small party this evening and would be honored if you and your friend would attend. There are a few matters I need to discuss with you."

Randy jabbed her elbow into Akbar's ribs. "If I am one of those matters, I had best be included in the discussion, my brother."

Akbar drew her close and hugged her. "Of course, little sister. There will be no more secrets, I swear," he assured her with a hearty laugh.

But the levity in his voice didn't extend to his eyes. James could see the concern in the depths of Akbar's gaze. With a curt nod, he accepted the prince's invitation to dinner and the unvoiced request for his help. Together, they would take care of the young woman who was very important to them both.

Chapter 7

James was pacing the salon waiting for Randy to appear when the mantel clock chimed nine. He hadn't seen her since she rode away with Akbar that morning. After the confrontation in the stable, he wasn't sure what to expect from her.

"Good evening, my lords. I trust I haven't kept you waiting too long."

Stephen rushed forward as Randy came into the room. He took her hand and kissed it. "Miss Collins, you are a vision. If I had waited a month, it would have been time well spent."

Honoring her father's request not to wear mourning colors, Randy's European-styled gown was a feminine confection of ivory lace and satin. Her auburn hair was swept up in a cluster of curls. A strand of pearls circled her neck, and dainty diamond clusters adorned her ears.

For several moments, James couldn't speak. She was feisty, stubborn, and infuriating, but Randy was also very beautiful. He had known prettier women, yet none had ever beguiled him as she had. Since his arrival, he had searched for a way to fight his attraction to her. The truth could no longer be denied; he was fighting a losing battle.

Randy looked expectantly at him. "You certainly are quiet, James. After finding me dressed as a man this morning, I thought my choice of apparel tonight would please you."

"I am more than pleased, my dear lady, but how does one compliment perfection?" James grinned at the rosy blush his words brought to her cheeks.

Recovering her composure, Randy pulled the brooch from her drawstring bag and handed it to James. "This was hidden in the doll you brought me from Nana."

"By God, that's the Bloody Tear of Allah. I've seen Nana wearing this piece many times."

"Can you tell me anything about it? In Nana's note, she implied that the brooch had special powers."

James shrugged. "Well, all the stones are diamonds. The center gem is a red diamond, the rarest of its kind. I don't believe in magic or superstitions, but according to the old legend, the owner of this gem would be protected from their enemies and blessed with good fortune." He put the brooch in Randy's hand. "Why don't you wear it this evening? I know Nana would be pleased if you did."

Randy walked to the mirror hanging on the wall and held the jeweled piece against the bodice of her gown. "I've never worn a brooch. Should I wear it on the right side or the left?"

James stood behind her at the looking glass. "On the left," he suggested as she moved it into position. "Just below your shoulder. Yes, that's perfect."

The point on the pin was dulled with time and wear. Randy tried unsuccessfully to push it through the layered fabric of her gown. "Oh, this is fine," she muttered to herself. "If I get past the lace, I will probably impale myself with this pin."

"Give it to me," James told her with a dramatic sigh. "I can't allow you to ruin your lovely gown with a lot of holes and bloodstains."

They were both laughing as James repeatedly tried to pierce

the heavily patterned lace. Trying not to injure her, he slid his hand under the edge of her bodice while he worked. It was only when he finally got the point through the thick fabric that the reality of what he was doing caused him to tremble.

The fullness of Randy's breast was warm beneath his knuckles. Her skin was like velvet. In his mind, he envisioned what his eyes could not see. A globe of soft, womanly flesh that could easily fill his hand. It would be pale in color with a nipple of rosy pink. He imagined how the nipple would become rock-hard when he took it into his mouth and suckled on it. Randy would moan as—

Beads of perspiration erupted above his brow. James dared not look into her eyes. He was sure his lusty thoughts were emblazoned across his face.

Randy was too busy waging a battle of her own to notice his discomfort. When James lowered his head to view the progress of his work, she had wanted to run her fingers through his gold-flecked brown hair. The heat of his breath tickled her exposed skin, while his hand pressed gently on her breast. Unaccustomed to feelings of desire, she burned with shame. James could never know how much he affected her, she decided. Randy squeezed her eyes closed and caught her bottom lip between her teeth when James suddenly stood up and stepped away from her.

"There. It looks perfect," he said, turning to Stephen. "Let's go. The carriage is waiting to take us to the palace."

Akbar's palace, the Opal Court, dwarfed the Collins home in comparison. Constructed of polished marble, the enormous structure shone like the gem it was named for. Pale shades of pink, gold, and blue shimmered beneath its milky surface. The ornate iron gates, grillwork, and large domed roofs were sheathed in gold.

The reception room was crowded with people. Though most of the guests were wealthy native men, there were many Europeans wearing Western-styled clothes and military uniforms in attendance as well. Randy and her escorts had just entered the party when a small Indian boy garbed in fine clothes and a gold turban came running toward them.

"Aunt Randy, you came!" he shouted. "I knew you had not forgotten me."

Randy ignored the delicacy of her gown and knelt on the floor to gather the little boy in her arms.

"I could never forget you, Naresh," she assured him with a hug. "Are you being a good boy and doing all your lessons?"

Naresh smiled, his head bobbed vigorously. "Oh yes, Aunt Randy. I work hard at my lessons. My English is good, yes? I want you to be proud of me!"

Tears filled Randy's eyes. "I'm already proud of you, Naresh. You are my dearest love. Always remember that you hold a special place in my heart." She hugged him tightly.

Naresh returned her embrace until he suddenly pulled away. "Remember? Does that mean you are going away, Aunt Randy?"

When she didn't respond quickly, Naresh turned to James. *"Angrezi,* are you trying to take my Aunt Randy away? I will not allow it, do you hear? I will not allow it!"

James didn't understand the foreign words Randy suddenly began saying to the child, but from the cowed look on Naresh's face, it was obvious that he was being scolded. A few moments later, Randy stood up and nodded to the little boy.

Naresh bowed respectfully to James. *"Huzur,* I beg your pardon. My temper ruled my tongue and I am heartily shamed by my actions. Please accept my apology and my hand in friendship."

James took the child's small hand while Randy completed the introductions. "My lords, may I present His Highness, Prince Naresh Murad Javid Kahn of Mysore. Naresh, this is Viscount Ryland, Captain James Grayson of England, and his friend, the Duc du Laurent, Etienne Michel Charles Morgan-Bouchard."

"But what kind of a captain are you, my lord?" Naresh asked. "If you are in service to your king, then why do you not wear the regimental uniform that is required? To do less would be disrespectful to your ruler."

James was hard-pressed not to smile at the authorative way the young prince spoke. "I am loyal to my king, your highness, but I am in service only unto myself. I am the owner and captain of the ship *Diana.*"

The boy's eyes glowed with childish exuberance. "You own a real ship? How fast does she travel? May I see her? I like—"

Naresh stopped in mid-sentence when a jeweled hand came to rest on his shoulder.

"My son, that will be enough questions for now," Akbar advised him in a low voice. "You will tire our guest with such foolishness. If I am not mistaken, I believe you were sent on an errand for your mother."

Sheepishly, Naresh looked up at his father and then to the gallery that overlooked the reception room. Remembering the duty he was sent to carry out, he bowed to Randy.

"My mother, Princess Leila, requests your presence up on the gallery in her bower so she and the ladies of the *zenana* may greet you and welcome you into our home." After completing his speech, Naresh turned for his father's approval. With a hint of a smile, Akbar nodded.

Randy dipped into a formal curtsey. "I gladly accept her kind invitation and would be honored to have you escort me to her side, Prince Naresh. If you gentlemen will excuse me, I shall return shortly."

When Randy walked away with Naresh, James signaled Stephen to follow her. That afternoon they had discussed the attempts on her life and decided to take turns watching over her. Hidden beneath their waistcoats, each carried a small, loaded pistol. With so many strangers about, James didn't want to leave anything to chance.

Akbar chuckled and patted James's back. "Captain, you

have no cause to fear. Randy is quite safe in my home. In addition to the uniformed guards you see, my finest men are dressed as guests and are scattered throughout the room." Looking at James's formal black-and-white apparel, the prince shook his head and sighed dramatically.

"You English amaze me. You dress your army in bright shades of red and blue when they do battle, but your party attire lacks the same luster. Is there some rule that says men's formal wear must be black, white, or brown?"

The inane topic caught James by surprise. He realized his host was trying to ease his mind by changing the subject. James smiled and turned to look at Akbar.

Akbar was resplendent in a royal blue tunic and trousers. A large jeweled medallion was displayed on his chest. His cloth-of-gold turban, which matched his long, sleeveless robe, was adorned with a sapphire the size of a hen's egg. He had rings on most of his fingers and gold loops on his ears. Even his soft leather slippers were gold and encrusted with gems.

James chuckled. "Compared to you, Akbar, a peacock would be a dull, colorless creature."

"I know," Akbar agreed with a shrug. "I am not altogether comfortable like this, but it is what they expect," he admitted, nodding toward a group of European guests across the room. "Now the ladies can attend their little tea parties and brag about seeing the savage prince in all his glory."

James suddenly noticed that there was only a few women in attendance, and all of them were Europeans. "Don't Indian ladies come to your celebrations?"

"Of course they do, but not in the way you might imagine, Captain. They are up there, on the balcony behind those carved wooden screens. The ancient rules of *purdah* forbid them from attending celebrations with the men, so they have a party of their own.

"India is an old country, rich with values and traditions," he continued. "We protect our women by keeping them in a *zenana*. It is secluded and the best-guarded apartments in the palace. After dinner, I will take you to the gallery and introduce you to my wives.''

James was startled. ''Wives? How many do you have, Akbar?''

''Only three at this time. Leila, who is mother to my sons, Naresh and Kedar. Kalinda, mother of my daughter, Chandra, and my newest wife, Bibi, who will deliver a child by year's end,'' Akbar explained. ''But enough talk about my family. Come, Captain, I want to introduce you to a few of the local planters. My fellow countrymen are wary of dealing with foreigners. Perhaps with my intervention, we can change all that.''

Almost an hour later, Stephen came rushing across the room and broke into their conversation. Akbar followed as Stephen dragged James into a nearby alcove.

''James, she's gone! I can't find Randy anywhere. The guards wouldn't let me on the gallery, so I stayed near the staircase and waited for her to come down. Lieutenant Gerard stopped and we talked for a while and drank some wine. When he left, I asked the guard to check on Randy. He reported that she had returned to the main floor by another set of stairs.''

''Calm down, Stephen. Akbar assures me that the entire room is crowded with his best guards,'' James confided to his nervous friend. ''I'm positive that nothing has happened to Randy. She is probably busy talking to some of her father's friends.''

''It is a bit warm in here. Perhaps Randy has stepped out into my gardens for a breath of air,'' Akbar suggested.

''I don't know anything about that, but I have searched this entire room, and she's nowhere to be found,'' Stephen declared. ''And James, you wouldn't be so relaxed if you had spoken to Gerard. It seems that Major Spencer returned to Calicut this afternoon and came to the party with him. What's worse is that I haven't been able to locate Spencer either!''

James ran to the archway that the Prince said led to the

gardens. While Stephen and Akbar alerted the guards to search for Randy and Spencer, James was confident that his gut instincts would lead him to her first.

"Major Spencer, I would advise you to let go of me," Randy warned. "Perhaps your injury addled your mind as to what occurred the last time you tried to force yourself on me. I am more than willing to refresh your memory!"

She was seething with anger. While visiting Akbar's family in the gallery, she had been overwhelmed by sadness. The thought of leaving India and her friends brought her close to tears. Not wanting anyone to see her in such a state, she had gone to the gardens to calm herself. She had barely taken a breath of cool evening air when she was set upon by Brandon Spencer.

"Please, Miranda, I must talk to you," he implored her. "It is imperative that we speak privately. You're in danger and I'm here to protect you. What we have to discuss could make all the difference in your life." His good arm was wrapped around her waist like a steel band as he rushed her along the torch-lit garden path, away from the palace.

A glimmer of hope coursed through Randy. "Is it about Papa? Do you know who killed my father?" They had reached the bubbling fountain in the center of the gardens when she dug in her heels and refused to take another step. "Please, Brandon, tell me why you've brought me here."

In the light of the full moon, Brandon gazed into her eyes and gently touched her mouth with his finger. "You said my name. From your lips, it is the sweetest of sounds. Oh, my dearest, I've waited so long for this moment."

Suspicious of his intentions, Randy stepped away from him. "This has nothing to do with my father's murder. Exactly what kind of danger are you protecting me from?"

"The danger you have brought upon yourself, my sweet." His voice reeked of his patient, patronizing air. "It was bad

enough when you insisted on remaining in that pagan home
with a staff of uncivilized servants, but now you have two
Englishmen residing there with you. When word gets about
that you have men staying under your roof without proper
chaperons, your reputation will be in shreds, Miranda.''

"I have done nothing wrong, Major Spencer," she informed
him, emphasizing the formal use of his name and rank. "Abu
and Jarita are more than civilized and they are proper chaperons,
I assure you. Aside from that, whatever transpires in my home
is my business and has absolutely nothing to do with you.''

"Of course it does, Miranda. I love you and I mean to protect
you from the foul gossip that will no doubt taint your otherwise
flawless character. Once we are married, no one will dare
question your honor. I've already procured a special license so
we can be wed on Saturday.''

Randy glared at him. "Major Spencer, you must be insane
if you think you can get away with this. You tried to charm and
seduce me, but to no avail. Then Papa died and you threatened to
contact my uncle. But this time, sir, you've clearly outdone
yourself. Blackmailing me with attacks on my reputation!''

"I am not blackmailing you, Miranda. I love you, and as an
officer and a gentleman, I can do no less than forgive your
minor indiscretion and do the right and proper thing to protect
your honor. As your husband—''

"I wouldn't marry you if you were the last men alive on
God's green earth," Randy told him sharply. "You are nothing
but a ignominious bigot, with the soul of a jackal and designs
on sainthood. I would sooner spend eternity in purgatory than
be your wife for a single day!''

Brandon's face was nearly the color of his scarlet tunic.
Seeming to forget the sling on his right arm, he angrily took
a menacing step toward her.

"Damn you, Miranda! I won't allow you to get away from
me. My plan is perfect. To become a general, a man must have
a proper wife, wealth, power, or influential familial ties. With
you as my spouse, I could have it all. And you shall be mine,

Miranda. If I have to drag you behind those bushes and take you by force, I will have you!"

When he lunged for her, Randy was ready for him. All of her concentration was centered on his attack. Using Oriental skills of self-defense, she grabbed Spencer by his forearm, shifted her weight, and flipped him over her shoulder. By the time he recovered his senses, she was holding his twisted arm taut and pressing the heel of her foot against his throat.

"I could kill you right now," she hissed through clenched teeth. "With just the slightest pressure, I could crush your windpipe, Major. You would suffocate, drowned in your own blood. When you accosted me at the party for Lieutenant Reynolds, I took pity on you and only broke your wrist and fingers. I even allowed you to salvage your pride by letting you tell people that it happened in a riding accident.

"Be forewarned, Major. If you attempt to hurt me again with any more threats or contemptible lies, I won't be so charitable. The next time, sir, you will die."

Randy lifted her foot from his throat, straightened the fall of her skirt, and walked toward the palace. She was out of sight when Brandon Spencer struggled to his feet.

"Damn silly bitch," he muttered to himself, "with nothing but a lot of empty threats. Miranda could never kill me."

"Maybe, maybe not," a male voice called from the shadows, "but I have no such reservations, Major. I could easily kill you where you stand."

The sight of James Grayson stepping in front of him caused Spencer to stumble in retreat. The pistol James was carrying was aimed at the major's chest.

James had never wanted to kill a man as badly as he did now. Running through the garden, he had come upon Randy and Spencer arguing. He had kept himself concealed, hoping the officer would reveal his involvement in Sir Jonathan's murder. But the more he heard, the less likely it seemed that Spencer was responsible.

The thing that shocked James more than learning how Spencer had sustained his earlier injury was witnessing Randy's swift and mysterious retaliation to his attack.

"Grayson, you could never get away with killing me," Spencer warned him in a near shout.

James raised his brow, and a sardonic smile curled his lips. "But I can. All I have to do is report how you attacked Miss Collins here in the gardens. Shooting you is the least I can do to defend the lady's honor."

"Miranda Collins is no lady. The wench is a she-cat from hell," Spencer spat out viciously. "A good thrashing would tame that witch—"

The sound of James pulling back the hammer and cocking his pistol stopped the major's spiteful tirade.

"Ah, blessed silence," James announced with an exaggerated sigh. "Now that I have your attention, Major, I wish to tell you that your days of threatening Miranda Collins have come to an end. I am going to teach you what intimidation really is.

"When we met, I knew your name was familiar. After thinking about it, I remembered why. You believe your career is safe because your family are accepted members of the nobility. Your father is an earl, but as a businessman, he is sorely lacking in skill. He has outstanding debts all over England. If Miranda's grandmother discovered what you have tried to do to her only grandchild, the dowager would happily buy up all your father's notes and bankrupt him in a matter of weeks. What good is a title without money to back it up?"

James tapped the barrel of his gun on Spencer's chest. "Then there are your two brothers. Harold is your father's heir, but if word gets out about his proclivity for young boys, no decent woman will have him—especially those with large dowries. And I know brother Alan from our days at Cambridge. How he became a barrister is truly a mystery. Alan was never much of a scholar. He drank to excess and was constantly in brawls. It was rumored among the students that he boasted of buying his passing grades with—"

"Enough, Grayson!" Spencer demanded. "Why drag my family into this? Why don't you just shoot me and be done with it?"

"Killing you would be too easy and over much too soon. The possible downfall of your noble family will be a far greater punishment for you to endure. Your torment will repay only a portion of what you've put Randy through these past weeks."

Brandon's eyes narrowed. "What must I do to appease you, Grayson? I give you my word as a gentleman that I'll stay away from Miranda and I will not interfere with you and your business dealings here in Calicut."

James nodded. "Perhaps you're not the fool I've taken you for, Spencer. Live up to your end of the bargain, and no one will learn your family secrets from me."

"But after I've done all that I have promised, what will prevent you from damaging my family and destroying me in the process, Grayson?"

"My word as a gentleman, of course," James replied with a smug grin. "And before you leave, I'll make you another promise, Major. Should you fall back on your word and try to hurt Randy in any way, I will kill you. Not only that, but I will take my revenge on your entire family. You will go to your grave knowing you were responsible for their destruction as well as your own."

James was deep in thought when Akbar found him standing alone near the fountain. His arms hung loosely at his side, the loaded pistol forgotten in his hand.

"You can put your weapon away, Captain. Randy is safe inside with your friend and my guards to protect her. Spencer departed several moments ago—though I don't know why you were so concerned about him."

James tucked the pistol inside his coat. "I thought Spencer was the man responsible for Jonathan's death and the attempts on Randy's life. When I learned that the killer had lost a finger, I recalled the bandages on Spencer's hand and believed—"

Akbar laughed heartily. "The man is a pretentious fool, eager to acquire a beautiful wife. The major is many things, but being Papa Jon's murderer isn't one of them. Besides a lack of courage, Spencer was home in bed nursing his broken hand and wounded pride when the foul incident occurred. Do you know how he obtained his injuries?''

"From the argument I witnessed, Randy claims that she was the one who crippled his hand. At first I doubted what I had heard, but then I saw her fend off his attack and literally throw him to the ground, and I wasn't so sure. Did my eyes deceive me, or did I actually see her do that?''

"Your vision is not impaired, James. Like myself, Randy has been trained in the ancient arts of combat. In my position, assassins are a constant worry, so my father hired the finest masters of these skills to teach me. Since I was living with the Collins family at the time, Randy was educated with me. I ask that you be discreet about this. If she knew that you witnessed her unladylike actions tonight, it would hurt her more than the injuries she inflicted on Spencer pained him.'' Akbar shook his head. "After what happened the first time he accosted her, I thought the major was wise enough to stay away from her.''

"Tell me about that night,'' James said.

"In mid-August, Jonathan Collins gave a party to honor his departing military liaison, Lieutenant Nigel Reynolds. During the festivities, Spencer managed to corner Randy in the library and proposed marriage. When she turned him down, he tried to seduce her into complying. Randy demanded to be set free. He refused, a struggle ensued, and in a matter of seconds, it was all over. That's when Randy sent for me.

"She told me what happened and how she had struck Spencer with several blows, breaking his wrist and fingers. She asked me to take him to the compound so he could get medical care for his injuries. I was to tell no one how he had been hurt.''

"But that was foolish. At least Jonathan should have been informed of the attack on his daughter,'' James interjected.

"I agree with you. I planned on telling him about it the next day, but I never got the chance. That night after the party, Papa

Jon was killed." Shaking his head, Akbar sighed. "Sona Ag deserves far better than what life has given her."

"Sona Ag? Is that what you call Randy?"

"Actually, it is the name my father bestowed on her when we were children. Sona Ag means golden fire and refers to the burning spirit that glows brightly in her eyes," Akbar explained. "Only a very special man can nurture that flame without trying to smother it. Tell me, Captain Grayson, are you up to the task?"

James understood the challenge in Akbar's words, but could not reply. His mind, body, and heart battled inside of him.

His mind warned him of the dangers to be found with a woman as complex as Randy. There were parts of herself that she kept hidden. Could he trust her? In the past, secrets had nearly cost him his life. Was she worth the risk?

His body said yes. But virgins demanded commitment, and that was something he had learned to avoid. Yet Randy's innocent sensuality inflamed him with needs too strong to deny.

His heart gave him the biggest battle of all. More than lust, a strong emotional need had overtaken him. Somehow, this irascible young woman with the face of an angel had captured his heart. He had fallen in love with her.

This discovery made James feel amazingly free. He would have to be cautious and not expose his feelings too quickly. Gaining Randy's love wasn't going to be easy, but it was a challenge he would gladly accept. Chuckling, James shook his head and thumped the prince on the back.

"Am I up to the task? Damned if I know, Akbar, but I promise you that I will give it my best."

"In you, James Grayson, I believe Sona Ag has met her match. Be patient. Guard her heart as you guard her person, and a treasure of inestimable value will be your reward."

"I hope so, Akbar. With my wanting to protect her and her fighting me at every turn, Randy is going to lead me a merry chase."

Akbar slapped James on the back. "Ah, yes! But what an adventure it will be for you, my friend!"

James and the prince were laughing as they returned to the palace. They never saw the man dressed in black watching from behind the flowering hedges.

"Damn your bloody interference, Grayson!" he growled angrily. "When Miranda finished with Spencer, I could have had her. She would be dead and I would be free at last."

Using the familiar paths of the palace grounds, the intruder made his escape without being seen by the guards. Though foiled in his latest attempt, he suddenly decided on his next move.

"It's all so simple. Why haven't I thought of it before?" he chided himself. "I know you well, Miranda Collins. Your love for your creatures and your predictable habits will soon lead to your demise and my ultimate success. I can hardly wait."

Chapter 8

"Jarita, if you pull my hair any tighter, I think my eyes will be permanently crossed," Randy scolded her ayah. "Be careful with those hairpins or you will draw blood."

Jarita shook her head and secured the chignon at the nape of Randy's neck. "You are as nervous as a mouse lost in a herd of elephants, my baby. Stop your complaints and tell me what is vexing you this morning. Did you not enjoy the reception?"

"Other than having to deal with Major Spencer for a bit, I really had a lovely time." While Jarita applied the liquid that temporarily stained Randy's skin a tan color, she related the events that took place in the palace gardens. When she had finished, she sighed. "Well at least no one saw what happened. Spencer has his wretched pride and I am still considered a poor defenseless female, but a lady nonetheless."

Using a small, pointed brush, Jarita lined Randy's eyes with a paste of black kohl, giving them a dark, exotic look. "If all went as you said, my baby, then why are you so affected this morning? Do you think the major will accost you again?"

Her cosmetics complete, Randy stood and began to dress in her Indian attire. She secured a long yellow petticoat around her waist and put on a short blouse called a choli before she replied to Jarita's question.

"The major doesn't concern me. If he makes another attempt, I will deal with him. My current problem has more to do with Captain Grayson," she said, attaching gold hoops to her earlobes.

"Has the *Huzur* Captain done something to harm you, my baby?"

"Oh, no, Jarita. James has been a perfect gentleman."

"So, this is a problem?"

Randy laughed at Jarita's confusion. "Only for me, I suppose. I know he'll be leaving soon and I should be putting distance between us, but after the way he treated me last night, it's becoming an impossible chore. He was sweet and attentive. When he learned I was going to work at the mission today, he insisted on coming along. No matter what objection I made, he had an answer. Not even telling him that he had to dress in Indian clothes could dissuade him."

"Aha!" Jarita exclaimed. "This is why Abu went to the *Huzur* Captain's room early this morning. He is helping your man to prepare, my baby."

"He is not my man, Jarita, and I want you to remember that." Randy pulled several bangle bracelets onto her wrists. "James is a guest in my home, a friend of Nana's, and the last man I want to get involved with. Now, help me arrange my sari so I won't be late."

The sari was saffron-yellow trimmed with a border of deep gold. Jarita wound the long length of semi-sheer fabric around Randy's trim waist, draping the final layer over her shoulder. A matching veil over Randy's head completed her native attire.

James nervously stood outside her suite wearing the clothes he had borrowed from one of Akbar's advisors at the palace the night before. Though the boots were of a soft leather and the cut of his pants and tunic allowed him easy movement, he was uncomfortable. His face, ears, neck, and hands were colored to match the natives' skin tone. The turban he wore completely covered his tawny hair. He fussed with the wide green sash that circled his midriff and the medallion that hung from a chain around his neck as he knocked on her door. But when Randy opened the door looking like an exotic lady from an Eastern fairy tale, his uneasiness vanished without a trace.

"You are a vision of beauty," he declared with avid appreciation. "How do I measure up to your local gents?"

Randy felt herself blushing beneath the stain on her cheeks. "Oh, James, in spite of your blue eyes, you remind me of a Kashmiri prince, so tall and handsome. Has Stephen seen you?"

"No, Stephen left before I was up, and I'm pleased about that. If he saw me in this disguise, he would take great joy in teasing me about it." James held up his hand and regarded its altered color. "Was all of this really necessary?"

"It is if you insist on coming with me. The people we treat at the mission are very poor and fearful of foreigners. If I can save them a moment's worry by coloring my skin and dressing as they do, then it is a small price to pay."

The mission was located in the ghetto of Calicut. James and Xavier rode horses on either side of the palanquin that held Randy. The six muscular bearers of her enclosed litter were not servants, but the strongest warriors in Akbar's guards. Able to see through the sheer draperies, Randy told James about the points of interest that they passed along the way.

People were already lined in the street when they arrived at the mission. When James helped Randy out of the palanquin, he was surprised to hear many of them calling out to her, using the name the maharajah had chosen for her. As she turned and greeted them in their language, bestowing a smile on each and every one, James could see the caring warmth in her eyes. Sona Ag, the golden fire, was an apt and fitting name for her.

For the better part of the day, he watched her from across

the crowded infirmary. Though he didn't understand the words she said or the methods she used to help the sick and injured people, he could see what a difference she made in their treatment. Small crying children, frightened and in pain, went willingly to her. Randy would hold a small one in her arms and close her eyes for a moment before whispering softly to the child. When the physician took the child from her, they'd share a few words and then she would go on to the next one who needed help.

But it wasn't only the babies and children who benefitted from her concern. Elderly people, some too old or infirm to speak, were brought to her. Randy would take their hands and silently console them. From her simple touch, they seemed to receive great comfort.

It was well after noon when one of the monks who worked in the infirmary brought her some very distressing news. Without being told, James knew how upset she was. When she turned to face him, there were tears in her eyes.

James rushed to her. "What's the matter, Randy?"

"The baby boy I helped deliver the other day is very ill, and his mother isn't expected to live much longer. Brother Casper asked me to see them."

"But what can you do for them? You're not a doctor."

Randy shook her head. "No, but if I can tell the doctor where the pain is located, perhaps he can find a way of at least saving the baby."

Filled with purpose, Randy walked to the rear of the clinic with Brother Casper, a short, rotund man in a brown cowled robe. James followed close behind them to the small room where the sick mother and child were being kept.

It was only when Brother Casper moved to the side of the room that James could see the person on the bed. Randy had said the woman was young, but nothing had prepared him for this. The young Indian mother couldn't have been more than twelve years old. She was a tiny creature with long black hair and big brown eyes. Her gaze was glassy, fixed on the ceiling over the bed. She seemed totally unaware of her surroundings and the child whimpering in the cradle beside her.

Randy sat on the bed and held the young woman's hands. She didn't move for several minutes. James thought she was praying. In a soft voice, Randy began to speak.

"Too hard to breathe . . . very hot . . . burning inside . . . much pain . . . so weak . . . my baby . . . my poor baby—"

Suddenly, she stopped talking and pulled away from the bed. Even though he was untrained in the healing arts, James knew the young mother was dead. When the monk stepped forward to cover the body, Randy removed the crying baby from his cradle.

"Poor precious child," she crooned to the tiny infant in her arms. "Your mother's last thoughts were of you. Don't worry, little one. I'll take care of you and you won't be alone."

James had never felt so helpless. The questions that arose in his mind when Randy held the dying woman's hands were lost as he watched her with the baby. From the worried look on Brother Casper's face and the dismal shake of his head, James knew there was no hope for the ailing child.

During the next hour, Randy sat in a chair, cuddling the infant. No amount of talking by James or the monks could convince her to put the baby down. She bathed him and tried to force fluids past his lips, but nothing helped to break his fever. His breathing was labored, and soon he was too weak to cry.

"Look, James, he's fallen asleep. Maybe the herb tea and the bath helped him," Randy said hopefully. "Do you think he's getting better?"

James knelt beside her. "He's not getting better. I'm afraid the poor lad has gotten worse."

Randy shook her head. "No, that's not true, James. Can't you see that he's not so flushed anymore? He must be improving."

"I'm sorry, love. Your eyes are only showing you what you want to see."

But Randy couldn't accept his words. "No, James, you don't

understand. I don't need my eyes to see. I know it because of what I feel in here," she said, patting her own chest.

"Whether you use your eyes or your heart, the outcome will be the same. This baby is very sick. He's going to die."

"No, I can't let that happen. He must not die." Cradling the child, Randy began rocking from side to side. "Come on, little one, show James that he is wrong. Don't let me fail you like this. Please don't let me fail you."

Without warning, Randy went still. Her entire body became taut as she stared at the lifeless baby in her arms. Suddenly she put her mouth over the infant's nose and mouth and tried to force air into its lungs.

"Breathe, baby, breathe," she begged like a litany between each breath. "You must breathe."

She continued trying to revive the child until James and Brother Casper were finally able to subdue her and remove the small, inert form from her. Randy's anguish cut through James like a knife as he took her into his arms and held her close.

"He's dead and it's all because of me," she cried.

"That's nonsense. The babe and his mother were seriously ill. You had nothing to do with that."

Randy pulled away from him and removed a handkerchief she had tucked into the sleeve of her choli to wipe her eyes. "It *is* my fault, James. Had I been here yesterday, perhaps I could have told the physicians what was wrong sooner."

"You can't blame yourself, Randy. The two of them were in poor health. That girl was only half grown and needed a mother herself. She was a child giving birth to a child."

"That child and her baby needed me, but I was too caught up in my own life to come and see them yesterday. I may have failed them, but I won't let that happen to the others."

"Randy, what are you talking about?" James asked as she turned away from him and walked toward the door. "Please speak to me. I don't understand what you're implying."

When she turned around, her tears were gone, and the expression on her solemn face was tranquil. "Thank you for your concern, Captain Grayson, but I won't be accepting your offer of passage to England after all. You see, I've decided to stay in India.''

James shook his head. ''You can't mean that, Randy. There's a man here who is trying to kill you.''

''Yes, I know, but after three tries, he has yet to get it right. I refuse to let fear of him dictate my life.''

''Randy, you must listen to reason. The next time that bastard could succeed and kill you.''

Randy shrugged; a serene smile graced her lips. ''Then so be it, Captain. I am one person, a single life that will come to an end someday. But while I am alive, I can stay right here and save many others. These people need me. I won't spare my own life at the cost of theirs.''

James was momentarily dumbfounded by her statement. Before he could say a word, she turned and made her way through the clinic. As he watched her speaking to the monks, he couldn't quell the fury building up inside him.

''Damn her and her noble cause! If Randy wants to be a sacrificial lamb, then let her. I don't care what the hell she does with her life!''

Even as he spoke, James knew he didn't mean what he said. He shook his head. His anger was real, but his apathy was false. He cared about Randy too much to let her remain in India without him. Somehow, he had to find a way of showing her that he was right.

Randy spent a sleepless night prowling the confines of her bedroom. After returning from the mission, she had bathed, had her dinner brought to the suite, and dismissed Jarita. With her mind beleaguered by so many conflicting thoughts, she didn't want to deal with anyone, not even her beloved ayah.

She had told James that she was going to remain in India. But even without the danger of the killer looming over her, staying in India had more than its share of complications.

Randy dragged her fingers through her tousled hair. "I could take Abu and the others and flee to the northern provinces until I come of age, but what about Nana? If I ran away, would she be upset? Could she possibly understand?"

Though they had never met, Randy felt a special bond with the woman she had been named for. From the stories her mother had told her and the letters the dowager sent, she knew her grandmother was a spirited lady who thrived on challenges.

"Maybe going to England *is* the solution. Nana would help me deal with Richard, and James and I could . . ." She sighed. "Once James knows about my empathic gift, he will probably have nothing to do with me."

Biting her lip, she considered another thought. "Maybe if James fell in love with me, he would learn to accept my strange talents. At the mission yesterday, he didn't understand what I was doing with those sick people, but he never questioned me. He was patient and attentive, and offered me comfort when I broke down and cried over the baby."

Sadly laughing to herself, Randy opened the terrace doors that overlooked the gardens. "James in love with me? What a fool's dream! After the way I turned on him yesterday, he likely thinks I'm demented. Besides, he may already have a lady waiting for his return. Perhaps it's that woman Diana he's talked about. You can hear his affection for her in his voice. I wonder if she holds his heart?"

Randy yawned. The answers to her questions would have to wait until she got some sleep. Turning toward her bed, she realized that Sidra had not come home. Since James and Stephen arrived, Sidra had spent every night on her pallet in the corner of the bedroom. The guards assigned to the rear perimeter of the grounds that edged the jungle knew about the tiger and were told never to interfere with the creature's comings and goings.

Sleep was forgotten as Randy became concerned with the well-being of her precious pet. Wearing a silk nightgown, robe, and slippers, she ran out to the garden to look for Sidra.

The first rays of sunlight were coming over the horizon. Her calls to the tiger went unanswered. She covered the entire garden twice before an idea suddenly occurred to her.

"Drat! I was so involved in my troubles, I didn't open my door for her. Sidra's probably in the stable loft pouting."

At the stable, Randy found that one of the large double doors had been left ajar. "All right, Sidra, come on out," she called as she stepped inside. "I know you're angry because I forgot to leave my door open, but I won't do it again, I promise."

While she was looking up at the opening to the loft, Randy heard a sound behind her. Before she could turn, a hard object struck the back of her head and sent her crashing to the floor.

James bolted upright in bed. His head throbbed with pain. "This is a bloody way to start the morning," he groaned, rubbing the back of his head. "No more brandy for me. Next time, I'll stick to wine when I want to drown myself. On second thought, I'll use water. It won't taste as good, but at least I won't feel so rotten."

When he tried to lie down again, the ache in the base of his skull grew worse. Rather than expose himself to more discomfort, he decided to get up. Struggling to his feet, he carried out his morning ablutions. It took some effort, but he was soon washed and dressed. The pain was so severe, he didn't trust himself to shave. After he had a few cups of strong black coffee, he would find a servant to handle the task for him.

Standing at the window that faced the gardens, James realized how early it was. The sun had been up for only a few minutes. He doubted if the kitchen staff had started breakfast. It might be a while before he got his much-needed dose of coffee.

"Maybe a breath of air will help this bloody headache of mine," he muttered, walking out onto the veranda adjacent to his room. He sat on a tall rattan chair and closed his eyes while he filled his lungs with the sweet morning air.

* * *

Randy's lids fluttered open to find herself surrounded by darkness. Her hands and feet were bound, and she was lying facedown on the stable floor. Dry straw scratched her cheek. The air was stifling and strange odors assailed her. A blinding pain shot through her head as she recognized the acrid smell of lamp oil and smoke. Seconds before she lapsed into unconsciousness, the gag in her mouth muffled the three words that fought to escape her lips.

"James . . . help . . . me. . . ."

James jumped and looked around, startled by what he had heard. The voice had definitely belonged to Randy. Since he was alone, James decided that he must have been dreaming.

"But it seemed so real. It sounded like Randy was calling out to me, begging me to—"

An icy chill enveloped him. Fueled by instinct rather than logic, James leaped to his feet and began running through the garden. Seeing the smoke billowing from the stables, he knew Randy was inside.

The sound of footsteps joined his on the path. He was surprised to find Abu Nazir running at his side.

"I have sent for help, *Huzur.* Xavier and the others will see to the fire and the horses, while you and I get Missy Collins out of there."

James should have been curious as to how Abu knew that Randy was in the stable, but he was much too involved in his own thoughts of her peril to question the older man. When they arrived at the burning structure, flames were licking up the walls in various places. They could hear the trapped horses inside, bucking and screaming, fighting to get out.

Two beams of wood were braced against the doors, holding them shut. James kicked them out of the way and yanked the doors open. Dense gray smoke filled the air. Pulling off his coat, he dipped it in the water trough near the well, draped the wet garment over his head and entered the stable. Abu unwound his turban and mimicked his actions. Within minutes, the two men were forced back outside by the smoke and intense heat.

"Damn!" James bitterly exclaimed. "I know Randy is in there but how can we find her? The smoke is so thick, it's blinding. Even if she could answer my calls, I would never hear her over the ruckus those poor animals are making."

"Then perhaps you are searching the wrong way, *Huzur*. Do not use your eyes and voice alone. Open your mind, and your heart will lead you to her."

The old man's advice sounded strange, but with the fire growing quickly out of control, James was willing to try anything. Keeping close to the floor, he once again entered the stable with Abu.

By this time, help had arrived. While Xavier and the grooms gathered the horses, the guards and gardeners fought the blaze.

James tried hard to follow Abu's advice and put all his concentration on finding Randy. Crawling along the floor, he peered into each stall and found nothing but growing frustration.

"Maybe I was wrong, Abu. Perhaps Randy's not here."

"She is here, *Huzur*. I can sense her presence, yet I do not possess your insight to find her. Call and she will respond."

In spite of his doubts, James shut his eyes and willed himself to think of nothing but Randy. Fear and thoughts of the fire were cast aside. Only the message he wanted her to hear filled his mind.

"Randy, where are you? You must answer me if I'm to find you. Please, answer me now, love."

James, help me. I'm here.

As before, he heard Randy's softly spoken words. But he realized that it hadn't been his ears that caught her reply. Her voice seemed to be inside him. And this time, James knew for a certainty that it hadn't been a dream.

"Randy, I can't find you. Can you describe where you are?"

It's dark, very dark, James. I can't see anything, but I know one of the horses is very close to me. He's kicking the wall because he's so afraid of the fire.

Two horses remained in their stalls at the end of the barn. They both seemed crazed by the smoke and the approaching flames. James crawled to the nearest one and lifted the latch on the gate. The beast bolted quickly past him, making good his escape. There was nothing but a manger for the feed and a water trough in the abandoned stall.

James recognized the occupant of the last enclosure. The golden stallion, Garuda, reared up on his hind legs when they entered the stall. The horse's eyes were not drawn to the fire, but to a blanket-covered figure on the floor. Garuda pranced nervously as if he were trying to prevent them from getting too close to it. But James would not be deterred. Even before he saw the length of auburn hair sticking out from beneath the wool blanket, he knew they had found Randy.

"Nazir, take this," James ordered, shoving his wet coat into Abu's hands. "When I grab Garuda's bridle, I want you to throw my coat over his head. With his eyes covered, you should be able to lead him out of here while I tend to Randy."

Working together, they quickly subdued the stallion, and Abu led him from the barn. As James gathered Randy's wrapped body in his arms and carried her toward the open doors, the rafters over Garuda's stall crashed to the floor in a roaring blaze. Sparks flew through the air, catching the back of his shirt, igniting it in small pinpoints of fire.

When James emerged from the stable, Abu draped a sopping wet blanket over his shoulders. James was oblivious to the heat of the flames and the cold water that doused the fire on his back. Dropping to his knees a safe distance from the burning structure, he placed Randy on the ground and removed the wool blanket that covered her.

Randy squinted against the bright sunlight that touched her eyes. Dirt streaked the pale skin of her face. Her hair was loose, bits of hay tangled in its dark length. A muzzle of soiled white linen was tied snugly over her mouth, but to James, she had never been more beautiful.

"Thank God you're alive, Randy. I was so afraid of not being able to find you."

Tearing the strip of cloth away from her face, James pulled her into his arms and captured her lips in a kiss filled with relief. His tongue swept into her mouth and savored her living sweetness until he suddenly felt her struggling against him.

"My animals . . ." she rasped, turning her face toward the burning stable. "I've got to go back and get them out of there."

"Abu and the others are taking care of the animals for you, sweetheart."

Randy shook her head defiantly. "You don't understand. If she's in there, she won't come out for anyone but me."

James held her tightly. "You're not going anywhere, Randy. I'm sorry, but I can't allow you to risk your life because of one of your pets."

"She could be trapped in the loft. Even an animal doesn't deserve to die that way." Randy pushed aside the blanket that covered her and tried to pull free of his embrace. "Please, James, I have to go back and save her."

"Don't be foolish. If one of your pets was in the stable, it probably escaped on its own." James grabbed her bound hands and held them up to her face. "Need I remind you that you were almost killed this morning? Some bastard tied you up and left you to die in that heinous fire." While freeing her hands, he looked at her soiled nightclothes and shook his head. "Evidently this man knows of your concern for your animals and set this trap for you. How could you be so careless?"

Randy jerked her hands away from him. "I don't appreciate being lectured to. If you will help me untie my ankles, I would like to see what damage this madman has wrought to my stables."

Biting back a retort, James removed the ropes from her legs and assisted her to her feet. When the wet blanket fell from his shoulders, revealing his scorched shirt, Randy gasped.

"Your shirt has burn holes all over it! Oh, James, you must be suffering great pain."

The concern in her voice and the gentle touch of her hand on his arm calmed his ire. Looking over his shoulder, he shrugged. "I'm fine, Randy. I suspect my shirt took the brunt of the damage. I was so involved in getting you out of there, I never realized that the flames had reached me."

Randy lifted the burnt fabric from his back and looked at the mottled red marks on his skin. "The wet blanket helped, but you're going to have a few blisters. My cook, Kira, has ointment that we use for burns that could help—"

A wave of dizziness swept over Randy, causing her to sway against James. He caught her around the waist and held her up.

"What's the matter, Randy? Are you in pain?"

Closing her eyes, she raised her hand and touched the back of her head. "The intruder hit me on the head. I think the blow has left me a bit addled."

James lifted her up into his arms. "I'm putting you to bed and sending for the physician at the British compound."

"Put me down this instant," Randy demanded, poking his chest with her hand. "I'm dizzy, not mortally wounded. Besides, I wouldn't have that English doctor tend a dead dog. When the man's not tipping his elbow with a pint of gin, he's sleeping off a drunk. I am feeling fine now, so please put me down!"

"You're being a stubborn brat," James complained, setting her on her feet. "A blow to your head could be very dangerous. You must let a physician examine you. Since you don't trust the man at the compound, we can send for Brother Casper."

Randy shook her head. "No, Brother Casper has enough to do without tending to my needs. If I require care, I'll send for Kahlid Jovar. He is Akbar's physician at the Opal Court."

"Missy Collins, Allah be praised! You are safe." Abu smiled broadly as he hurried toward them, brushing his unruly hair from his face. "It is good to see you well."

"She's not unscathed, Nazir," James informed him. "Randy suffered a blow to the head and I want her to see a physician."

Randy glared at James when Abu frowned with worry. "I told you my injury is minor, Captain. Right now, my concern is only for my home and the safety of my animals."

"All the livestock has been accounted for, Missy Collins. Other than soot and smoke, the creatures are well. But I regret to inform you that the stables are a total loss. In spite of our efforts, the fire was much too large to contain."

Turning her back to James, Randy walked toward the smoking ruins with Abu. "We can put up temporary corrals for the horses and store their feed in the barn with the goats until the stables can be rebuilt. If we get to work on it right away, I'm sure we can have the new structure completed in just a few weeks. I can begin working on the plans after breakfast."

Angered by her callous disregard of his concern, James caught up to her and grabbed her arm. He pulled her around to face him. "Have you lost your mind, Randy? A maniac tried to murder you again this morning and all you're concerned with is building a new stable. You should be making arrangements to leave India before that bastard succeeds in killing you."

Yanking free of his hold, Randy braced her hands on her hips. "I was foolish to go to the stables alone this morning, but I will not make that mistake again. I'll hire additional guards and be more vigilant in the future. Should I decide to go to England, it will be when I say so and not before. I have no intention of going anywhere until my home and property have been set to rights." Turning away from him, she moved closer to the smoldering remnants of the stable.

James noticed the way Abu's attention was drawn to the jungle beyond the stables. "What's the matter, Nazir? Do you see someone out there?"

Abu stared at the copse of trees and shook his head. "No, *Huzur*. It is just a feeling that plagues me, but I think it would be best if Missy Collins returned to the house."

Randy heard his words and frowned back at him. "Abu, you

are worrying over nothing. Certainly that man is miles from here by now. Send guards to search the jungles if you wish, but I'm going to see how Garuda and Ratri are faring."

She had barely taken two steps when Abu suddenly spun around and rushed toward her. The sound of a gunshot exploded in the morning air as he grabbed Randy and shielded her with his body. James saw a blossom of red blood erupt on the back of Abu's white tunic seconds before the older man crumpled to the ground.

Randy screamed and dropped down beside Abu. "I am so sorry, old friend," she cried as James shouted orders for the men to search the area for the shooter. "Had I listened to you, Abu, this wouldn't have happened. You were wounded because of me."

Lying on his side, Abu winced with pain and shook his head. "You ... are not at fault, my lady. The jackal ... the jackal is desperate." His voice was low, his breathing labored. "I could not let him harm you. Do not cry, Sona Ag ... my duty ... to protect you," he whispered as he lapsed into unconsciousness.

James knelt down and tore off the back of Abu's tunic to inspect the wound. After a moment, he wadded up the cloth and pressed it against the bleeding flesh.

"The shot has entered beneath his left shoulder blade. From the way that he's breathing, he might have a punctured lung. God only knows if the ball has damaged his heart. I'm sorry, love, but I don't think Abu's going to make it."

Racked with tears, Randy put her trembling hand against Abu's chest and closed her eyes. The gift that had helped her aid so many others now told her that her old friend and mentor was gravely wounded. His lung was pierced, but his heart seemed to be uninjured. A ray of hope suddenly filled her soul.

"James, please send one of the men to the Opal Court to fetch Kahlid Jovar. Kahlid will be able to help Abu survive this wound. But we must hurry."

With the amount of blood seeping through the cloth in his

hand, James didn't believe anyone could save Abu's life. But something in Randy's eyes as she looked up at him made him doubt his own judgment. He found her optimism was contagious.

After sending one of the guards to get Kahlid Jovar, James carefully lifted Abu into his arms and, with Randy's help, carried the slightly built man into the house.

Late that afternoon, James and Randy waited in the salon for word on Abu's condition. Jovar had been working on his patient for several hours and no one other than Jarita had been allowed in the bedroom with the physician as he went about his tasks. Bathed and dressed in a Western-styled gown of emerald green, Randy impatiently crossed the room, berating herself for the almost tragic events of the day.

"If only I had listened to Abu this morning, he never would have been shot trying to protect me. But no, I had to look at my ruined stables. I ignored his warning and set myself up as an easy target!" She looked over at James where he sat silently on the sofa watching her. "Well, aren't you going to tell me what a terrible mistake I made this morning?"

The shoulders of his loose-fitting shirt rose in a shrug. "Why should I? You're doing a fine job of it all on your own. Besides, you made your worst mistake long before today."

Randy stopped in front of him. "What do you mean?"

"If you had listened to Abu and the rest of us, you would have agreed to go to England days ago and none of this would have happened. Your stable would still be standing and Abu wouldn't be having a lead ball removed from his chest."

"Don't you think I know that?" Heaving a disheartened sigh, Randy sat down beside him. "But going to England would cause as many problems as it would solve."

"You're talking about losing your freedom and having to deal with your uncle, aren't you?"

She nodded. "And much more than you will ever understand."

The sadness in her voice was laden with pain. James reached over and stroked her pale cheek. "Then tell me about it, Randy. Help me understand what's troubling you."

Randy swallowed back the tightness in her throat. "Some people are born with the talent to create wondrous works of art. Others are endowed with beautiful voices and can sing like angels. Gifted poets compose verses that stir our hearts with emotion, while others are blessed with the ability to heal, like Jovar and Brother Casper. My God-given talent makes me a freak."

James's brow creased with confusion. "But you have a gift to heal, Randy. I saw how you treated those people in the clinic. You touched them and helped them feel better."

She opened her hands and looked at her palms. "My gift is not in healing, James. When I touch people with my hands, I can feel their pain as if it were my own. I tell the physician where the pain is, and they decide what treatment should be used to help the patient."

James gasped. "That's how you knew about Abu's injury this morning! You touched his chest and knew where the ball was lodged inside him. What an extraordinary gift you possess."

The awe in his voice made Randy smile. "You're quite surprising, James. While the people here in India value my ability as a precious gift, most Europeans would think me daft for making such a claim about myself."

"I am not your typical European, Randy." Using his finger, James turned her face toward his. "My mother and her sister are identical twins, who have shared mental contact with each other all their lives. When one is sick, the other feels her pain. Once, when my mother was abducted, it was her sister's link to her through dreams that led to her being rescued. So, although I don't possess such a gift, I know they exist."

Randy smiled brightly at him. "But you too have a gift,

James. How else can you explain how you were able to find me in the stable this morning?''

''Don't be absurd, Randy. I called to you and you answered me. There's nothing special in that.''

''I was gagged with a cloth and couldn't speak. You didn't hear me with your ears, James. You heard me with your mind.''

James pulled slightly away from her. ''I said I heard you, so let's leave it at that. I got you out of the bloody stable and you're safe. That's all that matters. Now, why do you think your ability to feel the pain of other people will cause you problems if you went to England?''

The stony expression on his face told Randy that James wasn't ready to admit to the mystical link they had shared that morning. Arguing with him about it would be a waste of time.

''My ability is not limited to feeling the pain of humans. I share a similar link to animals and birds. Over the years, I've found many wounded creatures, nursed them back to health, and made them my pets. That's how I knew that Garuda's hoof was injured. If people in your world learned of my gift, they would use me, or worse, ridicule me because of it.''

James scoffed at her words. ''It's not just my world, Randy. You may have been born in India, but you are as English as I am.''

''You are missing the point, James. More than geography separates me from the land my family calls home. I have been schooled in the ways of both cultures, and I don't think I can survive in England with its oh-so-perfect society.''

Despite Randy's attempt to remain calm, desperation crept into her voice. ''I can pour tea, arrange dinner parties, and display all the fine attributes of a properly bred English lady. But it's all a facade! I am not an actress. It wouldn't take people long to see that I am not what I appear to be.''

''Randy, sweetheart, you must listen to me.''

Lost in her own thoughts, she turned away from him and shook her head. ''I would be a misfit there. Denied the freedom to be myself, I would grow bored and find a way to use my gifts to help others. But being the niece of the Duke of Maidstone would put me on public display, and I would be caught. My grandmother would likely be disgraced, and Uncle Richard would devise a ghastly way to punish me.''

James placed a consoling hand on her shoulder. ''I told you Nana wouldn't allow that to happen. She will petition the courts to be named your guardian. After your father's killer has been found, you would be free to return to India if you wished.''

Tears held back for far too long burned her eyes. Tension caused her to tremble. ''I cannot count on that happening. Even with all Nana's wealth, Richard has the title and the upper hand in this matter. My uncle hates Nana and would gladly use me as an instrument to cause her pain. I know the law, James. Richard could sell this house, put Abu and the others out in the street, and marry me off to some crone of his before Nana could do a thing to stop him. I don't fear for myself, but everyone would suffer because of me. James, what am I supposed to do?''

James pulled her into his arms. ''Don't worry, Mira. We'll find a way of dealing with this, I promise.'' His lips touched her cheek with a soft kiss before he hugged her against him.

The way he called her Mira and sealed his promise with a kiss reminded Randy of her father. Aching with a bone-deep weariness, she eagerly allowed James to comfort her. She could trust him. In just a few days, he had become an important part of her life. Even before he had saved her from the fire that morning, she had come to rely on him. As his fingers stroked her back, she knew he was trying to think of a way to help her, and she was glad.

Randy knew that his heroics and the way he reminded her of her father were only a small part of the feelings she had for this handsome, headstrong man. Against all logic, she had fallen in love with James. But that knowledge gave her no ease. With his home in England and hers in India, there was little hope their relationship would grow into anything lasting.

Burrowing her face into his shoulder, she prayed she would

learn to survive the loss when he was gone. She let out a moan of disappointment when James suddenly eased away from her.

He lifted her chin with his hand and made her look up at him. "Marry me, Randy."

She gaped with surprise. Her pulse raced. "Marry you?"

"Yes, marrying me would be the perfect solution," he replied with a curt nod. "Tomorrow I'll procure a special license from the government offices and we can be married immediately."

For several moments, Randy didn't trust herself to respond to his announcement. Every woman dreamt of the day when a man proposed to her, but none of her musings had been quite like this. He hadn't made any declaration of love or even mentioned the possibility of fond feelings between them. His eyes were cool and direct; not a bit of tenderness was evident in their azure depths. She struggled to conceal her confusion.

"You want us to be married immediately?"

James nodded and stood up. "Most definitely. We must have the marriage certificate with us when we get to England if we're to avoid problems with your uncle."

"My uncle? What does my uncle have to do with this?"

James didn't respond. Deep in thought, he walked the length of the room with his hands clasped behind his back. "If Abu is up to it, we could lay in supplies for the journey, get your things brought to the ship, and set sail on Friday morning."

"Friday?" she gasped. "That's only three days from now."

"Yes, I know. But with Stephen overseeing the loading of the ship and Akbar's aid with the local merchants, it can be done. The servants can begin packing your things right away."

The dizziness that engulfed Randy had little to do with the injury she had sustained that morning or watching James as he paced back and forth across the room. "This is moving much too quickly for me. Packing, supplies, and sailing away in three days' time?" She slumped back against the sofa and shook her head. "All this and a wedding too? It can't be done!"

"Of course it can," James boasted confidently. "We're only

going to have a quick civil ceremony at the government offices, not a flowery affair in church with family and friends.''

"But, James, I always thought . . .'' Randy closed her eyes and fought to keep the pain she was feeling out of her words. "I don't think marrying now is going to solve anything.''

Not looking up, she felt James sit beside her on the sofa.

"Marrying now is the best solution for you, Randy,'' he explained. "If you're my wife when we return to England, Richard Wentworth will have no say over your life or your inheritance.''

Randy's eyes popped open. "You offered to marry me to thwart my uncle?''

James nodded. "Of course. I may not have a title as lofty as his, but my family's wealth and power are more than enough to stop the Duke of Maidstone from bothering you if we were married. Lord knows I wasn't looking for a wife, but it is the simplest way of protecting you.''

"Protecting me?'' Randy felt heat building in her cheeks. The effort to keep her voice low felt like a noose tightening around her throat. "It's very noble of you, James, but I can't allow you to make such a sacrifice on my account. I will have to find another means of dealing with my problems.''

The portrait of nonchalance, James eased back in his seat and shrugged. "I won't be sacrificing much, Randy. As soon as we get word that your father's murderer has been caught, we will have our marriage annulled and you can return to India. That shouldn't take more than a year.''

"Our marriage will be annulled? On what grounds can this be done?'' She hoped her polite tone didn't reveal that the words felt like acid rolling off her tongue.

"We won't consummate the marriage. Our relationship will be in name only,'' he informed her. "After the annulment, I will turn all your funds over to you and bring you back here. Then you will have the freedom to live as you choose.''

Randy's fingernails bit into the flesh of her palms as she clenched her fists in her lap. "Your kindness is overwhelming,

Captain, but again, I must decline your offer. There must be another way of handling this situation."

James's posture stiffened. There was no mistaking the rancor in his voice. "You don't understand, Randy. There is no other way. Your father's killer is getting closer to doing away with you. It's a miracle that you survived this morning. Abu nearly paid the price for your foolishness. Whose life are you willing to forfeit the next time the bastard comes after you?"

Randy felt as if she had been physically struck by his words. Tears burned her eyes. "How can you ask something like that? You know I never wanted anyone to be hurt because of me."

James gave her a reassuring smile and drew her into his arms. "I know, sweetheart, and I'm sorry I had to be so blunt about this, but I had to make you see that there is no other way. Your being hurt or killed is something I can't accept, Mira. If I'm willing to be a part of this marriage in name only to keep you safe, the least you can do is comply."

Torn by conflicting emotions, Randy closed her eyes and rested her cheek against his chest. The wisdom in his words battled her fears. She had no choice. A sigh escaped her lips.

"All right, James. I'll marry you and go to England for a while. But I expect you to honor your pledge regarding my pets and the servants I told you about. I will not go without them."

Hugging her, James shook his head. "You won't have to, Mira. We'll be a bit crowded in the cabins, but there will be room enough for your people. Are you going to take Sidra to England as well?"

"Of course I'm taking Sidra—" Startled, Randy pulled away from him. "Who told you about Sidra?"

"Abu told me how Sidra fought off the intruder and saved your life the night your father was killed. With such courage, I'm looking forward to meeting her. Has Sidra been a servant in your household a long time?"

James frowned with confusion as Randy stumbled over her

response. "Sidra has . . . um, been with me for several years, but . . . ah, she's not . . ."

"My baby," Jarita cried out, running into the salon. "The gods be praised for their goodness! Abu is going to live. The *hakiim* has surely performed a miracle this day. Come, my lamb! Abu is asking to see you."

As he watched Randy hurry off with her ayah, James fell back against the sofa. A triumphant smile curved his lips.

"You will marry me, Randy, but our marriage will never be annulled," he boasted out loud to the empty room. "During our months together, I'll make you love me. I shall convince you that being my wife is worth the loss of your freedom and that your home is with me in England."

Stephen walked into the salon grumbling to himself as he yanked off his dust-covered coat and loosened his cravat. "I don't know what's worse about this country, the damned heat or the gritty dirt from the roads. I swear I will never complain about the cold weather and rain back home ever again."

Before James could comment, Stephen wearily sat on the sofa beside him and closed his eyes as he talked. "The footman at the door told me that Nazir is doing well. Randy must be pleased about that. And how's your back, James? Did that ointment take away the pain from those burns?"

"Yes it did, but I wanted to tell you—"

Oblivious to his friend's answer, Stephen rambled on. "I just can't believe that I slept through that fire this morning. Must be the heat and all the running around I've been doing on your behalf that tires me out so much."

James scowled at Stephen's reclining form. "Eating everything in sight and drinking endless glasses of wine and brandy like a starving wretch doesn't help either. All those spirits and rich food can do you more harm than good."

Stephen yawned. "I still think the climate is at fault."

"But not for much longer," James replied. "We will be leaving for England on Friday."

"That's only ten days from now. Not much time to get—"

James interrupted him. "Not next Friday, Stephen, this Friday. On the morning tide."

Stephen bolted up in his seat and glared at him. "Are you insane? We can't be ready to leave in three days!"

"With your help and Akbar's aid we will." James stood up. "I'll go to the library and write a list of things that must be handled before our departure."

Stephen gaped with disbelief as James turned and walked away from him. "But, James, why are we rushing off this way? We are still negotiating with the local growers, and so far we haven't secured any shipments to deliver in England. Have we come all this way to return home with an empty hold?"

James stopped in the archway to the hall and looked back at his friend. "The hold will be far from empty, Stephen. With Randy's pets and servants and their belongings, we're going to need all the space we can spare. By the by, you'll be bunking with Emmet for the voyage home. Abu will be using your cabin while he recovers. Randy will be in my quarters."

"So, you've convinced Randy to go to England. That's wonderful news." Smiling, Stephen nodded with understanding. "After this morning, I can see why you want to leave quickly. Are you afraid she might change her mind?"

"Randy won't change her mind," James declared in a serious tone that clearly dissuaded Stephen from arguing with him. "She knows what we are doing is for the best." His grave demeanor disappeared when he suddenly grinned and leaned his shoulder against the wall. "Furthermore, old chum, I won't be able to pay you the winnings on our wager until we get home. I'll probably be needing the money to bribe Major Spencer in the morning."

Stephen was totally perplexed by his friend's change of subject. "What wager did I win? And more important, why are you bribing that twit Brandon Spencer?"

James shrugged with feigned indifference. "I don't think Spencer would sign my marriage license without a little monetary encouragement. A thousand pounds and my promise not to squelch his career with my connections in England should get his signature as the acting governor on the document.''

"Marriage license? You and Randy?'' In the blink of an eye, Stephen's disconcerted frown grew into a full-blown smile. "I knew you and Randy were meant to be together. So which one of you broke down first and admitted how much you love each other?''

"Neither. The lady thinks that we're going to have a marriage in name only to stop her uncle's interference in her life. With my name and living with me, she'll be protected from him. Our union will not be consummated so it can be annulled when her father's murderer has been caught and she will be free to return here to India in a year or so.''

Stephen sputtered with disbelief. "And you went along with this crazy notion?''

James smiled. "Of course. It was my idea.''

"Of all the moronic . . . how could you think . . . ?'' Stephen jumped up and rushed to where James was standing. Touching his shoulder, Stephen's voice dropped to a conspiratorial tone. "Randy is a very desirable woman. You would have to leave the country yourself or lock her in a convent for the year if she is to remain untouched.''

The only response James offered was an amused smile. His brows rose expectantly. Stephen suddenly realized his friend's true intent and laughed heartily.

"Why, you sly dog! By getting Randy to agree to a mock marriage, you've given her your protection and gained yourself the time to win her love. You're going to seduce your own wife.''

James nodded. "Yes, but I won't rush her. When the time is right and I'm sure it's truly what she wants, I'll make Randy my wife in every sense of the word.''

"That shouldn't take long. Even I can see that the lady's half besotted with you already. Getting her to give up her home in India might take some effort, but if she loves you, I don't think it will be a problem.''

Turning away from Stephen, James shook his head. "Randy giving up India isn't the only thing worrying me about this. After what Caroline Sutcliffe tried to do to me a few years ago, I detest any form of manipulation. Yet that's exactly what I'm doing to Randy. But what choice do I have?

"Every day she remains here puts her in more peril. When I nearly lost her in that fire, I realized how much I cared for her, so I decided that I'd do whatever was necessary to keep her safe. Even if it meant trapping her into a marriage she didn't want. I fear she'll hate me if she figures out what I've done. It has me wondering if the end truly justifies the means."

"Of course it does," Stephen scoffed. "You're doing it for the purest of reasons, James. You love her. Randy could hardly fault you for that." He playfully slapped James on the back. "Now let's get to work on that list of yours. If we're sailing on Friday, I'm sure you will have plenty for me to do."

Walking toward the library with Stephen, James chuckled. "I haven't put ink to paper yet and you're already complaining."

"Of course I am, Jamie. If I didn't complain, you would think me dead. With all you have on your mind, replacing your best friend is one worry you shouldn't have." In front of the open library door, Stephen stopped and grabbed James by the arm. "I am your best friend, am I not, James?"

James heard the doubt in Stephen's voice and quickly reassured him. "Of course you are, Stephen. Never doubt it."

"Then why are you making me share a room with Emmet for the voyage home? The man snores so loudly, it's a wonder he hasn't knocked the door to his cabin off its hinges!"

James shoved Stephen into the library and shook his head. "It's good to know you're alive, friend, but just once, I wish you weren't so bloody predictable."

Chapter 9

It was almost noon on Friday when James angrily made his way through the bustling crowds at the docks to the berth where his ship, the *Diana,* lay at anchor. Yanking off his cravat, he stormed up the gangplank ready to do battle with anyone who got in his way. Seeing dozens of cages of loudly clucking chickens littering the deck of his proud vessel stopped him in his tracks.

"What in the bloody hell is going on around here?"

Stephen sauntered over to his side, shaking his head in mock concern. "Tsk, tsk, is that any way for a titled noble to present himself on such a lovely day, my lord? The sky is blue, the sun is shining, and all is right within the world, so what's put you off, Jamie boy? Have you lost your taste for fresh poultry, my friend?"

James glared at him. "I have just spent the past four hours dealing with that prig Spencer, and I am just in the mood to wring someone's neck! If you don't want to be the scapegoat for my foul temper, I suggest you tell me what is going on around here." His stormy gaze swept the expanse of the deck.

"I leave you in charge to oversee the final loading, and I return to find my ship looking like a barnyard!"

Fighting a smile, Stephen wearily leaned back against the ship's railing and muttered, "It's more like a menagerie."

James turned back to him. "What was that?"

His unconcealed anger caused Stephen to snap to attention. "Did you—ah, have more trouble with the major this morning?"

Letting out a breath laden with frustration, James used his discarded neckcloth to wipe the sweat from his brow. "Trouble is that greedy bastard's middle name. I went to the government offices to pick up my marriage certificate, and Spencer tried to rob me of another thousand pounds!"

"He tried to blackmail you again for his signature?"

James shook his head. "No, the major was far more clever than to try that. Tried to call it some kind of an exportation shipping fee, for goods he claims I am taking out of India."

"But you're not exporting anything. With this rushed departure, we didn't have time to arrange for a single contract or consignment. Financially speaking, this voyage was a loss."

"I know, but Spencer refused to believe me. Since I would not pay him, he threatened to send a squad of soldiers here to prevent our sailing until his excise agents could do a thorough search to verify my claim. Said it would take at least a week to get the task completed."

"Another week?" Stephen sputtered. "Why, that's ridiculous! Knowing how badly you want to depart, he really must be desperate for funds if he's willing to risk your ire to get it."

"My thoughts exactly. That's why I knew his ploy had less to do with money and more with delaying my departure with Randy. He denied it at first, but after we argued a bit, I persuaded him—physically—to tell me the truth." James rubbed the knuckles on his right hand. "Too bad I didn't break his jaw."

"What did he say?"

"Not much. Just that he had sent word of Jonathan Collins's

death to Richard Wentworth the day after the murder. By now, the Duke of Maidstone knows that his niece is orphaned, and he has been declared her legal guardian.''

''But Spencer told Randy that he hadn't done that yet.''

James cocked his brow. ''He did even more. In the letter he sent to the duke, Spencer stated that he and Randy were betrothed to be married. He even claimed that her father had blessed their upcoming union.''

''Why, that lying cur!''

''Oh, but it gets even better, Stephen. Major Spencer was contacting her new guardian not only to gain permission for the marriage, but to arrange the payment of her dowry.''

Stephen fell back against the railing and shook his head. ''I can't believe the gall of the man. How did Spencer think he would get away with it?''

''He had help. The man who carried his message to Wentworth was Nigel Reynolds, Sir Jonathan's former aide. Lieutenant Reynolds owed Spencer a favor for helping arrange his transfer back to England. Reynolds's repayment was delivering the letter to a friend of his family, the Duke of Maidstone. The major got the missive to Reynolds's ship minutes before it sailed that day.''

A crash of splintering wood and loudly squawking chickens caused James to spin around. Looking down at the broken cage and his crewmen scrambling to catch the escaping birds, he sighed out loud. ''Can you tell me why we have so many chickens and why they haven't been secured in the hold, Stephen?''

Stephen smiled. ''There isn't any room in the hold.''

''That's impossible. We don't have any cargo to transport back to England. With Randy's possessions and our provisions, there should be room enough to store these chickens.''

Stephen shook his head. ''Sorry, Jamie. Between Randy's servants, supplies, and all her pets, we couldn't squeeze another thing down there.''

''What the devil are you talking about?'' James demanded.

"I told Randy she could bring along six servants and a few of her pets. That shouldn't take up the entire hold."

"Well, there are only four servants, but as far as pets"— Stephen shrugged—"how many is a few? And do horses and some rather exotic creatures qualify as pets?"

Stephen ignored the incredulous look on James's face and continued. "Let's see. There are two Arabian horses, one black, one gold. Funny, but that stallion looks exactly like the one you wanted to purchase the day after we arrived. Then I saw an owl, a peregrine falcon, a brass cage filled with colorful little birds, an ugly little beast she said was a mongoose, a furry gray kitten with a bandaged paw, a long-haired goat, and a large—"

"Enough!" James shouted. "Just tell me where Randy is and I will have this out with her."

With a cocky grin, Stephen pointed over his shoulder. "Your wife is in the captain's cabin, where she's been since dawn. The last time I saw her, she was busy removing your clothes from the wardrobe and having Jarita carry them down to Emmet's cabin. We are definitely going to be crowded for the trip home. Tell me, Jamie, would you prefer a hammock or the floor?"

James stuffed his ruined cravat into his pocket. "Neither. If anyone is going to be moved from the captain's quarters, it won't be me. Randy can sleep with her animals for all I care."

Realizing his teasing banter had pushed James over the edge, Stephen caught him by the arm and tried to stop him from moving toward the entrance to the passageway. "I don't think you should confront Randy while you're so upset. She's got—"

"She's got to grow up and face her responsibilities," James replied, slapping away Stephen's hand. "And Randy doesn't need you interceding on her behalf. Have the men get those damned chicken crates below or have them lashed together and secured so they won't get in the way. Once I've finished talking to my wife, we will be ready to sail."

* * *

"But my lamb, moving your husband from his room is only going to enrage the *Huzur* further. How can you have a happy marriage if you go out of your way to anger him?"

Randy gave Jarita the two pairs of James's boots she was holding. "Why can't you understand that this marriage is nothing but a sham? James only went through with that mockery of a wedding to keep me safe from my uncle. The last thing he wants is a wife. Most especially not me!"

Jarita sighed and carried the boots toward the door. "Do not be harsh with your husband. I know you were disappointed with the ceremony, my baby. But with our hasty departure, you can hardly expect to have a big church wedding, with flowers and friends in attendance. The *Huzur* did the best he could."

"If that was his best, I shudder to think what his worst would have been." Randy sat on the edge of the bed to tighten the ribbon that kept her hair tied back at the nape of her neck. "James couldn't even secure a minister to perform the ceremony. We exchanged vows before a magistrate in my father's old office. I swear the magistrate was drunk. Instead of friends like you, Akbar, and Javid in attendance, I had to put up with the likes of Brandon Spencer leering at me through it all. Seeing him behind Papa's desk, acting so smug and superior, made me feel sick."

Jarita stood at the door and smiled at her. "For a sham of a marriage, you are most upset, my lamb. I think this union with the *Huzur* means more to you than you are willing to admit."

"You are reading too much into it, Jarita. I wanted you, Akbar, or Javid there for support. Having one of you with me would have made my task an easier one."

"My place was at home with my husband. Had he been well, you know Abu and I would have been at your side. As for the prince and his father, there simply was not time to find them. *Sahib* Stephen told you the servants at the Opal Court reported their lord had gone to Mysore."

Randy fell back against the bed. "I know I sound like a petulant child, but I really wanted to see them both before we sailed. James said no, we couldn't wait. He doesn't understand that Javid and Akbar are like family to me, and I'm going to miss them while I'm away. We had a frightful argument about it last night." Her fist hit the bed. "That man's high-handed attitude truly annoys me."

The ayah smiled. "Your annoyance would have been soothed had your husband taken you to his bed rather than left you to sulk in your apartment after your spat. The fire you both possess should be shared in passion, not in anger."

Randy jerked up to glare at the older woman. "How many times must I tell you that this marriage is a sham, a charade, an act of trickery? James doesn't want me any more than I want him!"

Clasping the boots with one arm, Jarita pointed at her eyes. "These eyes may be ancient, my lamb, but they know what they see. In the two of you, I see desire hot enough to break into flames with its intensity." Her hand dropped to her chest. "In my heart, I sense the love within you both that you keep hidden from each other." Patting her chest, she nodded. "And in my soul, I know that you and *Sahib* James are meant to be together."

"But Jarita, I told you—"

The ayah shook her head and crossed the threshold into the hall. "Do not waste your strength arguing with me, my lamb. In time, you will learn that I am right." Laughing, she pulled the door closed. "And then there will be new babies for me to care for and joy shall be mine."

Randy yanked the pillow from the bed and tossed it at the door. The cushion struck the wooden portal with a muffled thud. "There will be no babies, you foolish woman! How many times must I tell you . . ."

Her anger dissipated as quickly as it had flared. A deeply

rooted sadness overwhelmed her and she felt weak with the pain it caused. Her eyes dropped to the ring on her left hand.

The wide gold band had belonged to her mother. Randy had found it in her father's things after he died. Hoping it would give her solace during the months ahead, she had insisted on using her mother's ring for the ceremony. Now she realized that doing so had been a terrible mistake.

"This ring was once given and received in love, but now it's merely a prop in our little melodrama. God forgive me. How could I have cheapened its worth like this?"

A harsh hissing sound drew Randy's attention to the far side of the room. Lying in the corner, to the right of the door, Sidra sleepily raised her head and stared at her mistress.

"I'm sorry, Sidra. I didn't mean to wake you from your nap." Randy stood up and went to her pet. She reached down to stroke Sidra's soft, furry head. "I know you're still angry about the cage that brought you to the ship, but it couldn't be helped. There was no other way to get you here without causing an uproar. Xavier built it out of the finest wood and materials for your safety. He padded it with cushions and brought along your favorite rug from my room so you would be comfortable."

Her hand touched the jeweled leather collar that Sidra wore, and she smiled. "You shouldn't complain about this either. Akbar had it made for you last year and I think it makes you look beautiful. Not every tiger gets to wear emeralds around her neck." The thought of facing James with the truth about Sidra robbed Randy of her levity. "Sidra, we have to make a good impression on James. After losing Papa and now not having Akbar and Javid to rely on, I don't want to leave you."

Sidra hissed again. Rather than draw away from Randy, the tiger butted her head on the skirt of her mistress's traveling gown and rubbed against her leg.

Randy recognized Sidra's actions as an attempt to comfort her. The notion brought happy tears to her eyes. "Thank you, my friend," she said, scratching the tiger's velvety ears. "You always know how to make me smile."

Looking around the cabin, Randy shook her head. The captain's quarters were quite spacious for a ship, but nothing to compare with the size of her rooms at home. On board, space was at a premium. With the exception of the chairs around the dining table, all of the furniture was firmly fixed to the walls and floor. Even the large bed that dominated the center of the room and the cast-iron stove in the corner were bolted in place. A narrow door that slid into the wall gave privacy to the small alcove that held the necessary and washing stand. Several of her trunks sat opened on the polished wood-plank floor, adding to the clutter of the usually neat room.

Randy hadn't been surprised to find James's quarters clean and orderly. Like the man himself, the room was handsome in appearance, but not overly embellished. The fabrics that made up the coverlet on his bed and the hangings for the three small windows were of the finest quality, but in subdued shades of brown.

Everything about James and his surroundings was controlled, neatness personified. Even his clothes hanging in the wardrobe were pristine in their appearance. With the exception of the morning of the fire, she had never seen him look rumpled or dishevelled. She doubted if the man even perspired.

The only thing that didn't fit into this perfect room was an oil portrait that adorned the main wall of the cabin. Set in an ornate gilt frame, the painting was that of a beautiful young woman wearing a rose-colored gown. Her large, expressive eyes were green and her long, dark hair fell over her shoulders in glistening curls. The artist had given her a smile that was both entrancing and full of mischief. The small brass nameplate attached to the frame told who the subject of the painting was.

Diana

It had been seeing the name on the portrait that morning that sent Randy into a rage. She admitted their marriage had not been a love match, but couldn't James see how offended she might be by having the reminder of his past love adorning the walls of the room they were going to share during the voyage?

James had convinced her before the ceremony that they should follow through with their portrayal of a newly married couple by staying in the cabin together. But unlike other couples, she and James would sleep apart—he in the bed and she in the smaller trundle that was built below it. No one, save Abu or Jarita, would know that they were not truly living as man and wife.

"Well, James Grayson can sleep in your cage, Sidra. I won't have that man anywhere near me!" Giving Sidra one last pat on the head, Randy walked to the door and picked up the pillow. She tossed it onto the bed and looked at the offensive painting on the wall. "I will get Xavier to remove this, and my husband can take it with him. A man of his restraint deserves a woman on canvas to keep him company."

The door to the passageway crashed open and slammed into the wall, causing her to spin around. Her heart was nearly pounding out of her chest from the unexpected noise. The sight of James in his shirtsleeves, red-faced, sweaty, and unmistakably furious, filling the entryway didn't frighten her. In fact, she couldn't help but laugh at his appearance.

"My God, James, what's happened to you? Were you caught in an elephant stampede on your way to the ship?"

"Chickens!" James snarled, slapping feathers off his dark britches. "I had to make my way through hordes of chickens to get down here. They're on the deck, the steps, blocking the passageway, and all over. I nearly broke my neck. Thanks to you, my ship has more livestock than a bloody farm!"

Randy put her hand in front of her mouth to control her laughter, but it didn't work. Giggles spiked her words. "I really am sorry about that . . . but seeing you . . . the master of neatness and control . . . oh, James, this really is funny."

"You will not be laughing when I throw your animals and all those blasted chickens into the harbor, Randy! Now explain to me what's going on around here."

James was too busy shouting to hear the snarl coming from the corner of the room, but Randy had. When he charged into the cabin and moved toward her, she held up her hands to stop him.

"James, don't come any further. Please stay where you are."

Seeing the smile vanish from her face caused him to halt in mid-stride. He could see the fear in her eyes, the trembling in her hands. She was so frightened, she couldn't even look at him. He sighed and shook his head. "I am angry with you, Randy, but I would never harm you."

"I know that," she replied in a low voice, looking past him. "But if you don't want to be hurt, please don't shout at me."

James couldn't believe she was issuing him orders. "This is my ship, and I can shout anytime I feel like it," he boasted, bracing his hands on his hips. "And save your threats of hurting me. Even with all your skills in Oriental fighting, you can't best me on my own ship."

Randy looked at him with surprise. "I never threatened to hurt you, James. I was simply trying to warn . . ." Confusion creased her brow. "Who told you about my training in the Oriental disciplines? It was to be kept a secret."

Not wanting to betray a confidence, he replied, "I saw you and Brandon Spencer together in the gardens of the Opal Court."

"You were following me?"

James shook his head. "No, but when you left the reception, I became worried and went looking for you. A broken wrist and a few fingers was too small a price to pay for what that bastard tried to do to you, Randy. My biggest regret was not being the one to cripple him in the first place."

His words brought a smile to her lips. "Thank you, James. That's probably the nicest thing you've ever said to me."

"If you'd give me a chance, I would gladly add to that list of nice things, sweetheart." Forgetting the chickens and the problems of his day, James was suddenly filled with the need to take her into his arms and lose himself in her kiss.

When he moved toward her, Randy's eyes darted past him

and she held up her hands to ward him off. "Stop. Don't move!"

"Stop, don't move? I will not tolerate being ordered about, Miranda. If you think—"

James felt a warm puff of air on his right hand. Something wet and oddly rough brushed his flesh. When he looked down to discover its source, he found himself paralyzed with fear. Two bright amber eyes gazed up at him. A huge feline head marked in orange and black fur rubbed against his thigh as its broad tongue licked his hand.

"Randy," he gasped, "that's a tiger."

"I know. James, I want you to meet Sidra."

Sidra sat beside James and pressed her long, brightly colored body against his legs while he watched her. Her tail whipped back and forth as she playfully bumped his dangling hand with her head, inviting his touch. His failure to respond to her entreaty gained him a hiss from the impatient tiger.

Randy knelt beside Sidra. "Don't be a naughty girl. James does not know that you're just a big, overgrown house cat. I won't let you frighten him."

Sidra rolled over on the floor and showed off the golden white of her underbelly. She purred with unabashed pleasure when Randy scratched her furry stomach.

Surprised by the unlikely display, James chuckled. "Am I imagining things, or is that beast actually purring?"

Randy looked up at him and smiled. "Of course Sidra purrs. All cats purr when they're content. And don't call her a beast. She saved my life and deserves your respect. Why don't you come down here and get to know her better? Sidra likes you already."

"How can you tell?" James asked warily.

"She didn't pounce on you when you charged in here ready to do battle with her mistress."

"This is the Sidra that attacked the intruder? But I thought she was a servant. You never said—"

Randy colored with embarrassment. "I was going to tell you

the other evening, but Jarita came with news about Abu and I never got around to it." She patted the floor beside her. "Why don't you sit with us for a few moments, and I will tell you how Sidra became a part of my life."

Ignoring his misgivings about being close to a wild animal, James sat on the floor beside Randy. As she spoke, he found himself envious of the big cat. Not just because of the warm way Randy talked about Sidra, but watching her fingers travel across the creature's fur became pure torture for him. He could well imagine how her hands would feel caressing him like that. It would be heavenly when it happened.

Perspiration broke out on his forehead when his body began to respond to his thoughts. He had to wriggle his hips slightly to relieve the pressure inside his snug-fitting britches.

Misreading the cause of his discomfort, Randy reached over and touched his hand. "I assure you, James, you have nothing to fear from Sidra. She's been with me since she was a tiny cub, and other than attacking the man in my bedroom, she has never harmed anyone."

James laughed dryly. "With those claws and that mouthful of teeth, that's hard to believe. The size of her alone is quite intimidating. She must weigh as much as two grown men."

"Not quite. Sidra is small for a tiger. Her breed is usually twice this size, but the injuries that left her without a voice and unable to bear offspring seem to have stunted her growth as well."

"Stunted growth or not, a creature like her would be better off in the jungles."

Randy grabbed the cat's furry jowls and playfully tugged on them. "That's not possible. Her mother was killed before she could teach Sidra how to hunt for food." Smiling, she looked at James. "My poor baby could never survive in the wilds. She has a healthy appetite and would starve on her own. That's why I've brought along the chickens for her to eat."

Her referring to the tiger as a baby only reminded James of the unpleasant task before him. Rather than delay it any longer, he stood up to tell her what had to be done. "Having a tiger on board during a long voyage would be extremely difficult, but bringing such a creature into England is unthinkable. I'm sorry, Randy. I can't allow you to bring Sidra with us. You'll have to send her back to your house. The servants you left behind can take care of her."

Randy's smile became a frown laden with icy disdain. "No one besides Xavier or me can handle Sidra. She is well-behaved but, like a truculent child, must be watched closely. If I left her behind, I fear she would get herself killed."

"I am sorry, Randy, but I won't be swayed in this. I will allow you to keep the rest of your pets on board, but Sidra will have to leave the ship."

"Then I'm leaving, too," she replied, standing to confront him. "I owe Sidra my life. If she's not welcome on your noble ship, than neither am I."

When Randy turned to walk away, James grabbed her arm. "Don't be ridiculous. You must go to England with me."

"Take your hands off me, Captain. You can't force me to do anything, and it's high time you realized that. If Sidra leaves this ship, then so do I."

"The hell you will! You're going to England if I have to keep you tied up for the entire voyage!"

Hearing the anger in their voices, Sidra roused from her place on the floor and forced her way between them. Her eyes glared at James. A warning growl, deep and guttural, emanated from her damaged throat.

James pulled back, more amazed than frightened by the change in the animal's demeanor. Minutes before, the tiger had been playful, licking his hand. The rough tongue that had tickled him had disappeared, and feral white teeth showed beneath the tiger's curled lip. There was no mistaking the animal's intent.

"Sidra doesn't seem to be very fond of me at this moment."

Randy touched Sidra's head. "Stop growling and be a good girl. James would never hurt me." When the tiger immediately followed her command, Randy looked at him. "Don't judge her behavior by this. Sidra was only trying to protect me."

James crossed his arms over his chest and sighed. "Then she and I have something in common. We both mean to keep you safe. Taking you to England is the only way I can be sure that your would-be killer doesn't succeed at his task."

"I know, but I just can't desert Sidra." Worrying her lip, Randy scratched the tiger's ears. "There must be some way I can convince you to change your mind. Sidra wouldn't cause any trouble. Xavier handles her care and feeding. He even built her a cage so she can be transported to and from the ship without incident. Please, James, I'm begging you to say yes."

"Randy, I think—"

"Wait a minute, James," she interrupted. "Just to show you how badly I want Sidra, I am willing to make a deal with you. If you allow Sidra to come with us, I will give Garuda to you."

"You'd give up your stallion for her?"

Randy's fingers entwined possessively around the tiger's collar. "Garuda is a beautiful animal, but Sidra is my friend. I cannot abandon her. I will do anything to keep her."

James stroked Randy's cheek with his fingertips. One day, he prayed she would be as loyal and committed to him.

"Keep your horse, Mira, and your tiger, too. I just hope that I don't regret this decision."

"You won't, James, I promise." Ruled by her happiness, she reached up on her toes and sealed her pledge by placing a quick kiss on his lips. "And I'm still giving Garuda to you. After I return to India, you will have him to remember me by."

Knowing he had no intention of ever letting her go, James felt awkward and searched for a way to change the subject. His gaze fell upon the open door of the empty wardrobe closet. "I know ladies are notorious for needing lots of space for their things, but where have you put my clothes, Randy?"

Randy took a cautious step behind Sidra. "Since we're to be married in name only, I have decided that we should not stay in this cabin together. I will remain here with Sidra, and you can share Stephen's accommodations for the voyage home."

James shook his head. "That's not possible. Stephen gave his cabin to Abu and moved in with my first mate, Emmet. There is no way the three of us can share that one small room. Besides the lack of space, the voyage to England is going to take many weeks."

"Then share the cabin with Abu. Jarita can stay with me."

"Abu is recovering from his wound and will need to be with his wife. Like it or not, I'm staying in this cabin."

"Fine, you can stay here, and I will sleep on a pallet next to Sidra's cage in the hold."

His earlier remark to Stephen about letting Randy sleep with her animals had been made in a fit of temper. Now that she had suggested it herself, he refused to consider it. "The hell you are! I won't have my wife sleeping in the cargo hold."

Randy shrugged. "If a sleeping pallet in the hold is good enough for Xavier and Kira, then it's good enough for me."

"The hold may be good enough for your animals and servants, but you won't be there to find out. The only place you will be sleeping is in this cabin, and that's final." James closed his eyes for a moment to contain his anger. When he spoke again, his voice was low and calm. "I'm not trying to be difficult, Randy, but I would like to know why you're dead set against sharing this room with me. Am I really such an ogre?"

Seeing Diana's portrait on the wall just past his shoulder strengthened Randy's resolve. Though she was jealous of the woman from his past, she wasn't about to admit it to him.

"I'm sorry you took offense at my decision, but I really don't know you at all, James. Truth be told, we only met a matter of days ago, and the prospect of living with you after such a short acquaintance is quite unnerving for me. I know that for appearance's sake, we must reside like a married couple, but I am not ready for that yet. Can you please be patient and give me a little time to get used to the idea?"

With obvious reluctance, James nodded. "All right, Randy,

but I insist that you remain in this cabin. I don't want my men thinking I abuse my wife by making her sleep in the hold.''

"I really feel a little guilty about this. How will the three of you sleep in one small cabin?"

"Don't worry, sweetheart. That's what hammocks are for. If it gets too bad we can sleep in shifts." He nodded toward the empty cabinet. "Would you mind if I keep my things in here? With the abundance of clothes Stephen brought along on this voyage, poor Emmet will barely have space enough for his own possessions, let alone mine."

Returning his smile with one of her own, Randy nodded. "It's the least I can do. I'll have Jarita . . ." A wave of dizziness caused her to stumble.

James caught her around the waist. "Randy, are you feeling all right?"

"I am fine. My lack of sleep last night must be catching up with me." Anxiety caused by his touch made Randy nervous. She eased herself away from him and sat on the bed. "My fatigue is partially your fault, James. Your refusal to postpone our departure until I could contact Akbar and Javid left me so distraught, I didn't get a wink of sleep."

Her accusation set off his anger. "I am sorry that you will not be able to see your friends before we sail, but I won't risk your life another day. As soon as I go topside, we're leaving."

"But James, could we—"

"No more talk, Randy. This ship is getting under way within the hour, so accept it!" When Sidra hissed, he pointed at her and scowled. "And I will not tolerate any more interference from you. Get in my way and you will spend the next two months below decks in that cage Xavier built for you."

As the door slammed shut behind James, Randy knelt beside Sidra to stroke her head. "My lord husband seems quite put out by us, my friend. Well, that can't be helped. I provoked James to gain my own way, and I won." Remembering his tenderness and the way he called her sweetheart before his anger forced him to leave the room, she sighed. "Why does the thought of celebrating my victory suddenly seem so wrong?"

The deck was bustling with activity when James emerged from the passageway. As he waited for his eyes to adjust to the bright sunlight, Emmet joined him to make his report.

"All is ready to sail, Captain. Your lady's man, Xavier, saw to the chickens. The crates that wouldn't fit in the hold have been lashed together and secured near the prow." The wind swept Emmet's shaggy red hair off his forehead. "We can catch the afternoon tide if you're still meanin' to depart."

James nodded. "Excellent. Let's get under way, Emmet. The sooner we leave this place, the better I'll feel." He looked up at the tall ship's riggings. "Get Bradshaw and Higgins to—"

"Jamie, get over here!" Stephen was standing at the rail, pointing at the crowded docks. "You've got to see this!"

"You look for me, Stephen. I've got a ship to sail out of this port within the hour." James turned to some of his crewmen. "Barstow, you and Cummerson lift that gangplank."

Stephen ignored the rancor in his friend's voice. Taking out a telescope, he looked at the cavalcade approaching the ship and laughed. "You better delay that order, Jamie. I do believe that we're about to be boarded."

James snatched the spyglass from him and used it to search the docks. "If Spencer thinks I am going to stand idly by while his troop of . . . oh, my God."

Instead of British soldiers, at least a hundred guards on horseback, wearing the royal livery of Mysore, were making their way toward his ship. They accompanied six elephants in jeweled harnesses that bore large wooden chests on their backs. Prince Akbar rode at the front of the colorful procession with an older man on a white steed at his side.

From his regal bearing, there was no doubt in James's mind that this was the Maharajah of Mysore. Randy had told him about Akbar's father, but nothing had prepared James for the sight of Javid Surat Kahn. The Indian monarch appeared to be a strong, vigorous man, in the prime of his life. As trim and handsome as his son, he rode his white stallion with the ease of a man half his age.

"Emmet," James called over his shoulder. "Send young Harry down to my cabin. Have him tell my lady wife that we have company."

Javid Surat Kahn came on board the *Diana* with all the pomp and ceremony due to a man of his station. With a neatly trimmed beard and flashing dark eyes, he was dressed in white and gold. Jewels adorned his turban and the front of his tunic. Six of his guards and Akbar solemnly stood by his side on the deck waiting silently for Randy to appear.

When Randy came on deck, she reverently approached the maharajah and addressed him in a combination of Hindu and Muslim greetings. She translated the words so none of the Englishmen would be offended by her use of the foreign languages.

"*Namaste, pitaji.* I bow to thee, Father," she told Javid with her palms held together and her chin lowered to the tips of her fingers. "*Salam alejyn, valid sab.* Peace be on you, most honored Father."

"*Valekum as salan, Khavand.* And also on you, Daughter," he replied with a nod. Suddenly, a brilliant smile erupted on Javid's face. "Now, enough with formalities, Sona Ag. Come give this tired old man a hug and a kiss. It has been too long since I have seen you, my child."

Randy hugged her foster father and kissed his cheek. "You are not an old man and you saw me only a few weeks ago. Are you trying to play on my sympathies with such talk, my lord?"

The maharajah laughed. "After riding at the pace Akbar set for this trip, I feel like an ancient. But being able to see you before your departure, I can say it was well worth the effort."

He kissed Randy's forehead. "Now, Sona Ag, introduce me to the man you now call husband. I have much to discuss with him."

Her brow arched. "Who told you that we were married? There wasn't time enough for me to contact Akbar about it, let alone you in Mysore."

"Abu sent a message to my son after the reception at the Opal Court that you were going to marry the *Angrezi* captain and that I should make haste if I wished to see you before you sailed."

"But how did Abu know about this days before I did? Was this all a clever plot to get me to—"

Javid tapped his finger against Randy's lips to stop her tirade. "Sona Ag, my golden fire, I can see the outrage in your eyes. There was no plot, my child, only destiny being fulfilled. Besides, you know your old teacher, Abu, occasionally has a way of knowing things long before the rest of us." He put his left arm around her shoulders and turned to face the others assembled before him on the deck.

Without being introduced, Javid smiled directly at James and offered him his hand. "Captain Grayson, as honorary father of Sona Ag, I welcome you into our family. I hope you will value this treasure I am bestowing on you, sir. Randy is the daughter of my dearest friend, Jonathan Collins. I love this girl as my own and I would see her safe and happy at any cost."

James stepped forward and shook his hand. "I swear I will do my best, your majesty."

"See that you do, young man." Javid gave Randy's shoulder an affectionate squeeze. "I regret that we were not here for the ceremony, but Akbar and I have brought your wedding presents along with us. I hope they will please you."

Randy shook her head. "But we cannot accept wedding presents. You see, our marriage isn't going to be . . . um, that kind of a . . ." She looked to James to help explain the terms of their union, but all he offered was a shrug. She sighed and tugged on Javid's arm. "Can we speak privately, Papa Javid? I have something important to tell you."

"Certainly, my child." As Randy led him away from the others, Javid called to his son. "Akbar, while I am talking to Sona Ag, have the men bring up the things we have brought along with us."

"As you command, Father." After Akbar had issued orders to the guards, he turned to James. "For a newly married man, Captain, you do not seemed pleased. Is matrimony not to your liking?"

James frowned. "How would I know? We've been married less than a day, and most of the time we have spent arguing over one catastrophe or another."

"From your tone, I assume you have yet to celebrate your wedding night. I told you Randy was stubborn."

"Being stubborn is only a part of it." James looked across the deck. Seeing Randy a safe distance away talking to Javid, he told Akbar about tricking her into becoming his wife and his plan to make their marriage real.

Akbar smiled. "A sea voyage would make a wonderful wedding trip, James. Long starry nights. The subtle rocking of the ship riding the waves. You could—" His attention was drawn to the men coming up the gangplank with the cumbersome wooden chests.

James didn't understand the orders Akbar shouted at his guards and bearers, but there was no mistaking the authority in his words. Six large coffers were soon lined up on the deck.

The prince proudly waved his arm over the wooden chests. "These three contain bolts of silks and threads. Herbs and spices, including quantities of saffron, cinnamon, and ground pepper fill that one. The finest teas grown in India and Ceylon is contained in the large red chest, over there. And this last one has—"

"That will be enough, my son." Javid rejoined them and scowled at Akbar. "You always like to spoil everyone's surprise. Let Randy and James have the pleasure of discovering what's contained in this last wedding present for themselves.''

Randy gasped at his side. Her cheeks were flushed. ''Papa Javid, I told you—''

The maharajah held up his hand and halted her words. ''I know. But indulge me, Sona Ag. Open the chest and see what this old man has brought for you and your husband.''

Randy sighed and knelt beside the black enameled coffer trimmed with brass and lifted its heavy lid. ''I do not see what this will accomplish . . . oh, sweet heaven above!''

Looking over her shoulder, James gaped in surprise. The large chest was filled with a fortune in jewels, silver, and gold. Precious gems in a rainbow spectrum of colors flashed in the midday sunlight before she snapped the lid shut. James reached down and helped an unsteady Randy to her feet.

''Papa Javid, we appreciate your generosity,'' she began in a whisper, ''but after what I just explained to you, surely you can understand why we cannot accept these gifts.''

Javid leaned forward and answered her in kind. ''You feel that your marriage is a sham, so you are refusing my gifts?''

''Of course. How can you expect me to do anything else?''

The maharajah laughed heartily. ''Because I deem it so,'' he boasted, patting Randy's back. ''You will stop this foolishness and accept my presents. I command it. If it will ease your mind, let this bounty be considered a going-away gift from your adopted family. You will be gone for a year at least and could use the silks for new gowns. The spices will enhance the *Angrezi* fare that is reputed to be quite bland, while the tea can quench your thirst and warm you during the cold English weather.''

Randy sighed. ''I will accept the tea, the fabric, and the spices, but I cannot take the rest of it.''

''Then I will give it to James. It shall be a down payment.''

James frowned in confusion. ''A down payment for what, sir?''

"On future shipments, Captain," Javid said. "While you show me below decks to see my old friend, Abu, I will tell you about the shipping contracts I am proposing between us."

"But Papa Javid—"

The maharajah halted Randy's objection with a kiss on the cheek. "Go visit with Akbar while I conduct business with James, Sona Ag. A woman should not be involved in such dealings."

James saw the anger in Randy's eyes as Javid took his arm and turned him toward the opening to the passageway. Before he could call out an apology to her, the Maharajah leaned over and whispered to him.

"Do not worry, Captain. She is furious with me now, but I will be forgiven. I prefer her ire to arguing with her about the validity of your marriage. Be patient, my son. In time, Sona Ag will accept her fate. You are a part of her destiny."

In the shadows of the passageway, James turned to face Javid. "You're talking about that chart you had drawn up for Randy when she was a child. I don't believe in such things."

A perspicacious smile curved Javid's lips. "Your belief is not required, James. Only your love and devotion to my cherished Sona Ag matters. You do love her, do you not?"

"Yes, but Randy thinks—"

Javid held up his hands in a dismissive gesture. "What she thinks is unimportant. With knowledge, thoughts can be changed. Her protection and getting her away from the one who has tried to kill her is my primary concern. That you as her husband are the instrument by which this can be accomplished was preordained by the gods. I pray your marriage will bring you both happiness."

"Then the wedding gifts are exactly that. The talk about a shipping contract was only a diversion to placate Randy."

"Not at all, Captain. My proposal is as genuine as your marriage. With numerous plantations, mines, and ownership of many weaving shops, I could use a firm such as yours to ship my goods to European markets." Javid put a companionable hand on James's shoulder. "Come along, my son. Let us visit with Abu while we discuss the terms of our agreement. I do not wish to hold up your departure any longer than I already have."

Chapter 10

Four days into the voyage, the *Diana* was making record time skimming across the open seas. Her full white sails billowed like clouds in the wind as the regal ship moved powerfully through the waves. But her captain noticed none of it. His mind was on another lady—an auburn-haired beauty, with tears of anguish glistening in her eyes.

It was noon when James relinquished his position at the wheel to Emmet. Instead of going below to take his rest, he sat on a large coil of rope on the deck and stared out at the clear blue skies.

"James? Harry wants to know if you will be eating dinner before you turn in." When James failed to respond, Stephen shook his shoulder. "Did you hear what I said?"

Raking his fingers through his hair, James sighed. "Yes, I heard you. Why don't you just leave me be?"

Stephen leaned against the rail behind him and studied James with deep concern. "You cannot go on like this. You did all of your watch and half of Emmet's. Twelve hours is too long for anyone to work. Even someone who is bound and determined to avoid the problem that's really troubling him. Have you had a chance to talk to Randy?''

James shook his head. ''No. I haven't seen her since we left Calicut. You saw her, standing there, watching the shore of her home grow smaller and smaller in the distance. Randy looked so lost, so alone. The tears in her eyes when I tried to comfort her cut through me like a finely honed blade. But she wouldn't let me hold her. She pushed me away. I could see the accusation in her eyes. I was the one who robbed her of her friends and her home. I was guilty of causing her pain.''

''That's ridiculous, James. There was a madman trying to murder her. You took her out of India—''

''I know all the reasons,'' James declared tersely, ''but I had my own agenda as well. I tricked Randy into marrying me, and now I may have compounded her problems with my own selfish needs. She refuses to answer the door when I try to reason with her. As far as I know, she hasn't left the cabin in days.''

''Randy is just being stubborn. Give her another day or two, and then if she doesn't come to her senses, try using some of your charming wit to cajole her out of her pout.''

James frowned and shook his head. ''I know this sounds odd, but I have a strange feeling that something else is bothering Randy.''

Jarita's voice calling his name drew James to his feet. The tiny older woman rushed across the deck to his side, panting with exertion.

''*Huzur* James, you must come to see my lamb. She does not come to the door and I am worried about her.''

''I wouldn't be so concerned, Jarita. Perhaps Randy is sleeping.''

''You do not understand. In all her life, my lamb has never locked herself away from me.'' Jarita wrung her hands. ''I should have known there would be trouble when she had Xavier keep Sidra in the hold last night.''

Stephen shivered. "I will be sure to avoid the hold today. That bloody beast doesn't like me."

James glared at his friend before returning his attention to the ayah. He put his hand on her shoulder and ushered her toward the passageway. "We'll go below and see what I can do, Jarita. Though I doubt it will do much good. Randy hasn't spoken to me since we set sail on Friday."

"My lamb was upset by the departure, but she had accepted her fate and was going to make the best of it. She told me so, *Huzur*." James assisted Jarita down the narrow stairs. "I fear my baby is ill. Yesterday, she barely picked at her food, and today she has not eaten at all. See, her breakfast is still by the door."

As Jarita had reported, a tray of food sat untouched on the floor. James stepped around the dishes and knocked on the door.

"Randy, will you please open the door? Jarita is beside herself with worry and wants to see that you are well." When there was no response, James knocked again and tried a different ploy. "I know you are still angry with me, sweetheart, but please unlock the door so I can apologize face-to-face."

The continuing silence caused him to knock harder on the door. When it suddenly pushed open beneath his hand, the sight of Randy leaning against the jamb, pale and struggling for breath, left him shocked and momentarily speechless.

"I'm not ... angry, James," she wheezed, "just ... sick. Go away. You will get ... sick too."

Before James could reply, Randy's knees buckled. He caught her and lifted her up in his arms. Carrying her to the bed, he felt heat radiating through the thin fabric of her sleeping gown. Her auburn hair hung over his arm, a fiery comparison to the pale, ashen color of her complexion. As he carefully placed her head on the pillows at the top of the bed, he noticed that her lips were tinged with blue.

"Oh, my poor baby," Jarita cried, bustling in behind him. "Let me take care of her, *Huzur*."

James was surprised when Randy grabbed his arm. Her eyes implored him for help. "Please, James, make Jarita leave. Abu needs her."

Jarita clucked her tongue while she gathered towels and a basin of water. "That is nonsense, my lamb. You are the one who needs my help."

Randy's fevered gaze turned to her ayah. "Too dangerous . . . for you to remain here," she whispered. "This illness . . . killed a mother and her baby at the mission."

"Who will care for you, if not me, my lamb? I have nursed you through much during your life."

"The task belongs to me." James blocked Jarita from coming too close to the bed. "I will take care of my wife."

"Huzur, you are an important man, the captain of this ship. Who will see us to your England if you fall ill as well?"

He understood Jarita's reluctance to give up the care of her mistress and offered her a reassuring smile. "My second-in-command can handle the ship without me. Besides, I don't believe I am likely to get this ailment. I was at the mission with Randy when the woman and child died. So far, I've not suffered any of their symptoms. My ship's surgeon has some basic skills—perhaps he can advise us as to what can be done to help Randy."

Jarita shook her head. "No, my Abu studied with the great *hakiims* at the court of Mysore. When he awakens, I will ask him what can be done to ease my baby's breathing."

"If you and Abu tell me what to do, Jarita, I promise that I will follow all of your orders to make your mistress well again."

The ayah looked over at Randy lying on the bed. Tears filled the older woman's eyes as she gave James the basin and the towels. "So be it. First, we must combat her fever. While I gather the herbs from Abu's jars to brew in a tea for my lamb, you must bathe her. She may fight you on this, but if she is to survive, it must be done."

As the cabin door closed behind Jarita, James placed the basin on the bedside table and turned to face Randy. She appeared to be sleeping. He was sitting on the edge of the bed, washing her brow with a damp cloth, when she opened her eyes and spoke to him. Her voice was little more than a whisper.

"Dangerous for you, too. Go away. Save yourself."

James smiled and dropped a quick kiss on her cheek. "This is where I belong, sweetheart. You are my wife and I mean to see you through this, Randy, so don't try to send me away."

Fighting to keep her eyes open, she shook her head. "Not a real wife. Do not endanger yourself for me."

James gently cradled her chin in his hand. "In spite of your misgivings, you are my wife. I would gladly sacrifice myself to keep you safe."

Randy's strength suddenly seemed to ebb. Her eyes drifted shut and she sighed. "Such a sweet dream . . . must be very sick."

Kissing her forehead, James wiped her cheeks with the cool, wet cloth. "It's no dream, my love. Just get well and I will convince you how sweet reality can be."

During that next week, Randy drifted in and out of consciousness. When not plagued by fevers or bouts of sweats, her body was shaken by coughing fits that left her gasping for air. In her delirium, she cried out in pain, sometimes begging God to end her torment once and for all.

Through it all, James never left her side.

Rather than risk anyone else contracting her illness, no one was allowed inside the captain's cabin. The young cabin boy, Harry, delivered fresh laundry, water, and food to the door several times a day. Following the advice Abu sent with the potions and teas that were blended from his store of medicinal herbs, James tended to all the rest of Randy's needs.

James was grateful that she was not fully awake through the more personal aspects of her care. He could well imagine how humiliated Randy would have been during those countless sponge baths and times he aided her in handling her bodily functions. His deep concern for her health kept his desire for her in check.

It was during this time that he witnessed a side of Randy's personality that she had carefully kept hidden away from him. When the fever ruled her mind, she would sometimes talk out loud. James could ask her questions, and more times than not she would answer him. He learned a great deal about her, from the pain of losing her mother to her fears about her future in England. But the most astonishing information he uncovered was Randy's feelings about him and her jealousy of Diana.

On the evening of the seventh day, he was holding her on his lap on the bed, coaxing broth between her lips, when Randy's eyes fixed on the portrait of Diana hanging on the wall.

"Xavier was supposed to take that bloody painting out of here," she announced without warning.

Though her words were low and raspy, James could hear her vehemence and his curiosity was piqued. "Why is Xavier taking the painting away? What is he going to do with it?"

"Hang it in Sidra's cage."

"Sidra wants a painting in her cage?"

Closing her eyes, Randy shook her head. "No, James does." Before he could ask why, she continued. "He can sleep in the cage with *her* portrait. I will not have that woman's picture hanging in my room."

"Do you know who that woman is?"

She nodded, her head drooping against his shoulder. "Diana. The woman James really loves."

James set down the cup of broth to stroke Randy's hair back from her face. "Sweetheart, you sound so unhappy. Why shouldn't James love Diana?"

"He is my husband. James should love me, not her."

"Do you want your husband to love you, Randy?"

"Of course I do." Randy sighed. "But how can I compete with Diana? He even named his ship for her."

Her indignation made James smile. Randy was jealous of
Diana. But why would she be jealous of his sister? Surely, he
must have told her that Diana was his twin sister.

James suddenly realized that other than a vague reference
or two in passing conversations, he had never spoken to Randy
about Diana or the rest of his siblings. In his efforts to protect
his heart, he had not shared anything of a truly personal nature
about himself with the woman who was now his wife. How
could he expect to win her heart if he never let her close enough
to get to know him? Had his need to shield his feelings already
destroyed his chances of gaining her love?

James ignored the guilt of prying into Randy's thoughts while
she was so unguarded by her illness and asked the question that
was assailing his peace of mind.

"Randy," he said, prodding her awake with a gentle squeeze
to her shoulders. "Randy, do you love James?"

After a short fit of coughing, she sighed. "I love James with
all my heart, but he must never know that. It has to be kept
secret."

"Why must you keep it a secret? James is your husband.
Surely that must prove that he cares for you too?"

"Married me for duty, not for love. James was hurt in the
past by a woman and doesn't want a wife. I will not trap him
with words as she did."

James had to call on all of his control not to explode with
anger. The only one who could have told Randy about his
dealings with Caroline Sutcliffe was Stephen. When he got his
hands on his friend's scrawny throat, he would—

Randy patted his chest. "Don't be upset. I don't know her
name, but I hate that woman, too. She should be taken out and
shot for what she did to James!"

Her unexpected announcement made James smile. With his
fury in check, he asked, "Who told you about this woman?"

"No one. When James is overwrought, I sometimes feel his
emotions. Only a betrayal of the heart can cause the pain he
has suffered." She burrowed her head against his shoulder.

"Don't tell James. I cannot control my ability, but he will think my seeing into his soul is far worse than anything that woman ever did to him."

That night, after Randy had fallen into a deep sleep, James sat in the chair beside the bed and considered everything she had said. Learning that her mental gift enabled her to sense his emotions disturbed him. His privacy had been violated, and he didn't like it at all.

Then the truth of what he had done suddenly slapped hard at his offended sensibilities. While Randy had innocently touched his thoughts, James had blatantly and without contrition invaded hers when she was delirious. He had plied her with questions and induced her to answer him, even when it was clear that she wasn't aware of who he was. At least twice she had demanded that James not know what she had confessed.

Could he accept Randy as his wife, knowing that she had the ability to share his thoughts, his pain, and his emotions? How could he question her jealousy of Diana and her feelings for him without admitting his part in learning the truth from her? And if he couldn't accept Randy because of her mental gifts, how could he let her go?

Hours later, James awoke with a start in the dark cabin. The candles had burnt down to nubs, and the oil lantern on the wall sconce was out. Only a dim shaft of moonlight came through the small row of windows into the room.

A sound, low and mournful, came from the bed. Now fully awake in his chair, he recognized the noise. Beneath the quilts, Randy was whimpering in her sleep.

James stood up and leaned over the bed. His hand quickly found her head as it trembled against the pillows. "Randy, I'm here, sweetheart. Are you feeling worse?"

"Same bad d-dream woke me again. Can't s-sleep. C-c-cold. I have never f-felt s-so cold."

He tucked the covers around her. "You already have a down comforter, two quilts, and a sheet over you. I don't know how much more you can stand without suffocating."

Her head tossed on the pillows. "Don't worry, James. Go b-back to sleep. I will be all r-right."

Though her words were brave, James could hear the shivering in her voice. There was no way he would let Randy deal with her discomfort alone. Not wanting to injure her pride, he thought of a way to divert her attention.

"Why don't I climb in bed and hold you in my arms for a bit? Shared body heat is supposed to be a good source of warmth on a chilly night."

"B-but you can't sleep in b-bed with your c-clothes on."

Even freezing with cold, his wife was obviously embarrassed by the thought of sharing a bed with him. James carefully kept the amusement out of his reply.

"I will remove my shoes and shirt. I'll only loosen the top of my trousers for comfort. It's dark, so you won't have to worry about being disconcerted by my appearance."

Moments later, James eased beneath the covers and drew Randy into his arms. At first she was stiff and unbending, shivering under his hand, but soon, lulled by his warmth and his comforting touch as he stroked her back, she rested peacefully against him. Her breath tickled his chest, causing him to shiver for an entirely different reason. He started talking to distract himself from his own tormenting thoughts.

"You said it was the same bad dream you had before. What was it about, Randy?"

After a slight hesitation, she sighed. "I was being chased through a dark jungle. I could not see who was stalking me, yet I knew it was someone evil, meaning to do me harm."

"So your fear of this person frightened you."

Randy shook her head. "No. What I feared the most was my ignorance of who this person was." She sniffled. "How can I defend myself when I don't know who my enemy is?"

Feeling the wetness of her tears on his chest, James hugged her close. "Don't cry, sweetheart. No matter who he is, I will never let him hurt you again." He leaned down and kissed her forehead. "Sleep now, Randy. I promise I will be here to keep you safe."

"Thank you, James," she murmured softly. "I don't know what I would do without you."

Randy snuggled against him. A minute later, her breathing eased and he knew she had fallen asleep. A need to protect her overcame all his earlier doubts and apprehension. Whatever the future held for this woman, he intended to be right by her side.

James rested his cheek on the top of her head and whispered into the darkness. "When you finally trust me with all of your secrets, Randy, I will tell you that I love you and you will believe me. I only pray that you will still love me then."

Sunlight, bright and golden, flooded the cabin the following morning. Randy could see its glow through her eyelids, and it made her smile. She was weak, but for the first time in days, she felt happy to be alive.

Her senses began to function. Beneath her cheek, she felt something warm and sleek and solid. Her nose detected a strange, but not unpleasant scent that combined nicely with the familiar fragrance of the sandlewood soap that had been made in her household. A low, rumbling sound under her ear caused her to lean up on her elbows and open her eyes.

The sight of James sleeping in bed beside her jerked Randy from her lethargic state. Pulling her hands away, she took a moment to study him. In repose, the face she had found handsome, yet cold, looked boyish and gentle. Locks of brown hair, flecked gold by the sun, tumbled over his forehead. His upper torso, muscled and lightly tanned, was revealed by the sheet that was hung dangerously low on his hips. She felt her cheeks burn when she wondered if the rest of him was as bare as his chest.

Randy's tension caused her throat to become very tight, sending her into a spasm of heavy coughing. James was instantly awake, sitting up beside her with his arm around her shoulders.

"Randy, are you all right, sweetheart? The fever must have left you very dry. Let me fetch you some water."

In the middle of a cough, Randy held up her hand to stop him from leaving the bed. When she realized he was getting up despite her efforts, she closed her eyes. But curiosity overcame discomfort, and she turned to look at him standing at the table filling a glass with water. With a note of frustration, she discovered he was wearing trousers. Chagrined by her thoughts, she fell back against her pillows. The position irritated her throat and her coughing grew worse.

James sat on the edge of the bed and lifted Randy up. He braced additional pillows behind her head before he carefully eased her back against them. When her coughing abated, he straightened the covers and held the glass of water to her lips.

"Sip this slowly, Randy," he instructed. James put his hand to her brow and smiled. "Your fever seems to have broken."

Randy pushed the glass away from her lips. "I've had enough, thank you. I just want to catch my breath."

James set the glass on the bedside table. He touched her neck and studied her face. "There is still some swelling on your throat, but your eyes are clear and your color is improved. The blue tinge around your lips seems to be fading as well."

"For a sea captain, you make an admirable nurse," she teased with a smile. "One would think you had medical training."

"After taking care of you all by myself for the past eight days, I've learned a whole new respect for physicians."

Randy frowned. "You've taken care of me for eight days?"

"Of course I have. Since it wouldn't have been wise to subject anyone else to your illness, I was the best choice. Abu sent me lots of advice and potions made up from his herb jars to aid your recovery, but I was the one who carried out his orders and tended to your care. Don't you remember any of it?"

Shaking her head, Randy closed her eyes. "Not really. Just

bits of things here and there. It's difficult to distinguish the dreams from the reality.'' Her fingers nervously twisted in the blankets. ''I am sorry that I was such a burden to you.''

James took hold of her hands and squeezed them gently. ''You were never a burden, Randy. As your husband, it was my duty to take care of you. And I would gladly do it again.''

With marked surprise, Randy looked up at him. ''But our marriage is little more than a business arrangement, James.''

''Does it have to be, Randy?'' He brushed kisses across her knuckles, keeping his gaze steadily locked with hers. ''Why can't we try and make this marriage a true one in every sense of the word, sweetheart?''

The knot in Randy's throat had nothing to do with her illness. As much as she wanted to say yes, there were still too many questions left unanswered between them.

''James, I think—''

Pressing a finger against her mouth, James shook his head. ''I don't want your decision just yet, Randy. We have another week or two of isolation together in this cabin. While you are building up your strength, you and I can get to know each other. I will tell you all about my family, my life, and the hopes I have for the future. Then you will share yours with me. Perhaps by the end of this voyage, I shall be able to convince you that our being together as husband and wife was destined by the fates.''

Randy pulled his fingers away from her mouth and gave him a shaky smile. ''James, you're beginning to sound like Abu with all his talk about Gopal's chart of my destiny. You, sir, are a realist. I didn't think you would believe in mysticism.''

''Since meeting you, I have learned to accept a great many strange things, Randy. Sensing pain in others, making friends with wild animals, communicating by thought.'' James shrugged. ''God only knows how many more wonderful revelations I am going to experience now that you are a part of my life. I am looking forward to discovering each and every one of them.''

Randy tried to tamp down the hope mounting in her heart. "Are you sure about this, James? Aren't you afraid that you will learn something about me that might shock you?"

"The only thing I'm afraid of is losing you." James kissed her cheek. "Give me a chance to prove that a marriage between us is possible? That you and I can be friends as well as lovers?"

"Friends first?" she asked warily.

James chuckled. "Don't be such a skeptic, Randy. After taking care of you for over a week, I think I have earned your trust. When we become lovers, you will be fully recovered from this illness and it will be what we both want, I assure you."

Hoping to cover her embarrassment, Randy looked around the cabin. "Other than talking, what will we do to pass the time during the next two weeks?"

"We can play cards or chess. I also have quite a few books you might be interested in reading." James scratched his chin. "I could also use your advice on the decoration of this cabin. Do you think I should hang my sister's portrait in the wardroom instead? That way everyone on board can see who the ship was named for."

"Diana's your sister?" When James nodded, Randy started laughing. Her laughter started another fit of coughing.

But the pain it brought made Randy feel very good.

Chapter 11

Several weeks later, as the *Diana* carried her crew and passengers closer to their destination, Randy was plagued by indecision. Fully recovered from her near-fatal illness, she sought the advice of her old friend and teacher.

It was a blustery, sun-filled afternoon when the two of them strolled the decks of the tall-masted ship together.

"Abu, I apologize for bothering you with this, but I have no one else to turn to. Jarita cannot be impartial in helping me with my dilemma."

Walking with his hands clasped behind his back, Abu nodded. "Yes, I know Jarita wants you to accept *Huzur* James as your true husband. My wife does not understand all the problems you will have if you stay married to a man like James Grayson."

"Jarita has a romantic—" Randy came to an abrupt stop, knocking her hood off her head. Her cloak rustled against the hem of her gown. "What did you mean when you said a man like James Grayson? What fault do you find with my husband, Abu?"

Abu pulled his chilled hands into the long sleeves of the

Take 4 FREE Books!

Zebra created its convenient Home Subscription Service so
you'll be sure to get the hottest new romances delivered
each month right to your doorstep — usually before they
are available in book stores. Just to show you how
convenient Zebra Home Subscription Service is, we would
like to send you 4 Zebra Historical Romances as a FREE
gift. You receive a gift worth up to $24.96 — absolutely
FREE. There's no extra charge for shipping and handling.
There's no obligation to buy anything - ever!

Save Even More with Free Home Delivery!

Accept your FREE gift and each month we'll deliver 4 brand
new titles as soon as they are published. They'll be yours
to examine FREE for 10 days. Then if you decide to keep
the books, you'll pay the preferred subscriber's price of just
$4.20 per title. That's $16.80 for all 4 books for a savings
of up to 32% off the publisher's price! What's more...$16.80
is your total price...there is no additional charge for the
convenience of home delivery. Remember, you are under no
obligation to buy any of these books at any time! If you are
not delighted with them, simply return them and owe
nothing. But if you enjoy Zebra Historical Romances as
much as we think you will, pay the special preferred
subscriber rate of only $16.80 each month and save over
$8.00 off the bookstore price!

Check out our website at www.kensingtonbooks.com.

We have 4 FREE BOOKS for you as your introduction to
KENSINGTON CHOICE!

To get your FREE BOOKS,
worth up to $24.96, mail the card below.
or call TOLL-FREE 1-888-345-BOOK

Take 4 Zebra Historical Romances FREE!

MAIL TO: ZEBRA HOME SUBSCRIPTION SERVICE, INC.
120 BRIGHTON ROAD, P.O. BOX 5214,
CLIFTON, NEW JERSEY 07015-5214

YES! Please send me my 4 FREE ZEBRA HISTORICAL ROMANCES (without obligation to purchase other books). Unless you hear from me after I receive my 4 FREE BOOKS, you may send me 4 new novels – as soon as they are published – to preview each month FREE for 10 days. If I am not satisfied, I may return them and owe nothing. Otherwise, I will pay the money-saving preferred subscriber's price of just $4.20 each... a total of $16.80. That's a savings of over $8.00 each month and there is no additional charge for shipping and handling. I may return any shipment within 10 days and owe nothing, and I may cancel any time I wish. In any case the 4 FREE books will be mine to keep.

Name _____

Address _____ Apt No _____

City _____ State _____ Zip _____

Telephone (   ) _____ Signature _____

(If under 18, parent or guardian must sign)

Terms, offer, and price subject to change. Orders subject to acceptance.

KC10A9

AFFIX
STAMP
HERE

KENSINGTON CHOICE
Zebra Home Subscription Service, Inc.
120 Brighton Road
P.O.Box 5214
Clifton, NJ 07015-5214

llltllltllltllltllltllltllltllltllltl

wool coat he had borrowed from Stephen. "It is common knowledge that European men prefer their ladies quiet and docile. Even your education would be frowned upon by them."

"James isn't like that," Randy protested. "He admires my intelligence and thinks I can be of great help to him and his new business. He wants me to teach him to speak Hindi and Urdu before we return to India next year."

Abu turned toward the railing. "If you keep *Huzur* James as your husband, he will be in charge of your inheritance. Western men are known to control their wives with their purse strings."

Randy shook her head. "James has no intention of touching my inheritance. He believes a woman should be able to handle her own wealth."

Stroking his bearded chin, Abu stared out at the ocean. "Then it must be his quick temper and cruel behavior that keeps you from accepting James as your husband."

"What a vile thing to suggest, Abu! James does not have a quick temper. He is wonderfully patient. When I think of all he did for me while I was ill, I could . . ." Randy suddenly saw what Abu was doing and shook her head. She leaned on the rail so she could look into her friend's wizened face. "It seems my old teacher is still trying to give me lessons. Have I proven to be a very stubborn pupil, Abu?"

Abu's dark eyes darted toward her. His lips curved with the hint of a smile. "You require no lessons, my child. I merely remind you of the knowledge you already possess." He patted her hand resting beside his on the rail. "Tell your old teacher what is the real reason you delay in accepting James as your true husband. Are you so fearful of him?"

The wind blew Randy's hair into her eyes when she looked across the deck to where James stood at the wheel talking to Emmet. She felt her heartbeat quicken at the sight of him, and she smiled. "That man evokes many emotions in me, Abu, but fear is not one of them."

Abu shook his turbaned head. "Then what fear governs you?"

Randy sighed. "Would you think me daft if I confessed that the thing I fear most is being myself? For years, I have been whatever was required of me—Akbar's companion, my parents' daughter, the governor's hostess, and Sona Ag, friend of the poor Indian people. I hid behind costumes, cosmetics, or a facade of mannered civility, but as a wife to James, there would be none of that. He would see me for what I am. A desperate woman with mental capabilities that mark her as a freak among most people in the civilized world."

"James would see a beautiful young lady with a compassionate soul and a pure heart. He would also see a woman who loves him."

"And a woman who was keeping secrets from him." Randy's gaze dropped to her hands grasping the rail. "I simply cannot find a way to tell him that my gift has enabled me to sense his inner emotions. James might be hurt if he knew."

The old Indian's brow rose quizzically. "Has he revealed all of himself to you?"

"Yes ... well, almost. James told me about his childhood and family. He briefly mentioned a woman named Caroline whom he had been seeing a few years back. I sensed his discomfort, so I didn't press him for details about her." A shiver that had little to do with the chill in the air caused Randy to pull up her hood. "I am positive she was the woman who hurt him."

"And there is the crux of your dilemma. You cannot discuss this woman with *Huzur* James without revealing how you came by your knowledge." At her nod, Abu took her cold hands from the rail and gave them a reassuring squeeze. "Set aside your worry, my dearest child, and accept James as your husband. In time, these troubles will work themselves out."

"A promise of things to come?" she asked hopefully.

His lips curled in a mysterious smile. "The gods would have it no other way, my lady." A movement behind Randy caught his attention. Steepling his fingers in a praying position beneath his chin, Abu bowed. "Continue your walk while I go and see to the preparations for this evening. A bride deserves the best for her wedding night, and you will have nothing less."

"But Abu, wait," she called as he walked away from her. Without warning, the subject of their conversation was standing at her side.

"Randy, do you think standing here in the cold is wise? You've only been out of bed a little more than a week." James gently turned her toward him and pulled her hood fully over her head. "I didn't nurse you back to health so you could fall ill from exposure, sweetheart."

"Your concern is appreciated, but I feel fine. The chill in the air is refreshing after being cooped up for so long." She reached out and stroked his wind-reddened cheeks with her hands. "You have been out here all day. Surely you must be freezing?"

James shook his head and prayed his smile didn't betray the tension coursing through him. After a month of sharing a cabin with Randy, his hunger for her had grown a thousandfold. His promise not to pressure her into consummating their union until she was ready had kept him on deck working for long hours in the bitter cold. Her gentle touch on his face nearly drove him over the edge. It took all of his control not to pull her into his arms and end his weeks of self-imposed restraint.

"I've grown accustomed to the cold weather during my life, but you haven't had to deal with it." He took her hands from his face and enveloped them within his own. Bringing them to his lips, he blew warm air over them. "Randy, you should be wearing gloves. Your fingers feel like ice."

Randy gazed at his hands rubbing her fingers and smiled. "My hands feel very nice right now. You seem to have a talent for curing my ills, James. What do you suggest for my lips? At this moment they feel very chilled and terribly neglected."

Her flirtatious banter caught James by surprise. Since her illness, he had been the one who teased her for playful bits of affection. Chaste kisses and holding hands were the extent of his actions since that one and only night he had slept with her in his bed, cradling her in his arms. Loneliness had been his sole companion when he sought his rest on the trundle bed after that. Standing there on the deck with her looking so lovely and desirable, gazing up at him, he hoped he wasn't misinterpreting the invitation in her words.

He decided to proceed slowly and go along with her game.

James lightly traced her soft pink lips with his fingertip. "A bit cool and dry perhaps, but not chapped," he said, trying to keep his voice low and his reactions to her in check. "If I were you, Randy, I would—"

His power of speech deserted him entirely when Randy's tongue darted out to moisten her lower lip. A shudder cut through him as he felt it brush against his finger. Then she did it again, and his shudder became a groan.

"Oh, sweetheart, you don't know it, but you are playing with fire," he warned, staring intently at her mouth.

Randy ran her fingers over the dark wool coat covering his chest until her hands were clutching his shoulders. "If you are the fire, James, then warm me. Share your heat with me and make me burn with it."

Oblivious to his crew working around them on the deck, James pulled Randy into his arms. He had planned to be gentle with his kiss, but her eager response changed all that. Her soft lips parted. The tip of her tongue reached out to touch his. When his mouth closed over hers in a caress that was blatantly possessive and hungry with need, he felt her trembling beneath his hands. He tried to ease away, but Randy wouldn't allow it. Her arms were around his neck, holding him while she met him kiss for kiss.

James was feasting on the sweet taste of her mouth when a sudden crosswind snapped a portion of the rigging on the mainsail and sent it crashing to the deck just a few feet away from where they were standing. He quickly gathered Randy into his arms and began shouting orders to his men regarding repairs.

Once he saw the work was under way, he carried her down to their cabin.

Cursing to himself, he kicked the cabin door shut with his foot and dropped into a chair with Randy held tightly in his arms. "Bloody hell, you could have been killed up there."

Pushing the hood from her head, Randy turned to face him. "I am fine, James. Some rigging fell, but I was not hurt."

He shook his head. "You don't understand. This is my ship, and I should have been more vigilant regarding your safety while you were on deck. If anything had happened to you, Randy, I would only have myself to blame."

She prodded his chest with her finger. Her eyes sparkled with irritation. "Stop talking like that! None of this was your fault, James Grayson. It was mine. If I had not been trying to seduce you on deck—" Her cheeks flushed with embarrassment as she clenched her hands together and turned away from him.

Randy's admission put a smile on James's face. He hoped it was true, but disbelief made him ask, "You were trying to seduce me?"

When her only reply was a slight nod, James took pity on her discomfort and kissed her cheek. "You don't have to resort to seduction if the man in question is more than willing to comply with your ah . . . ideas, sweetheart."

Randy shrugged and continued to divert her eyes from his. "You haven't tried to hold me or really kiss me in weeks. I thought you had lost interest in me."

Hugging her close, James playfully nuzzled her neck. "I was trying to be a gentleman, patiently waiting for you to accept me as your husband." He cupped her chin and made Randy face him. "Though I must confess, my noble gesture was all but forgotten when you kissed me a few minutes ago. I was so damned interested in what we were doing at the time—"

His words were cut off by Stephen calling to him from the passageway. "James, I hate to disturb you, but Emmet wants you on deck immediately. Something about the rigging needing more work than you ordered."

"Tell Emmet I will be right there." After Stephen left to deliver his message, James sighed and rested his forehead against Randy's. "I am sorry, sweetheart, but your safety and that of everyone else on this ship is my responsibility. We're apt to hit a winter storm or two before we get to England, so it's best to be prepared." He placed a tender kiss on her lips. "I pray you won't change your mind before I return."

Randy smiled and put her arms around his neck. "Not a chance of that happening. I have waited my whole life for you, James. Another few hours of anticipation could only add to the pleasure we will eventually find together."

The slight apprehension he sensed in her brave words touched his heart. The warmth of her smile and the unconcealed desire in her bright gold eyes caused him to regret his duties as captain. "With you looking at me like that, I have half a mind to give this ship over to Stephen. He enjoys titles; let him be captain. He can deal with the repairs while I stay here with you."

"And your friend Stephen would have us all marooned in a matter of hours." Randy stood up and removed her cape. "Go along, Captain Grayson, and see to your ship. When you return, we will celebrate this union as we should have weeks ago."

The sun had been down for a couple of hours and Randy was nervously pacing the cabin, wondering if her courage had finally deserted her. In spite of her confident words to James that afternoon about celebrating their marriage, she was riddled with insecurity and shyness.

Abu and Jarita had helped her make the preparations. The cabin had been transformed from a stolid masculine room to a sanctuary that titillated the senses.

Colorful satin pillows were arranged on top of the scarlet coverlet on the bed. Incense made with patchouli smoldered in a brass burner, wafting its scent around the room. A supper of curried chicken and vegetables sat on the small iron stove that warmed the room. Covered dishes of sweetmeats and little spice cakes laden with sesame seeds and honey sat on the bedside table with a bottle of red wine and two crystal goblets.

Looking around the cabin, Randy shook her head. "This was a silly idea. All I need is a trio of musicians playing in the alcove to complete the setting of this fairy tale."

She walked to the ornate mirror that hung on the wall where Diana's portrait had been before James moved it to the wardroom. Wearing a flowing sleeping gown and a robe of white batiste trimmed with lace, her reflection revealed a young woman both excited and frightened by what was to come. The snowy white of the fabric contrasted to the vivid red highlights in her hair that tumbled over her shoulders and down her back. Her gold eyes were bright and alert staring back at her.

Randy's hand trembled as she touched her flushed cheek. "I hope James doesn't think I am trying to manipulate him with all this."

A sudden draft of cold air caused her to turn toward the door as James stepped inside the cabin. He was wearing a long wool robe and carrying his boots. After securing the door, he turned to face her.

"I, ah . . . washed up in Stephen's cabin when I was, ah . . . done working." His face was pink from being recently shaved, and his clean, damp hair was brushed back from his brow. "After hours spent laboring on those repairs, I knew I wasn't fit company for my wife." James shifted his bare feet on the cool floor as he looked at her. "My God, you are truly exquisite, Mira."

The awe in his voice and the vulnerability she sensed in him helped allay her discomfort. Trying to ease the tension between them, she moved toward him and took the boots from his hands.

"Thank you for the lovely compliment, James. You're looking quite handsome as well." Too nervous to stand still, she carried the boots to his cabinet and placed them inside with the rest of his things. "That blue robe matches the color of your eyes perfectly. I don't recall seeing it before."

"It's not mine. I borrowed it from Stephen."

Randy avoided looking back at James and busied herself with straightening out his wardrobe. "I will have it laundered in the morning so it can be returned to him as soon as possible." Shutting the door of the cabinet, she hurried toward the stove. "You must be hungry. Why don't I serve dinner now?" She lifted the lid of the pot and stirred its contents. "Kira made curried chicken just the way you like it. Or would you prefer a glass of wine first?"

"The only thing I want, Mira, is you."

His softly spoken reply wasn't made from across the room, but directly behind her. Randy dropped the spoon into the pot when she felt James stroking her hair. She shivered as his hand followed its length from the top of her head to just below her waist and then began again.

"Flaming satin. Touched by the lamplight, that's what your hair reminds me of, Mira. Shimmering satin that rivals burning embers for its color." He lifted a thick tendril and rubbed it on his cheek. "It feels so silky against my skin."

She closed her eyes and tried to suppress the nervous excitement his nearness caused her. "Jarita makes a rinse for my hair to keep it soft and shiny," she babbled. "It's a mixture of aromatic herbs, lemon, dried flowers—" Feeling his face nuzzling her hair robbed Randy of thought. She heard him inhaling near her right ear. His warm breath tickled her.

"Mmmmm," he hummed in appreciation. "That must be what gives it such an amazing fragrance. Reminds me of sunshine and summer gardens." His lips brushed against her neck.

Randy moved her head to allow him more access to the sensitive area of skin beneath her ear while she tried to continue their conversation. "She . . . Jarita makes all my soaps . . . and bath oils." His unexpected nip on her earlobe caused her to jump. When he laved it with his tongue, she nearly swooned against him. "Oh, James, what are you doing to me?"

"I'm trying to arouse you, sweetheart. Is it working?"

With his mouth so close to her throat, his words vibrated on her skin. Randy laughed from the strange, but very pleasant sensation. "If arousal makes one giddy and yearn for more, then you are doing very well, husband."

James put his arms around her waist. He took the lid from her hand and put it on the pot. "Dinner can wait, sweetheart, because I cannot. The only sustenance I require at this moment is you. What can you offer this starving man?"

Setting aside her trepidation, Randy turned to face him. Her hands circled his neck. "I can offer you everything, James. All that I am and all that I will be is yours, for as long as you need me."

"Count on forever, Mira. I'm afraid not even death can end this hunger I have for you."

"Then kiss me, James, and let forever begin right now."

Without further urging, James pulled her into his embrace and captured her mouth with a kiss that was both gentle and demanding. His tongue traced her lips before delving inside to deepen the caress. Randy answered his actions by stroking his tongue with her own. The moan he made when she suckled on him, drawing him deeper into her mouth, told her he was pleased by her bold behavior. The hard length of his manhood she felt pressing on her belly through the layers of their clothes let her know that his body was responding favorably as well.

Caught up with the heady new feelings of desire mounting within her, Randy didn't balk when he carried her to the bed. His lips never left hers as he set her on the floor and untied the belt of her robe. When she became aware of her surroundings again, her nightgown and robe were pooled at her feet and James was looking at her.

Randy felt herself blushing while he regarded her nude body, but she refused to hide herself from his gaze. There was no mistaking the passionate gleam in his eyes as he carefully lifted her in his arms and placed her on the bed.

Lying beside her, James reverently touched her pale breasts and smiled. He tenderly cupped one of the full orbs in his hand. "You are so incredibly beautiful, Mira. I have envisioned making love to you for weeks. Now that my dream is about to become a reality, I can hardly believe that it's true.''

Randy rubbed her fingers on the satin lapels of his robe. "This is a very nice robe, James, but aren't you a bit over-dressed for the occasion?'' she teased.

He kissed the tip of her nose. "Since this is your first time, I thought to spare you the shock of seeing an aroused man too quickly. I would not want your first look at me to frighten or upset you.''

"You could never frighten me, James. Besides, I already know what a naked man looks like.'' Sensing his shock and surprise, she spoke quickly to assure him. "Though I have never seen a living man naked, I've viewed dozens of statues in India. Did you know they have temples dedicated to making love? They are quite beautiful, with entire walls carved in the images of people making love to one another. In India, the people believe that making love is an art, a celebration of passion between a man and a woman.''

James frowned. "Who took you to these temples? Akbar?''

His peevish tone made Randy smile. "No, Abu took us both to many temples and houses of worship when we were children. It was a part of our education.''

"Was Abu a good teacher?''

"The very best. His instruction spanned topics from history to mathematics to philosophy. Moreover, he taught me to always be confident and open to new ideas.'' She reached out and stroked his furrowed brow. "But visiting temples and hearing lessons about what transpires between a husband and wife is not enough, James. I need you to complete this part of my education.''

Feeling somewhat chagrined by his jealousy of Akbar, James stood up and looked away from Randy as he removed his robe. When she gasped, he cursed himself for revealing himself too quickly to her. His regret became amazement as he turned and found Randy boldly staring at him with a brilliant smile on her face.

"Oh, my! None of the figures in the temple were as splendid as you, James. You are so muscular and virile. Compared to you, those statues resemble young boys."

James laughed at her enthusiasm. "Randy, I have never met a woman like you before."

Her smile dimmed. "Is that bad? Are you ashamed of me because I speak my mind and don't cower like a proper lady?"

"Not at all, sweetheart. I just meant that you are honest and not afraid to voice your opinion. I admire those qualities, and I will thank God every day that you are mine."

Her smile restored, Randy leaned back against the pillows and held out her arms to him. "Come to me, James. Teach me how to be your lover. Let us be husband and wife at last."

After dousing all the lights except the brass lantern on the side table, James joined her on the bed and took her lips in a tender kiss. Propped up on his arm, he eased away from her mouth and watched as his fingers caressed the length of her body. His right hand looked large and dark against her pale, soft skin. He cupped her breast and brushed his thumb against her pink nipple, causing her to whimper with pleasure.

James touched his tongue to the sensitive tip before he drew it into his mouth. He suckled on her nipple until it became pebble-hard. Randy cradled his head in her hands and moaned with pleasure from his ministrations.

While switching his attentions to her other breast, his hand moved smoothly down her belly to the nest of dark auburn curls that shielded her femininity. He shuddered when he pressed his finger between her nether lips and found her honey-moist and warm. Stroking the small, sensitive nub hidden there caused Randy to arch her hips, opening herself more fully to his touch. She nearly came off the bed as he lightly rubbed the pulsing kernel between his forefinger and thumb, then pushed another finger into her tight passage.

Not wanting to rush her completion, James gentled his touch and sought her mouth with his own. His tongue moved slowly, skillfully exploring her mouth, imitating the movements of his fingers caressing her at the apex of her thighs. It wasn't long before she was squirming against his hand, inviting him to increase the teasing pressure.

Randy's eager response to his loving spurred James into satisfying a need of his own. Brushing kisses across her breasts and stomach, he lowered himself between her thighs and placed his mouth on her fragrant woman's flesh. His fingers parted her plump nether lips to his questing tongue, letting him savor the sweet, yet salty nectar of her arousal.

Hearing her soft sob of pleasure, he pushed a pillow beneath her hips, opening her further to the sensual probings of his mouth. He laved her slick pink flesh for several minutes before ending her torment by touching the tiny jewel of her need. He capture the throbbing nub with his lips and gently sucked on it.

A torrent of pure male satisfaction swept over James when he felt Randy's body quaking with her first climax. Ignoring his own need, he sat up and stroked the satiny skin of her inner thighs as he watched her luxuriate in the warmth of her release.

Randy's color was high and her eyes were bright when the tremors finally subsided and she met his gaze. "Oh, James, I never knew it would feel so . . . so magical."

Returning her smile, James stretched out beside her and brushed back the damp tendrils of hair that clung to her forehead. "Your response to my caresses was magical, sweetheart. You were so beautiful in your passion. I can hardly wait to witness it again."

Randy rolled toward him and tentatively stroked his chest with her hand. "Will it be a long wait for you, James?"

Grinning, James eased her back onto the bed and loomed over her, rubbing his muscular chest against her breasts. "Not if I can help it, love."

Fueled by his drugging kisses and the fervor of his renewed caresses, Randy's passions flared again. She wrapped her arms around James as he kissed her, and explored the muscular lines of his back and buttocks with her hands. Without conscious thought, her body moved of its own accord.

The tip of his manhood rubbed against her sex, seeking entry into her narrow, untried passage. Stimulated by an inborn carnal need, her thighs parted, inviting him to complete the union that would make them one. She groaned when she felt his hips surge toward her, pushing his thick length deep inside her. The moment of discomfort was quickly forgotten, and Randy found herself returning his movements with actions of her own.

Leaning up on his arms to avoid crushing Randy beneath his weight, James tore his mouth away from hers and gasped to catch his breath. His blue eyes were glazed with desire when he looked down at her. "My God, you are so tight! I don't know if I can hold back much longer, Mira."

She raised her hips, rhythmically accepting his thrusts with a welcoming sigh. "Then don't try, James."

"But I wanted to make it better for you."

"You already have, James. Much more and I would likely perish from the pleasure of it all."

A triumphant smile curved his lips. "Ah, yes, but wouldn't that be an incredible way to leave this life, my love?"

Before she could reply, James slid his hand between them and began stimulating the pearl of her femininity with his fingertips. The combination of his touch and the welcome force of his tumescence plunging deep inside her caused Randy to cry out with pleasure and sent her spiraling to the peak of another completion. Suddenly, she felt James stiffen against her as he found his own explosive release.

After bathing each other with scented soap and a basin of warm water, the two lovers cuddled together beneath the covers on their bed. James was nearly asleep with his arm wrapped around Randy when he heard her sighing.

He opened his eyes and looked down at her. "What's the

matter, sweetheart? Are you already having regrets about this? Are you sorry that we made love?''

Randy scowled up at him. ''Of course not. I was just lying here wondering if you were going to have second thoughts about having me for a wife. You came to India a happy single man with the goal of building a shipping company of your own. Now you're plagued with me, a troublesome wife with more than her share of problems to interfere with your life.''

''I am not plagued with you, Randy. You are my wife and I could not be happier about it.''

''Sure you are,'' she mumbled, burrowing her face into his shoulder. ''Until you have to deal with my uncle and all the other baggage I have brought into this marriage. Then you will likely put me on a ship back to India and be well rid of me.''

James gave her an affectionate squeeze before leaning back on the pillows and closing his eyes. ''When you go back to India, it will be for a visit with your husband at your side. As to Richard Wentworth and the rest of your problems, I've already told you that we will handle them all together. Don't fret, sweetheart. No matter what it takes, I swear that you will be safe and happy with me.''

''And you are doing all this because you are my husband?''

''Certainly. You are my wife and it's my duty to see that you are taken care of.''

The word *duty* made Randy wince, and she was grateful that James hadn't seen her facial reaction to his declaration. Like any new bride, she longed to hear tender words of love and devotion from her husband. But their marriage had been based on circumstances and family loyalty, not a romantic melding of two souls.

James seemed to like her well enough. During the past few weeks, a special friendship had developed between them. From his passionate response to their lovemaking, she knew he desired her as a woman. But could he love her? Would he ever set aside the pain inflicted on him by the mysterious Caroline and allow himself to fall in love with the woman he had married?

What would James say if he knew that his wife was desperately and hopelessly in love with him? If she said, "I love you," how would he react?

Perhaps he would thank her for her consideration. Or overcome by male pride, he would smile and gloat at her easy defeat. Maybe he would prove to be a gentleman and return her words without truly meaning them.

Randy frowned and made an important decision as she drifted off to sleep. She would be a good and dutiful wife to James, but until he admitted that he was in love with her, the extent of her feelings for him would remain a secret. Only then would she know that her heart had not been given in vain.

Chapter 12

The winter sun was glinting off the icy waters of the Atlantic as James stood on the deck of the *Diana* and caught his first glimpse of the English coast with his telescope. He was deep in thought when Stephen, bundled up in his greatcoat and wool muffler, joined him at the railing.

"Emmet said you wanted to see me up here, though I can't imagine why. It's as cold as purgatory!" Stephen shivered and yanked his scarf over his wind-reddened nose. "Couldn't we have this chat in the wardroom over a cup of hot tea instead?"

Tucking his spyglass into his coat, James pulled his knit cap over his ears and turned to face Stephen. "No. I wanted to speak with you alone. I've made plans regarding our arrival in Chatham tomorrow, and I will need your aid in carrying them out."

"Chatham? But I thought we were going to dock in London."

James shook his head. "Going to Chatham makes far more sense. My parents have docking facilities there, and it's closer to Miranda Wentworth's estate, Mirage."

"So, you're taking Randy to her grandmother's home."

"Yes. Nana's birthday is tomorrow and I thought a reunion with her only grandchild would be a wonderful present for the occasion."

Stephen raised his brow. "Why do I feel that getting Randy to Mirage has more to do with protecting your wife than giving Nana the perfect gift?"

"Because you know me too well, my old friend." James looked out over the water. "Until I see my solicitors regarding the validity of my marriage to Randy, I don't want anyone to know that I have brought her to England, especially not Richard Wentworth. By now he's probably learned of Jonathan Collins's murder and has been declared her guardian."

"If we had come directly to England instead of making all of those port stops so you could show your wife the exotic sights along the way, we might have gotten here before that first message from Spencer arrived, Jamie."

Leaning on the rail, James scowled over his shoulder at Stephen. "With all the animals and extra people on board, you know very well that we had to replenish our supplies more often. That it gave me the opportunity to spend some time alone with my wife was an unexpected reward I will treasure always."

"Can't fault you for that, James." Stephen grinned and slapped him on the back. "Now what part am I to play in your plans tomorrow?"

"While Randy and I make our way to Nana's home with Abu and Jarita, I want you to deliver her pets and the other servants to my family's estate. My parents are visiting Diana in America, so tell my father's steward that Xavier is to have full use of the heated barn we built last spring for new foals. It's empty now, so it should suffice for my wife's animals."

Stephen chuckled. "That's a good idea. I can well imagine the furor Sidra would cause at the dowager's house if she arrived unannounced. A full-grown tiger isn't a typical pet in England."

"A tiger wouldn't be a typical pet anywhere," James quipped.

"I don't envy you the task of dealing with that beast."

James shrugged and looked toward the horizon. "The beast you refer to saved Randy's life, and I'm willing to do all I can to take care of her. Poor Sidra won't be allowed to roam the countryside, so I'm going to have a solarium built for her use on my estate. It will be similar to my mother's greenhouse with lots of plants and bushes, but it will also have a small waterfall and a stone-bottomed pool for bathing. Tigers like to swim."

Stephen whistled low. "Sounds quite elaborate. Randy must be impressed by your generosity toward her pet."

James glowered back at him. "Randy knows nothing about it, and I want it kept that way. The solarium is to be a surprise for her. I've drawn up the plans and Emmet will be taking them to my estate manager up the coast when the *Diana* leaves tomorrow night. By the time the problems are solved with my wife's uncle, the construction should be completed for our homecoming."

"I will not say a word to Randy, James. I promise."

His friend's solemn reply made James regret his cross tone. "Forgive me for being terse with you. I just want everything to be perfect for Randy. If her pets and family of servants are well taken care of, perhaps she won't regret leaving India."

"Well, you can count on my help whenever you need it."

Smiling, James clapped his arm around Stephen's shoulders and began walking him toward the passageway. "I am so glad you said that, my friend. Because when the *Diana* departs tomorrow night, I would like you to be on board."

"But you said you wanted me to go to your family's estate."

"I do. You will have plenty of time to get there and back before Emmet sets sail on the evening tide."

Stephen stopped short and frowned. "You're not being fair, James. You know I've been miserable during this voyage. Besides the constant rocking, I've had to deal with narrow bunks, limited shipboard cuisine, and snoring companions. I am really looking forward to a soft feather bed, a thick beef-steak, and possibly a lovely lady to warm me through the night. What could be so important that you would deprive me of these few pleasures?''

James crossed his arms over his chest. ''Money? Or would you rather wait until next summer to collect your wager?'' Sensing his spendthrift friend's interest, he sweetened the offer. ''I will also instruct my estate manager to pay you a bonus of another thousand pounds when you accompany the ship to my Ryland holdings.''

''Exactly how am I to earn this bonus?''

''See that the chest of gold and jewels I received from the maharajah are safely delivered to the cellar vault in my home,'' James explained, watching Stephen nod, ''and remain as my guest at my estate until I send word for you to meet me in London.''

Stephen arched his brow. ''Why do you want me to stay at your house? Afraid your staff will abscond with your loot?''

''No. I simply want to keep you out of sight for a bit. Everyone knew you went to India with me, and until I've had a chance to get matters straightened out with Randy's uncle, I would prefer that no one knows that I've returned.''

''But your estate is nearly in the wilderness,'' Stephen complained. ''Don't misunderstand me. I think your Ryland property is quite wonderful, but it's so ... bucolic and isolated. Not a decent gaming house, restaurant, or men's club anywhere around.''

Shaking his head, James sighed. ''Stop complaining. If you get bored, there's a new inn down in the village, and the pretty young widow who runs the establishment is said to be the finest cook in the county. I'm told they have a card game every night in the public room.''

''A pretty young widow who can cook? Well, maybe it won't be so bad after all. Perhaps a few weeks of rest in the country is exactly what I need to consider my options and decide how to spend my newly found cash.'' After a moment, Stephen seemed to warm up to the idea even more. Excitement glowed in his eyes as they moved toward the entrance to the passageway. "While I'm there I can oversee the construction of Randy's solarium. With all of my expertise on plants and fauna, it should resemble an enclosed jungle when you arrive home."

Panic swept over James. "Your mother is the expert on gardening, not you. I doubt if you know one end of a shovel from the other. Stay away from the workers and let them do their jobs without your interference."

As if James hadn't spoken, Stephen swept his arms up in a dramatic arch. "I can see it all now. A tall, majestic framework of wood and glass made to capture God's sunlight while housing a fine collection of nature's perfect greenery. Where are the plans? I would like to take a look at them. Who knows? Maybe helping out on this little project of yours is going to open a whole new career for me."

Rolling his eyes, James shook his head. "Just like the time you became enamored of that opera singer and fancied yourself her next singing partner. You hired that voice coach and spent a fortune buying a new piano for your townhouse."

Stephen scowled at him. "Don't be cruel, James. How was I to know that I was tone-deaf? I had never heard myself sing."

"Then there was your foray into writing the world's greatest novel," James continued. "Your spelling was atrocious, your thoughts disjointed, and the manuscript was haphazardly written in French and English."

"The two languages were constantly used in my home when I was growing up. It was natural for my thoughts to bounce back and forth between them. I didn't want to squelch my creative fervor by sorting them out too closely when I was writing."

"Your attempt at being an artist had its difficulties as well," James reminded him. "The colors of the mural you painted in the salon of your family's manor house were painful to the eyes. Did it really take four coats of whitewash to cover that forest scene you painted in shades of crimson red, olive green, and purple?''

''So I have a little problem with seeing colors. But you have to admit my trees were marvelously done.''

''For purple trees, they weren't so bad, yet the red hedgehog was even better.'' James laughed and allowed Stephen to precede him down the stairs to the passageway. ''Let's go to your cabin and I will show you the plans for the solarium. Just remember, Randy isn't to know a thing about this. I'll blacken your eye if you spoil her surprise.''

Stephen held up his hands in submission. ''I won't say a word, Jamie, I swear it. You won't regret this.''

Watching his friend enter the cabin, James shrugged and shook his head. ''So why do I have a feeling that I'm going to do exactly that?''

It was shortly before dawn when the *Diana* dropped anchor at the Grayson shipping dock in Chatham in Kent, downriver from London. Within a few hours, the animals and passengers with their belongings were loaded onto hired conveyances and sent on their way, with select members of the crew riding along to guard their safety.

Rather than be confined in a slow moving coach, James and Randy ignored the cold weather and chose to ride on ahead to Mirage on horseback. Wearing the fur-lined cape and a riding habit with a split skirt that James had purchased for her during one of their port stops on the voyage, Randy was eager to see this new land that would now be her home.

She had been told that England was a verdant land of rolling hills and thriving forests. The trees were there, but the winter had stripped them of their greenery, leaving them like tall, dark sentinels devoid of color. No one had mentioned the rutted roads thick with slush and mud or the frigid air that burned the throat if one inhaled too deeply. She thought the tiny hairs inside her nose had frozen from the cold.

Randy's discomfort was forgotten and her excitement renewed when the two of them arrived at Mirage. It wasn't the opulent home she saw, but the thought of finally meeting her grandmother that boosted her spirits.

James, who had been strangely quiet during their ride, dismounted and lifted her to the ground. A gentle smile curved his mouth after he gave her a slow, lingering kiss and hugged her against him.

"Nana is going to be very pleased to see you, Randy. Call me selfish, but I simply don't know if I'm ready to share you just yet. Once the dowager and you get together, there will be such celebration, I doubt if either one of you will even notice if I'm here or not."

Randy patted his cheek with her gloved hand. "Don't be silly. You are a very large man. I would definitely miss you if you were not lingering nearby," she teased.

Her smile dimmed when the sound of the double doors opening drew her attention to the house behind James. A white-haired butler dressed in black stood in the entry staring out at them.

"James, I am suddenly feeling a little nervous about all this," Randy whispered, ducking her head further back into her hood. "Please, promise that you won't leave me on my own. I don't know what I would do if I suddenly made a fool of myself in front of my grandmother."

James kissed her forehead and gave her an affectionate squeeze. "You couldn't make me leave if you tried, sweetheart. Come along. It's time Nana got her birthday present."

Taking her arm, James led Randy into the house where he greeted the butler by name. "Good morning, Percival. Is her grace up and about yet?"

The elderly servant closed the doors. "I've not seen her as yet, My Lord, but a breakfast tray was sent to her suite an hour ago. Let me take your coats so you and your guest can be comfortable while you wait in the salon. . . ."

Percival saw the hood fall back from Randy's face and he

gasped. A grin brightened his somber face. "Good gracious! Is it possible? Can this lovely young lady be the daughter of our precious Lenore? It has to be! Except for her being taller than Lenore, she's the very image of our gel."

The old man's sudden exuberance put Randy at ease. She couldn't help smiling at him. "You knew my mother?"

"Of course I did," the usually stoic butler boasted happily. "I was in service to your grandfather for several years before your mama was born. Lenore was the joy of the entire household. I could tell you stories about her—"

"Mr. Percival," a stern female voice called from the top of the staircase, "her grace would be most aggrieved by your lack of decorum. Your duties do not include entertaining guests with idle talk in the foyer."

"But Viscount Ryland and Miss—"

"Be off with you, Percival, before I decide to inform her grace of your flagrant indiscretion."

Visibly struggling to contain his ire, Percival bowed to James and Randy before he turned on his heel and walked away.

A tall woman dressed in a gray gown descended the stairs. Her silver hair was pulled into a tight chignon that emphasized the pointed features of her face. She moved with a confident air when she dropped into a curtsey before Randy and James.

"Good morning, my lord, miss. I regret to inform you that her grace is not receiving any callers today. If you would like to leave your card, I will see that she is apprised of your visit."

When Randy was about to object, James stopped her with a shake of his head. "We are not callers, but family," he explained. "Tell the dowager that James Grayson is here and I assure you, madam, she will see us."

With her hands folded primly at her waist, the woman released an impatient sigh. "I have worked for the Wentworths for many years, my lord. I do not recall ever hearing the name Grayson associated with this family."

James cocked his brow. "And I doubt your household duties

include interrogating all of the dowager's guests without cause. Now, I insist that you tell her grace that I am here.''

Before she could answer, an attractive, dark-haired lady dressed in a gown of rose pink wool came rushing into the foyer with Percival close at her heels. The petite woman's light blue eyes shone with worried urgency as she came to stand between James and the female servant.

"Please forgive Ida, my lord. I'm afraid her protective concern for the dowager's health and welfare governs her actions a bit strongly these days.''

"Is Miranda ill?'' James asked.

Sighing, she nodded. "The weather has been dreadful this winter—not much snow but bitterly cold. Her grace was afflicted with influenza several weeks back and has been very slow in recovering. For the past ten days, Ida and I have been staying here, seeing to her care.'' Brushing a tear from her eye, she smiled. "Perhaps a nice visit with friends will be just the tonic Miranda needs.''

"Beg pardon, my lady," Percival interrupted, "I told you Viscount Ryland was a friend to her grace, but I did not—''

"Oh, dear, Percy, what has become of our manners? A drafty foyer is no place to properly welcome people. Help our guests off with their wraps and have cook prepare a tea tray immediately. Ida, while I'm entertaining our guests in the salon, I want you to look in on her grace. If she's napping, let her be. The poor dear really needs her rest.''

Randy found herself admiring their self-appointed hostess as she and James followed her into the drawing room. The soft-spoken lady was barely five feet tall, but issued orders with great authority. With strands of silver shining in her black curls, she appeared to be in her mid-thirties. Thoroughly poised and gracious, she was the picture of refined elegance. Randy couldn't help feeling a little awkward and shy around her.

"Now, why don't the two of you sit on the settee near the fireplace while I take the chair beside it. We can get acquainted while we warm ourselves and wait for our tea. Percival told me that you've known the dowager for a long time, my lord, but little else. Do you live close by?''

James laced his fingers with Randy's when he noticed the woman was looking intently at his wife. ''Actually, my family have been friends and neighbors of the duchess for years.''

''Oh, really. Which estate ... ah, do you ...'' The dark-haired woman nervously laughed over her own distraction as she looked at Randy. ''I really must apologize for staring at you, my dear. I know we have never met before, but something about you is so familiar. Perhaps if I was not so vain about wearing spectacles, I could figure out why,'' she admitted with a derisive sigh.

From the side pocket of her gown, she removed a pair of wire-rimmed spectacles and put them on, making her pale blue eyes appear large and round. Her expectant smile froze as she got her first clear look at Randy's face.

''Oh, my word, it *is* you!'' she gasped only a second before her complexion paled and she collapsed into her chair.

''I frightened her into a faint,'' Randy complained as James carried the woman to the settee. ''Do you think she knew my mother and the shock of seeing me did this to her?''

James tucked a pillow beneath the woman's legs and elevated her feet. ''It's a mystery to me. I didn't want to be rude to a woman who is apparently a good friend to Nana, but I don't even know who she is.''

Percival chose that moment to enter the drawing room with the tea service. The sight of James and Randy hovering over the figure on the sofa nearly caused him to drop the heavy tray.

''My lord, has her grace suddenly come down with influenza, too? Should I send for the physician?''

''I don't believe influenza is the cause for her swoon, Percival. Why don't you set those things down and fetch smelling salts and a blanket. We will see if that will revive her.''

The old butler was nearly out the door when Randy called out to him. ''Percival, who is this lady?''

Looking back with surprise, he replied. ''Forgive me for not making introductions, but I thought you knew. She is your Uncle Richard's wife, Amelia Amanda Wentworth, the thirteenth Duchess of Maidstone.''

With a quick bow, Percival closed the door behind him and rushed off to carry out his orders.

The silence in the drawing room was nearly absolute. Only the crackling of the burning logs in the fireplace and the shallow breathing of the room's three inhabitants marred its purity. James suddenly moved away from the settee and gathered Randy into his arms as the reality of their situation hit him full force.

''Bloody hell! After all my efforts to keep your presence a secret from your uncle, I've practically delivered you into his hands. She's married to that damned bastard.'' Feeling Randy tense in his embrace, he kissed her forehead. ''I am sorry, sweetheart. Nana mentioned that Amelia visited occasionally, but I had no idea she would be here.''

Randy turned to look at Amelia. ''Perhaps we are not as badly off as you imagine.''

''What do you mean?''

''Amelia must really care about Nana. That's evident in the fact that she has been here nursing her back to health for the past ten days. Maybe my grandmother can convince Amelia not to tell Richard that I am here.''

James arched his brow. ''I would not count on it. Amelia's been married to your uncle for almost fifteen years and—''

A low moan drew their attention to the settee behind them. Randy rushed over to assist Amelia as she struggled to sit up on her own.

''Don't rush yourself, your grace. If you move too quickly, you may faint again.'' Randy sat down beside Amelia and put a steadying arm around the slight woman's shoulder. ''James, will you get the duchess a cup of tea with sugar. The stimulus should help her regain her bearings."

Dabbing her face with the handkerchief she had tucked in the pocket with her spectacles, Amelia looked at Randy and laughed with embarrassment. "I have never swooned before in my life. Here I should be hugging you and thanking God that you're alive, dear niece, not plaguing you with an untimely display of my weakness."

Randy couldn't conceal her surprise. "You know who I am?"

Amelia patted her cheek and smiled. "Of course I do, Miranda. Your grandmother has shown me all of the miniature portraits your dear father sent her over the years. Since she received the report of Jonathan's murder without a single mention of your condition or whereabouts, looking at those miniatures and your letters have been all that sustains her." She gave Randy's hand a consoling squeeze. "May I offer my heart-felt condolences on the tragic loss of your father? Though I never met Jonathan, I know through her grace that he was a wonderful man."

James gave Amelia the cup of tea he had prepared for her and sat in the chair beside them. "You said there was no mention of Miranda in the report?"

Sipping her tea, Amelia shook her head. "No, none at all, my lord. That made it so frustrating. The official notification that was sent by the government offices didn't have a word about this dear girl in it. We've been at sixes and sevens, just waiting to get some news about our Miranda."

"What about the letter Major Spencer sent to your husband? According to the major, he sent a letter to the duke the morning after the murder, informing him of Jonathan's death and his assurance that Miranda was alive and well."

The Duchess smiled sadly. "I have absolutely no idea what letter you are talking about. Though I really shouldn't be surprised. You see, my husband and I have not been on the best of terms recently. He prefers staying in London with all the parties and social engagements. Visiting gambling halls and attending horse races are his favorite pastimes. I enjoy the quieter, more restful atmosphere of living in the country with my gardens and my books." Moisture welled in her eyes behind her wire-rimmed spectacles. "It's a dreadful thing to admit, but I haven't seen Richard in several months. Even my Christmas present was delivered to me by messenger."

At that moment, Percival rushed into the room with a blanket and an ampule in his hand. Going to the settee, he gave Amelia the small glass bottle. "It's good to see you have recovered, your grace. I got the smelling salts from Ida, but I was careful not to reveal who they were for."

"Thank you, Percy," Amelia replied with a gentle nod. "Your understanding of the situation is impeccable, as always. The less Ida knows about my business, the better off I will be."

Her remark made Randy ask, "Doesn't Ida work for you?"

A strange look passed over Amelia's face. "Yes and no. Ida Brody is my personal maid, but ofttimes I feel she is more like my keeper. Richard hired her to take care of my needs when we were first married. He's the one who pays her wages and to whom she is loyal. I know for a fact that she sends word to him about everything I say and do."

"Then dismiss her," Randy demanded. "You shouldn't have to live under such scrutiny."

Amelia sighed. "I'm afraid that would only make matters worse. I have nothing to hide from my husband. If I dismissed Ida, he would become highly suspicious of my motives and find other ways to spy on me."

James nodded with understanding. "You would rather deal with the devil you know."

"Exactly!" Smiling now, the duchess turned her attention to James. "And you must be James Grayson. The handsome young man who was going to make Nana's dreams come true by bringing Miranda home to her on your new ship. I can hardly wait until she sees how well you have succeeded."

"I beg your pardon, your grace," Percival interrupted, "Ida wanted you to know that the dowager is still napping, but should be awake within the hour."

"That's splendid, Percy. While we're waiting for her grace to wake up, I want you to show Miranda to the pink guest suite and Captain Grayson to the green one. You will be staying with us a few days, won't you, James?"

Randy shook her head. "But we don't need—"

"Yes, thank you, your grace," James replied, effectively cutting off Randy's objection. "With my own family still away visiting my sister in America, Foxwood would be a lonely place to come home to."

Randy's confusion made her scowl. "But James, Aunt Amelia should be told that—"

He leaned over and patted her hand. "Of course, my dear, just leave everything to me."

"Is there a problem?" Amelia asked.

"Not really a problem," James replied. "You see, Miranda brought along two of her personal servants from India. Abu and Jarita should be arriving soon with our luggage, and she's a bit concerned about their welfare."

"Well, don't spend another moment worrying over such things, my dear. Percy will find accommodations for your servants and all shall be taken care of." Removing her spectacles, Amelia stood up and put them in her pocket. "While Percy shows you to your rooms, I will inform Cook that there will be additional guests for dinner."

Amelia turned to Randy, who was now standing beside her with James, and stroked her cheek. "I pray that having you here will give my dearest friend a reason to get better, Miranda. She deserves the happiness that only your presence can provide. And all of this is due to you, my lord captain." She offered James her hand. "My thanks for bringing Miranda safely home where she belongs. This family will be forever in your debt."

After James kissed her hand, Amelia smiled brightly and

hurried from the room chattering happily. "My, my! What a celebration this will be!"

Percival was about to lead them up the stairs when the brass knocker banged loudly on the front door.

"That could be our baggage," Randy suggested to the elderly servant with a warm smile. "Why not see if it is while the captain and I make use of the tea that you brought in earlier. It's still warm and I'm suddenly dying for a cup of tea."

As Percival went off to do her bidding, Randy shut the door to the salon and turned to confront James. Her posture was taut, her hands propped on her hips. The smile she had given to the butler had changed to an angry frown.

"Why didn't you tell Amelia that we were married and that we wouldn't be needing two bedrooms? After weeks of sharing a room with me, have you suddenly changed your mind and decided that you're tired of having a wife around?"

Without the hint of a smile, James strode towards Randy and caused her to step back until she felt her spine pressed against the door. Dipping his head, he captured her lips in a kiss that was filled with passion and carnal possession. When he eased back slightly to look at her, there was no mistaking the desire—and the annoyance—she saw in his eyes.

"She could give us a dozen rooms and the only one I would be sleeping in is yours, Randy. You are my wife, and I would have to be dead not to want you in my bed every night."

"Then why didn't you tell Amelia that we were married? She is such a lovely lady. I'm sure she wouldn't betray us to Uncle Richard."

James pulled her into his arms. "Amelia seems nice enough, but that maid of hers can't be trusted. So take off your wedding ring and place it safely away for a while. Until we know more of what's going on around here, I would prefer that no one finds out that we are husband and wife."

Randy playfully nipped his chin with her teeth. "Not even, Nana? Since she was the one who orchestrated our meeting in the first place, I think she deserves to know the truth about us. It will probably make her very happy.''

''All right, Randy. We can tell Nana, but nobody else. Before any public announcements are made, I need to be sure that our marriage is valid.''

She tightened her hold around his waist. ''If it's not, would you be willing to marry me again?''

''A thousand times if it were necessary, sweetheart,'' James replied in a husky whisper as he lowered his mouth to hers. ''Gladly, a thousand times.''

Chapter 13

Randy's bedchamber was bright and cheerful, with lacquered white furniture and carnation-pink walls. Even the large canopy-covered bed with its lacy hangings and spread was finished in the color of snow. The upholstered loveseat and chair that sat before the white marble-faced fireplace were done in a pale pink floral print and matched the draperies on the windows. Exquisite porcelain figurines of full-blown pink roses and peonies adorned the mantel and tables. The only thing that deviated from the color scheme of the room was the gilt-framed mirror on the dressing table and gold-trimmed pier glass that stood in the corner.

But Randy noticed none of it.

Sitting before the hearth on the Aubusson rug, she stared into the flames. It was nearly midnight as she sat alone and contemplated the events of that day.

After years of anticipation, her reunion with Nana was hardly what she had expected. Nana was nothing like the woman James had told her about. Propped up in her bed, she looked frail and tired. Her smile, though genuinely given, appeared forced. The eyes James had once vividly described as brilliant as emeralds now appeared clouded and dull.

Randy was so miserable and deep in thought, she never heard the door to her room opening. It was only when James knelt down and drew her into his arms for a warm, passionate kiss that she found a reason to smile again.

"I'm so glad you're here, James," she sighed a few minutes later as they cuddled naked beneath the covers on the bed. "I wasn't sure if you were going to join me tonight or not."

James cradled her head against his chest and stroked her hair. "Keeping our marriage a secret and not making love is difficult enough, but not being able to sleep with you in my arms is downright impossible."

"I am sorry about not making love, James. With Amelia only across the hall and Nana next door and all the servants running about, I'm afraid someone might hear us. But once Nana is better and we share our news with her and the rest of the world, we can make up for the lost time."

"Don't worry, sweetheart. I promise not to press you into making love until after everything has been settled. The door's locked just in case your aunt or someone else tries to look in on you during the night." He leaned over to kiss the crease in her brow. "You know, I think maybe Amelia's right about Nana. Now that you are here and she knows you're safe and out of danger, I'm certain your grandmother will be on the mend very soon."

Randy shook her head. "I'm not so sure. While you were checking on Abu and Jarita, Percival offered to escort me to my room. After talking to him, I have my doubts that Nana's concern for my well-being has anything to do with her lingering poor health."

"What did he tell you?"

"He said Nana had been fine up until three weeks ago. Even after learning of my father's murder the month before, her confidence in you finding me and bringing me back to England never wavered. Nana was full of plans and enthusiasm for my homecoming. Presents were purchased and wrapped, party menus selected, and the house was made ready for the many guests she was going to invite to share her joy. When she wasn't scurrying about Mirage personally overseeing the preparations, she was writing long, detailed letters to her solicitors.

"Yet almost overnight, Nana became ill and took to her bed. The physician thinks it's influenza, but she isn't responding to any of the remedies he's prescribed. Her color paled, and her usually healthy appetite for food waned to almost nothing. The only things she eats with any regularity are tea, broth, and the crispy little almond biscuits Ida makes for her. I wish I knew what kind of ailment she is suffering from."

James gave her a consoling squeeze. "Couldn't you use your little talent to see where her pain is?"

Randy was warmed by James's acceptance of her mental gifts and his encouraging her to use them. "After Percival left me, I went to my grandmother's room and tried to do just that. Nana was sound asleep and Ida was sitting in the corner doing her knitting. I held Nana's hand and directed my mind to search her body for pain and the source of her illness, but I couldn't find any. My grandmother is weak and lethargic. Other than a mild stomach upset probably brought on by not eating properly, she seems to be fine."

"Maybe it's a brain disorder or a form of dementia that's causing her symptoms," James offered.

She shrugged. "I don't know. That's why I want Abu to have a look at Nana tomorrow. With all the knowledge he acquired from the Indian physicians in Mysore, he might be able to discern exactly what is wrong with her."

"Do you honestly think Amelia or Ida is going to allow you to bring a strange man into Nana's room?" James chuckled. "You might succeed in convincing your aunt, but that maid of hers is cut of a different cloth entirely. When she first saw Abu standing in the foyer directing the footmen with our baggage, I thought she would keel over from the shock of it. I don't know if she was put off by his strange clothes, the dark color of his skin, or the fact that he was wearing gold earrings."

"Yes, I know," Randy admitted. "Ida told Percival that I should have left my heathen servants back in India where they belonged. Goodness knows what she would do if she ever saw Xavier."

James laughed out loud. "The old witch would likely run off screaming in fear of your gentle giant. It's not every day that one sees a man who is nearly seven feet tall. Now, go to sleep, sweetheart. We can come up with a plan to get Abu into Nana's room in the morning."

Lying there in the dark, Randy recalled something Nana's old butler had said, and she knew what had to be done. "James, I know a way to do it. Percival was complaining that Ida was going to be in the kitchen making up another batch of almond biscuits for Nana after breakfast. That means Amelia will be sitting at her bedside. I will offer to take Amelia's place while she takes you on a tour of the house."

"Fine, fine. I'll do whatever you want in the morning," James yawned, patting her back. "But I must go to sleep now. If I'm to be up and back to my room by dawn, I need some rest."

Randy leaned up on his chest to kiss his cheek. "Thank you, James, for being so understanding."

A warning growl emanated from deep within his throat. "Understanding be damned! Rub your breasts against me one more time, sweetheart, and I will forget about your aunt across the hall and ravish you until you scream with pleasure."

His sensual threat both frightened and excited her. "But this morning in the drawing room you said we had to be careful. That I was too vocal in my passion to risk taking the chance of being heard."

"Yes, but I could also use a pillow to muffle the sounds if I was desperate enough."

"You wouldn't dare!" she gasped.

In the dim light from the fireplace, James looked down at

her and scowled. "Of course not, you silly goose! I was just teasing you about the pillow. You see, I rather enjoy listening to those delightful sounds you utter when I'm making love to you. They're quite inspiring and they spur me on to more vigorous endeavors in pleasing you." He playfully patted her behind. "Now, enough talk, sweetheart. Go to sleep."

"Just you wait, James Grayson," Randy countered, with her head resting on his shoulder. "As soon as everything has been resolved with Nana and we can make love again, I'll show you who can be vocal. When I start pleasuring you, husband mine, your lustful howls will be heard clear out to the stables and back."

Randy dozed off a while later, watching James sleep with a rakish grin on his face.

It was mid-morning when Randy was finally able to put her plan into motion. With Jarita watching Ida in the kitchen, and James keeping Amelia busy in the library on the other side of the house, she ushered Abu into the dowager's bedroom.

"You see, Abu, she's sleeping again. According to Percival, Nana has never been one to wile away time in bed. Before she became ill three weeks ago, she rarely slept more than four hours a night and never took naps during the day."

Stepping to the bed, Abu took hold of the dowager's hand. He checked her pulse and rubbed his thumb over the sleeping woman's fingernails. After carefully setting her hand down on the blankets, he leaned over and lifted her eyelids for a silent inspection of her eyes.

"Amelia says the doctor thinks Nana has influenza," Randy continued, "but I believe he is wrong."

"And what do you base your belief on, my child?" Abu asked, not looking up at her as he put his open palm on the dowager's forehead. "Have you used your gift and found a problem the *Angrezi* physician knows nothing about?"

"It's nothing that I found, Abu," she admitted with a sigh.

"It's more like . . . like a feeling I have inside me. I know it's not logical, but I sense something else is making Nana ill."

Abu's wizened gaze fixed on Randy's face. "Then accept your feelings as fact, my lady, because they are far more accurate than those of your grandmother's learned physician."

"You mean, I am right?"

Abu nodded. "It appears that the dowager has been the victim of arsenic poisoning. Have you not noticed the strong scent of almonds on your grandmother?"

Randy felt herself sagging with relief. "That's only from those biscuits Ida makes for her. Since Nana's been sick, it is one of the few things she will eat."

The old Indian shook his head. "Eating biscuits would not make the odor linger on her flesh like this. The smell of bitter almonds on her skin and breath is only the first of several things that led me to know that arsenic has been used."

Abu picked up the dowager's hand and showed it to Randy. "The color of her nail beds and the yellowish tint in the whites of her eyes are telling signs. She has a slight fever and is too weak to stay awake. Arsenic would also cause nausea, making eating a painful experience."

"But that's insane. Why would anyone want to kill Nana?"

"It is not my place to say, but whoever is doing it has been very clever. By giving it to her in small doses and increasing it over time, the dowager's death could be deemed a natural passing instead of murder."

Abu went on to explain that he had witnessed a similar crime when he was a young man in the court of Javid's father, Niranjan. "One of the maharajah's wives tried to eliminate a new member of the *zenana* by giving her almond coconut candies that were dosed with arsenic for several weeks. Niranjan's *hakiim* recognized the ailing girl's symptoms and saved her life. The jealous wife was beheaded for her crime."

Randy sat on the bed and held her grandmother's hands. "Is there anything you can do to save her, Abu? Surely in your jars of herbs and medicinal powders you have something that will make her well again.''

"I can give her something to help fight the fever, but plenty of juices, broths, and fluids to clean out her system is the best remedy for this kind of poisoning.'' Abu put his hand on Randy's shoulder. "You remain here with the dowager while I seek out *Huzur* James. He will know how to find the jackal responsible for this.''

As Abu closed the door behind him, Randy leaned over and brushed some wisps of hair from her grandmother's face. "Don't worry. We are going to take good care of you, Nana, I promise," she pledged, kissing her cheek.

The scent of almonds that wafted toward her reminded Randy that someone in the household was capable of committing murder. Her grandmother's servants seemed devoted to her, so it wasn't likely that any of them were involved. That left Amelia and her maid Ida to consider.

Amelia had been the dowager's dearest friend for a long time. According to Percival, the petite lady even risked her husband's wrath to spend time with her at Mirage. During one such visit the previous year, Richard Wentworth had come to the door and demanded that she leave with him. When Amelia rushed out to do his bidding, the duke struck her in the face before shoving her into his coach and ordering his men to drive on.

"Then it must be Ida Brody. Amelia said that Ida worked for Richard. Were her almond biscuits a means to hide the arsenic she was poisoning you with? Could it be that he was the one who ordered her to do this to you?'' Randy sighed. "Oh, Nana, I wish you could tell me why Richard would suddenly want to harm you like this.''

"Richard is a cruel bastard.''

Randy nearly fell from the bed when she heard the dowager's raspy voice answering her question. "Nana, I didn't mean to wake you. How are you feeling? Can I get you something?''

Miranda Wentworth looked up at her with tired eyes. "A

sip of water for my parched throat would be most appreciated, my child.'' Once Randy had helped her to take a drink and plumped up her pillows, the old woman patted her hand. ''Now explain to me what you were talking about when I woke up. It was something about Ida and that dastardly stepson of mine.''

After Randy told her of Abu's diagnosis of arsenic poisoning and her own suspicions that Ida and Richard had been responsible for the vile deed, Miranda Wentworth sighed. ''I believe you may be right. Richard is desperate for funds and will do anything to get them—even doing away with me, I suspect.''

''How will killing you get him the money he needs? You told James that father and I were your only heirs.''

The dowager shook her head. ''It's not my wealth he's after, child, but yours. With the generous inheritance you would be receiving from my estate and that left to you by your father, you would be an extremely wealthy young lady. If he were made your guardian, Richard would have the right to do what he wished with your holdings.''

Randy was confused by her grandmother's statement. ''Nana, what do you mean, if he were my guardian? As my oldest male relative, won't the courts declare him my guardian anyway?''

The elderly lady smiled. ''Not if my petition to be named as your guardian was signed by King William and was accompanied by a letter from your own father asking that you be placed in my care in the event of his death.''

''When did Papa do this? He never mentioned it to me.''

''It was shortly after your mother, my dear Lenore, passed away.'' A teardrop rolled down her pale cheek. ''Your father did not want you to fall prey to my stepson if anything happened to him. When I received word of Jonathan's death, I had my solicitors file the proper documents, and within days you were made my ward.''

Randy shook her head with disbelief. ''Did you really ask the king to help you?''

''Of course. They say rank has its privileges, though being godmother to his niece, Princess Victoria, certainly didn't hurt my request." The dowager yawned behind her hand and closed her eyes. "Poor Amelia. She's going to be devastated when she learns of this, but she should not be surprised. Richard has been excessively cruel to her over the years. He beats her and demands her obedience in all things. Amelia would be well rid of him and Ida if they are found guilty of trying to kill me."

"And they will, Nana. James and I won't let them get away with this."

"That's fine, my child, though I am going to miss those biscuits." The dowager sighed, her eyes misting with the memory. "I have always adored almonds. Amelia's brother occasionally ships them to her from the Orient. Ida would grind them up and bake those crispy little biscuits and send them to me. That's why I didn't suspect anything was amiss four weeks ago when the tin of biscuits arrived."

"Perhaps my cook, Kira, has a recipe for almond biscuits that you will like just as well," Randy suggested.

With a slight shiver, the elderly lady shook her head. "Don't trouble yourself, Randy dear. After all this, I doubt if I will ever be able to eat almonds again."

"I understand, Nana. Why don't you try and rest now? When you wake up, Abu will have one of his remedies prepared for you and we can begin ridding your system of the poison."

Snuggling against her pillows, the dowager's eyes drifted shut. "I knew Richard hated me, but I never imagined he had the pluck to try anything as devious as this to gain control over you. It would serve the bounder right if I married you off before I died. Then all his plans will have been for naught."

Randy took hold of her grandmother's hands. "You're not going to die, Nana. I won't let you. Besides, Richard's plans are already ruined. James and I were married by a magistrate back in India. So, if anything befalls you or me, your stepson isn't going to gain a solitary penny. I hope you can forgive me for not telling you about our marriage sooner, Nana."

The dowager's reply to her declaration was not what Randy

expected. A soft snore escaped the elderly woman's lips, letting her granddaughter know that she had fallen back to sleep.

A short time later, Randy entered her grandmother's library and found James at the desk glaring at the woman seated before him. Dressed in her blue gown and pristine white apron, Ida Brody sat on a chair with her hands primly folded in her lap. Her posture was taut, the expression on her face cold and aloof.

James slapped his hand against the desk. "I cannot believe the temerity of this woman, Randy. Not only did we find her with the arsenic, but she had just completed another batch of biscuits for your grandmother. We fed one to a rat that the grooms had trapped in the stables and it died within minutes. Yet in spite of all this, she claims to be innocent."

"I am innocent," Ida countered in a brisk tone. "I have no idea how arsenic got into the canister with the ground almonds. If there's trouble afoot, search out the dowager's own staff for someone to blame. With the laxity I have witnessed in this household, any of them could have done it."

Randy went behind the desk and stood beside James's chair. Her hand rested on his shoulder. "The people who work for my grandmother have nothing to gain by harming her, Miss Brody. In actuality, the only one who could profit by her death is your employer, the Duke of Maidstone."

Ida's brow lifted. "Exactly what are you implying?"

"Only that you are a loyal servant of my Uncle Richard and have been for nearly fifteen years. If he gave you orders to do something, you would probably do it without fail."

"I have been a devoted maid and companion to the duchess for a long time, but I would never do anything illegal or underhanded for her or the duke."

"Nothing underhanded?" Randy shook her head in disgust. "What do you call those secret reports you send to my uncle regarding his wife? Do you deny that you spy on the duchess constantly so you can tell Richard where she is and what she is doing? If betraying the woman who employs you in this manner isn't being underhanded, then I don't know what is!"

James leaned forward and stared at the maid. "You know, I can't help but wonder why Richard Wentworth is so concerned with the activities of a wife he hasn't taken the time to see in months. Was Amelia the only cause of his interest, or was the duke using you to spy on his stepmother as well? Did he order you to do away with the dowager?"

Ida flushed with indignation. "I have absolutely no intention of discussing his grace with you or anyone, my lord. Suffice it to say, I am a true and honorable employee of the Duke of Maidstone, and as such have served him to the very best of my abilities. My duties are none of your concern."

With a haughty air of disdain, Ida Brody stood up. "If you mean to accuse me of poisoning the dowager, then I insist that you contact the village magistrate. Once the proper authorities deal with this investigation, I am sure to be vindicated."

"You seem quite sure of yourself, Miss Brody," James replied. "Are you expecting his grace to come rushing to your rescue if you are charged?"

"There will be no charges. Your evidence is conjecture at best. There is no proof that I was the one who tainted the almonds and you know it." Ida turned and moved toward the door. "I will wait in my room for the constable to arrive."

When James angrily rose to pursue her, Randy held him back. "Let her go to her room. There's a terrible snowstorm blowing outside and I doubt if she would risk trying to escape into it."

James grabbed the bellpull that hung on the wall behind the desk. "I won't have that woman roaming freely about this house. Percival can assign several of the footmen to take turns standing guard at her door until we can send for the magistrate."

At that moment, Amelia came rushing into the library. Her face was pale and her eyes were swollen with tears. "Please tell me it isn't true. Has Ida really poisoned her grace? Am I to lose my dearest friend because of that woman's foul interference in my life?''

Randy gently helped her into a chair. ''It is true, Aunt Amelia, but Nana is going to be fine.''

Amelia dabbed her eyes with her handkerchief. ''When I stopped in Miranda's suite to visit her, your Jarita told me about the poisoning. Arsenic is very dangerous, Randy. Your grandmother needs to see a physician immediately, but with weather conditions as they are, I'm afraid that's impossible.''

''Abu has dealt with this kind of poisoning before, and he knows what must be done to counteract the arsenic Nana has ingested during the past few weeks. Evidently, Nana's symptoms began shortly after she ate from the tin of biscuits that Ida sent to her last month.''

''Then poor Miranda never had influenza. My maid's act of kindness was actually an attempt at murdering her. No doubt Ida was taking orders from my wretched husband.'' A shudder racked Amelia's petite form and she sobbed. Tears flooded her eyes. ''Dear God, I feel so responsible. If I had stayed away from this house and not befriended Miranda, Richard could not have attempted such a vile scheme.''

James filled a glass with brandy from the crystal decanter on the desk and handed it to the duchess. ''Drink this, my lady. It should help calm you.'' As she sipped the potent liquor, he silently motioned Randy to follow him out of the room.

Closing the door, James pulled Randy into his arms and gave her an encouraging hug. ''Amelia is close to breaking down. You stay with her while I see to the arrangements for Ida.''

''James, I need to tell you what Nana did—''

''I don't want you to worry about any of this,'' he continued. ''As soon as the weather lets up, I will get that woman out of this house. Perhaps I should engage a Bow Street runner to discover why Richard suddenly decided to harm your grandmother.''

Randy freed herself from his embrace and shook her head. ''That won't be necessary. I already know his motives.'' As she explained what Nana had told her earlier, the look of concern on James's face turned to a triumphant smile.

He dropped a quick kiss on her lips. "You see, marrying me was the cleverest thing you've ever done, sweetheart. Nana will certainly not object to our union and you are safely out of Richard's reach."

"But my uncle doesn't know that. Until he learns of our marriage, Nana is still in danger."

"Then we will post the announcement of our marriage in the London dailies for everyone to see. To be sure Richard doesn't miss it, I'll have copies forwarded to his townhouse and all of the clubs he frequents." James dropped another quick kiss on her lips. "Why are you frowning, sweetheart? I thought the knowledge of being free of your uncle once and for all would please you."

"I am pleased, James, it's just that I don't want Richard getting away with what he tried to do to Nana. If Ida Brody does not confess to following his orders in this plot, my uncle will never be punished for his crime."

James scowled. "Even if Ida does implicate Richard, I fear it won't be enough to convict him. She's only a servant while he is the Duke of Maidstone, a peer of the realm. He may have had a motive to kill your grandmother, but it would still come down to a contest of Ida's word against his. In our class-distinctive society, Richard would likely win."

Randy suddenly smiled. "If our marriage can be kept a secret a while longer, maybe there's a way *we* could trap him."

"If you think I am going to allow you to endanger yourself in any way, you are sorely mistaken."

Seeing Percival coming toward them, she gave James a kiss on the cheek. "Don't frown so, James. I will tell you all about it this evening after dinner. Go on and take care of Ida. Her testimony might not condemn Richard, but it would certainly add validity to our case against him."

Before James could voice a protest, Randy hurried into the library and closed the door in his face.

"I apologize for taking so long to answer your summons, my lord," Percival said with a bow. "I was detained in the kitchen overseeing the search for additional arsenic, and I am pleased to announce there isn't another bit of it to be found. You look upset. Is something wrong, my lord?"

Staring at the library door, James sighed. "Nothing an education in female logic wouldn't solve."

"What was that, my lord?"

James shook his head and faced the old retainer. "Ignore my mood, Percival. We have much to do before I can keep an appointment with a very headstrong and determined young lady."

Randy was more than happy to see James when he crept into the pink guest room late that night. He was barely through the door when she threw herself into his arms.

"Oh, James, I have missed you so much," she said, pressing her face against his shoulder and hugging him. "After hours of consoling poor Amelia and reassuring her that Nana is going to be fine, I am emotionally drained. I need someone to hold me for a while. I need someone to tell me that everything is going to be all right. But above all, I needed that someone to be you."

James gently kissed her and cradled her in his embrace. "I know, sweetheart. That's why I am here, now."

Without warning, Randy pulled away from him and yanked on the top cape of his sodden greatcoat. "Where have you been? Percival told me you had gone off on an errand this afternoon. When you didn't return in time for supper, I became frantic with worry. What was so all-fired important that you would risk your life by going out in the middle of a blizzard? Have you lost your mind? You could have died out there in the storm!"

Her scolding made James smile. The knowledge that Randy worried about him warmed him better than a flaming hearth after his icy ride across the countryside. Grabbing the shoulders of her red velvet robe, he jerked her back into his arms. "If you must know, I went to my parents' estate to check on Xavier, Kira, and your pets. I wanted to be sure that they were well. Sidra is a bit restless, but thanks to the stoves in the barn, she and the rest of your creatures aren't suffering from the cold."

A mask of contrition covered her features. "You did this for me, and here I am acting like a shrew. I'm sorry, James."

He kissed the tip of her nose. "You are not a shrew, just a concerned wife. But if it will ease your conscience, you can help me out of these wet clothes."

"Of course, James," she replied, pulling off his coat. "And then I will warm you up in my big comfortable bed. Doesn't that sound cozy?"

After handing Randy his wet shirt, James unbuttoned his doeskin britches and sat on the chair near the hearth to remove his boots. "Your invitation sounds wonderful, sweetheart, but I know you are trying to distract me. Until we discuss this plan you have come up with to trap Richard Wentworth, I am not getting into that bed and neither are you."

Striding to his chair, Randy frowned at him. Her unbound hair swirled around her like a satin cape. "You are too clever for my own good, James Grayson. Why should I bother telling you about my idea when you have obviously decided that I am wrong?"

James put his arm around her waist and drew her down to sit on his lap. "If that were true, I would have jumped into that bed, made wild love to you, and hoped that someone would hear us so our marriage wouldn't have to be kept a secret any more. Now, just sit there and tell me about this plan of yours."

"If you insist." Randy leaned back against his shoulder, twisting her hair with her fingers while she spoke. "I liked your suggestion that we post a formal announcement in the papers so Richard will know that I am here in England. As soon as the roads are fit for travel, we can send the news of our betrothal to all the dailies in London."

"Why not just announce that we're already married?"

Randy stroked his chest with the end of her hair. "It's all very simple. Once my uncle knows I am your wife, he would have nothing to gain by going after Nana again, so we couldn't catch him in the act. But if Richard believed that the two of us were merely betrothed, he would have to deal with you as well."

James cocked his brow. "Deal with me in what way?"

"By trying to eliminate you before our wedding, of course. For that reason, we would have to set a wedding date that wasn't too far off. If Richard thought he was going to lose me soon, it would force his hand and cause him to move quickly."

Her almost glib attitude about using him as bait began to rankle James. "Do you think I'm just going to sit idly by and wait for your bloody uncle or one of his hired assassins to come after me?"

She shook her head. "Of course not. We will deal with Richard head-on. As soon as Nana is recovered enough to travel, we are going to London to face him."

James jolted forward, nearly knocking Randy from his lap. Grabbing her by the shoulders, he turned her to face him. "I will not risk taking you or your grandmother anywhere near Richard Wentworth. If he so much as touched a hair on your head there would be no need for a trap to catch him because I would kill the bastard myself."

Randy put her arms around his neck and hugged him. "I know that, James, and I thank you for it. But what I was suggesting was confronting my uncle at a public gathering, such as a party or the opera. Surrounded by his peers and the members of London society, Richard's not likely to try anything foolish. It will doubtlessly enrage him and that will be his downfall."

His wife's sweet, womanly scent and the feel of her velvet-covered breasts crushed against his bare chest filled James with longing. The effect of her buttocks rubbing on his groin left him only half listening to what she said. After weeks of enjoying the passionate freedom of making love to Randy, his two days of abstinence seemed more like years.

Biting back a groan of disappointment, James eased away from her embrace and shook his head to clear the sensual cobwebs that were invading his logic. "What did you say about Richard's downfall?"

"By making Richard lose control of his temper, he will react like the animal he is and come after you without thinking of the consequences. There won't be any danger for you or any of us, because we know what he's up to and we will be prepared to capture him." Randy smiled with excitement and wriggled happily against him. "Now, don't you see what a great plan it is?"

James lowered his hands to her hips and gently stopped her innocent but arousing movements. "Your ... ah, plan has definite merit, sweetheart, though there are some details that still have to be dealt with."

Randy looked at him expectantly. "Such as what?"

James closed his eyes to concentrate more on the subject they were discussing and less on the tempting sight of Randy's tongue as it reached out to moisten her lips. "Well, we do have to consider what's to be done about Ida. If we turn her over to the magistrate, there will be an investigation, and even if she doesn't implicate Richard with a confession, as her employer he would be notified of the charges against her."

"Then we won't give her to the magistrate until we've captured Richard. We can keep her locked up here, or better yet, why not take her to your family's estate? Ida can stay in the barn with my pets. With Sidra and Xavier guarding her, that woman could never make good an escape."

James almost flinched when he felt Randy's hand gently stroking his jaw. "Are you feeling all right, James? Your cheeks are flushed and your breathing seems a bit labored. I hope you haven't taken a chill."

"No, I am fine. Just a bit tired."

"Well if you're tired, why don't we go to bed now? We can finish our talk in the morning."

Knowing there was no way to hide the swollen ridge of his manhood from his young wife if he stood up, James opened his eyes and helped Randy to her feet. "Why don't you go on to bed without me, sweetheart? I want to stay here for a little while so I can think about this marvelous plan of yours."

"Are you sure that's what you want me to do?"

"Yes, Randy," he replied tightly. "You hurry off to bed and I will join you soon."

Randy brushed down the hem of her heavy velvet robe and gasped. "The back of my robe is very damp from sitting on your lap. Your britches must be sopping wet."

"Um . . . perhaps they are. I will deal with them as soon as I . . . ah, find the energy to stand up."

"Well, I'm not going to bed until I get those off you." Before he could stop her, Randy knelt beside his chair and began tugging on the unfastened waistband of his pants. "Now lift your hips so I can get these down your—oh, my! It does appear that someone is feeling a bit neglected tonight."

Ignoring the pleasant sensation caused by the warmth of Randy's breath so near his exposed member, James tried to cover himself with his hands. "I didn't mean for you to see me like this. Just give me a few moments and it will pass."

"But why should we waste such a marvelous opportunity, James?"

James glared at her. "You know damned well I made a promise not to make love to you with Amelia across the hall and your grandmother in the next room."

Randy's lips curved into a siren's smile. "That's true, but I never made any such pledge about making love to you. After all my efforts, the least you can do is allow me to complete my first real attempt at seduction."

"So your little hugs and touches were deliberate? You were trying to provoke my lust?"

Tossing her hair over her shoulder, she emitted a coy sigh.

"Of course. And now that you know what I was about, I will never know if I am truly any good at this seduction thing."

A knot caused by intense desire tightened in his throat. "Madam wife, I assure you, with your feminine guile and innate charm, you could tempt a monastery full of monks into abandoning their vows."

"But all I want is you, James." Keeping her gaze locked with his, Randy moved his hands away and lightly dragged her fingernails along the sensitive flesh of his inner thighs. She pushed his legs further apart and leaned toward him. "Let me ease your discomfort and pleasure you."

Realizing her intent, James tried to stop her. "You don't have to do this. I can wait a few more days."

"This is something I want to do for you, James. You have made love to me like this many times. I thought you would enjoy receiving some for a change."

James lost all rational thought when Randy's lips touched his throbbing manhood. Though untutored in this form of making love, her enthusiasm could not be denied. Again and again, her tongue swirled around its tip and flicked down the length of his erection, bringing him closer to the taunting brink of his release. His hips rocked of their own volition and he entwined his fingers in her hair when she began sucking on him, drawing his turgid length into her mouth. Seconds later, his back arched and James cried out, powerless to stop the climax that exploded from deep within him.

The light from the fireplace cast a golden glow over the darkened chamber. Covered with several quilts, James lay beside Randy as she told him about her evening with Amelia.

"Aunt Amelia has such a kind heart. In spite of what Ida did to Nana, she refuses to place all the blame on her maid. Amelia says Richard is quite forceful when he wants something and isn't above making threats or hurting people. God only knows what he did to gain Ida's compliance in this."

"If we decide to go ahead with your plan, can we count on Amelia not to tell her husband that Ida was caught?"

"I don't believe that will be a problem. He would be the last person she would talk to about this. From the way Amelia talks, I think she is afraid of him." Randy yawned and turned to face the fireplace. "We had better get to sleep. Jarita will be waking us up shortly after dawn."

After the way Randy had made love to him, James couldn't believe that she was now acting so shyly. Since they had gotten into bed, she had carefully avoided looking at his face. Could it be that she was embarrassed? Was she ashamed of what she had done? Somehow, he had to find a way to reassure her.

"Randy, sweetheart, I wish you would not turn away from me. After what happened between us a little while ago—you know, over there by the hearth—I think we should talk."

Randy's only response was a slight shrug of her shoulder.

"All right. Until you're feeling more up to it, I will talk while you listen. You shouldn't feel awkward or embarrassed by anything we do together when we are making love. What transpires between a married couple in the privacy of their bed—well, we weren't in bed exactly during that—but you understand what I am trying to say, don't you?"

In spite of the darkness, the light from the fireplace outlined Randy's body, allowing James to see her silent nod.

"The—ah, generosity of your loving attentions have humbled me, sweetheart. Never before have I experienced such a—a phenomenal release. It literally shook me to my vitals."

Randy's face was turned into her pillow, but James could hear the gasping sounds she was making. Reaching over, he touched her shoulder and felt her body quaking beneath his hand.

"You mustn't cry, Mira. What you did should not bring you tears of mortification. That you would give of yourself so freely, so passionately, deems me the luckiest of men."

"And most certainly one of the loudest," Randy replied when she turned over to face him.

Her smile and the glint of merriment in her eyes told James that his wife hadn't been crying at all. "By God, I can't believe this! While I've been struggling with a way to soothe your tender feelings, you were lying there laughing at me."

Randy nestled against him and patted his taut jaw with her hand. "Don't be cross, James. I wasn't laughing at you. Consider my giggles a form of nervous release. I simply couldn't figure out how to tell you the truth about yourself."

James cocked his brow. "To what truth are you implying?"

"That you are every bit as vocal as I am when caught up in the moment of glorious sexual release."

"Surely you must be exaggerating."

Randy shook her head. "Oh, no, I'm not. I wouldn't be surprised if your passionate shouts were heard down in the wine cellar on the other side of the house."

Throwing off the quilts, James loomed over his naked wife. When he began kissing her breasts and caressing the apex of her thighs with his hand, Randy gasped with surprise.

"James, whatever are you doing?"

He lifted his head and grinned. "I thought it was obvious, sweetheart. I'm making love to my wife."

"B-but what about keeping our marriage a secret and my rather boisterous response to lovemaking? Aren't you afraid someone is going to hear us?"

James offered her a rakish smile. "Have you heard the saying, 'in for a penny, in for a pound?' I just decided that as long as I may have already botched things up with my enthusiastic response to your seduction, you deserve to be heard as well. If you're concerned, try muffling your mouth with a pillow. But know this, Mira. When I'm done making love to you tonight, you will be far too sated to care about anyone hearing us."

Chapter 14

Abu was serving breakfast in the morning room the next day, when Percival arrived with Amelia on his arm. From the caring way the elderly butler led the sobbing woman to a chair at the end of the table, it was clear that something was terribly wrong. James and Randy left their places to join them.

Randy knelt down beside the duchess. "What is the matter, Aunt Amelia?"

"Her grace has had the most horrific shock," Percival rushed to explain. "Perhaps we should send for her physician."

James shook his head. "After last night's storm, the roads will be impassable for quite a while. If she requires a doctor's care, I am sure Abu could help her. What has upset her so?"

"Ida Brody is dead, my lord. Her grace and I took up a breakfast tray to her room and found her sitting in a chair, all cold and stiff." Percival leaned closer to James and spoke in a low voice. "I feel so badly that poor Lady Maidstone actually touched the body before she realized her maid was dead."

Hearing his sympathetic words, Amelia raised her flushed face to look up at him. "It's not your fault, dear Percy. Had I been wearing my spectacles, I would have seen her condition and acted accordingly.'' The duchess turned to Randy. ''I simply cannot believe it. Before retiring, I visited Ida for a few minutes and she seemed fine. What could have happened to her?''

As James and Abu followed Percival from the room to see to the dead woman, Randy gave Amelia's hand a reassuring squeeze. ''I don't know, but the men have gone upstairs to see what they can discover. Why don't you have a nice hot cup of tea while we wait for them to return?''

Moments later, Amelia was staring into the cup Randy had given her when she suddenly sighed. ''Last night I tried to convince Ida that things would go easier for her if she would simply admit what she had done to Miranda and why. I told her that I knew my husband had forced her into this and even offered to testify on her behalf. Ida said she would consider it and bade me a good night. Now she's dead, and the truth of her actions went with her.''

''I wouldn't say that,'' James announced, walking into the morning room with a piece of folded parchment in his hand. ''According to this letter I found in Ida's Bible, her guilt over her crime and her inability to betray her employer, the Duke of Maidstone, was too much for her to deal with.'' He placed the letter on the table in front of Amelia. ''I'm sorry, your grace. Rather than deal with it, your maid apparently gave herself a lethal dose of arsenic and ended her own life.''

Amelia shook her head. Dismay shone from her eyes. ''This is all too much for me to accept. Ida Brody had her faults, but she was a God-fearing Christian, and committing suicide is a mortal sin. That she felt compelled to take her own life makes me hate Richard all the more.'' She snatched up the letter and held it toward James. ''Surely the authorities can use this to prosecute my husband for what he has done.''

James sat beside Randy on the other side of the table. ''I don't believe so, your grace. You see, the letter in itself is little more than hearsay and can be explained in several ways. A clever solicitor could defend the duke by saying Ida was merely a deranged woman looking for someone else to blame for her sins, or that the betrayal she wrote of came from bringing disgrace on her employer's good name by what she had done.''

Amelia heaved a disheartened sigh. ''I should have known. Once again, Richard will go unpunished for his actions.''

''That's ridiculous!'' Randy objected. ''We know why Ida poisoned Nana, and who gave her the orders to do it.''

James patted her hand. ''Be that as it may, we can't prove it with this letter alone. We have no choice except to proceed with the plan we discussed last night.''

''What plan is that?'' Amelia asked, dabbing her light-blue eyes with her handkerchief.

''James and I are setting a trap to catch Richard,'' Randy explained. ''First, we are announcing our betrothal and our upcoming wedding in all the London dailies. It won't be true of course, because James and I—''

''Have already decided that, as a couple, we really don't suit,'' James cut in, nudging Randy's leg with his own. ''We know Nana had hopes that we would marry, but with my interests here in England and Randy's in India, a match between us is impossible.''

Amelia shook her head. ''That's too bad. Poor Miranda will be so disappointed. I had no idea that you were going back to India, my dear.''

Randy was confused by James's words and his obvious attempt to keep their marriage a secret from her aunt. Knowing he must have a good reason, she decided to follow his lead.

''India is my home, Aunt Amelia. I only came to England to visit Nana while the authorities in Calicut search for the man who murdered my father. Once the killer is found, I have every intention of going back there.'' Randy turned to James. ''Why don't you explain the rest of our plan to my aunt? I wouldn't want to leave anything out.''

''It's all rather simple, your grace. By naming me as Randy's betrothed husband, I will become the duke's new target. With a wedding date only a few weeks away, he will have to move quickly if he means to stop our marriage from happening.''

Amelia nervously twisted the handkerchief in her hands. ''Do you think Richard would actually come here?''

''He won't have to,'' James continued. ''When Nana is better, we're going to London. I will confront the duke in full view of the *ton.* How do you think Maidstone will react to such a public display, your grace?''

She visibly shuddered. ''My husband will be furious. Though I have never much cared for the lauded dictates of the social elite, Richard swears by it all. James, you must be careful. The duke is a very prideful man and he wouldn't think twice about killing you just to save face.''

James looked over at Randy and smiled. ''That's exactly what I am counting on. Don't worry, your grace—when Richard makes his move, I will be ready for him.''

''Well, James Grayson, it's about time you came up to see me. Come here this second, and give your Nana a proper greeting.''

James had entered the ailing dowager's suite late that day and found the lively matriarch sitting up in bed, holding court over her assembled visitors. While Randy and Jarita sat in chairs beside the bed, Abu stood like a silent sentinel near the window. Percival was busy serving tea to everyone from a rolling cart that held an assortment of cakes, buttered scones, and small finger sandwiches.

''Nana, I should have known that you wouldn't let something as insignificant as arsenic poisoning get you down for long. I can't believe how well you are looking today.''

The dowager patted the curls that escaped her linen cap and adjusted the satin ribbons on her pink bedjacket. ''Of course I look well. Abu has been taking wonderful care of me, with all his potions and broths. And you, James, have given me the greatest cure of all. You have brought my little Miranda, or should I say my Randy, home to me. Now, get over here this instant so that I may hug you and give you my thanks for bringing this miracle about."

After receiving his hug and kissing the dowager's soft, pale cheek, James stood behind Randy and put his hand on her shoulder. "Is your granddaughter everything that you expected?"

"Oh, yes, and so much more. Jarita was just telling me all about Randy's childhood when you came in. Did you know that when Randy was five, she disrupted a state dinner by allowing her pet mongoose to run loose in the dining room?"

"Nana," Randy interrupted, "could we delay any more discussions about me until later? I'm curious to know how things went with Amelia's departure." Looking up at James, she scowled. "I think my aunt would have been safer here."

"Amelia brought up certain points, and I agree with her. She is taking Ida's body back to Maidstone Hills, where her steward can send word to Richard that their maid died of heart failure. Amelia was also concerned that the duke might pay her a visit just to verify the woman's passing. The last thing we want is for that man to come here before we are ready for him."

Randy crossed her arms over her chest. "I still think you are wrong, and no amount of talking is going to change my mind."

James shook his head. "You know, Nana, I really should take you to task for not telling me more about this granddaughter of yours before I left for India. I was expecting a child with copper curls, not a temptress with golden eyes and a will every bit as stubborn as your own."

The dowager smiled and gave him a playful wink. "I could have told you many things, but wasn't learning for yourself a lot more fun, James? Besides, if I had said more about her, you might have thought I was playing the matchmaker."

His brow arched. "Wasn't that exactly what you were doing?"

"Well, you can't blame an old woman for trying. I thought the two of you would be perfect for one another," she sighed as she looked down to fuss with the row of buttons on her sleeping gown. "Earlier, Amelia told me how sorry she was that my hopes for bringing you together had been dashed. She thought I already knew. But you mustn't worry about me. I will treasure each day that I have with my granddaughter until she goes home to India."

Randy looked at James. Her gaze was filled with hope. He smiled and answered her unspoken question with a nod. Standing, she took his hand and moved toward the bed with him.

"Nana, your hopes were never dashed. Although we are far from perfect, James and I were married before we set sail. I will miss India, but England is my home now."

The dowager's eyes welled with tears of happiness as she looked from Randy to James, and then back again.

James laughed. For the first time that he could recall, the ever-exuberant and effusive Miranda Wentworth was speechless.

During the next few weeks, everyone at Mirage was kept busy getting ready to put "the plan" into motion. While Abu continued nursing the dowager back to health, Percival saw to the packing and travel arrangements. Jarita and several of the household maids helped a local modiste create an entire new wardrobe for Randy's grand entrance into London society, using some of the exquisite silks, cashmere wools, and satins Javid Kahn had brought to the ship on the day of their departure.

James sent word to the staff at his family's town home that he would be arriving by the end of the month with five guests for an extended visit. He wrote and prepared the announcements that would be delivered to all of the dailies the day before their arrival in London. A letter instructing Stephen to join them in town was also forwarded to his Ryland estate.

When the weather permitted, James rode over to the Graysons' estate at Foxwood with Randy so she could visit her pets.

Using a long leather leash, they took Sidra for walks through the neighboring forest. The wild cat seemed unaffected by the cold and enjoyed playing in the snow like an overgrown kitten.

Everything was going well with "the plan" until an argument about Sidra nearly stopped it from being carried out at all.

"I will not go to London for more than a week without Sidra, and that's final, James!" Randy paced the library in Mirage, the split skirt of her gold riding habit snapping against her legs. "If I am away too long and she doesn't see me, Sidra will escape and come to find me."

James leaned on the edge of the large desk and shook his head. "That's ridiculous, Randy. Sidra is a clever animal, but she certainly isn't capable of breaking out of a locked building and making her way to town. Do you have any idea how far away we are from London? Traveling time by coach is well over three hours."

Coming to an abrupt stop in front of him, Randy decided to explain her concern. "Besides the fact that tigers have an acute sense of smell and can successfully track prey over great distances, Sidra and I share a special relationship. Since I rescued her, she has become my self-appointed guardian. It was that loyalty and regard that led her to save my life when that murderer tried to kill me. She's only content if I am nearby."

James frowned. "I think Sidra can survive being separated from you for a few weeks. As long as she is fed and Xavier takes her out for exercise, she should be fine. You saw for yourself how well she's getting on living at Foxwood."

"You don't understand," Randy declared. "Sidra has only accepted her place there because I have been to see her nearly every day. When I was ill during the voyage and unable to visit her, Sidra almost tore her cage apart trying to get to me. If I stay away too long, I know she won't be easily appeased and she will find a means of coming after me. Then some fool armed with a gun will shoot her."

Marked by defeat, James rubbed the back of his neck. "Our plan may take weeks to come to fruition, and we certainly can't take Sidra to town with us. I suppose we have no choice other than to return to Foxwood every few days to see her.''

Randy rushed forward and threw herself into his arms. ''Thank you, James. I truly appreciate your kindness.'' She put a quick kiss on his cheek. ''You know, if we took Garuda and Ratri to town, the two of us could ride them and make those little trips in a fraction of the time it would take by coach.''

Pulling from their embrace, James scowled at her. ''I thought you understood the proprieties we must adhere to until our marriage is officially recognized. If Richard is to believe that we are only betrothed, then you and I cannot be seen going about without a proper chaperon. That is the only reason why I have agreed to take Nana along with us.''

''I know, I know. The silly *ton* and its ridiculous rules of behavior.'' Randy sighed, rolling her eyes. ''Why anyone would want to acquiesce to the dictates of such a group of snobs is beyond my comprehension.'' A sudden thought made her smile. ''We could avoid the need of a chaperon if I dressed as a man and—''

''No. I won't risk your safety that way.''

Randy struggled to contain her impatience over his denial. ''There would be no risk if we were careful. I could wear a beaver hat and a greatcoat just like yours. By leaving before dawn, staying away from the main roads and going cross-country, we would make good time and avoid being seen.''

His brow arched. ''What would you do if we were set upon by thieves? This isn't India, Randy. You won't be riding with a troop of imperial guards at your back.''

''For all the good they did! If the truth be known, I took better care of myself than those fool guards ever could,'' she boasted. ''When that cretin, Brandon Spencer, assaulted me, I tossed him flat on his back and broke his wrist. . . .''

The realization of what she had admitted pushed Randy into a strangled silence and left her wishing the floor beneath her feet would open up so she could escape. After carefully keeping that part of her life from James, she wasn't sure how she could explain it without shocking him with her unladylike prowess as a fighter. It was only then that she noticed that James was smiling at her.

"I forgot you knew I was the one who injured Spencer!" she gasped. "Who told you?"

"Akbar told me about that incident with the major and the training you both had as children in the Oriental arts, but I—"

More chagrined than angry, Randy moved away from James. "Why, that loathsome magpie! He couldn't keep a secret if his life depended on it." She crossed the room and stood at a window that overlooked the snow-covered gardens. "Now you know that your lady wife is flawed in yet another way."

Randy felt the welcome strength in the arms that James wrapped around her waist. She leaned against him and sighed. "I hope you're not too disappointed in me."

"I will only be disappointed if you don't show me that move you used on Spencer in the palace gardens." He playfully nuzzled her neck. "When I saw you throw him—"

"You saw me!" Randy spun around to face him. "What were you doing, spying on me?"

James pulled her back into his arms and kissed her forehead. "Not spying, sweetheart. Just attempting to protect the woman I had already decided to have for my own."

"And seeing how I thwarted Spencer's attentions didn't scare you away?"

He shook his head. "Absolutely not. As a point of fact, I became even more determined to make you mine after that."

His reply left Randy perplexed. "Why?"

"With all the desperate mothers of the *ton* looking for husbands for their daughters, I thought having you protecting my back would definitely be to my advantage," James said with a teasing wink. "Can I count on your help when we get to London, my lady, or will I be forced to fend for myself?"

Growling playfully, Randy put her arms around his neck and drew his face down to hers. "If one of those blighted females dares to come near you, I won't think twice to protect what is mine." She brushed her lips against his in a lingering kiss. A moment or so later, she asked, "Would you like me to teach you some of those Oriental defense lessons now?"

A hint of desire sparkled in his eyes as James shook his head. "Not now. I suddenly have a few lessons of my own that I would like to show you this evening. Are you interested?"

"Without a doubt," she purred. "Shall we go to my suite and get to work on furthering my education?"

James pulled Randy against him, cupping the curves of her derriere in his large hands. "Since the door is locked and a library is a place of learning, I suggest we stay right here."

When Randy smiled and nodded, he sighed. "Thank goodness. For the life of me, I don't think I could make it up the stairs if I had to wait any longer to do this."

James hungrily sealed Randy's mouth with his own.

On the rug before the blazing hearth, the two young lovers came together in a union that needed no teachers or lessons to be understood. Following nature's urging and the needs of their own passionate hearts, they attained perfection.

Chapter 15

The morning of their departure was cold and clear. The sun was shining, but it did little to allay the bitter nip of winter in the air. Their group consisted of the dowager's large traveling coach, a luggage wagon, and six men-at-arms on horseback. One of the grooms from Mirage also came along with Ratri and Garuda.

Randy was swamped with conflicting emotions. In spite of the comfort the spacious coach offered, with soft leather seats and foot-warmers, she felt closed in and would have preferred the freedom of riding her horse. A part of her was excited at finally getting to see the city of London, while she also dreaded the reality of coming face-to-face with her uncle, Richard.

James leaned over from his place by the window and whispered near her ear. "We still have another hour of traveling ahead of us. Why don't you try to nap like Nana and Jarita?"

Randy looked beside her and saw her grandmother dozing in the corner, the orange plume on her hat bouncing with each bump of the road. On the seat across from them, Jarita, enveloped in a thick wool cloak, was snoring softly with her head resting on Abu's shoulder as he read from a thin leather-bound book.

"I'm far too tense to sleep, James. Meditation usually helps, but even that ability is evading me at the moment."

James had his arm draped over her shoulder. He cuddled her close to him. "Why don't you relax and look out the window while I point out the sights we are passing?"

For quite some time, Randy was content to listen to James as he described the historical events that had taken place along their route. When she noticed that the blue sky overhead had suddenly turned into a murky gray, she asked him about it.

"James, is it my imagination, or has the sky gotten darker? Do you think we're in for another storm?"

"It's not a storm, Randy. We are just entering the outskirts of London. The gray comes from the soot and smoke of the city mixing with low-lying fog."

Randy leaned over and gazed through the window. "The sun is out, though you can barely see it through the haze. Is it always like this in London?"

James shook his head. "No, though it happens often enough. People tend to get used to it."

The closer they came to their destination, Randy saw more and more sights that surprised her. English citizens she had met in India over the years had constantly bragged about the beauty and grandeur of their beloved London. The drab skies, filthy streets, and crowded rows of tenement houses they passed had never been mentioned. The smells that wafted through the open windows were far from pleasant.

When Randy saw a group of children wearing dirty, tattered rags, playing barefoot in muddy water that ran along the gutter of the street, she shook her head sadly.

"This isn't much better than the ghetto in Calicut. How can people live in a place like this?"

James shrugged. "Perhaps like the poor in India, these people don't have a choice. Poverty is a worldwide problem. It can be found even in the richest countries of the world."

* * *

The Grayson town home was an impressive four-story mansion located in the finest area of London. Set well off the street, the stately gray residence had a circular drive, an evergreen maze, and manicured grounds.

Keeping up appearances for the benefit of the household servants, Randy and her grandmother were given a two-bedroom suite that shared a small, elegantly furnished sitting room. Abu and Jarita's accommodations were adjacent to theirs on the second floor wing reserved for special guests.

Following a sumptuous dinner, the dowager retired to bed while James took Randy on a tour of the house. After viewing the library, the drawing rooms, salons, and a ballroom that would have befitted the finest palace, they arrived in a gallery that contained the portraits of all the earls of Foxwood.

When they finally stood before the last painting, James held up his hand towards it. "And this is the current earl and countess of Foxwood, my parents, Miles and Catherine Grayson."

Unlike the rest of the portraits in the collection that showed people in formal poses in rich courtly attire, this painting depicted a smiling young couple who seemed far more concerned with their comfort than impressing anyone with their finery. The darkly handsome Miles Grayson was wearing an open-collared shirt; he leaned against a tree with his arm around his beautiful wife. Catherine's simple empire-waisted gown appeared to be a soft yellow muslin. Her long blond hair was unbound, tumbling over her shoulders like a golden waterfall of curls.

James laughed. "As you can see, my parents are rather unconventional, but I like them that way."

Randy didn't try to hide the awe in her voice. "They make such a magnificent couple. Are they as happy as they seem to be in this portrait?"

"More so, if that's possible. Theirs was a love match that has continued to grow over the years. Even after five children and an abundance of problems, my mother and father still act like a pair of young lovers when they are together.''

The mention of the Graysons' loving relationship reminded Randy of the strange circumstances of her own marriage. Driven by a need to protect her, James had not given her declarations of love when he proposed. During her illness, they had developed a close friendship. Then caring and desire took over, resulting in the passionate melding of their bodies. Their lusty encounters were incredible, but sadly they weren't enough. Randy longed to have more than her husband's body. She wanted his love.

Her attention returned to James when he slipped a ring on the third finger of her left hand. The large center stone, a square-cut emerald, was framed with white diamonds.

''This is the Ryland betrothal ring that has been in my family for generations. I know it can't compare with the jeweled brooch Nana gave you, but I hope you will wear it.''

Hearing the apprehension in his voice, Randy smiled. ''Of course I will wear it. I would be honored.''

James nodded. ''Good. That will help convince Richard that we are truly affianced. For this plan to succeed, we need to see that all these little details are taken care of.'' He missed seeing the crestfallen expression on Randy's face when he looked up and spied one of the footmen coming toward him.

''My lord, there is a messenger from your factor waiting to see you,'' the servant in blue and silver livery reported.

''Fine. Show him to the library and see to his comfort. I will be down momentarily.'' When the footman was out of sight, James drew Randy into his arms and sighed. ''Another new member of the staff I have never seen before. That's precisely why we can't sleep together. We must be mindful of everything we do, even in this house. A bit of gossip spread about by the servants could spoil our charade before we get a chance to trap your uncle.'' He gave her a quick kiss. ''Come along, sweetheart. As a dutiful gentleman, I will escort you back to your suite before I deal with the man waiting for me down-stairs.''

* * *

Randy was crossing the sitting room of her suite when she noticed the light shining from beneath the door of the dowager's room. Suddenly needing someone to talk to, she knocked on her grandmother's door. From the bright smile on the elderly woman's face when she entered, she was clearly pleased to see her.

"Do come in, my child. With all this work of catching Richard in his own web and preparing for this trip, we rarely have time to visit. We shall have some sherry and chat for a while, just the two of us."

Wearing a royal-blue robe trimmed with gold braid, Miranda Wentworth ushered Randy toward a pair of upholstered chairs near the fireplace. As the dowager filled two glasses with wine from the decanter on the console table, Randy smiled over the fact that her grandmother hardly resembled the pale, debilitated creature she had met several weeks before. From her bouncing curls, to the sparkling mirth in her eyes and the lightness of her step, everything about Nana now seemed vibrant and full of life.

"Now, tell me what brings you to my door," the dowager asked after handing Randy the wine and taking her own seat. When Randy didn't reply quickly enough, she continued, "I expect being newly married and having to stay away from your husband because of this plan isn't easy for either of you."

Randy shook her head. "It's not just that, Nana. Of course I will miss being with James, but . . . well, there's something more that is lacking in our relationship and I have no idea what to do about it." Sighing, she held up her left hand. "Just a few moments ago, James gave me this betrothal ring. It has been in his family for many years. Instead of sharing tender words that should be associated with such an event, he informed me that my wearing it was another important detail of this plan. As though the ring held no special significance to our marriage."

"Don't be too harsh on James, my dear. I suspect that ring evokes painful memories for him."

Randy frowned. "What are you referring to, Nana?"

The dowager took a sip of the amber wine and contemplated her reply for several moments before she spoke. "What I am about to tell you must remain between the two of us, Randy. If in the future, James tells you about this incident, I trust you will not let him know that I was the one who told you first."

When Randy nodded, Miranda began to speak. "Seven years ago, James came to London with his family. As a rule, he never enjoyed the parties or events of the *ton*, but it was his sister Diana's debut into society that brought him here that season. He knew Diana was ill at ease dealing with strangers, so he began escorting her around to the balls, teas, and gatherings. It was during one of those parties that James met Caroline Sutcliffe."

"James mentioned her once, but never gave me any details about her," Randy said. "What was she like?"

"Caroline was a very pretty girl with pale blond hair, blue eyes, and fine manners. Many people thought her countenance was that of an angel." The Dowager scowled with distaste. "Poor James fell in love with her at first sight. Like the rest of us, he didn't know demons came in such heavenly-looking packages."

The vehemence in her grandmother's voice made Randy ask, "What did Caroline do to James?"

"She used him to gain another man's attentions. All the while Caroline was flirting with James and encouraging him with her smiles and stolen kisses, she was putting on a show to gain a marriage proposal from a reluctant suitor, Aaron Wexler, Marquess of Montrose."

Randy sniffed indignantly. "James is very handsome and comes from an excellent family. That other man, Aaron, must have been very special if she chose him over James."

"What Aaron was, my child, was extremely wealthy. Wexler had barely passable looks, but he had made a fortune in mining, armaments, and foreign investments. Greed overrides many faults. Money-hungry Caroline wanted him in spite of his being over forty and having a foul temper.''

The dowager stared down into the glass she held in her hand. ''Caroline fooled everyone. James had no idea what the chit was about. He worshiped Caroline and decided he was going to call on her father, Viscount Hedly, to offer for her hand in marriage. But first, James wanted to propose to her in a very romantic way. His parents were away on business, so James asked me for advice.''

''A romantic proposal? I can hardly credit we are discussing my husband, the cool and pragmatic James Grayson.''

Miranda's saddened gaze fixed on the embers glowing in the hearth. '' 'Twas all that witch's doing. Back then, James was trusting and eager to love. After the blow Caroline struck to his ego, I worried that he would never be able to put his faith in anyone ever again.''

Randy leaned forward and patted her grandmother's hand. ''Go on, Nana. Tell me the rest of it.''

''Your grandfather and I were holding a ball for a visiting dignitary. It was arranged for James to take Caroline out to the garden terrace shortly before midnight while I stood watch at the French doors. From there, I could act as a chaperon for their meeting, while keeping others from intruding on them. The roses were in bloom and a string quartet was playing music from behind the hedge. The moon was full and the stars sparkled like the row of diamonds on the Ryland betrothal ring that James had tucked away in his waistcoat pocket.''

The dowager sighed. ''Caroline looked quite lovely in a gown of pale-blue silk when James led her out to the terrace that night. I couldn't hear what was said, but I saw James take the ring from his pocket and slip it on her hand. Caroline looked away for a moment, her attention fixed on the far end of the terrace. A second later, she threw herself into James's arms and kissed him. It was then I noticed a massive figure stepping out from the shadows of the house.'' Miranda shivered. ''Dark and foreboding, Aaron Wexler looked totally enraged as he rushed toward James and jerked Caroline from his arms. A terrible fight ensued, and heated words were exchanged. A duel was scheduled for the next morning.''

"A duel?" Randy gasped. "I thought such things were illegal.''

"They are, but that doesn't stop an ardent young man bent on defending a lady's honor or an older gent needing to punish the man who cuckolded him from meeting at dawn over a pair of dueling pistols.'' The dowager sipped her wine. "Your grandfather agreed to act as James's second, but he gave me quite an argument about my attending the duel. As usual with the duke, I got my way. In thinking back, I wish I had not.''

Randy felt the knot in her stomach growing tighter. She wanted to know about James and the woman in his past, but she dreaded it as well. Unable to stay seated, Randy got up and carried her untouched glass of wine to the tray on the console table as her grandmother continued speaking.

"James was bruised and a bit battered that morning, yet he looked very proud standing there in the meadow. From my coach, I saw Caroline among the very small group of spectators who had come to witness the event. As the one challenged, Aaron chose pistols, and sooner than I would have liked, the two men were positioned back to back, and the count of ten paces was begun. In his anxiety, Aaron turned on nine and fired. His shot would have caught James squarely in the back, but being a heavy man, he slipped on the wet grass and his aim was off.''

Randy let out the breath she was holding. "Was James hurt?"

"Only slightly. The shot nicked the top of his left arm. When he spun around to face his opponent, James moved his hand toward his wound and the gun he held went off by accident. Thanks to a faulty firing mechanism on the pistol and Aaron's hulking size, the shot found its way into Wexler's right shoulder. A blossom of crimson red erupted on his white shirt as he fell to the ground.''

"James wasn't punished by the authorities for the incident, was he?"

The elderly lady morosely shook her head. "No, though what transpired next was far worse. Caroline ran to Aaron and cradled his head in her lap while the doctor tended his wounds. When James came forward to see how Wexler fared, Caroline called him vile names and damned his soul to the devil. In front of everyone assembled, she told James he was a silly fool, that she had never loved him, that her affections were naught but a sham to get Aaron jealous. She yanked the betrothal ring from her finger and threw at him, saying she wanted to be a wife to a real man with his own fortune, not a young pup who needed his family's wealth to live on."

The dowager dashed a tear from her cheek with her hand. "I can still see James standing there in the pale morning light, a look of shock and heart-wrenching pain etched on his handsome features." She shook her head. "The assault on his pride was devastating. James was never the same after that. The gentle, caring dreamer he had been was gone. A hard-driven realist, bent on being a success on his own, took his place. I was hoping your marriage would lessen his pain and bring James back to himself again."

Moving toward the window, Randy pulled back the drape. The sky was dark and starless beyond the frost-covered pane, the view much like the gaping void in her heart. It was obvious that the emotional block she had sensed in James had been caused by the betrayal of Caroline Sutcliffe. For the pain to have been so great, he must have loved the beautiful young woman very much.

"Nana, I wouldn't count on James changing because of me or our marriage. Our union was a necessity, not the product of an all-healing love."

"But James loves you, my child," the dowager insisted. "I can see it in the way he looks at you. The man's in love with you."

Stepping away from the window, Randy shook her head. "If

you see anything, Nana, it's a healthy bit of old-fashioned lust. Don't misunderstand. James treats me very well. He is friendly, loyal, and dependable. It's just that the word love doesn't seem to have a place in his vocabulary.''

"You love James, don't you, Randy?"

Randy bit on her lower lip and nodded. ''Yes, Nana, I love him very much.''

The Dowager studied her granddaughter's face. ''Something tells me that you have never told James about your feelings. Why won't you tell the man you love him?''

"I couldn't do that to him," Randy said shaking her head. ''Our marriage was supposed to be a temporary way of protecting me from Richard, but my illness on board ship and the circumstances it caused drew us together. It trapped James in a marriage he didn't want or need, to a woman he barely knew. I won't force him into returning my words of love because he feels obligated to appease me.''

"But my child, I know James—"

Randy held up her hand. ''Please, Nana, I don't want to talk about this anymore. Perhaps someday James will be able to tell me he loves me. Until then, I will accept what he has to offer and I shall make the best of our relationship.''

The dowager smiled. ''All right, my child, we will do things your way. But soon you're going to see that I am correct and it will give me the greatest pleasure to say that I told you so.''

The next morning, James and Randy were in the drawing room with the dowager discussing invitations that had arrived since their engagement notice appeared in the dailies, when Abu came in to announce a visitor.

He closed the door behind him and bowed. ''Lady Maidstone is here. I instructed your man, Fenton, to remove her wrap and show her in after I informed you of her arrival.''

"What's Aunt Amelia doing in London?" Randy asked.

James shrugged and patted her hand. ''We'll soon see. Just

remember, Amelia doesn't know that we are married. With our plan already in motion, it wouldn't do to have that news bandied about by anyone."

Randy scowled. "Amelia isn't just anyone. In spite of her marriage to Richard, she's been a good friend to Nana."

"It's because of her connection to your uncle that we must be especially careful around her," James explained as he stood up in preparation for greeting their visitor. "As I told you before, I doubt Amelia would ever willingly forsake us, but what if Richard forces her to reveal what she knows? The less she knows, the better off we all shall be."

Randy was still frowning when Amelia came into the drawing room wearing a veiled hat. Her look of irritation became one of concern when Amelia lifted the tulle netting from her face and revealed a colorful bruise on her swollen jaw.

"Oh, Aunt Amelia!" she gasped. "What happened to you?"

The dowager rushed forward and took hold of Amelia's arm. "I'll wager that devil of a husband has put his hands on her again. Come, sit beside me on the sofa, Amelia dear. We can send for tea."

Perched on the edge of her seat, the duchess shook her head. "Forgive me, Miranda, but I can't stay for refreshments. I simply wanted to tell you all what Richard has been up to before I return to the country. With my husband in such a rage, I cannot risk remaining in town a second longer than I have to."

Randy sat down on the sofa next to Amelia and looked at her damaged face. "Did Richard do this to you?"

Amelia touched the side of her jaw with her gloved hand and offered Randy a weak smile. "It really looks far worse than it feels, but yes, the duke did this to me last night."

Her pale-blue gaze turned to James, who was seated close to Randy. "You were correct about Richard, my lord. As soon as he learned of his niece's presence in England and her betrothal to you, he flew into quite a rage. The library of our townhouse is in shambles. He summoned me from Maidstone

Manor and demanded to know why I hadn't informed him of the news myself. When I tried to deny having any such knowledge, the duke called me a liar and struck me several times. He spent the night drinking himself into a stupor. His temper is so volatile, I fear for my life.''

James ignored the *I told you so* glare he was getting from his wife and spoke to the trembling woman in comforting tones. ''I am truly sorry you were put into such danger, Amelia. I never suspected the duke would try to implicate you in this. Why don't you come and stay with us until all of this is over? While you are here, I can see that you are well protected from him.''

''I appreciate the kind offer, my lord, but I have already made other arrangements. My old friend, Beryl, has a small estate in Dorset that Richard knows nothing about. Using some funds I had set aside, I hired a coach and driver to take me there. My new maid and I will be leaving within the hour.''

The dowager sniffed with indignation. ''The injustice of it all! My stepson is the criminal and you're the one who must flee. Why, if I were a man, I would shoot the bounder myself and be done with it!''

''Now, Miranda, you must calm yourself and accept the fact that I have no choice but to leave London until all this is resolved,'' Amelia said, patting her arm. ''Staying here with you would only endanger everyone else. I simply cannot allow that to happen.''

Amelia drew a piece of folded parchment from her drawstring purse and handed it to James. ''Here is a list of my husband's social engagements that I copied from his appointment book early this morning. As you can see, Richard plans on going to several balls and receptions during the next few days. This evening, he will be attending the opening gala at the opera. If you still intend to confront him in a public place, any of these events should suffice.''

James looked at the list and gave it to Randy. ''We have

invitations to all these parties as well as the use of my family's private box at the opera house.''

The dowager nodded. ''The opera would be a splendid place to begin your assault on my stepson. Everyone who is anyone in the *ton* will be there.''

''Nana, I never realized seeing an opera would be such a popular pastime. Are most members of the *ton* music lovers?''

Miranda chuckled. ''You misunderstand, my dear. The value of the occasion has nothing to do with viewing the production. The importance lies in seeing what's going on among those attending the event. At an opening such as this, more time is spent gossiping than actually listening to the music.'' The Dowager turned to James. ''Your parents' box is directly across from Richard's. My stepson will be very aware of our presence in the theater this evening.''

At that moment, the clock on the mantel chimed, marking the noon hour. Amelia leaned over and gave the dowager a hug and a kiss on the cheek. ''I must be off, Miranda. Richard should be awake now and I want to be well away from here by the time he leaves the house this afternoon. I will get word to you after I have settled in with Beryl.''

After Amelia departed, the dowager dropped back against the sofa, shaking her head. ''What that poor woman has had to put up with being married to my stepson is beyond belief. No one deserves the kind of cruelty Richard metes out on her, Randy.''

''Then why hasn't Amelia left him before this?''

Miranda sighed. ''And where is she to go? Amelia and her brother were orphaned as children and raised by their uncle, a cash-poor baron from Faversham. The old man died years ago and her brother is in the army, serving at some outpost in the East. I offered to help her financially so she could start a new life for herself, but Amelia is too proud to accept charity.''

''A divorce seems far more sensible than remaining married to a man who seems intent on killing you.''

James reached over from his seat and gave Randy's hand a

consoling squeeze. "Obtaining a divorce isn't an easy thing. The grounds are limited and the costs are high. Besides, Richard is a duke and it would take an act of Parliament to get one."

Randy was incensed. "But the man brutalizes her! You saw the bruises on her face. God knows what damage Amelia had hidden beneath her gown. He should be arrested for what he's done."

"As unfair as it sounds, sweetheart, the law is on Richard's side in this. I don't agree with it, but according to English law, a man has the legal right to beat his wife. Richard could be fined by a magistrate for abusing his horse, but beating his wife simply isn't a crime."

"All my life I've been told that England has the finest law and justice system in the world. If this is an example of it, then it is highly overrated." Randy scowled. "I suppose if Richard beats Amelia to death, he would get away with that too."

James shook his head. "No, he would be arrested and put on trial for her murder."

"At long last, something a husband can be prosecuted for," Randy snapped caustically. "The victimized wife would be dead, but justice, as dictated by this moronic society, would be served."

Without warning, Randy stood up and moved toward the door. "If you both will excuse me, I have to go up to my room so I can select my ensemble for this evening. The sooner we trap Richard for a crime he can be punished for without additional harm to his wife, the better."

Standing beside the doorway as Randy hurried out, Abu nodded to James. "As you see, *Huzur,* the golden fire is bright in my mistress's eyes again. Guard her well tonight and do not let her temper endanger her life or your own."

Before James could question the old Indian's strange warning, Abu bowed and quickly followed his mistress up the stairs.

Chapter 16

"The theater is much bigger than I imagined it would be, Nana. I've never seen anything quite like it." Seated in the Graysons' private box beside her grandmother, Randy looked over the rail at the well-dressed crowd filling the auditorium. "The cost of the jewels and clothes these people are wearing would add up to a sizable fortune."

"It's the way things are done, my dear. Everyone tries to outshine everyone else to gain attention." The dowager waved the lace-trimmed hanky that matched her peach-colored gown, greeting a friend in an adjacent box. "That is why I insisted that you wear my diamond necklace and earrings tonight with your new emerald gown. With your bright auburn curls and beauty, every eye in the place will be on you."

Feeling suddenly embarrassed, Randy turned toward James and found him glaring at someone across the theater.

"If that blasted fop in the ruffled shirt over there doesn't stop staring at you with those blasted opera glasses, I am going to shove them down his throat."

Randy patted his hand. "Now, James, don't take on so. He is probably trying to decide if my jewels are real or paste."

James looked at the bit of cleavage revealed by the fitted bodice of her gown and scowled. "That man is more likely trying to determine if certain parts of *you* are real or paste." Leaning toward her, he muttered angrily, "Why did the seamstress make that neckline so bloody low? One good sneeze and your breasts will be out on display! For all I paid that modiste, the least she could have done was see that your gowns fit you properly."

The jealous tone of his words caused Randy's heart to beat rapidly. Tamping down her excitement, she smiled and tried to reassure him. "My gown is not too low. Nana and the modiste both said this style was the very height of fashion. And as for that man staring at me, let him. When we finally face down Uncle Richard, he can be one of the witnesses. It must be done this way if we are to succeed."

James took her gloved hand and entwined his fingers with hers. His eyes sparkled as he smiled at her. "It may help our plan, but that doesn't mean I have to like it. I never realized that using you as pretty bait would bother me so much."

"Pretty bait?" Randy teased. "If that is your best attempt at a compliment, then you better try again, my lord. Comparing one to an attractive bucket of worms or chopped-up fish surely doesn't qualify as a statement of high praise."

"So it's praise you're after. Well, let me see, surely there is something about you that merits such things."

"James, I wasn't asking for compliments."

Ignoring her objections, James lowered his brow and studied her. "The color of your ensemble is quite lovely, though the cut of the gown reveals too much of a figure that belongs to me alone. Your hair is nicely coiffed into a cluster of curls on the top of your head, but I think it looks much better fanned out against my bare chest after we—"

Randy clapped her fingers on his mouth. "All right, I admit

I wanted to hear your compliments, but don't tease me about it.''

James pulled her hand from his mouth and kissed it. "No more teasing, sweetheart. I know full well I am with the most beautiful woman in the theater. The thought that other men are looking at you has a tendency to irritate me.''

"I know exactly what you mean, my lord," she sighed. "Being with the handsomest man here tends to set my teeth on edge too. I wish you didn't look so outrageously attractive in your formal attire. It only adds to my discomfort when all the ladies gape so longingly at you.''

"Now you're exaggerating, sweetheart. I haven't noticed any women turning my way.''

"How could you when you were so busy glowering at all the men looking at me? There were a half-dozen females in the lobby alone who were drooling over you when we passed them." When James rolled in eyes in disbelief, Randy sniffed. "So you doubt what I'm saying. Fine, just give me a moment and I will prove it to you.''

Randy turned in her seat and looked out over the crowded theater until she found one of the women she had described. "The blonde wearing blue in the box across the way was among those in the lobby. She hasn't taken her gaze off you since she sat down and spied you sitting beside me. If that's not admiration or lust in her pretty blue eyes, then I don't know what is.''

Shaking his head, James playfully squeezed her hand and sought out the woman Randy had directed his attention to. A second later, Randy winced in pain when his hand clenched hard around hers. She pulled her hand free of his hold.

"James, what's the matter? Do you know her?''

At that moment, the dowager nudged Randy. "There he is at long last. My stepson has finally arrived. It really is too bad that Richard inherited his father's good looks and none of his wonderful temperament.''

The woman in blue was forgotten when Randy turned to

meet the stormy gaze of the man staring at her. Even at a distance, she knew the attractive gentleman with graying dark hair was Richard Wentworth, the Duke of Maidstone.

Randy wanted to move closer to James, but thinking her uncle would view it as a weakness, she stayed seated as she was. With her head held high and her eyes firmly linked with his, she offered the duke her most beguiling smile.

Richard's brow lifted and he gave her a curt nod. One of his companions drew his attention to the guests sitting in his box and the duke took his own seat just as the orchestra began playing the overture.

It was then Randy noticed that the woman in blue was among the eight people in her uncle's box and that James was still looking at her. Randy leaned toward her grandmother and whispered. "Nana, who is the woman in blue sitting with Richard's party? Do you know her?"

The dowager raised her opera glasses. A gasp escaped her lips. "Why, that's Caroline Sutcliffe, or I should say Caroline Wexler. Montrose hasn't been dead a year and already the chit is on the prowl again. I wonder which of Richard's friends she's set her sights on this time."

Randy felt the blood suddenly draining from her face. She suspected Caroline's expectations didn't involve any of her uncle's friends. From the undisguised expression on her face, the man who had taken her interest was James Grayson. And from the way James was looking back at the pretty blonde, the interest was definitely shared.

Randy turned to the stage as the curtains parted, but she was too numb with pain to appreciate the colorful scenery or the performance of the singers. Even when James draped his arm around the back of her chair and pulled her closer to him, she could not take comfort in his embrace.

Disparity over what might have been enveloped her like a shroud. How could she ever hope to gain James's love when it was obvious that he cared for another? That part of his emotions he had kept deeply hidden from her was not pain, as she had once guessed. No matter what Caroline had done to him in the past, it was very apparent to Randy that James still loved her.

It was during the intermission, while standing in the lobby sipping lemonade, that Randy forced herself to talk to James about Caroline. "Nana told me the lady in blue was Caroline, the woman you courted years ago. Did you know she was a widow?"

James downed his glass of wine and shook his head. "No, but I'm not surprised that Wexler's dead. With a woman like Caroline about, death would be a welcome retreat." He put his glass on a passing waiter's tray and slid his arm around Randy's waist. "Your uncle is coming this way. From the set of his jaw, I don't think he is in the best of moods."

"Good," Randy replied through clenched teeth hidden behind a smile. "I am fed up with this entire charade. The quicker this is resolved, the better I will like it. Did you see where Nana went? I don't think she wants to be left out of this."

The dowager suddenly appeared at her side. "I am right here, my child. I was just gathering a bit of gossip from Lady Trusdale and her sister, Elizabeth. We will discuss what I have learned later. Right now we have other business to—" Miranda's voice abruptly took on an overly bright tenor. "Why, Richard, seeing you here this evening was quite a surprise. I had no idea you would be attending the opera."

The Duke of Maidstone took his stepmother's proffered hand and brought it to his lips. "You are looking very well, madam. It's good to see your recent bout of influenza hasn't robbed us of your lively presence here tonight." He looked at Randy and smiled. His hand lightly touched her cheek. "Even without an introduction, I would know you anywhere, my dear. Though your hair is darker, you have Lenore's face. Your Mama would be so proud if she could see you now, Miranda Juliet."

Randy swallowed back the tightness in her throat. "I am called Randy, your grace, not Miranda. I was honored to be named for my grandmother, but I wanted a name distinctly my own.''

Richard chuckled. ''An independent miss, not unlike your grandmother. Then Randy it is.'' He picked up her hand and kissed it. ''Welcome to England, my dear.''

''Thank you, your grace.''

''No formalities are needed between us, my dear. You are my sister's child. I would deem it a true privilege if you would address me as Uncle Richard.''

It took all of Randy's control not to cringe when the Duke kissed her forehead. Forcing a smile, she nodded, ''Thank you, Uncle Richard.''

The duke turned to James, and his brow rose over his deep-set hazel eyes. ''Well, now I get to meet the young man who captured my niece's heart. Viscount Ryland, I was told it was your ship that brought our dear child home to her family.''

James smiled, the warmth of the gesture never reaching his eyes. ''Yes, your grace. Though I must admit my reasons for bringing her to England were selfish ones. I fell in love with your niece in India and decided to make her my wife. When my parents return from America in a week or two, Randy and I are going to be married. We hope you can attend the ceremony.''

''But why so soon?'' the duke inquired with an air of disdain. ''My niece has just returned to the bosom of her family, and here you are rushing her off to be married. Are you afraid, if given time, my niece will reconsider your proposal and find another man to wed?''

''Someone like Brandon Spencer?''

The duke frowned at James. The expression in his eyes was cool and unreadable. ''Brandon Spencer? I have no idea who you are talking about. Is this Spencer someone my niece has met since she arrived here in England?''

''I know full well that you don't approve of our betrothal,'' James continued. ''Word has it that you read the notices in the dailies and destroyed your library in a fit of temper.''

"And who was the source of this slanderous bit of gossip? My wife?" Richard chuckled and shook his head. "If you give credence to anything that troublesome woman says, you're a bigger fool than I thought."

"The bruises on Amelia's jaw speak for themselves."

"Amelia is clumsy and loses her balance. I certainly can't be held accountable because she injures herself on occasion."

James sneered. "Tell me, your grace, do you get much pleasure out of beating your wife?"

Richard's face flushed, and his voice rose with irritation. "Grayson, you don't know what you are getting involved in. My dealings with Amelia have nothing to do with you, so just stay away from her. You would be wise not to ignore my warning."

"Why? Are you threatening me, your grace?"

The duke leaned forward and spoke in a husky whisper to James. "It's not a threat, you impertinent pup, but a solemn vow. If you side with Amelia, you will regret it."

Hoping to use her gift of sensing pain and emotions in others, Randy reached out and touched Richard. She could feel the tension in his arm, but little else. Only the flexing of his taut muscles beneath her fingers and the memories of Amelia's battered face reminded her that in spite of his well-mannered demeanor, Richard Wentworth was a very dangerous man.

In a dismissive gesture, the duke turned away from James. He smiled and patted Randy's hand. "I really must be going, my dear. My guests will think I have deserted them. Should you ever need my help, please feel free to call on me at any time."

As Richard made his way through the crowded lobby, Randy sagged against James's embrace. "That man makes me nervous. How can he stand there and act so pleasant to me when we know what he's capable of?"

"My stepson is a master at pretense," the dowager explained. "As long as Richard values his status in the *ton*, he must adhere to their strict code of behavior when he is in public. With so many of them in attendance tonight, he had no choice but to be civil. Congratulations, James, on being the first person I've ever seen to put a chink in my stepson's social armor."

James sighed with disgust. "It galls me that the duke could be the Devil's own disciple in the privacy of his own home, but as long as he uses proper manners, dresses well, and is seen with the right people, his position in polite society is assured."

"Come along, children," the dowager ordered, turning toward the stairs that led to the private boxes. "The next act is about to begin and I don't want to miss a minute of it."

Randy took hold of James's arm and rushed to catch up with her grandmother. "I had no idea you were such a devotee of Mozart's music, Nana."

The dowager laughed. "Can't stand it! The performance I am concerned with is going to take place in the box across from us. Watching my stepson maintain his facade is a far better comedy than anything we might see on the stage. I wager he will crumble under the pressure and leave before the final curtain call."

A windy rainstorm had started by the time the opera was over. The well-dressed assembly quickly became a crowd of angry, sodden people as they pushed their way toward the line of waiting carriages at the curb.

James shook his head. Water dripped from the curved brim of his beaver hat. "I knew we should have left the moment your uncle departed at the beginning of the third act. The last thing your grandmother needs right now is a bout with pneumonia."

Pressed against the wall of the building to avoid the wind, Randy held her fur-trimmed hood over her head. "Stop worrying, James. Nana is busy chatting with her friends in the lobby."

"You should have stayed inside with her. There's no reason why the two of us should be wet and cold."

She snuggled closer to him. "I am fine. The rain has eased off and my cloak is quite warm."

James frowned. "I know, sweetheart, but I don't want to risk your health." He kissed her forehead. "Go stay with Nana. I will come for you when our carriage is here."

Randy nodded and moved back toward the doors of the theater. She had only taken a few steps when a female voice caught her attention and caused her to turn around.

"James Grayson? Is that really you?"

A cloaked figure was rushing toward James. The wind caught the woman's hood and revealed a fluffy cap of golden curls. Even before James acknowledged the woman or said her name, Randy knew the identity of the pretty lady smiling up at him.

"Good evening, Caroline," he said in a detached, formal tone. "I didn't expect to see you this evening."

Caroline laughed nervously. "No one did. I just couldn't stand another minute of staying in the country."

James looked around at the milling crowd. "I heard a rumor earlier that Montrose had passed away. Is it true?"

"Yes. My husband died ten months ago and the title went to his brother, Giles. I am no longer Marchioness of Montrose," Caroline admitted with a sad smile.

"You have my condolences. I had no idea your husband was in poor health."

"Aaron's health was fine," she sighed. "It was his foul temper that did him in. He got into a terrible row with some business associates that led to fisticuffs. Afterward, Aaron got drunk and was thrown from his horse while he was riding home. He broke his neck and died instantly."

"That doesn't surprise me. I learned firsthand that Wexler was a bully and a hothead."

Tears filled Caroline's eyes. She grasped his arms with her hands. "Oh, James, I am so sorry for what I did to you back then. My father was in a financial bind and I thought having a wealthy husband would solve everything. I wanted Aaron to get jealous so he would propose to me, not challenge you to a duel.''

James visibly stiffened at her touch. "Tell me, Caroline, did marrying Aaron solve your problems?"

She shook her head, loosening some of her golden curls to fall around her face in disarray. "No. For all his wealth and claims of wanting me, Aaron was miserly in sharing his wealth and affection. He stopped me from seeing my family, insisting I needed no one but him." Caroline wiped the tears from her face. "I wasn't a cherished wife, but a beautiful trophy he could show off to his friends. You can celebrate the fact that my marriage to Aaron brought me nothing but sorrow, James."

Pain shot through Randy when James put his arm around the sobbing woman. Until that moment he had appeared irritated and aloof, but Caroline's misery seemed to have dissolved his anger. After seeing him stare at his former love in the theater, this display was more than she could handle without trying to do something about it. Carefully hiding her vexation, she hurried back to her husband's side.

"James, darling, is this lady feeling sick? If she's not well, bring her into the lobby while we send for a physician."

Brushing the dampness from her cheeks with her gloved hand, Caroline turned to Randy and shook her head. "That will not be necessary, my lady. I apologize for letting my emotions get the better of me."

An expression that looked like relief passed over James's face. "Sweetheart, I would like you to meet an old acquaintance of mine, Caroline Wexler. Lady Montrose, may I present my betrothed, Miranda Collins." He put an arm around Randy and drew her close to him. "Caroline was just telling me how her husband died last year."

Randy reached over to pat Caroline's hand. "You have my sympathies, my lady. If there's anything we can do for you during these trying times, please feel free to call upon us."

"Why ... ah, thank you." Caroline seemed jittery as she

cast a look over her shoulder. "There is a matter I need to discuss with James, but my friends are waiting and it would be wrong to delay them. I will call on you in a few days."

As Caroline disappeared into the crowd, Randy pulled herself away from James and spoke to him in a barely controlled whisper. "It was bad enough watching you moon over her in the theater without having to see her draped all over you like that. Has that woman no morals, no pride?"

James chuckled and appeared quite smug. "Your jealousy warms me, sweetheart, but it's quite unnecessary. Caroline means nothing to me. She was just a woman whom I attended a few parties with years ago."

Randy didn't want to betray her grandmother's trust, so she withheld her knowledge of his past with Caroline and offered him another explanation for her anger.

"Jealousy has nothing to do with this," she explained in a low voice while attempting to smile at an elderly matron who was staring at them. "If you really want this plan to work, we must appear to be a happily betrothed couple. I doubt that tear-wrenching reunions with your former lady friends will signify as acceptable behavior by the *ton* or my uncle."

James frowned. "I have done nothing to endanger our plan, Randy. Caroline was the one who—"

"Isn't that our carriage just pulling up to the curb?" Randy asked curtly, effectively cutting off his explanation. "I will go and get Nana."

When she tried to walk away, James grabbed her arm. His voice was low, but definitely tinged with anger. "Deny it if you like, sweetheart, but I know that you're piqued over Caroline's presence here tonight. What must I do to convince you that she doesn't mean a thing to me?"

Randy yanked her arm free. Thoughts of their plan and protecting Nana's trust were eclipsed by a fury that suddenly overwhelmed her common sense. "A good dose of pure truth would certainly help."

"What are you talking about?" James demanded, pulling her back to his side.

A crack of gunfire rang out a split second before the shot hit the brick wall next to them. Women screamed and people scattered as James pushed Randy to the ground and covered her body with his own. When no additional shots were fired, he helped her to stand and took her into his arms.

"My lord!" Henry, the Graysons' footman, cried out as he ran toward them through the melee, "the shooter got away on horseback. With the darkness and all the coaches penning us in, we couldn't go after him. We didn't even see his face. I'm very sorry, milord."

"That's all right, Henry. It couldn't be helped. Fetch the dowager from the lobby and see her safely to our carriage. We will be there shortly." While the footman went to carry out his orders, James hugged Randy to him and gave her a quick kiss that was filled with relief.

"Damn it all, I never thought your uncle would attempt to kill me this quickly." Studying the shattered brick near his shoulder, James stroked Randy's cheek with his fingers. "By God, that ball could have struck you! If you had been hurt, I would have torn that bloody bastard to shreds."

"Do you really think Richard fired that shot?"

James shook his head. "Not him personally, but one of his paid minions could have carried out the deed for him. The duke left the theater in plenty of time to arrange this." He put his arm around Randy's shoulder. "Come along, sweetheart. If this is an indication of how desperate your uncle is, we may have to reconsider our plans."

Moments later, as their carriage pulled out onto the street, a plain black coach with its curtains drawn passed them going the other way. The woman sitting beside the window peaking out at the Graysons' coach muttered angrily to her male companion.

"I can't believe that fool you hired made such a muck of this. After all I went through to set things up properly, that idiot missed the target. Now James Grayson will be more on his guard than ever."

"Patience, my pet. We have waited this long, a few more days won't make much of a difference."

Shaking her head in the darkness, the woman scoffed at his words. "Since you failed before, forgive me if I find it difficult to share in your confidence."

"Of course I'm confident. I suddenly realized that we've been going about this all wrong, my pet." His gloved hand reached across the seat and patted hers. "Killing our prey would solve certain problems, but with the courts and other delays, it would take months to get our hands on the money we need. Rather than strike down our quarry, I suggest you and I remove it to a place of our choosing and hold it for ransom."

"A kidnapping? Won't that be dangerous?"

He shrugged. "Not if it's done properly."

"Even if the ransom is paid, won't we have to worry about being identified?"

"The only one who will be able to identify us will be dead. I look forward to putting that particular problem out of my life, once and for all."

The coach hit a rut in the road, causing the man to groan in discomfort. "Next time I hire a coach, remind me to find one with better springs, my pet. My old bones can't take much more of this rattling about."

"Have no fear, my love. When we get back to my lodgings, I will make you feel better, just like always."

The anticipation had the man smiling into the darkness.

Chapter 17

Over the next few days, James escorted Randy and the dowager to many parties, teas, and functions around London, hoping to cross paths with the Duke of Maidstone once again. He even went out on his own to the clubs Richard frequented, as well as the horse auction at Tattersall's the man always attended, but it was all to no avail. Richard Wentworth was nowhere to be found.

"The duke must know we're on to him and is keeping out of sight for a while." James crossed the salon of Randy's suite and dropped onto the settee beside her. "I just wish I could think of a way to bring him out of his lair."

Abu handed him a cup of tea and stood next to the dowager's chair. "The best way to trap a hungry animal is to offer him a reward he is not likely to find on his own, *Huzur*. Her grace and I have been discussing the matter, and we may have come up with a solution. You and my mistress will be married on Saturday morning."

"But that's only three days away," Randy pointed out. "How can we stage such an event in such a short period of time?"

The dowager smiled. "I have already seen to everything. Thanks to my solicitors and the staff, the license, invitations, bishop, church, wedding breakfast, even the ball on Friday night have been taken care of."

"Do you think your stepson will attend the ball Friday night?" James asked. "No one has seen the man in days."

"Richard will be here," the dowager boasted. "We are going to use his position in the *ton* and his facade of following its proprieties to our advantage. Once the announcement appears in the papers tomorrow, stating that he will be escorting his niece down the aisle for the ceremony, he will have no choice but to attend the ball. As Randy's only male kin, it is his duty to be there."

Abu nodded. "The hired guards who have been following you about and seeing to your protection these past few days can be dressed as footmen during the party. If the duke or one of his men try to assault you this time, *Huzur,* we will be ready."

"And what am I to do in the meantime?" James inquired with a frown. "Just stay in the house and wait until Friday night?"

"We can go to Foxwood and take some of the guards with us," Randy declared. "I have not seen Sidra in nearly a week. Unless I visit her soon, I'm afraid my pet will come looking for me. If we take the horses, we can be there and back again within a day."

When James was hesitant in replying, Randy thought of a way to win his agreement. "If you like, we could stay the night there and return early Friday morning." She leaned forward and whispered near his ear. "Or doesn't being alone with me for an entire night interest you, husband mine?"

James smiled, and his ominous mood quickly brightened. "As a good captain, I know when I'm being out-maneuvered. All right, we will leave in the morning. Since Nana and Abu have everything in hand, we may as well make good use of our time."

                        * * *

The ride to the Grayson family's ancestral estate was blessed by sunshine and unseasonably warm weather. Later that night, after enjoying a delicious meal and touring the manor, James and Randy curled up on a rug in front of the fireplace in his room, discussing Sidra and the events of their day.

"Xavier told me Sidra hasn't been in the best of moods lately." Randy leaned back into her husband's arms. "He takes her for walks several times a day, but she's restless. She probably misses her freedom."

James kissed the frown line on her forehead. "I think Sidra was just lonely for you, sweetheart. The moment that beast saw you this morning, she began rolling around on the floor, playing like a kitten. When we get her to my Ryland holdings, I'm sure she will be content."

"Why? Does your estate have a warmer climate?"

"No, the weather's the same, but the area around the estate consists of forests and raw land. The few neighbors I have are not going to mind your pets, especially when they see what I . . . ah . . ." Realizing he had almost revealed his surprise of the huge greenhouse for her animals, James feigned a long, drawn-out yawn. "Sorry," he said stretching his arms. "I must be more tired than I thought. We had better get ready for bed before I fall asleep here on the floor."

Randy grabbed his shirt as he stood up. "Wait one minute, my lord, and finish what you were saying. Why are you so sure that your neighbors aren't going mind my pets?"

James pulled Randy to her feet and drew her into his arms. "Once they see what a lovely lady I have taken as my wife, the lot of them will forget everything, but that."

There were no more questions or objections when he captured her mouth in a deep, arousing kiss. With the servants dismissed, and no one about to witness their sleeping arrangements, James was determined to make up for the nights he had been deprived of Randy's welcome presence in his bed.

Clothes were quickly removed and tossed aside as they made their way across the room. Lips and mouths fused together while their tongues tasted and explored each other with sensual abandon.

James lifted Randy onto the bed, covering her with his larger, muscular form. "Oh God, I have missed this," he moaned. "Your skin feels like warm silk rubbing against my flesh."

"You sound as though we've been apart for months," Randy laughed, "not just a few days."

"Days, weeks, months," he said, nuzzling her neck with his mouth, "is irrelevant to me. Without you in my arms, any amount of time is an eternity."

Randy sighed, luxuriating in the feel of his hard body rubbing against her softer one. "You sound like a passionate philosopher, so wise, so knowing."

James cupped her breasts, flicking her sensitive nipples with his tongue. "What I am, my sweet, is very hungry for you."

He took a nipple into his mouth and suckled on it. Randy arched up, cuddling his throbbing manhood with her hips. Her actions made him groan, "Oh, Mira mine, I promised myself our coming together this night would be slow and lingering, but if you do that again, I don't think it's going to be possible."

"Good," she replied, splaying her hands over his buttocks to knead his firm flesh. "Go slowly next time, husband dear. I am just as starved for this joining as you are."

James slid a finger into her feminine delta. "You are wet and warm, Mira, but I want more. I want you hot and burning for me when I take you."

"But, James, I don't want to wait. I . . . I . . . want . . ."

Randy's words faded on a moan as James caught the tiny pearl of her desire between his fingers and gently rubbed it, making the nerve-filled nub swell under his touch. It wasn't long before her hips rose to meet his hand, begging for a release that only a deep, full penetration would give her. The sight of his wife totally enveloped in a sensual haze that he had caused was all the encouragement James needed.

He pushed the turgid length of his member inside her. The moist, clenching depths of her passage surrounded him, wrenching a cry of pleasure from his lips. The rhythm of their mating began, hard and fast, then hesitant and slow. The two lovers took turns setting the pace, tormenting each other to just the point of release, before changing their course to delay the final climax of their union.

James fell to his side on the bed, and without unlodging himself from her sultry depths, turned on his back and brought Randy up to straddle his hips. He could feel the mouth of her womb rubbing on the end of his member.

"Ride me, love," he gasped, taking hold of her full breasts to squeeze them with his hands. "Ride me to the end of this passionate journey we have started."

With her unbound hair cascading around her, Randy braced her hands on his shoulders while she raised and lowered herself on his length. Though new to this way of making love, her natural instincts guided her movements and soon the two of them were on the brink of fulfillment.

Wanting their joy to be a shared experience, James eased his hand between them and found the swollen little kernel in the folds of her femininity. His gentle caress was all that it took to push Randy into the sensual explosion of her release. The grasp of her inner muscles milked his length and forced him to shoot his seed inside her with a shout of surrender.

A few minutes later, while lying awake in her sleeping husband's arms, Randy couldn't help thinking about the changes that had come into her life. Since her father's death a few months before, she had been inundated with new people, places, and experiences. The cherished daughter of a government official in India was now a married woman and a viscountess, embroiled in a treacherous plot of greed and attempted murder. The crimes were horrible, yet the circumstances of her marriage tormented her more. She was married to a man who desired her, who had wed her out of loyalty, but had never said he loved her.

Feeling suddenly melancholy, Randy turned away from James to lie on her side. She had barely put her head on the pillow when she felt him roll toward her and wrap his arm around her waist. His body came up behind hers in spoon fashion.

"I won't let you get away from me," he mumbled near her ear in a sleep-roughened voice. "This is where you belong, Mira, and where you are going to stay."

Randy settled against her husband. When she heard him softly snoring near her ear, she sighed and closed her eyes. "I do love you, James Grayson, with all my heart. Maybe someday you will get over your past disappointments and learn to love me, too."

The sound of the bedroom door crashing loudly against the wall woke the sleeping couple shortly after daybreak. A woman's enraged voice filled the room.

"James Garret Grayson, if you think you can use this house to despoil young ladies, you had better think again."

There was no doubt in Randy's mind that the tall figure wearing snug britches, a tailored shirt, and knee-high boots was a female. The attractive blond woman with a thick plait hanging over her shoulder walked toward the bed and scowled at James.

"There are just so many things I can permit, and this isn't one of them, young man."

James leaned back against his pillow and grinned. "And a very good morning to you, too, Mama. Did you have a pleasant voyage?"

Randy wanted to shrink beneath the quilts. Being caught in bed by a stranger would have been humiliating enough. That the beautiful woman glowering at James was his mother was just too much to accept. Randy knew without looking at a mirror that her cheeks were a flaming crimson red.

Catherine Grayson stepped up to the bed and poked her son

in the chest with her fist. "The voyage was fine, but I am not here to discuss my trip and you bloody well know it."

James yawned. "Is Sarah here? I've missed the princess more than I would like to admit."

"No, I sent her on to stay at your grandfather's in Chatham for a few days," Catherine snapped. "After seeing what you have been doing, I am glad your little sister isn't here to witness the disgrace you have wrought upon this household."

"Did Father come home with you?" James asked.

Male laughter erupted at the open door. "I'm right here, son, but don't count on me to rescue you."

It was then that Randy noticed Miles Grayson, the Earl of Foxwood, casually leaning against the door jamb. An older version of James, with darker hair, Miles seemed unconcerned by his wife's anger or his son's apparent lack of propriety.

Pulling the sheet over her head, Randy closed her eyes and prayed that the entire episode was just a bad dream.

James sighed. "Calm down, Mama. I can explain—"

"You don't have to," Catherine replied tersely, "the clothes strewn around the room and that sweet child cowering beneath your covers says it all. My own son, a seducer of young ladies. I am amazed, I am shocked—"

"I am married!" James announced.

A minute of pure silence fell over the room. Randy peeked over the edge of the sheet to see the look of total astonishment on Catherine's face. The moment of tension broke when the earl crossed the room, laughing.

"Congratulations, son. On your marriage and your success at leaving your mother speechless. I haven't been able to do that in years," he confided, draping his arm over Catherine's shoulder. "Come on, my love. Let these two get dressed. We can get to know our daughter-in-law over some breakfast."

Miles was leading his stunned wife to the door when she suddenly stopped and rushed back to the bed. Catherine sat on the bed beside Randy. Tears glistened in the older woman's emerald-green eyes as she placed a kiss on Randy's cheek.

"I want to welcome you to our family, my dear. For far too long, my son has been alone and I worried about him. Evidently he must love you very much and that gives my heart ease."

Randy was assailed by remorse. In good conscience, she couldn't allow James's mother to believe that their marriage was a lovematch. "But madam, you don't understand—"

"I understand that you two could not wait for us to get back so we could share your joy, but having experienced a great love myself, I forgive you." Catherine glanced over at her son. "Are you going to introduce us to your wife or have you forgotten all the manners you were taught, Jamie?"

James put his arm around Randy and drew her close to him. "Mother and Father, I want you to meet my wife, Randy. She is Nana's granddaughter and we were married in India before our voyage to England. Sweetheart, may I present my parents, Miles and Catherine Grayson, the Earl and Countess of Fox-wood."

Catherine frowned. "Randy? I thought Lenore named you after her mother."

"She did. Miranda is a splendid name, but I prefer being called Randy."

Smiling, Catherine nodded. "I can appreciate that. For a good part of my life I was called Cat."

"Not anymore," Miles interrupted with a terse frown. "You outgrew that name, remember?"

Randy was confused by the tone of annoyance she detected in the earl's voice. "You outgrew your name?"

Catherine leaned over and kissed her cheek. "One day, when we have time to chat, I will tell you all about it."

"Mama, do me a favor?" James asked. "Save the telling of that tale for at least five or ten years from now."

A hint of mischief sparkled in Catherine's eyes. "Why? Are you afraid your wife would run off in horror if she knew the truth about your mother?"

James shook his head and chuckled. "Not at all, Mama. But

after hearing of your exploits, Randy might decide that I am too boring a fellow to stay married to.''

Randy laughed with the others, though she couldn't help wondering what in the countess's past would be so intriguing. But all of that would have to wait, she decided. With so many other mysteries in her life, she did not need another to solve.

Chapter 18

The two couples and their armed escort arrived in London before noon. The Graysons' house and grounds were swarming with servants and extra hired help in preparation for the ball that was taking place that night.

James had just entered the front door with his parents and Randy when the household butler, Fenton, hurried to his side and gave him an envelope. "Milord, this arrived for you yesterday morning. The messenger intended to wait for a reply, but I informed him that you would not be returning until tonight."

It had been years since he had seen the feathery penmanship that addressed the missive, but James knew all to well who had written it. "Thank you, Fenton. I will deal with this."

Randy tried to look at the envelope. "What's the matter, James? Is it bad news?"

Shaking his head, James stuffed the packet into his coat. "Nothing important, sweetheart. Simply some old business I should have taken care of long ago." He kissed her cheek and smiled. "Why don't you and my mother go find Nana? With all that's going on around here, I'm sure she could use some help. I'll go to the study with my father and see to the final plans regarding the placement of guards during the party.''

"Armed men disguised as footmen and guests.'' Randy sighed with disgust. "Do you really think all this is necessary?''

"Other than shooting me at the altar tomorrow morning, this celebration will be your uncle's last chance to eliminate me from your life. It's a sorry state of affairs, but I am willing to do whatever it takes to trap him.''

Randy shook her head. "Maybe I am the one who doesn't want you to take that risk! I lost my father to a murderer and nearly died myself at his hands. If something happens to you, James, I don't know what I would do.''

Catherine put a consoling arm around Randy's shoulders. "Nothing bad is going to befall Jamie, my dear. All evening, he will be surrounded by guards whose sole purpose is to keep him safe.'' Leading her daughter-in-law to the stairs, she laughed. "You mustn't blame Jamie for being this way. He comes from a family of risk-takers and none of us have suffered for it. Now, you must introduce me to your Jarita. After weeks at sea, I could use a bit of that hair preparation she makes for you.''

When the women were out of sight, James removed the envelope from his pocket and gave his coat to Fenton. "The earl and I will be in the study. I am relying on you to see that we are not disturbed.''

The two men were sitting on the leather couch in the study sipping brandy when Miles asked, "Are you going to tell me what's really bothering you, or would you like me to guess? I saw the look on your face when you got that letter, so you obviously know who wrote it and are not very pleased.''

"That's putting it mildly, Father.'' James broke the wax seal on the parchment. "If I am to be honest, it's the gall of this particular person that surprises and infuriates me.''

"Well, don't keep me in suspense any longer. Who sent it? The Duke of Maidstone?''

James shook his head and examined the pages. "No. It's from Caroline Wexler."

Miles was incensed. "That troublesome Sutcliffe chit who embroiled you in a duel years ago? Montrose married her. Is she suddenly not content being a marchioness?"

"Montrose was killed in a riding accident last year," James replied, still reading the letter. "Evidently, the title and all it entails went to Giles."

"And now the brazen wench is looking for another wealthy nobleman to take his place." The earl grimaced. "Hedly should have drowned that bit of his litter at birth and saved us all a lot of grief. It took me several months to convince your mother not to do the deed herself when she discovered what that blasted girl had done to you."

James glanced over the edge of the paper at his father. "That didn't stop Mama from doing her best to ruin Caroline with most of the *ton*. No hostess worthy of note would have anything to do with Montrose and his wife once the Countess of Foxwood declared them unfit company."

Miles looked chagrinned. "Damn! Didn't think you knew about that. I do my best to govern your mother's temper, but sometimes it's simply a lost cause. Who told you?"

"Caroline did. It's all in this letter." James handed the pages to his father. "As you can see, she is asking for my help in reclaiming her status in polite society. She goes on to imply that there is a new man in her life, and without my aid in this and some other problem she's been facing, he will not marry her."

Reading the missive, Miles nodded. "She also wants to see you right away. Something about time being of the essence. A life-and-death situation." The earl looked up and chuckled. "This chit certainly has a way of turning a dramatic phrase. She could use her talent to write a gothic novel."

James stared into the glass of brandy he held in his hand. A thought that had haunted him for days suddenly made a great deal of sense to him.

"I told you how Caroline approached me after the opera the other night. For all her sweetness and banter, she seemed nervous. I saw her looking over her shoulder as though searching for someone behind her. She was gone no more than a minute when that shot was fired, nearly hitting me."

Miles refolded the letter and handed it back to his son. "So now you think Caroline Wexler is involved in the attempt on your life?"

"It makes sense. She was sitting in Maidstone's box all evening. When he left, Caroline and several others in his group went with him." James raked his fingers through his hair. "That's why I was so surprised when she approached me nearly an hour later outside the theater. If I am correct, she was there to set me up for the assassin."

"Son, I know it's rather indelicate of me to ask, but do you still have tender feelings for this woman?"

James shook his head. "No, absolutely not. Caroline killed any affection I felt for her in that meadow seven years ago. When I saw her in Maidstone's box the other night, I couldn't stop staring at her. If looks could inflict pain, then surely mine would have caused her enough agony to pray for death."

"Such hatred is dangerous, James. You must be careful or it will destroy you."

Turning to his father, James nodded. "Yes, I know. While I was sitting there looking at Caroline, I suddenly realized that my hatred for her wasn't worth the effort. That I had a special new lady in my life on whom I had to concentrate instead."

Miles smiled and patted James on the back. "You sound like a man totally besotted with his wife. As one suffering from the same glorious affliction, I couldn't be happier for you, my boy. Randy must be a very extraordinary young lady."

"Yes, she is." James picked up the sheets of folded parchment and moved toward his father's desk. "I don't want Randy to know about this letter from Caroline or its possible connection to her uncle. With all she's been through in the past few months, this is one problem she shouldn't have to deal with."

"What do you plan to do about Caroline? You surely aren't going to meet her in the park as she requested, are you?"

James retrieved the quill from the ink well. "No. If Caroline wants to see me, she will have to come to the party this evening. I'll send her a personal invitation, one she would not dare to ignore."

An hour later, Randy came down the stairs and saw the butler coming out of the study carrying an envelope. "Fenton," she called, "is my husband still busy talking to the earl?"

"Yes, my lady. He wants this invitation to the ball delivered straightaway. Lord James was most adamant about it. Is there anything that you require?"

"No, Fenton. Since my lord is occupied, I will go to the kitchens and check on the final menu for tonight. Carry on with your duties."

"Yes, my lady." Fenton bowed before he turned and handed the packet he was carrying to the footman standing near the front door. "Mickey, take this missive to Lady Caroline Wexler at this address posthaste."

"Should I wait for a reply, Mr. Fenton?"

The butler shook his head. "That will not be necessary, Mickey. Lord James says the lady is expecting this invitation. Just deliver it and get back here as soon as possible."

As the two servants rushed off to their duties, Randy held onto the newel post at the foot of the stairs and struggled to contain the anguish she was experiencing. After the incredible night they had shared, the last person she thought James would want to see was Caroline Wexler.

His remarks about his former love had always been glib or tersely delivered when he spoke of her. But had his words only served as a way of masking his true feelings for Caroline? She had seen her husband staring at the blond beauty at the theater and later witnessed him holding the woman in his arms. Would

James be sending a frantic last-minute invitation to a woman he had no feelings for?

The answer was obvious to Randy. Despite the humiliation she had brought on him years before, James was still in love with Caroline. He was saddled with a wife he didn't love, while the woman who truly held his heart had suddenly become available again. From the way the pretty widow acted at the theater, it was clear James held a special interest for her as well.

Randy looked up at that moment and saw Fenton opening the door for a visitor. A tall, thin man wearing fine clothes and carrying a leather case burgeoning with papers stepped inside. Taking the man's card, the butler approached her.

"My lady, this gentleman is Sir Malcolm Addison, the dowager's solicitor," Fenton explained handing her the card. "He says it is most urgent that he speak with you or your grandmother right away."

Randy sighed and glanced down at the card. "Her grace is resting in her suite. I will see the gentleman myself."

Taking a deep fortifying breath, Randy greeted the solicitor and guided him into the drawing room. Once the door was closed and they were sitting down, Sir Malcolm explained the reason for his visit.

"Your grandmother sent me a letter, informing me that you and Viscount Ryland were married in India before you sailed to England. Her grace wanted all the proper documents filed regarding the holdings she had already put into your name as well as amending her will to include your husband and to remove a codicil she had added last year."

"I know. Nana told me about this weeks ago. That's why she asked me to send you my marriage certificate so the information could be easily verified. Is there a problem?"

The solicitor pulled a handkerchief from his pocket and mopped his brow. "Well—ah, yes, there is. I really should discuss this with her grace first, but . . . you see . . . ah . . ."

The man's apparent discomfort caused Randy to lean forward and touch his hand. "Sir Malcolm, are you all right?"

"I am fine, my lady, but until this problem is resolved, I cannot make the changes your grandmother wants on her will. The codicil and the rest of it stays in force and the dowager shall be most upset." Smiling sheepishly, he shook his head. "Though I really don't know why I am carrying on like this. After tomorrow, everything will be set to rights anyway."

His cryptic remark made Randy uneasy. "If this problem has to do with me, then I demand your reply this instant."

Sir Malcolm sighed. "Your marriage to James Grayson in India is not valid. The ceremony was conducted by a magistrate who had been recalled by the government due to various charges that your father, Jonathan Collins, filed against the man last year. The final decree was sent to India months ago. The man who took your father's place in Calicut should have received a copy of it in plenty of time to have avoided this debacle."

Recalling the drunken magistrate and the cocky expression on Brandon Spencer's face at her wedding caused a tight knot to form in the pit of Randy's stomach. There was no doubt in her mind that Spencer knew all about the government decree regarding this man and had employed him in carrying out his own little plan of revenge against her.

Sir Malcolm laughed nervously. "But as I said before, after tomorrow morning it will all work out. You and Viscount Ryland will be married and the error will be corrected. Would you like me to explain any of this to her grace or the viscount, my lady?"

Randy shook her head. "No, I would prefer to do it myself."

"Under the circumstances, I can appreciate your concern in handling this personally." As he stood up, Sir Malcolm removed a document from his case and gave it to Randy. "Here is the marriage certificate, my lady. I won't be needing it any longer."

Alone in the drawing room, Randy suddenly felt chilled and moved toward the fireplace for warmth. Gazing into the burning hearth, she thought of the discoveries she had made during the past hour and how things would be if she kept this knowledge to herself.

She and James could be married in the morning and everything would go on exactly as they planned. But what about Caroline? If James cared for the young widow, would he keep her as his mistress? Randy couldn't help wondering if she would be truly happy if she married the man she loved, knowing that he was in love with another woman.

She looked at the document in her hand. "This worthless piece of paper is only good for one thing now." Crushing it with her hands, she threw it into the flames and watched through tear-filled eyes as it was rendered to ashes.

"Oh, my lamb, you should have slept a little longer," Jarita scolded, bustling around Randy's bed. "Your face is the color of flour and your beautiful eyes are swollen with fatigue."

Wearing a chintz wrapper, Randy got up and crossed the room to sit at her dressing table. "I tried to nap, Jarita, but it was useless. I am tired, but I just cannot sleep. Besides, my stomach is queasy again. That's the fourth time this week. I hope I'm not getting sick."

"If you will not rest, then have some of the soup the countess has sent up for you." Jarita put the bowl and spoon on the tabletop next to Randy. "You must try to eat something."

The heady aroma of beef and vegetable soup filled Randy's nose when she dipped the spoon into the mixture and brought it to her lips. A wave of nausea swept through her, causing her to drop the spoon untouched into the bowl.

"Jarita, please take this away. I think I'm going to be—"

With a hand to her mouth, Randy ran for the clean chamberpot that was stored under the bed. After relieving her stomach, she sat on the floor with the porcelain bowl in her lap and rested her head on the edge of the mattress.

"My poor lamb," the old woman clucked, brushing Randy's

hair away from her damp brow. "What you are suffering from is not so bad. In a month or two it should pass."

Randy turned her head and frowned at Jarita. "A month or two? You must be joking!"

"No, no! Carrying a child is not a thing to jest over." A look of understanding suddenly lit the ayah's concerned features. "Surely you know that you are going to have the *Huzur's* baby. You have not had your woman's flow in more than three months and from the fit of your gowns, your bosom has already grown fuller. The stomach upset only confirms it."

The significance of Jarita's words left Randy stunned to silence. With her head leaning on the mattress, hot tears coursed down her cheeks. She was so caught up in it all, she never took notice of Jarita leaving the room or the loving presence of another sitting down beside her on the bed.

"Do not cry, Missy." Abu stroked her thick, unbound hair with his fingers. "There has been much disappointment in your life, but this is a time to rejoice."

"Oh, Abu, this was the last thing I would have wanted now. With all I have to deal with—" Randy shook her head. "What am I going to do?"

"You are going to have a beautiful baby and cherish it with all your being. It is fate that this child, created in love by you and James, be born. It was meant to be."

"I love James, but he doesn't love me," she cried, losing her tattered control. "He still loves Caroline."

Abu sniffed. "That cursed dog! I suppose he has told you this himself many times. A man capable of such cruelty does not deserve you, my dearest child."

Randy sat up and rubbed her cheeks with the sleeve of her dressing gown. "James is not a dog, nor has he ever admitted his feelings for Caroline to me. But I saw it, Abu. He was staring at her in the theater for the longest time. Only love for someone would cause a person to react that way."

"Or hate?" Abu arched a dark brow. "Love and hate are intense emotions. Of these passions, one feeds the soul, while the other drains our energy. You have told me what this woman did to James years ago. Knowing the *Huzur,* do you really think he would harbor tender feelings for such a viper as she?''

''But I saw the brightness in his eyes when he was looking at her that night.''

''Hatred can also glow like a flaming bonfire on a starless night. Could you not be mistaking his anger for affection?''

Randy frowned and shook her head. ''I don't think so, though it may be true. But what of the invitation to the ball I saw him send to her this morning? Why bring her here if he hates her?''

The old Indian shrugged. ''Revenge, perhaps?''

Abu's suggestion made Randy reconsider everything she had witnessed during the past week. Taking Abu's offered hand, she got up from the floor and began pacing the room.

''Revenge is a plausible reason, yet I saw James holding Caroline in his arms when she was crying. Would he do that if he truly dispised her?''

''The *Huzur* is a compassionate man. A woman's tears, even those of this jaded minx, could bring a momentary softening of his fury.''

Randy shook her head. ''You were not there, Abu. I saw—''

''You saw, you saw!'' Abu interjected in a voice thick with impatience. ''Since when do you allow your eyes to be your only guide, my child? Besides great intelligence and wit, you possess a gift that enables you to sense the pain and emotions in others. You rarely use your talent anymore. Why is that?''

Racked with frustration, Randy sat in the chair by the dressing table. She looked into the mirror before she dropped her face into her hands. ''I don't use it because I am afraid these people would consider me a freak. All these weeks, I have struggled to keep that part of me tightly reined. The only time I used my ability successfully was when Nana was very ill and I knew that no one else would witness what I was doing.''

Abu placed a reassuring hand on her shoulder. ''Denying yourself the freedom to use your gift is hurting you. The confidence that made you strong is waning and leaves you in doubt.

It grieves me to think that the girl I have watched grow into a woman has become such a coward.''

Randy jerked her head up and glared at Abu in the mirror. "I am not a coward."

"Then why have you not told James that you love him?"

"Because I . . . well, I wanted . . ." Shaking her head, Randy sighed. "All right, so I am a coward. I simply don't want to tell James of my feelings until I'm sure he loves me too."

"A man's pride is very important to him, and once wounded, he would guard himself wisely from another attack. Perhaps James has been waiting for you to admit your love for him first." Abu gently patted her back. "Is the reward not great enough to risk being honest with your husband?"

Randy turned around to face her old teacher. "James isn't my husband, Abu. According to Nana's solicitor, our marriage in India was not valid.'' After telling him everything Sir Malcolm had said, she shrugged. "I am torn as to what I should do about this. If I say nothing, James and I will be married tomorrow morning, and the problem with Nana's legacy and the rest of it will be solved. But is that fair to James? Do I have the right to trap him in a marriage that he never really wanted in the first place?''

Abu seemed unimpressed with her words and folded his arms across his chest. "A marriage is not governed by a piece of paper. Vows were exchanged, and in your soul, you know that you and James are already married. As I have said before, the union between the two of you was meant to be."

"Yes, I know. It is fate, kismet, providence, destiny, or whatever else you wish to call it." Randy turned back toward the mirror and frowned at her reflection. "Perhaps I would be a bit more optimistic if I were feeling better."

"Jarita is down in the kitchen even now, preparing an herb tea that I have blended as a remedy for your nausea."

Randy met Abu's wizened gaze in the mirror and smiled at him. "All of my life I have had you to depend on, Abu. You are my teacher, my protector, and my friend. How can I ever thank you for everything you have done for me?''

"Thank me by being the best woman you can be, my child. Be true to yourself and your beliefs, and never again doubt your abilities or fear what others will think of you because of their ignorance. Remember, when things seem the most hopeless, the best place to look for a solution is within your own heart.''

Randy's brow creased with confusion. "Are you trying to warn me about something, Abu? Is James in danger tonight?''

Abu spoke softly, his hand soothing as he touched her shoulder. "I do not know exactly what the gods have planned, my child, but I can tell you that evil is lurking close by. Keep alert, be guided by your instincts, and never, never lose faith in yourself or in those who love you.''

Chapter 19

"You look like a queen in all those diamonds," James told Randy as he swept her across the ballroom floor to the strains of a melodious waltz. "Nana's gift to you of the Crystal Tears is the talk of the evening."

Randy scowled down at her white brocade gown and the gems she was wearing. "I feel like the display case in a jeweler's shop, but Nana insisted that I wear the entire collection. Perhaps if people are too busy estimating the value of these jewels, they won't have time to notice how nervous I am."

James drew her closer to him. "What they are going to notice is how incredibly lovely you are tonight. Relax and enjoy the celebration, sweetheart. Leave the worrying to me."

"James, I have several important things to tell you." The curls dangling fashionably loose from her upswept hairstyle fell over her shoulder. "I wanted to talk to you before the party, but the guests began arriving and I never got the chance."

Brushing her curls back with his fingers, he placed a quick kiss on her brow. "I'm sorry, love, but whatever it is, you are going to have to wait a bit longer to tell me. Your uncle has arrived and we have to greet him.'' James tucked her hand into the crook of his arm and led her from the dance floor.

With his noble bearing and confident smile, the Duke of Maidstone, Richard Wentworth, stood at the entrance of the ballroom, looking every inch a gentleman. Even if he wore pauper's rags instead of his impeccable formal attire, Randy doubted if anyone could ever mistake him for a man of lesser rank. He exuded innate charm and power. It was too bad, she mused, that so many fine qualities had been wasted on a man like her uncle.

Richard stepped forward when they reached him, and with the enthusiasm of a doting father, he embraced Randy and kissed her cheek. ''Good evening, my dear. May I say you are looking quite beautiful tonight?''

''Why, ah . . . thank you, Uncle Richard,'' Randy replied, looking into his smiling face for a sign of deception. ''I am glad that you decided to come to our party.''

''As a member of your family, it's my place to be with you. My biggest regret is that your parents couldn't be here to celebrate your joy as well.'' Richard turned to James and held out his hand to him. ''I would be extremely grateful if you could forgive my dreadful behavior the other evening at the opera. My only excuse is that I haven't been well lately, and my condition tends to make me testy.''

James nodded and accepted his hand. ''Certainly, your grace. Consider it forgotten.''

Randy recalled her conversation with Abu about her gift for sensing ailments in others. She was curious to see if she could use it to prove that Richard was lying to them.

''Uncle Richard, would it be impertinent for me to ask you about your illness?'' Randy took hold of the duke's hand and held it between her own. ''My man, Abu, has been trained by many of the finest physicians in the Orient. He might know of a remedy or treatment that could help you.''

Richard patted the top of her hand. ''I appreciate your concern, my dear, but I have had these stomach ulcers for many years. Only simple food, no liquor, and less anxiety can reduce the occurrences. It's easy to follow the first two, but life has a nasty way of increasing the third, I'm afraid."

Randy hoped the look on her face didn't betray what she was doing. Within seconds, she had discovered that her uncle was telling the truth about his condition. Deep, burning pain was radiating from his stomach. There wasn't one afflicted area, but three. In spite of her mistrust of the man, she admired his ability to smile while suffering such discomfort.

"Well, well, my loving stepson graces us with his presence," the dowager announced when she stepped from the crowd to face Richard. "After all you said the other night, I didn't think you would support this marriage."

The duke turned to his stepmother and bowed to her. "What's the point, madam? I still think this hasty union is ill advised, but I am not Randy's guardian, so there's nothing I can do to prevent it. True love triumphs, they say."

"As well it should." The dowager stepped closer to Richard and spoke to him in a low voice. "I heard you were a bit put out when you learned that Randy was declared my ward. Was the loss of governing Randy's wealth the true reason for your rage, your grace?"

The duke's eyes flashed with anger. "How dare you accuse me of such a thing!"

The dowager smiled. "Then the rumor of your needing cash is not true?"

Casting a glance at the crush of people around them, Richard fought to control himself. His voice was an exasperated whisper. "My need for ready cash has nothing to do with this, Miranda. By applying to the king for guardianship of my sister's child behind my back, you thwarted my position as the head of this family. You made me look like a fool before my peers. Once again, you found a way to keep me out of your private little family!"

James put himself between Richard and the dowager, and grabbed the duke's arm. "This discussion is really pointless, your grace. Tomorrow morning, Randy will become my wife and as such will no longer be a part of the Wentworth family. The responsibility for her inheritance, wealth, and properties will belong to me, so why argue over it now?''

Richard freed himself of the younger man's hold. "You discourteous lout! I don't need you lecturing me on what I should or should not do. If you know what's good for you, you will cease interfering in my affairs.'' Not waiting for a response, the duke turned on his heel and made his way through the crowd.

James scowled at the dowager. "I thought I was the one who was going to provoke Richard this time.''

Lady Miranda snapped open the fan dangling from her wrist and waved it in front of her face. "Well, I was sick and tired of waiting around for Richard to do something, so I thought by giving him a shove we could get on with it.'' She dabbed the moisture from her brow with her handkerchief. "My, it certainly is warm this evening. All this intrigue has left me parched. I wonder if the lemonade is cold.''

Randy took pity on her grandmother and allowed her to change the subject. "Now that you mention it, Nana, I'm a bit warm too. Why don't you and I find a seat with some of your friends while James goes after some lemonade for us?''

Smiling over her grandmother's head at James, Randy led the dowager away. He nodded and went in search of the refreshments.

A few minutes later, a footman in blue Foxwood livery and a powdered wig approached Randy with two glasses of lemonade on his tray. "Lord Ryland asked me to bring this to you, my lady.''

Randy looked away from the spirited conversation the dowager was holding with a group of her friends to find a tall, bearded footman standing beside her. She found herself wondering if this was a new household servant or one of the many guards who had been hired to protect James. There was something about the man that seemed oddly familiar, though she couldn't remember ever seeing him before.

"Thank you, uh . . . I am sorry, but I don't know your name."

The footman bowed his head. "I am Heath, my lady. I have been assigned by the earl to see to your needs this evening. Should you require anything, please let me know."

The knowledge that Miles Grayson had selected one of the men to keep watch over her eased some of the tension she had been plagued with since late that afternoon.

"Thank you, Heath. That is very good to know. Where is Viscount Ryland?"

"My lord was by the entry a few moments ago greeting a guest." The footman looked over the room and nodded. "Yes, there he is, standing beside that woman in the lavender gown."

Randy stood up and nearly toppled the tray from Heath's hand when she saw James speaking to Caroline Wexler. Her doubts returned full force as she watched him leave the ballroom with the petite blond woman clinging to his arm.

"My lady, are you all right?"

Quick to hide her pain, Randy offered the concerned man beside her a smile. "I'm fine, Heath. Why don't you serve the dowager her lemonade and stay with her while I am gone. I have a matter of some urgency to attend to."

Hoping to follow James and Caroline, Randy hurried across the crowded ballroom. Before she reached the archway, a pair of strong male arms caught her by the waist and spun her around.

"Did you miss me, Randy?" Stephen asked, kissing her cheek.

"Stephen, it's good to see you. James thought you would be back two days ago." Randy looked anxiously over her shoulder. "If you want to catch him, he just went—"

"I saw him already. He was on his way into the—" Stephen suddenly stopped speaking as he seized a glass of wine from the tray of a passing waiter. "Would you like some, Randy?"

When she shook her head, he took a hefty sip from his glass

and sighed. "After spending the past weeks in the rustic wilds of James's estate, I needed that. With the possible exception of the wine cellar that only James has a key to, there isn't a decent bottle of spirits to be found in that entire area."

"Stephen, where did you say James was going?"

"He was going into his father's study." A look of stunned realization covered Stephen's face and he grasped her arm. "But before you—ah, go searching for him, I—uh, want to tell you something."

Randy knew the reason for Stephen's discomfort, but she wasn't going to let him deter her from her task. "Stephen, you can talk to me later. I have to see James immediately."

"Please, Randy, don't go in there now. James will blame me for telling you where he was."

She removed his hand from her arm. "Calm yourself, Stephen. I know he is in there with Caroline Wexler. Nana told me all about that witch and what she did to James. I simply have to know why he invited that woman to our party."

"You don't have to be jealous of Caroline. James loves you. With all the money it cost him to build that enclosure for Sidra on his estate—"

The unexpected reference to her cherished pet garnered Randy's full attention. "James built a cage for Sidra?"

"It's not a cage, exactly. There are plants and a bathing pool, and high, glass-enclosed ceilings."

"So, it's a big, fancy cage, but a cage nonetheless."

Her dull tone must have alarmed Stephen. "N-no, honey," he stammered, "it really isn't a cage. You don't understand."

"Does it have four walls, a roof, and a door that keeps the inhabitants inside?" she asked in a soft voice.

"Yes, but—"

"Then it's a cage." Randy patted his hand. "If you will excuse me, Stephen, I have to be by myself for a while."

Randy was relieved when Stephen didn't follow her from the room. Learning that James had built a cage for Sidra without ever discussing it with her felt like an act of betrayal and she wasn't up to revealing the pain it caused her with anyone. But her relief was short-lived when she ran into Catherine Grayson in the foyer of the house.

"Are you feeling all right, Randy? You look very pale."

Catherine wore a gown of deep gold lace over cream-colored silk. Randy thought this graceful woman was a living portrait of femininity. Her blond tresses were arranged in a coronet of braids. Jeweled butterfly pins adorned her hair.

Randy struggled to smile. "Between meeting all these new people and witnessing another encounter between James and my uncle, I guess the tension is taking its toll on me."

"It won't be much longer, my dear." Catherine put her arms around Randy and gave her a sympathetic hug. "Your uncle must make his move soon, and all this will be over. Even if Richard doesn't try to interfere, you and Jamie will be married in church tomorrow morning, and that pleases me immensely. Nana and I are looking forward to it."

When Catherine pulled away, Randy's brooch containing the Bloody Tear of Allah got caught in the bodice of the Countess's gown. The two women laughed as they stood head to head and fought to remove the antique piece of jewelry from the tightly woven lace without tearing it.

"Finally it's free," Randy sighed several minutes later. "I am glad the brooch didn't ruin your gown."

"I would have a jeweler check the closure on that pin. All our pulling on it might have weakened the clasp." It was then that Catherine noticed two uniformed footmen standing at the door of the study. "What are those men doing out here? They were assigned to watch over Jamie, not linger about in the foyer."

"I believe they are doing exactly that," Randy replied tightly. "Stephen told me James was in the study."

Catherine frowned. "There's a houseful of guests, a plan to catch a villain already in motion, and my son is holed up in the study. Well, I'll just put a stop to this!"

Ordering the guards aside, Catherine flung the door open.

When she discovered Caroline kissing James in the center of the room, her aggravation exploded into unbridled rage.

"What in the blazes is going on here? Get away from my son, you trollop, before I finish the chore of getting rid of you once and for all!"

James pushed Caroline behind him as his mother moved toward them. "Calm down, Mama. This isn't what you think—"

"I don't have to think, Jamie. I saw enough with my own eyes to know that this witch is up to her old tricks again and I won't have it! Who invited her to this house?"

"Well, I did, Mama, but I—"

"Are you demented?" Catherine prodded his chest with her finger. "That woman nearly cost you your life. How could you be so stupid as to invite her to a party honoring your wife? If Randy ever—" The color suddenly drained from Catherine's face. "Oh, my God."

The strangled gasp his mother emitted as she turned toward the opened door to the foyer told James that something was wrong. "Mama, what's the matter?"

"It's all my fault. Saints above, what have I done?"

James touched his mother's trembling shoulder. "Mama, what are you talking about?"

Catherine's green eyes sparkled with tears when she looked up at her son. "Randy was right behind me when I threw open the door. She must have seen you kissing Caroline."

Frowning, James shot an angry glare at the young woman cowering by the fireplace. "Caroline was the one doing the kissing. I had just agreed to help her with a problem she was having and she got carried away with her gratitude."

"Well, you are the one with the problem now, Jamie," Catherine sniffed, moving behind the desk. "You'd better go after Randy and pray she's not as hotheaded as your mother. If I were in her place, you would have to get on your knees and beg me to believe such a tale."

"It's not a tale, Mama. I swear what I've told you is true."

Catherine's eyes fixed on Caroline. "I know, Jamie. Go after your lady and make amends, while I remain here with this minx. I won't let this one out of my sight until you and Randy return happy and reconciled.''

"James," Caroline whimpered, "please don't leave me with her. Your mother hates me and I'm afraid of her."

A cool smile tilted the corners of Catherine's lips. "You have no idea just how accurate that observation is, and if Randy refuses to see reason, I am going to take great joy in proving it to you. And this time, no one will stop me."

Suddenly mindful of the odd looks people were casting her way, Randy found herself wandering through the crowded ballroom. After dealing with one shocking revelation after the other all day long, seeing James and Caroline together had simply been more than she could handle. The last place she wanted to be was lost and alone in the middle of a grand celebration surrounded by strangers, but in her confusion she had placed herself in just that situation. She was surprised and relieved when her rescue came from a most unexpected source.

Heath appeared at her side with a glass of lemonade on his tray and gave her a stiff bow. "I apologize for taking so long to find you, my lady, but here is the refreshment you requested. Has your migraine grown worse?"

As the people dispersed around her, commiserating with her plight, Randy took the glass from Heath's tray and whispered her appreciation while they made their way to the edge of the room. "Thank you for coming to my aid with that excuse. I was so deep in thought, I lost all perspective of where I was."

"Thanks are not necessary, my lady," he replied in a husky tone. "I told you earlier that it was my duty to take care of you. When I saw you come in so pale and shaken, I knew something was wrong. Why don't you sit down in private and collect yourself before dealing with any more of these people?"

Randy glanced at the man's thickly bearded face and gave

him a wry smile. "In this crush, that would be impossible. The entire house is filled with guests."

Heath lifted his gloved hand toward the glass doors that led to the gardens. "Then why not a breath of fresh air, my lady? The weather is quite warm this evening and you can sit on the veranda and enjoy a bit of solitude. I'll stand guard just inside the door so no one will interrupt your respite."

"That is an offer I cannot refuse, Heath. Thank you." Randy took a sip from the glass she was holding. "There certainly is a lot of sugar in this lemonade."

"The hothouse lemons were slightly bitter, so they used extra sugar to disguise the tartness. If you don't like it, I would be more than happy to bring you something else, my lady. Would you care for a glass of wine?"

Randy shook her head. "No, I will drink this. The last thing I need at this moment is spirits clouding my mind." She tipped her glass to Heath in a salute. "Thank you for your assistance, Heath. I will be back soon."

The evening air felt refreshing on her skin. She was pleased to find herself alone with only the stars glittering against the black velvet night sky as company. Sipping her lemonade, Randy sat on a stone bench on the far end of the dark terrace and contemplated what she should do next.

Thoughts of losing James to Caroline and the fact he was not her legal husband warred with the knowledge that she loved him and carried his child. Did he deserve being denied the woman he really loved because her own needs seemed to be greater than his?

"This is all my own fault. If I had stayed in India where I belonged, none of this would have happened." She drained her glass and set it on the ground as she stood up and gazed unseeing over the shadow-filled gardens.

The thought of India reminded Randy of the difficulties her trip to England had caused her servants and pets. Abu and the others could learn to adapt to the weather and strange customs, but the animals weren't as lucky. Poor Sidra would suffer by being enclosed in a cage for the rest of her life.

Wrought with melancholy and sadness, Randy felt tears welling in her eyes as she came to an important decision. "If I returned to India, everything would be solved. Sidra would have her freedom, James could have his Caroline, and I could have his baby." Her hand dropped protectively to her flat abdomen. "I wouldn't have James, but at least I would have a small part of him to call my own."

Suddenly, a shudder of weakness coursed through Randy. She stumbled back toward the bench only to find hard, punishing hands grabbing at her. A muscular arm wrapped around her ribcage as her assailant stuffed a rag into her mouth and covered her face with a rough, moldy-smelling sack. She fought him with all of her diminished might. The delicate fabric of her gown tore with the effort. Her hands slapped at the arm squeezing the air out of her, but it was to no avail. Seconds later, she fell limp against the man's unyielding chest.

The last thing Randy heard as she fell into unconsciousness was his raspy laughter near her ear. "You're not getting away from me this time. After all these months, I have earned my success, and I bloody well mean to enjoy it."

"This is insane! Randy doesn't know her way around London." James paced the length of the study, his fingers raking through his hair. "Even if she was angry with me, I can't imagine her leaving the house without telling someone where she was going."

Miles Grayson sat behind his desk and shook his head. "No one saw her leave, and none of the horses are missing from the stable, James. If she left this house, Randy went with one of the guests."

Fenton stood at the door. "I questioned all the household staff myself and none of them witnessed her departure, my lord."

"I should be out there looking for her myself," James declared, "instead of staying in here like a caged animal."

"Abu sent you back, my son, because you were getting in the way." The earl shrugged. "Something about your nervous tension interfering with his ability to do a thorough search. He is overseeing the guards and should be here soon."

At that moment, the dowager rushed in wringing her hands. "The entire house has been searched, top to bottom, and still there's no sign of my precious granddaughter. Have the guards found anything in the gardens, James?"

"Not yet, Nana." James put his arm around the elderly woman and led her to a chair near the hearth. "Why don't you sit down and keep warm while we wait for news? You won't be doing Randy or yourself any good if you wear yourself down with worry."

"If we don't find Randy, I really don't care what happens to me." Her gaze took in James's rumpled appearance and she sighed. "You are worried about her too. Do you know what could have driven her away from this house?"

James felt overcome with dread and guilt. "Yes, Nana. As much as I hate to admit it, I think Randy ran away because of me. If I had taken the time to explain a few things to her, she wouldn't have left this house on her own."

The dowager's brow rose expectantly. "Well, get on with it, young man. What did you do?"

From the shadows in the far corner of the room, a soft female voice answered her question. "James didn't do anything, your grace." Caroline stepped forward, looking more like a frightened child than a reputed seductress. "What happened was all my fault."

"What is this woman doing here, James? Isn't it enough that she nearly got you killed—"

"Please, Nana, don't remind me. I heard this lecture from my own mother a couple of hours ago."

The dowager sniffed. "Well, I should hope so. Your mother always has been very intelligent. It's just too bad you don't take after her more often. Now, what did this tart have to do with my granddaughter leaving the house?"

"I thought Caroline was a part of a plan Richard had contrived to gain control over Randy's wealth, so I agreed to talk to her tonight. But I never mentioned my suspicions to anyone except my father." Feeling like a small boy being chided in the schoolroom, James shuffled his feet nervously. "When Randy saw Caroline and me together here in the study, she must have gotten the wrong idea."

"Seeing you talking wouldn't have sent her off into the night, James. My granddaughter is made of sterner stuff than that. What aren't you telling me?"

"I begged James to help me," Caroline interrupted, "and when he said yes, I kissed him. But it wasn't a passionate gesture, your grace, simply one of gratitude."

Seeing the pallor of the old woman's complexion, James was quick to reassure her. "Caroline is telling the truth, Nana. We would have explained it to Randy, but by the time I realized what she had seen, I couldn't find her. I can't fathom why she was so upset by such an innocent kiss. It's not as if Randy knows about what happened between Caroline and me in the past."

The dowager stared down at her clenched hands. "Randy knows all about it. She was concerned by how dispassionately you acted when you gave her the betrothal ring. I wanted to ease her worry, so I told her about the last time you had given that ring to a woman, and the consequences that followed."

James shook his head. "But this still doesn't make any sense. Why would seeing Caroline kiss me bother her so much?"

"Perhaps my granddaughter believes you are still harboring feelings for your former love."

"That's ridiculous," James countered. "The only woman I am in love with is Randy. I love her with all of my being."

The dowager's eyes whipped up to meet his. "Then why have you not told my granddaughter that? Randy thinks she has you trapped in a marriage you didn't want in the first place."

"If anyone was trapped into marriage, it was Randy," James admitted dolefully. "I had to convince her that our union would be in name only before she would accept my proposal. But I was lying. I went into this marriage knowing full well that I was never going to let her go. When I find my wife, I am going to—"

"My mistress is not your wife, *Huzur.*"

James spun around and found Abu standing in the entry to the study. "Of course Randy is my wife, Abu. We were married before a British magistrate in Calicut."

The Indian bowed his turbaned head. "That is true, *Huzur,* but the magistrate was not authorized to perform marriages, so the union between you and my mistress was invalid. The dowager's solicitor came this afternoon and explained it all to my mistress and it grieved her very much."

"But how did Nana's solicitor get involved in any of this?"

"My mistress sent him your marriage certificate weeks ago when the dowager wanted to have your name included on her will and to remove a codicil that she had added to it last year. While verifying the certificate, her man discovered that the magistrate had been recalled many months prior to the ceremony."

Rage rushed through James. "Then Brandon Spencer knew our marriage wouldn't be valid. If I could get my hands on that bloody bastard, I would make him rue the day he was born."

Abu sighed with impatience. "Anger is a wasted emotion, *Huzur,* so deal with it another time. Your concentration should be on finding my mistress. She did not run away and in her present condition, she needs you more than ever."

Abu's comments garnered James's attention. "How can you be so sure that Randy didn't run away? And what do you mean about her condition? Is she ill again?"

"To begin with, *Huzur,* my mistress would never flee, even if her life was in danger. She is a fighter to the end."

James nodded. "You're right, of course. She refused to leave India in spite of the fact that a madman was trying to murder her. It was only her concern for you and those she loved that forced her to go. But what about the rest of it, Abu? Is Randy ill?"

The only movement on Abu's stoic face was the tiny lifting of his taut lips. "No, she is not ill, *Huzur.* I would never presume to tell you this on my own, but with matters as they are, I believe you should know. My mistress is with child. Even now, the baby created by the love you share is nestled inside her."

James shook his head with disbelief. "But Randy never told me about any of this. Not the baby, the magistrate, or anything else. Why would she keep these things from me?"

"She only discovered it all this afternoon, *Huzur.* She assured me that she was going to reveal everything to you before the celebration tonight."

Fueled by frustration, James rubbed his eyes with the heels of his hands. "That's what Randy was trying to do earlier, and I never gave her the chance. I was so caught up in this damnable plan to catch Richard that I told her whatever she needed to tell me would have to wait. I'm such a fool!"

"You are not a fool, Jamie. Just a man whose wife has been drugged and kidnapped," Catherine announced, entering the study. She handed the glass she was carrying to Abu. "The guards found this where you instructed them to search on the north end of the terrace. I think the dregs in this glass should prove to be laden with laudanum. Someone used it on me years ago and that odor still haunts me."

"But, Mama, what makes you think that Randy was the one who was drinking from that glass?"

Catherine turned to her son. "Because this was found on the ground near the glass." She placed the Bloody Tear of Allah in his hand. "The clasp on this brooch is badly bent and broken.

Only a struggle with someone very strong could have torn it from Randy's gown this way.''

"Oh, my God," the dowager gasped. "My Randy has been kidnapped. Call the authorities immediately. I want that stepson of mine arrested for his part in this crime."

Caroline cried out. "You can't do that. Poor Richard had nothing to do with it."

The dowager scowled at her. "What do you know about any of this, you detestable tart? Maybe James was right. You and Richard are in this vile little plot together. If a single hair is harmed on my granddaughter's head, I'll see you hanged."

"But we haven't done anything!" Caroline wailed. She rushed to James and pulled on his arm. "Please, James, I'm begging you. Tell her that it's not true. Show her the proof I brought here tonight. With all Richard has been going through lately, the very last thing he needs is to be brought up on false charges for a crime he didn't commit."

"Whatever is the chit suggesting?" the dowager demanded. "I simply will not abide anymore secrets, James, so you had best tell me now and get it over with."

"Jamie, your father and I deserve an explanation as well. It's not every day that our daughter-in-law is abducted."

"Please, James," Caroline wailed, "you promised to help me."

James held up his hands and shouted to be heard over the three women. "Enough is enough. This is going to have to wait until Stephen gets back here with the duke. My one and only concern at this minute is the fact that my wife"—he turned and frowned at Abu—"and Randy is my wife and no bloody piece of paper is going to say otherwise—has been kidnapped and I want her back, safe and sound."

Miles put a comforting arm around his son. "Of course you do, James. And we're all going to help." The earl nodded to his butler. "Fenton, send Thomas for the constable and have all the servants assembled for questioning. Catherine, my love, I want you and Abu to see that everyone is accounted for,

including the extra guards who were hired for this evening."
He turned to the dowager. "Miranda, please get your guest
list. Caroline can go over the list with you while you verify
how many of these people actually attended the ball. While all
of you are off taking care of these matters, James and I will
decide on our next course of action."

Alone with his father, James dropped into the chair behind
the desk and placed the brooch on the desktop in front of him.
"I feel so helpless sitting here. By rights, I should be out
scouring the city looking for whoever abducted Randy."

Miles sat on the edge of the desk beside him. "Exactly where
are you going to start, James? London is a large city, with
many places to hide. First, we need to know how your wife
was removed from this house and by whom. That would at
least give us a place to begin."

"You know, Father, this is all my fault. I thought my plan
was perfect. I was supposed to be the target, not Randy. If
she's hurt because of my arrogance, I will never forgive myself.
How could I have been so wrong about the Duke of Maidstone?"

"Caroline said she brought you proof of Richard's inno-
cence. What was she talking about?"

James opened the top drawer and removed a piece of folded
parchment. "Caroline gave me this letter that she's been holding for the duke. Evidently she and Maidstone have grown
quite close since her husband's death last year. She was hoping
I could use my influence to help him with this matter."

Miles was puzzled. "Exactly what does she want you to do
and why should you believe her? God knows, she has lied
before."

"Read it for yourself, Father. You will understand why I
know Caroline is telling the truth."

With an air of skepticism, Miles took the letter from his son.
His breath caught when he perused its contents. "My word,
this letter was sent to Richard by your grandfather, Geoffrey

Carlisle. I know his signature, and no one would dare to counter-
feit the ducal seal of Chatham."

"Yes, I know. As you can see, Grandfather is giving Richard
advice on obtaining a divorce from Amelia. Since it would
take the approval of Parliament, besides good evidence and
witnesses, he reminds Maidstone that he also needs the support
of his peers." James looked over the page and pointed to the
last paragraph. "Right here, Grandfather refers to the proof
against Amelia being quite incriminating and suggests the prob-
ability that she could face murder charges when the information
is revealed in the divorce hearing."

Miles shook his head. "Amelia Wentworth? She's a little
thing, with dark hair, pale blue eyes. She squints a bit. I've
only seen her a few times, but she hardly seems like a killer."

"I know what you mean, but apparently Grandfather has
gone over the evidence and believes Amelia capable of a crime.
I love Grandfather and I know how much he values truth. If
he thinks she is a murderer, then I have little doubt that she
is."

The Earl refolded the letter and handed it to his son. "This
may sound a little far-fetched, but do you think Amelia Wentworth could have something to do with Randy's abduction?"

James shrugged. "I doubt it. Amelia must have an inkling
what her husband is up to, and that's why she left town last
week. No, I think whoever took Randy is looking to ransom
her. She was wearing a fortune in diamonds and is the heiress
to one of the wealthiest women in the country." He steepled his
fingers and tapped his chin. "There's also another possibility."

"An enemy I don't know about, my son?"

The concern in his father's voice made James smile. "It's
not an enemy of mine, but back in India, there were at least
four different attempts on Randy's life that I know of. I can't
help wondering if that man has followed her to England."

"How can you be sure it was one man and not several who
tried to kill her?"

James stared at the fiery red gem on the desk before him.

"Call it a gut feeling, but I simply know it was the work of one man. Every time he tried, he failed. That kind of frustration could provoke a man to try again. The question is, would he be driven enough to travel halfway around the world to do it?"

Richard Wentworth strode into the study, tossing his cloak at Fenton, who was running to keep up with him. "Take this and go. I have sent word to the authorities. As soon as they arrive, get them in here immediately." The Duke of Maidstone then turned his attention to James. "Well, young man, you seem to have lost my niece. What are *we* going to do to get her back?"

James boldly met him eye-to-eye. "Whatever it takes, sir. Whatever it takes."

"Good," Richard declared with a curt nod. "You can count on my assistance as well. Since we have the ransom demands, we—"

James bound to his feet. "What ransom demands?"

Richard scowled and looked over his shoulder toward the foyer. "Your friend, Stephen, has it. The note was delivered to my home while he was waiting for me to dress to come here. Once I read it, that brash pup yanked it from my hands and wouldn't return it to me. There he is now."

Stephen rushed in with a small drawstring pouch and gave it to James. The usually dapper young noble wiped his brow on the end of his loose cravat. "Some crazy man has taken your wife. He wants fifty thousand pounds or you'll never see her again. Instructions for payment will be sent in three days with proof that Randy is alive."

James quickly read the note before handing it to his father. "Who delivered this? Did you get a good look at him?"

"It was just a street lad. Rather dirty and scruffy, but with the foulest mouth I have ever heard. When I tried to stop him from leaving, he cursed me, kicked me in the—well, then he ran." Stephen fell into the nearest chair and moaned in pain. Leaning up, he took something from his pocket. "I nearly forgot. I found this hidden in the lining of the pouch. It's a miracle that urchin didn't find it first."

James silently held the Ryland betrothal ring in his hand as Stephen scoffed. "That kidnapper must be a bloody fool to let a gem like that go. That emerald is at least ten carats."

"With the diamond collection she was wearing, it was a small sacrifice," Miles replied. "It simply confirms he has Randy."

Sitting down again, James clenched his fingers around the ring. "The house was filled with people tonight. In such a crush, it would be easy for a person to slip in. But how could anyone carry Randy off without being seen?"

As his father, Richard, and Stephen discussed the possible ways to escape the house undetected, James closed his eyes and prayed for guidance. The feeling of helplessness that assailed him was nothing new to him. Not being able to find Randy in the burning barn when he knew she was trapped inside had been just as bad as this. If he hadn't been able to contact her in that strange mental way Abu had suggested, she might have died.

That memory suddenly gave James hope. Could he communicate with Randy like that again? Remembering the old Indian's advice, James emptied his mind of everything else and concentrated on one single thought. "Randy, my love, where are you?"

Pitching from side to side, Randy awoke from her drugged stupor to find herself enclosed in a vibrating cell of darkness. She was sitting with her knees bent up near her chest and curved walls surrounded her. Noxious odors filled her nose, causing her stomach to clench in revulsion. Struggling with her bound hands, she knocked the rag from her mouth and gulped the fetid air to swallow back the bile welling in her throat.

Pain and despair were her unwanted companions. Her joints

burned and ached from inactivity; her feet and hands were numb. She was too dizzy and weak to do anything but rest her badly throbbing head against her knees. Tears fell from her eyes.

Randy, my love, where are you?

Randy heard the words with such clarity, she was left to wonder whether it was real or just a reaction to the potion that had rendered her so defenseless. When she heard them again and realized that they were coming from within her own mind, her doubts disappeared.

Randy, my love, where are you?

"James? James . . . is that you?"

Yes, my love, it's me. Where are you?

She shook her head. "Don't know . . . so cold and dark. Small moving prison. Smells awful."

Are you hurt, Randy?

"Too weak to move. Head spinning . . . feel sick."

Did you see who did this to you?

"No . . . just a man . . . an angry man. Find me, James . . . must tell you . . . I love . . ."

In spite of her best efforts to answer, Randy once again slipped into a deep, troubled sleep.

No . . . just a man . . . an angry man. Find me, James . . . must tell you . . . I love . . .

The weakness he heard in Randy's words told James that she was still suffering from the effects of the laudanum that had been mixed in her lemonade. Recalling some of the things she had told him, James ignored the curiosity of the other three men in the study and shouted for the butler.

"Fenton, get the cook in here right away."

The butler hurried in with the family cook, Betsy Wiggins. The stocky, middle-aged woman curtsied before the desk.

"Mrs. Wiggins," James began, "I know you were very busy preparing the supper for tonight's celebration, but did any of the tradesmen make a late delivery this evening during the party itself? You know, such as the baker or the butcher?''

"No, milord," she replied, the brim of her white mopcap bobbing with her curtsey. "All that was taken care of much earlier in the day I pride myself on having everything ready and waiting before the first guest arrives."

James felt his hope ebbing. "Then no one other than staff came in or out of the kitchen entrances all night?"

Mrs. Wiggins shook her head. "No, milord." A frown creased her brow. "Unless you count old Dan McGee, the fishmonger with those barrels of his. The stench left from the raw oysters and cod he delivered in them right put me off. Thank heavens one of the footmen helped Dan remove them from the kitchen."

"Which footman was that, Mrs. Wiggins?"

The cook was thoughtful for a moment before she replied. " 'Twas one of the new men, milord. Heath is his name. Tall, dark, with a bushy beard. Real mannerly, he was. Too bad about his scars, though."

"What scars are you talking about?" James asked.

"On the left side of his face. His beard covered most of them, but the one near his eye was plain. Lucky he didn't lose his eye, them being such a lovely shade of blue and all." She sighed and shook her head. "I couldn't help but wonder if Heath had been in a terrible accident. Poor soul! That would account for his missing finger."

James felt his heart lurch. "What finger was it?"

Mrs. Wiggins wiggled the small finger on her hand. "The pinkie of his right hand, milord. I would never have noticed it at all if he hadn't removed his white gloves to help old Dan carry them foul barrels out. When I saw Heath come through the kitchens a while later, his gloves were back on and he was carrying a tray with several glasses of lemonade. Is there anything else you require of me, milord?"

When James didn't reply, Miles dismissed the cook. As the

door closed behind her, he placed a hand on his son's shoulder. "What's wrong? Do you know who this man is?"

"I don't know his name, but I know what he has done. He murdered Jonathan Collins and tried to kill Randy. I will be damned if I let that son of Satan carry out his plan to destroy the woman I love." Standing up, James threw down the betrothal ring and moved toward the door.

"James, where are you going?" Miles asked. "You have to be here to talk to the authorities when they arrive."

James opened the door and looked back at his father. "You deal with them, sir. Abu and I are going to look for my wife."

Richard came to his feet. "James, don't you think—"

"I've already wasted too much time thinking, your grace. Abu once told me that Randy and I shared a link to one another that would help me find her when she was in danger." He touched his chest. "It was a knowledge in my heart and soul like nothing I had ever experienced before. I used it then and saved her life. My only hope is that we're not too late."

"But Jamie," Stephen said, "the kidnapper said he would send proof that she was alive with the ransom demands in three days."

"This madman is not going to let her live, Stephen. He has tried to kill her several times and it's become an obsession to him; he won't be appeased until he's completed the task."

"Then let me go with you. I can help."

James shook his head. "No, Stephen. Stay here and work with my father, the duke, and Nana. Go through the motions of arranging the ransom in case the kidnapper has someone watching the house. In the meantime, Abu and I will be looking for him."

"But son," Miles interrupted, "what will you do to find Randy if your—ah, special link with her isn't working?"

A wry smile curved the taut lines of James's face. "Randy has a similar bond with someone else. In fact, it may be stronger. If I can't find my love, I have no doubt at all that her friend, Sidra, will be able to find her for me."

Chapter 20

Randy woke up with the sun shining on her face. Her eyes were closed, but she could feel its welcome warmth on her skin. She was stiff and sore with her hands and feet bound, lying on what felt like a lumpy old mattress. The stale smell of dust permeated her nose. It was then she heard a woman's voice coming toward her, shouting in anger. In shocked recognition, Randy feigned sleep and prayed her suspicions were wrong.

"You're a stupid fool, Nigel! I thought you said she was wearing the brooch last night? The one piece I wanted more than any other and it still eludes my grasp."

"The chit had it on in the ballroom," he replied. "It must have fallen off during our struggle."

"I simply cannot fathom how careless you have become, Nigel. The Bloody Tear of Allah should have been mine. I searched that cursed house for more than three weeks and then she shows up with it."

"Calm down, dearling," he soothed. "You already have the rest of the collection. With that and the fifty thousand we will have by the end of the week, we will have more than enough to start a new life together on the continent.''

"Nigel, you know I won't leave England without everything I deserve, including that brooch. That red diamond gives its owner good fortune, making that person invincible to their enemies.''

"A lot of good it did for Miranda Collins,'' he snickered. "She is my prisoner and at my mercy. As I see it, that bauble hasn't done a damned thing to help her.''

"How can you say that? She survived all those attempts on her life with barely a scratch. The Bloody Tear of Allah was already on its way to her with Grayson, so its power protected her. With all I've had to contend with during my wretched life, I must have that gem for my own.''

Nigel laughed. "My poor dear Amy. You always were such a superstitious sort.''

"Call me what you like, Nigel, but I am also a great deal smarter than you.''

"Get away from that bed,'' he warned. "I prefer that our guest remain asleep a while longer.''

"Too late,'' she chirped, leaning over the bed. "You can cease the charade, young lady. I know you are awake and have been for quite some time.''

Opening her eyes, Randy met the icy blue gaze of Amelia Wentworth, who was standing beside her wearing a hooded cloak of black wool. "So, you were the one behind this plot, Amelia. Wasn't being the Duchess of Maidstone enough for you?''

"As if that exalted title could solve all my ills,'' Amelia scoffed, whirling away from the bed. "You know nothing of the mockery my marriage was, so keep your opinions to yourself. Get those manacles on her, Nigel, while I fetch Edith.''

When Nigel approached the bed from the corner of the small, drab room, Randy got her first look at him. The powdered wig and footman's uniform were gone, but there was no mistaking the full beard and blue eyes. Grinning, he snapped his heels and bent in a courtly bow. "I am at your service, my lady."

The military precision of his movements reminded Randy of someone she had known in India. His hair was long and darker than she remembered, but she instinctively knew it was him.

"You were on my father's staff in Calicut, Lieutenant Reynolds. I rarely saw you, but he spoke of you often. He referred to you as a fine spit-and-polish officer."

The shoulders of Nigel's brown riding coat lifted in a shrug as he removed the ropes and placed a set of heavy manacles around her ankles. "With Major Spencer trying to win your hand and your friendship with the native royals, I never thought you would notice a lowly lieutenant like me."

"I didn't encourage the major, and I never—" Her words came to an abrupt halt when Nigel reached over to test the bindings on her wrists and she saw his scarred hand with its missing finger. Anger surged through her. "Tell me, Lieutenant, how do you let a man host a party in your honor, knowing full well that you would be returning a few hours later to murder him in his sleep?"

Nigel pulled back his hand. "A man does what is necessary. My task would have been completed that night if that damned beast of yours hadn't maimed me. As it was, I tried six other times, and you continually evaded your fate. You have more lives than a damned cat!" His eyes shone with a feral gleam. "That's about to end. In a day or so I'm finally going to be rid of you."

Amelia came into the room with a white-haired old woman stumbling at her side. "Do be quiet, Nigel. Your insistent prattle is quite annoying. You know very well we cannot kill her until after we've collected the ransom. If something goes awry, young Miranda will prove a fitting hostage."

"But Amy, I think—"

Amelia glared up at Nigel and jabbed his chest with her

finger. "Stop thinking and do what I say. Have I ever been wrong, little brother?"

Randy gasped. "Nigel Reynolds is your brother?"

"Of course he is," Amelia boasted, patting his cheek with her hand. "Nigel is taller of course, but our eyes and coloring are just alike."

Amelia spoke to the old woman beside her in slow, deliberate terms. "Edith, I want you to help our guest see to her personal needs, but nothing else. Do you understand, Edith?"

Edith looked at the bed and nodded. Randy could see the vacant appearance of the elderly woman's eyes and her slack jaw. Her gown and apron were soiled, and her long white hair hung in a tangled disarray around her shoulders and back. Any hopes Randy had of possibly gaining this woman's aid were forgotten.

Amelia touched the old woman's shoulder. "I knew I could count on you, Edith. As our housekeeper, you always took such good care of us." She moved toward the door. "Come along, Nigel. While I'm writing the second letter, I want you to board up that window. We wouldn't want a snooping neighbor to see what we are up to."

Randy struggled to lean on her elbow so she could face her captors. "Amelia, since you've already planned my demise, can you at least tell me why Nigel murdered my father and then tried to kill me?"

Leaning against the door, Amelia smiled and counted off on her fingers. "Money, jewels, prestige, and all the rest that great wealth entails."

Randy was perplexed. "My father was only a government official. How did you think to gain all that from his death?"

"He was also an heir to the dowager's estate, just as you are. With the two of you dead, there will be no one in my way."

"Why would that make a difference to you?"

"Poor baby," Amelia said with a theatrical sigh. "Didn't your beloved Nana tell you about the codicil she added to her will last year? I found a copy of it in her library during one of my visits. In the event that you and your father cannot inherit, the dowager's entire estate comes to me.''

Questions that had plagued her over the past few months suddenly made sense to Randy. ''Until you recognized me in the salon, you thought I was dead. No wonder you fainted at the sight of me. You were the one who poisoned Nana.''

''When I discovered that Ida Brody was my husband's pawn, I decided to make use of her. She baked the biscuits for the dowager at my insistence, but I was the one who tainted the almonds with arsenic.'' Amelia pushed back her hood and patted her hair into place. ''Doing away with that traitorous wench was a pleasure.''

''Everyone thought Ida committed suicide.''

Amelia laughed. ''Of course they did. On the pretense of offering the poor woman solace, I brought her tea. Ida never noticed the laudanum in her cup and drank it right down. Once she was asleep, I pressed the pillow to her face and smothered her. Putting a touch of arsenic to her lips and in the cup was a stroke of genius.''

''What are you going to do after you kill me?'' Randy asked.

''Why, I am going to rush to the side of my dearest friend Miranda and console her through the tragic loss of her only grandchild.'' Deep in thought, Amelia frowned with concentration. ''I won't be able to use arsenic again, but hemlock should do quite nicely.''

''You seem to know a great deal about poisons.''

''Oh, yes,'' Amelia replied with a nod. ''My mother was an actress, but her father had been an apothecary in Birmingham for many years. I learned about herbs, poisons, and compounds in a journal she kept of his. I've often made good use of his knowledge when I needed it.''

The ease with which Amelia spoke of her crimes made Randy sick with revulsion. There was no remorse in her words. She was cheerful and proud of what she had done. If there was a

God above, this woman's conceit would lead to her downfall, and Randy prayed that she would live long enough to see it.

Nigel took his sister's arm. "Amelia, do you think it's wise to tell her all this?"

"Stop being such a spoilsport, Nigel, and let me enjoy my gloat a while longer. With those manacles and only this way out, our guest isn't going anywhere." She leaned up on tiptoe and kissed his cheek. "But if she tries to escape, you can shoot her."

Amelia glanced back at Randy. "By now Richard has received the ransom note and has probably been dragged in for questioning regarding your disappearance. With all the doubts I placed in James Grayson's head, your uncle is as good as convicted. Too bad your friend James didn't shoot Richard for me. It would have made matters far simpler."

"There's something you should know, Amelia," Randy declared, stopping her as she turned to leave. "James Grayson is more than my friend. He is my husband. We were married in India before we set sail for England. Even now, I carry my husband's child. As for the codicil to her will, Nana had it revoked weeks ago. If anything happens to me, James becomes Nana's heir. You will get nothing!"

Amelia whirled around and charged toward the bed. A glint of madness flared in her eyes. "Why, you unscrupulous bitch!" she screeched, raising her hand to strike Randy. "I should kill you this instant for robbing me of what should have been mine."

Nigel caught his sister's arm. "Stop it, Amelia. You were the one who told me that a dead hostage has no value when you're bargaining for your life. If what she said is true, Grayson and his whole bloody family will be coming after her. Should they find us before we can escape, Randy can guarantee our freedom."

Amelia angrily shook off his hold. "They are not going to find us, if you do as I say. Now, block that window and get that fishmonger's wagon with its smelly barrels out of here while I write the instructions for the ransom payment.''

When Amelia was out of the room, Nigel turned to Randy. "You would be wise not to goad my sister like that again.''

"What are you going to do if I chose to ignore your warning, Lieutenant?'' Randy asked, saying his rank with as much enmity as she could summon. "It's hardly a threat when I already know that you mean to kill me.''

Nigel leaned over the bed and pressed the tip of a dagger against her throat. "But there are many ways to die, my lady. I could make it quick and merciful, or long and lingering with a great deal of pain. The choice is up to you.''

He trailed the sharp-pointed blade across her throat, but Randy refused to be intimidated. She met his hostile gaze with a fiery one of her own. "Either way, Lieutenant, it doesn't matter to me. Because what my husband will do to you is going to be far worse, I assure you. James loves me more than life itself, and when he finds you, he will put you through the tortures of hell for killing me and his unborn child.''

It was only after Nigel had left the room that Randy let her real emotions surface. Lying back down, she closed her eyes and held her bound hands against her trembling lips. She took deep, calming breaths and tried very hard not to cry.

Her boast of being married to James had been a desperate attempt to keep Amelia and her brother from going after Nana. Though she knew their union wasn't valid and that the codicil was still in effect, she prayed they would believe her claims.

"Ye mustn't cry, milady.'' A low, weathered voice tempered with the burr of the Scots spoke near her ear. "The Devil's spawn would take great pleasure in it. Somehow, we'll find a way out of this dilemma, I promise ye.''

Randy turned to find the elderly woman named Edith standing beside her. There was a spirited flash of defiance in the old housekeeper's eyes that startled Randy.

Edith smiled and nodded. "Ye thought I was daft,'' she

whispered. " 'Tis the only way Amelia would trust me here with ye. The wee lass is the one addlepated, not me."

"You have known Amelia all of her life?"

"Aye, most of it." The old woman glanced over her shoulder. "But the tellin' must wait. Nigel will be at that window in a minute or two and we canna let him see us conversin' like this."

With surprising strength, Edith slipped her arm beneath Randy's shoulder and gently lifted her into a sitting position. "Come on now, darlin'. Let me help ye to the chamber pot in the corner. Then we'll get ye out of these clothes and bathe ye a bit. 'Tis a shame about yer gown. The lace might be repaired, but I doubt that horrible fish smell will ever fade."

As Edith guided her through the motions, Randy cursed her own weakness and the wretched aching in her head and battered body. The iron manacles on her ankles were connected with a very short span of heavy chain that made her shuffle across the floor in tiny, faltering steps. She could already feel the metal cuffs chafing her skin. When Edith sat her on a chair and removed the ropes from her wrists, the numbness in her hands disappeared and deep scalding pain shot through her fingers like molten lead. Randy gasped in agony.

"Ach, 'tis sorry I am," Edith apologized while carefully washing and rubbing the circulation back into Randy's tortured hands. "But I'll have to put the ropes back on ye when we're finished. I'll be sure not to tie them too tight so this willna happen again. Now let me fetch my wool dressin' gown for ye. 'Tis not fancy, though it will keep ye warm, milady."

Randy watched her go to the oak chest of drawers across the room and remove a red plaid robe. "Do you live here, Edith?"

The old woman looked at the door and window before she came back to where Randy was sitting. She helped Randy undress to her shift and put on the robe as she answered. "Aye, but 'tis more a hiding place than a home. Till just a few weeks back, I was livin' content in the Highlands with my sister, Meg.

Then his lordship sent word, and I knew 'twas time to come back to correct the wrong that has haunted me fer nigh on fifteen years.''

"Who was the lord who sent for you?"

"The Duke of Maidstone, o' course. But enough talk, milady. I hear Nigel scratchin' outside the window. Let me braid yer hair and get ye back on the bed afore he peeks in. And he'll do it. Nigel always had a curious nature. Got the lad in a peck o' trouble more than once.''

While Edith replaced the ropes on her wrists, Randy lay on the musty old bed considering all the things she had learned within that hour. It enraged her to think that Amelia and her brother had been responsible for inflicting so much pain and grief on her life. From her father's tragic death and forcing her to leave India, to nearly losing her grandmother, the two of them had done it all. Though they had not admitted it, she didn't doubt for a second that they had been the ones who nearly shot James in front of the opera house. Her inability to do anything to punish them made Randy all the more miserable.

Looking at the cracked ceiling, Randy suddenly felt dizzy, and her head ached. "How can I worry about retaliating against those two when I feel so sick? I should be thinking about escaping, but I don't have the strength to stand on my own."

" 'Tis that foul laudanum, milady," Edith whispered, pursing her lips in disgust. "Robs ye of yer senses and leaves a body throbbin' in revolt if ye had too much of it. There's naught to do but wait fer it to pass through ye. I'll do what I can to stop them from dosin' ye again.'' She stroked Randy's brow. "Rest a bit, milady, while I fetch ye some broth and peppermint tea. 'Tis the best thing fer an ailin' stomach."

With Edith gone, Randy tried to ignore her discomfort and the sound of Nigel nailing boards across the window by thinking about James. Though she remembered little of what happened after her abduction, she was certain her memory of speaking to him with her mind had really taken place. They had only shared a few words, but it was enough to give her hope.

"If we were able to communicate last night, perhaps we can do it again." Using her meditation skills, Randy relaxed and allowed herself to focus on the man she loved and the message she was sending to him. "James, can you hear me? I need you."

James seethed with impatience as he sat on a bale of hay in the Foxwood stables. "Abu, it's just not working. I've followed your instructions to the letter and I still can't reach Randy. What am I doing wrong?"

Clasping his hands behind his back, Abu sighed. "There are no set rules for this kind of thing, *Huzur,* but I believe your difficulty comes from trying too hard. Your emotions could be hindering your efforts."

"How can I not be emotional at a time like this? Randy was abducted more than eighteen hours ago. When I was able to touch her mind, she was weak and suffering. I could feel her confusion, and then she just faded away." James raked his fingers through his hair. "I've never felt so bloody helpless."

"Perhaps you cannot reach her, *Huzur,* because she is—"

"Don't say it, Abu!" James demanded, jumping to his feet. "Randy is alive. If she were dead, I would know it. I would feel it in my heart."

Abu smiled and touched the younger man's shoulder. "Of course she is alive. I was merely suggesting that she might be asleep. The drug she was given was quite potent."

Shaking his head, James wearily dropped back onto the bale of hay. "I am sorry, Abu. The frustration of not knowing where Randy is has left my nerves raw." He removed his watch from his coat pocket and snapped it open. "Shouldn't Xavier be back here with Sidra by now?"

"Kira told me that Sidra had been restless most of the night, and Xavier thought a long walk would soothe the beast."

James smiled with satisfaction. "Sidra must sense that her mistress is in danger. I know she will be able to lead us to Randy." A look of amazement suddenly appeared on the Indian's usually stoic face. "What's the matter, Abu? Don't you believe Sidra will be able to help us find her?"

Abu chuckled. "I have no doubt in Sidra's ability, *Huzur.* It is the change in you that astounds me. Touching minds. Speaking without words. Animals possessing mystical abilities. Only a few months ago you would have scoffed at such things. I am pleased to see you accepting these ideas without cynicism. For an Englishman, you show a great deal of Eastern logic."

At that moment, Xavier entered the stable with Sidra. The large orange-and-black beast was pulling hard on her leash, forcing her tall, muscular handler to strain in his efforts to force her inside. As soon as he secured the animal's chain to the pillar in her stall, Xavier began talking to Abu with his hand language.

"Xavier reports that Sidra did not want to return here," Abu explained to James, as the mute signed to him. "Sidra refused her food and spent the entire afternoon trying to go east. Do you know what that suggests?"

James nodded and approached Sidra's stall. "That victory is at hand." He leaned on the gate to the stall to watch the tiger pacing back and forth. Her agitated state seemed to mirror his own. "Why don't you and Xavier gather our supplies from the main house and have our horses readied? I will remain here with Sidra while you're gone."

"But, *Huzur,* it is nearly sunset. Would it not be better to wait until daylight to begin our journey?"

"No. There is going to be a full moon tonight, and I mean to take advantage of it."

Alone in the stable, James opened the gate and approached the high-strung animal. He knelt down with his hand outstretched and waited for her to come to him. Sidra butted her head against his hand, her long tail snapping rhythmically side to side.

"You know Randy is in trouble, don't you, girl?" James said, stroking the tiger's large, colorful head. "I won't admit it to Abu or the others, but I am worried about your lady. I haven't been able to contact her since last night. She was so weak and confused. I felt her pain as if it were my own.''

Emitting a soft hiss, Sidra's golden eyes lifted to meet his. As he looked into the tiger's gaze, he became aware of a soft voice calling to him. But he wasn't listening with his ears; the entreaty was heard in his mind.

James, can you hear me? I need you.

Recognition warred with relief as James smiled and closed his eyes. ''Yes, love, I can hear you. How are you feeling? Do you know where you are?''

I am feeling a little better, but I have no idea where I am. It's an old cottage. There must be people nearby. Nigel is boarding up the window so they can't see me.

''Is Nigel the man who abducted you?'' James asked. Several moments passed before he heard her reply.

Yes. Nigel Reynolds is also the man who murdered my father. He was a lieutenant on Papa's staff in Calicut.

James wanted to shout at Randy and remind her that this was the same man who had also tried to kill her. Someday he would help her break the habit of always minimizing the danger to herself. But someday would have to wait for a while.

''Randy, we are coming to rescue you. Do you know if Nigel is working alone? Does he have other men there helping him?''

I haven't seen any men, just his sister. Amelia Wentworth is Nigel's sister. You must be careful, James. Amelia is insane. She was the one who tried to poison Nana, and now she plans to kill me after ...

The sudden break in her message cut through James like a sharp blade. ''Randy, please speak to me. What's happening?''

When silence met his demands, James stood up and moved toward the gate. His failure to discover where she was being held only served to fuel the flames of his wrath. Unwrapping the chain from the post, he gave Sidra a slight tug.

''Come along, girl. Randy is waiting for us.''

The sun was setting as the unlikely pair walked out of the stable together.

Chapter 21

"Please, milady, ye must wake up. There's danger afoot, and we can stay here no longer."

Randy fought to rouse herself from her lethargic state. The light from the single candle sitting on the chest beside the bed hurt her eyes. Her head was throbbing, and her tongue felt swollen, sticking to the roof of her mouth.

"Water," she whispered. "Need water."

"O' course ye do, milady. Jest let old Edith help ye sit up a bit, so ye can have a sip."

The tepid water was served in a chipped cup, but to Randy it tasted like the sweetest nectar. After drinking most of the water, she licked her dried lips and struggled to speak.

"What happened to me, Edith?"

" 'Twas the broth I made fer ye. Amelia took the mug from me and put something in it. Don't ye remember me tryin' to knock it from yer hand when she gave it to ye?"

Randy closed her eyes and took several deep breaths. Her mind was cloudy, but she could recall most of what the old woman was talking about. "Yes, I remember what happened now. You attempted to knock it from my hand, and Amelia struck you and railed at you for being careless. Did she hurt you, Edith?''

''Ach, no! It would take a lot more than a slap from that wee one to harm me. If Nigel wasna standin' at the door holdin' that gun o' his, I would've struck her back and showed her how it was really done.'' Removing the ropes from Randy's hands, Edith looked toward the open door. ''Amelia is sleepin' in the spare room, and Nigel has dozed off on the settee in the parlor. I have to get ye out o' here afore they're up and about.''

Randy rubbed her aching temples. ''But where are we, Edith? I don't even know where I am.''

''We're in Faversham, milady. In the cottage Baron Reynolds willed to me for my years o' service to his family.''

Despite her headache, Randy recalled a conversation she had had with her grandmother. ''Wasn't the baron Amelia and Nigel's uncle, the man who took them in when their parents died?''

Edith frowned. ''Aye, he was that. Baron Reynolds was more soldier than gentleman. He had a cruel way about him that the Devil himself would have admired. 'Tis no wonder those two bairns fell to ruin with a beast like him to raise them.''

''I take it the baron wasn't a fit parent to his niece and nephew.''

Tears filled Edith's eyes. ''The man was a brute who hated his youngest brother for runnin' off with an actress instead of marryin' the wealthy heiress who'd been chosen for him. When they were killed in a carriage accident four years later, their babes were given to the baron.''

Her hands trembled as she blotted her eyes with her apron. ''He drank and took his loathin' out on the children. When Amelia started to blossom into a pretty young lady, I noticed a change in the baron. He became overly attentive and was always touchin' her. I feared for the lass and tried to warn her, but to no avail. She was but eleven when the baron did the unspeakable, and took her to his bed.

"I tried to find a way to stop him," the old lady continued. "When I told the vicar at the church, he reminded me that the baron was gentry and a war hero, while I was naught but a poor servant. Who would believe the likes o' me?"

Lost in her memories, Edith shuddered. "Even little Nigel suffered when he crept outta bed one night and spied that beast forcin' himself on Amelia. He jumped on his uncle's back to stop him. The baron whipped the lad and locked him in the cellar."

The nausea Randy was experiencing had more to do with her shocked reaction to the housekeeper's whispered declarations than the effects of the laudanum in her body. Reaching out to calm Edith, she could feel the depth of the woman's guilt and pain. "The baron was a depraved monster. It wasn't your fault. You cannot blame yourself for his actions."

"Oh, I know it, milady." Edith sighed, patting Randy's hand. "Forgive me for goin' on like I did. 'Tis old age catchin' up on me, I fear." She rushed to the chest and began going through the drawers. "Now let me find ye some clothes so I can get ye out of here. If we hurry, I think we can make it down to the village magistrate by dawn."

Randy tried to swing her legs from the bed. The pain from the heavy metal cuffs cutting into her ankles reminded her of another difficulty she was faced with. "Clothes won't solve this problem, Edith. I can't run with manacles on my feet."

Desperation lit the woman's troubled gaze. "Saints alive, I forgot about those foul things!"

"Why don't you leave me here while you go for help?"

Edith shook her head. "I dare not take the chance o' leavin' ye, milady. I heard those two discussin' yer plight over dinner. Nigel's had second thoughts and doesna want to wait for the ransom. With ye dead, he says there'd be naught to connect them to the crime. Amelia's a mite greedy and wants the cash in hand first, but I fear Nigel might act on his own."

"Aren't you afraid that Nigel will kill you as well?" Randy asked.

The old woman brushed the locks of her white hair away from her face and sighed. ''The thought o' livin' any longer with my conscience gnawing at my soul frightens me more than death, milady. What their uncle did to those two was awful, but their crime against him was even worse.''

''What did they do?''

''They murdered him.'' Edith sat on the bed beside Randy. ''Now yer probably thinkin' the man deserved to be punished, and I agree, but those two killed him for his wealth and estates. Many times over the years prior to that, I tried to convince them to run away with me to Scotland to escape the baron, but Amelia refused. Claimed her brother deserved his inheritance and was willin' to do whatever was necessary to get it for him. I ne'er thought she would resort to murder. The sight of the baron lying in a contorted heap, dead at the foot of the stairs, will torment me the rest of my life.''

When Edith became silent and seemed to drift away into her thoughts, Randy patted her hand. ''It could have been an accident. Why are you so convinced it was murder?''

''To begin with, Amelia bragged about it in her journal. She was nineteen when the baron arranged for her marriage to the Duke o' Maidstone, but she wanted no part of it. So one night, she put a powdered mixture into her uncle's wine to addle his wits. Half naked, she taunted and teased him into running after her. Once she got the old fool onto the landing, Nigel jumped out of the shadows to startle him and Amelia shoved the baron down the stairs.''

''You read about this in Amelia's journal?''

''Aye, but I saw it happen too,'' Edith replied mournfully. ''With the other servants in bed, I had gone to the study to fetch a book and was jest comin' out when I heard the ruckus on the stairs. It happened so quickly, the baron never got a chance to scream.'' The old woman trembled. ''From the crack o' the door I watched Amelia and Nigel, kissin' and pawin' one another in celebration of what they had done. 'Twas an unholy pairing, but their laughter was short-lived.''

Randy's curiosity made her ask, "Why? What happened?"

"Nigel wasna the baron's heir. The title and what was left o' his cash and property went to the son o' Reynold's second brother, who was livin' in the colonies. There was naught else for Amelia to do but marry the Duke o' Maidstone and use his money to help Nigel. I think the duke became wise to her, and all he would pay for was Nigel's commission in the army."

Tears trickled down the old woman's cheeks. "The duke was right nice to me. Shortly after their marriage, his grace pensioned me off with a yearly stipend."

Anger suddenly burned within Randy. "And you let him marry that witch, Amelia, knowing what she had done?"

"How could I do aught else when I blamed myself for what the lass had become?" Edith whimpered. "Had I ignored the vicar's warnin' to mind my own affairs and fled with the bairns when the baron first started sniffin' after Amelia, none o' this would have happened. But I was frightened and alone, with no one to help me. What choice did I have?"

Randy put her arm around Edith's trembling shoulders when she realized her rage should be directed at the injustices of society, not this woman. In a way, Edith was its victim, too. "I'm sorry for sounding cross with you. Please don't cry."

Edith wiped her eyes on the hem of her apron. "But I did try to make amends, milady. I wrote to the duke last year and told him what I knew. I suggested he look for the journals Amelia has always kept and find the proof for himself."

"Do you know if he found them?"

"Aye, he did," Edith replied. "The duke wrote me last fall and told me he had them in his possession, though they wouldna be enough to convict Amelia and Nigel. He begged me to come to London so I could testify in court as to what I had seen that night. I agreed, but rather than risk runnin' into Amelia in town, I decided to hide here in Faversham until the date for the trial was set."

The old woman snorted. "Was I surprised when Amelia herself appeared at my door a few days after I arrived! 'Twas the middle o' the night and my hair was a fright, much as 'tis now. She believed me demented and I did naught to convince her otherwise.''

Edith got up and moved toward the chest of drawers. ''Enough time wasted. I don't have a pair o' shoes to fit yer feet, and yer slippers must have been lost. Some good wool socks should keep you warm for the trek down to the village.''

''Don't bother,'' an irritated male voice called from the doorway. ''Our guest isn't leaving, Edith, and neither are you. Now, close those drawers and sit down in that chair.''

''But, Nigel, dear boy, ye don't understand—''

Nigel stepped into the room and pointed one of the pistols he was carrying at her. ''I understand enough to know that you can't be trusted, Edith. After all the years we were together, how could you betray Amelia and me like this?'' He moved toward the cowering old woman and put the gun barrel against her cheek. His face was a mask of rage. ''Thanks to your interference, we are going to lose everything. I could put this shot through your head for doing this to us, Edith.''

With her ankles chained together and her equilibrium marred by the laudanum, Randy knew she could never overpower Nigel to rescue Edith. But if she could find a way of distracting him, maybe the old woman would have a chance to escape.

''Shame on you, Lieutenant Reynolds,'' Randy mocked from her seat on the bed. ''Using your weapons and brute strength to subdue a helpless old lady. For a British officer, you certainly are a disgrace. Can you not find a better-matched opponent?''

Nigel's attention turned to Randy. ''Come on and give me a reason to pull this trigger, my lady,'' he taunted as he moved away from Edith and came toward the bed. ''Get up and see if you can toss me with one of those fancy moves those bloody heathens taught you in India. Amelia couldn't object if I told her that I was only trying to stop you from escaping.''

Lifting her manacled legs back onto the bed, Randy reclined on the pillow and crossed her arms over her chest. ''Shoot me where I am, Nigel. Your sister will see that you ignored her orders, and then you'll have to deal with her wrath and not me.''

''I don't take orders from anyone,'' Nigel boasted in a loud voice. ''Amelia and I are equal partners in this, and if I think you and Edith should be dead, no one is going to tell me otherwise.''

At that moment, Amelia came bustling into the room wearing her dressing gown and carrying a lantern. ''What in the devil is going on here, Nigel? I told you to leave this chit alone until I decide what's to be done with her in the morning.''

Nigel quirked his brow. ''Then it's a good thing I don't always take your advice, sister mine. Our hostage was about to escape and Edith was helping her. Once you hear what Edith has done to betray you, you will agree that it's time to end this charade now.''

With the full moon overhead, the three men rode along the deserted road with Sidra leading the way. After hours of running and tracking her cherished mistress, the large, tethered cat was tired, but refused to slow her pace.

''Where are we now, *Huzur?*'' Abu called out.

''On the outskirts of a village called Faversham. If I remember correctly, Amelia's family had an estate not far from here. Maybe that's where they are keeping Randy.''

All at once, Sidra changed direction and began moving off the road toward a forest. As they made their way through the trees, James saw the smoldering remains of a wagon in the clearing ahead of them. He pulled on the tiger's chain and rode toward the wagon. Handing the leash to Xavier, he dismounted and ran to the charred wreck.

James kicked over a plank of wood with lettering on it and knelt beside it. ''Look, Abu. It says McGee's Fish Market. This was the wagon that carried the barrels from the house during the party, and unless I miss my guess, Randy was inside of one of them." Standing up, he braced his hands on his hips and looked around. "Any sign of the barrels?"

Abu pointed behind a outcropping of rocks. "Over there."

They rushed to the partially destroyed barrels. The first one contained the body of an elderly man. A knotted silk scarf was entwined around his neck.

Abu studied the scarf. "This is the work of the same man who murdered Jonathan Collins. That Lieutenant Reynolds my lady told you of was obviously responsible for this poor soul's death as well."

The second barrel was splintered into smaller pieces. James bent down and retrieved Randy's white satin slipper from the debris. "This proves that Sidra's tracking abilities are truly remarkable. That animal puts my father's hunting dogs to shame."

"Sidra is tracking with more than her nose to guide her, *Huzur*. Her heart is linked to my mistress as well."

"I know, Abu, and so is mine." James pushed away the fears that were crowding his mind about Randy, and he stuffed the shoe into his coat pocket as they walked back to the horses. "From here on, we must be careful to keep a tight rein on Sidra. I have a feeling that we are close to finding Randy. We wouldn't want my wife's prized pet to get shot in the process of rescuing her. Randy would never forgive us."

"My lady would forgive you anything, *Huzur*. How could she not when she loves you with all her heart?"

James shot Abu a furtive smile as he remounted his horse. "I certainly hope you're right, my friend. With all the mistakes I have made recently, I pray her forgiving nature will hold out long enough for me to convince her that I love her too."

Nigel's telling of what Edith had said caused Amelia's temper to explode. "You always said you loved me, Edith. My husband has been looking for ways to be rid of me and you gave it to him, without regard to what would happen to me. Because of your blasted conscience, you have single-handedly destroyed my life, old woman. What am I supposed to do now?''

Nigel set one of his pistols down on the chest and put a consoling arm around his sister. ''Amy, all isn't lost. The journals that Richard stole from your bedroom are damning in themselves, but they are not enough to convict you. Without Edith's testimony, your husband doesn't have a case. If he had, Maidstone would have made use of them before now.''

''I suppose you're right, Nigel. As badly as Richard wants his freedom to marry that blond mistress of his, that's precisely what he would have done.'' Amelia rubbed her head. ''I have to think about what we should do next.''

''What's to think about, Amy? If I kill these two, we can set fire to the place and make good our escape before anyone is the wiser.''

Amelia shook her head, sending her long, dark hair over her shoulders like a sable cape. ''The ransom. We need the money from the ransom.''

Nigel grabbed his sister's arm and turned her to face him. ''Amy, you must be reasonable about this. The ransom isn't as important as keeping you safe. I heard Edith say that she has been in touch with Richard. He knows she's here waiting for the court date. It's only a matter of time before Maidstone comes looking for her.''

Confusion marred Amelia's brow. ''Is your concern for me or are you simply afraid of being caught yourself?''

''How can you ask that, Amy? Haven't I done everything you asked?'' Nigel embraced her. ''I couldn't protect you when we were children, but I love you and I would gladly die for you now.''

From across the room, Randy watched the two siblings. She despised them for what they had done to her father and family, yet she pitied them as well. She couldn't begin to fathom the depth of their strange relationship, but desperation and human need were universal. It was an incredible waste that two such attractive, intelligent people were also cold-blooded killers.

"And if I can't find a way to delay them, I am going to be their next victim," Randy mused bitterly to herself.

Amelia rubbed her temples with her trembling fingertips. "Forgive my doubts, Nigel. I know you love me and have only my best interests at heart."

"Of course I do, Amy. That's why I am telling you that we should forget the ransom and do away with these two. I have more than enough money to get us to France. The diamond jewelry young Miranda was wearing will bring a good price in Paris."

The mention of their captive drew Amelia's attention to the bed. Her renewed outrage was directed at Randy. She grabbed the pistol from the chest and moved toward the bed. "You have cost me more than anyone, you troublesome baggage. My only joy is knowing that when you are dead and your body is destroyed in the fire, no one will be able to connect me with the crime."

"I hate to disappoint you, Amelia, but James already knows that you and Nigel are responsible for my abduction," Randy said as she sat up on the edge of the bed. "If you do kill me, you had better be prepared to spend the rest of your life looking over your shoulder. No matter what it takes, my husband will hunt you down and make you pay for harming me."

"You're lying," Nigel snapped, moving to his sister's side. "Grayson was busy in the study when I stole you away from that house. He never even saw me, and it was probably hours later before he even realized that you were gone."

Randy shrugged. "That's true, but James knows that you and Amelia are holding me. I sent word to him several hours ago."

Nigel looked at the old woman whimpering in the corner. "But Edith never left the cottage—"

"Edith had nothing to do with it," Randy cut in. "I reached James all on my own."

Nigel threw back his head and snorted with laughter. "Sure

you did! I suppose you just willed yourself to Grayson's side and whispered in his ear!"

"Not exactly. The only thing I willed to James was my thoughts, and he answered me. I told him that you had kidnapped me and he said that he was on the way to rescue me."

Her stoic reply only made Nigel laugh harder. "If you are hearing voices, I must have given you too much laudanum."

Randy sighed. "The drug had nothing to do with it. I have a special mental gift that allows me to feel the pain in others. In some very rare occurrences, I can also exchange thoughts with certain people. James happens to be one of them."

"Try for another ploy, my lady. I would have to be an idiot to believe this drivel."

"Wait a minute, Nigel," Amelia interrupted, staring at Randy with fresh interest. "I have heard of such things. What if she is telling the truth?"

Nigel shook his head. "For an intelligent woman, you can be so gullible, Amy. You were always superstitious, with your good luck charms and gypsy soothsayers, but to believe this one's claim to special powers of the mind is too much to accept."

"What if I can prove it, Lieutenant?" Randy asked. "If I can show you one of my mental gifts, will you at least accept the possibility that I am telling you the truth about all of it?"

"Are you suggesting that you can read my thoughts?"

Randy shook her head. "No. I told you my ability to do that is limited to certain people. My gift to sense pain and ailments in others is far better." She looked at Amelia and found the woman frowning, rubbing the back of her neck. "Let me touch your sister for a moment and see if I can find the source of her discomfort."

"Let her do it, Nigel," Amelia replied. "I am curious to see how well she can do this."

Nigel aimed his gun at Randy. "I'm warning you, if this is a trick to get your hands on Amy so you can hurt her with one of your Indian tricks, I'll put this shot right through your head."

"Fine. If it will set your mind at ease, Nigel, I will only touch her with my left hand."

Amelia stepped closer to the bed so Randy could reach her. As her fingers grazed the woman's pale cheek, Randy closed her eyes and concentrated on the alien feelings rushing into her mind. "Your head is aching very badly. There is great pressure throbbing across your brow and reaching up from the back of your neck. Your stomach is queasy, and you sometimes feel feverish or develop chills. Even using your eyes causes you pain."

Amy pulled away, cradling the pistol she held against her chest. "Dear lord, how do you know all this?" she asked in awe.

"It is a gift from God," Randy replied. "I've used it to help physicians treat patients in Calicut. If Nigel was watching me, he must have seen me go to the mission many times."

"Do you know why I have been suffering? Is there anything I can do to take away the pain?"

Randy took a deep breath to quell her own dizziness and nausea. Not wanting to alarm Amelia with the truth, she carefully selected the words of her answer. "Tension is a great harbinger of pain, my lady. Your head aches because of the strain it is placing on you. The mind as well as the body needs a respite from too much activity. Using your spectacles more often could help alleviate the problems with your eyes."

Chuckling, Nigel shook his head. "I applaud your attempt, Randy, but I am not impressed. Of course Amelia is tense and out of sorts. She's been involved in a crime that could put her in prison for the rest of her life if we're caught. Amelia would have to be dead not to be bothered by such a worry."

"But Nigel," Amelia objected, "she described everything that I have been suffering with such accuracy. It was as if she were inside me, feeling the pain with me."

Nigel hugged his sister and kissed her brow. "Don't give her too much credit, dearling. Young Miranda is simply a very clever young woman. I know what's good for you, Amelia, and I won't allow her to sway your good judgment.'' He pushed her toward the door. ''Why don't you go and get dressed, while I take care of things in here? I want to be out of here by daylight.''

From the top of the ridge, James pointed into the valley below. ''There are several cottages down there, Abu, but only the one on the far end seems to be occupied. I can see light through two windows and smoke coming from the chimney. The barn behind it is large enough to conceal a number of horses. I would wager all I own that Randy is being held in that cottage.''

Churning with impatience, Sidra hissed and pawed the ground while Xavier held her lead chain taut.

''It appears Sidra shares your belief, *Huzur*. See how she pulls in that direction. If given the chance, I suspect the creature would be across the valley and into that house before anyone could stop her.''

James shook his head. ''We can't allow that to happen, Abu. Instruct Xavier to keep Sidra up here while you and I go down to the cottage for a look around.''

A cloud was passing over the moon, shadowing its light as the two men approached the cottage. Securing their mounts behind the barn, they entered the old structure and discovered several horses and a black coach. There were no emblems on the doors of the coach, but it seemed too fine a vehicle for people living in such modest circumstances to own.

James and Abu circled the cottage on foot. As they came to a window that was roughly shuttered with planks, they heard a familiar voice taunting someone inside the house.

''You're such a brave man, standing there with a pistol aimed at me, Lieutenant. You're nothing but a loathsome coward!''

At that moment a prickle of awareness shot through Randy,

and she knew James was close by. Hoping to stall for time until he arrived to rescue her, she decided to distract Nigel by nudging his temperamental ego.

"Well, at least at this range you shouldn't miss the target as you've done countless times before. Perhaps your vision is as poor as Amelia's and you need spectacles to see what you're firing at."

Nigel glared down at her. "There was a time when I could have bested anyone in marksmanship. But then I was set upon by that damned beast of yours and was maimed for life." He lifted his damaged hand for her to see. "This and the terrible scars on my face are what that animal did to me. The loss of this finger throws off my aim and nearly cost me my life when the wound festered and refused to heal properly."

Grabbing the headboard for support, Randy tried to ignore the weakness enveloping her. "Don't blame my pet for defending me. If you hadn't come into my room to murder me, Sidra would never have attacked you. It was your own greed and that of your saintly sister, Amelia, that caused your pain and suffering."

"Leave my sister out of this!" Nigel balked, pointing the gun at her. "You don't know the hell she has been through. Amy is an angel who was brutalized by our uncle, who beat me when I tried to keep him from her bed. He sated his lust on her and got her with child. When the midwife rid her of his babe, an infection set in and Amy was left infertile and nearly died."

"So you and Amelia murdered the baron."

Nigel shook his head. "Not murder, self-defense. The old blackguard was in need of cash, so he negotiated a marriage between Amy and the Duke of Maidstone for a sizable price. My sister knew problems would arise because of her lack of a maidenhead, but the baron insisted. I couldn't let Amy be shamed, so I helped her get rid of our uncle."

"But that didn't work out either."

"No. We were left with nothing, and Amy had no choice

but to go through with the wedding.'' Nigel's blue eyes took on an icy sheen. ''Richard Wentworth was more than piqued when he left his marriage bed. He shouted at her, claimed he had been cheated. She tried to tell him about the baron then, but he refused to listen. Poor Amy was miserable. Her husband wouldn't touch her and she had only me to comfort her. A few months later, he found us together. Rather than cast me out and disgrace himself before his peers, the duke purchased my commission in the army. Using his wealth and position, he saw to it that I was never posted in England ever again,'' Nigel admitted bitterly.

Getting into the cottage took a little more time than James had anticipated. The lock on the entry door was old, but well oiled. It took Abu several minutes to pick it open with the narrow point of his dagger.

An oil lantern on a shelf near the door showed that the small parlor was sparsely furnished with a threadbare settee and a rocking chair. There were remnants of a meal on the kitchen table and a low-burning fire in the hearth. The sound of voices led James and Abu to the small bedroom at the rear of the house.

The sight of Randy sitting on the bed talking to a tall, dark-haired man filled James with a modicum of relief. She was very pale, weaving slightly, but to him she had never looked lovelier. It was only the gun her captor was waving about that kept James from rushing to her side. Tossing Abu his coat, he pressed himself to the wall and watched for a chance to disarm the man without endangering Randy further.

Randy sighed. ''So because you feel guilty about deserting your sister, you murder innocent people to make it up to her.''

''It wasn't guilt, but love,'' Nigel defended himself. ''I love Amelia and will do anything to help her. Even if it means killing you and your entire family.''

"Love doesn't excuse the fact that your sister's needs have made you a murderer, Nigel. How can you live with yourself?"

A smirk filled with maniacal pride settled on Nigel's face as he raised his pistol toward her and cocked the hammer. "After the life I have been forced to lead, it gets easier all the time. Farewell, Randy."

A split second later, the room exploded into sound and motion. Randy threw herself away from the weapon and hit the back of her head against the headboard as James burst in and knocked Nigel to the floor. While the two men pummeled one another, Abu hurried to his stunned mistress's side. Edith began to scream. Without warning, she rose from her chair and began kicking Nigel in the back with her foot.

"Ye nasty bugger! I hope ye go to hell for yer crimes," the old woman screeched.

"Abu," James shouted over his shoulder. "Get this woman out of here before she gets hurt."

The Indian moved quickly, yet not fast enough to prevent Edith from being caught in the fray. Nigel whipped up his arm and struck her, sending her crashing to the floor with them. While James averted his opponent's blows and wrestled him for the weapon, the old woman did her best to inflict pain on the man she had raised from childhood. Abu joined the melee and pulled her from the battle as Nigel succumbed to the beating and his pistol skittered across the floor.

James stood, dragging a badly bruised and battered Nigel up beside him. "You bastard! I could kill you and your sister for what you've put Randy through. Get his gun for me, Abu."

"I think not." A soft but menacing female voice spoke out from behind him.

James turned to find Amelia, dressed in a prim black gown, standing next to the bed pointing a cocked pistol at Randy's brow. "Step away from my brother or I will shoot your lady," she warned. "I have no qualms about killing her. That Randy is barely conscious will only make my task easier."

Casting a glance at Abu, who stood in the corner with Edith,

James cursed himself for the helplessness of their situation. Nigel's pistol was on the floor beside the bed while his weapon was in his coat, which Abu had left in the kitchen. He backed away from Nigel and watched as Randy moaned and struggled to sit up.

"James, is that you?" she whispered, trying to center her vision on him.

"Yes, that's your heroic husband, for all the good it will do you," Nigel sneered, wiping the blood from his split lip on his shirtsleeve. He took the pistol from Amelia and took her place beside the bed. His free arm wrapped around Randy's neck, pulling the dazed woman against him. "Now, Grayson, if you want to see your precious wife again, I would suggest that you get in that corner with your man and let us leave peacefully. One false move on your part before we are safely away, and I will put a shot through this rather lovely head of hers."

"What makes you think that others aren't outside surrounding this cottage, Reynolds?" James asked, trying desperately not to look at Randy or notice the pain that was showing on her face.

Nigel chuckled. "Because I know what kind of a man you are, James Grayson. An arrogant nobleman who fancies himself capable of rescuing his love all on his own." He hauled Randy from the bed to the doorway, dragging her chained feet on the wood floor. "If you had arrived with a score of men, you would have attacked this cottage and caught us by surprise. Thank God that you're such a predictable fool. Grab my other pistol from the floor, Amy, and let's get out of here."

As Amelia moved away from her brother, a bloodcurdling roar erupted from the kitchen. Nigel spun around to face what was behind him and raised his gun. Terror was etched on his frantic features. Randy delivered a hard blow to his wrist with the side of her hand, knocking the loaded weapon to the floor. When Nigel bent to retrieve it, James made use of the distraction to run across the room and pull Randy from his grasp. At that moment, a large orange-and-black specter propelled itself through the doorway and crashed into Reynolds, taking the screaming man down to the floor with a single blow.

Nigel flailed his arms, but there was no way he could protect himself from Sidra. The usually quiet beast growled and snarled loudly, tearing into him with her claws. From the safety of James's embrace, Randy shouted orders to her pet to stop the attack, but the tiger continued to snap her teeth and massive jaw near Nigel's throat.

"Stop him!" Amelia shrieked in horror. "That animal is trying to kill my brother!"

When no one moved to aid Nigel, Amelia picked up the gun from the floor. Squinting her eyes to focus, she hastily took aim at the large cat and pulled the trigger. It was only when Sidra suddenly leaped off her silent victim that the result of Amelia's action became evident.

Nigel's pale blue eyes stared sightlessly at the ceiling. He was bloodied and torn from the animal's attack, but it was the bullet lodged in his brain that had ended his life.

Amelia dropped to the floor beside him, cradling his face to her bosom. "Poor sweet Nigel! Look what they have done to you, dearling," she wailed. Tears coursed down her face as she cried and rocked him in her arms. "It's all their fault, but don't you worry. I will make them pay for taking you away from me. They won't get away with this, I promise, Nigel. I promise . . ."

Xavier wrapped Nigel's body in a blanket and carried it out as Edith searched the cottage for the keys to the manacles. Abu tied Amelia's hands together and led her from the room while she cried and cursed them all for killing her brother.

Sitting on the edge of the bed with James, Randy shook her head at Amelia's piteous display. "She blames everyone but herself. Nigel may have been the one who murdered my father and attempted to kill me, but he was only acting as her puppet. He would have done anything she asked."

James hugged her close. "Amelia is deranged, my love. I'm afraid her insanity will land her in Bedlam for the crimes she has committed instead of the gallows. But even twenty or thirty years in that wretched place won't make up for the harm she has inflicted on you and your family."

Randy shook her head. Tears pooled in her eyes. "Amelia will be dead within a few months. To prove my abilities to her and Nigel, I touched her and discovered that she has a large growth inside her head. Besides impairing her vision and causing extreme pain, it is killing her. I can't help wondering if this growth was responsible for her dementia or whether her terrible abuse as a child was to blame for her actions."

"Who's to say, sweetheart? Ultimately, God will be the one to judge Amelia." James gently raised Randy's face with his hand. "The only thing that concerns me is that you are all right. Have you any idea how worried I have been about you?"

"You were really worried about me?"

"Of course I was. When I discovered the woman I love was abducted, I—"

"You love me?"

The disbelief and hope James saw on Randy's face made him sigh. "Of course I love you. You don't think I would marry a woman I didn't love, do you?" When he leaned down to take the doubt from her eyes with a kiss, she surprised him by bracing her hands against his chest and pushing him away.

"James, I have something to tell you."

He smiled at her wariness and kissed the tip of her nose. "I know what you're going to say, my love. You want to tell me that you love me, too."

Randy blushed. "No, that's not what I was going to say."

"Then you don't love me?"

She began to nod, then suddenly shook her head. "Of course I do. But that's not what I wanted to tell you—"

James feigned a frown. "Didn't you want me to know that you loved me?"

"I—um, of course," Randy sputtered, throwing her hands

up in surrender. "It's just that . . . oh, how can I say it? We're not really—"

James put his finger to her lips and halted her words. "If you are going to say that we are not married because that bloody magistrate in Calicut was recalled, I am going to turn you over my knee and warm your bottom for being a fool."

Smiling at her confusion, he stroked her cheek with his hand. "You, Miranda Juliet Grayson, are *my wife,* the keeper of my soul, the better half of my being. No silly piece of paper or government dictate can change that."

"But legally the marriage is invalid," she explained. "You don't have to stay with me, James. I have thought it all out. If you want to take up with your first love, Caroline, now that she's widowed, I won't stop you."

His unexpected laughter made Randy scowl. She poked him in the ribs with her elbow. "James, I am making you a very generous offer and you're laughing at me."

When she moved to poke him again, James grabbed her hand and fought to control his levity. "Now, Randy, I wasn't laughing at you, sweetheart. I just don't know where you got the idea that I was ever in love with Caroline. I admit I was a bit enamored of her years ago, but I was never in love with her. You, and you alone, are the only woman I have ever truly loved."

Randy was clearly astonished by his declaration. "But I sensed the emotions in you when you spoke of Caroline. Seeing her at the opera sent you into a highly impassioned state. You could barely keep your eyes off her."

"Evidently you misunderstood my feelings, sweetheart. What you thought was love and adoration for Caroline was actually hatred and a deep thirst for revenge. It was only when I knew how much I loved you that I realized my negative sentiments for that woman weren't important anymore."

"Are you sure you don't want to marry Caroline?"

James shook his head. "Positive. Besides, after your uncle gets his marriage annulled, he plans on marrying Caroline. It seems Richard attended Wexler's funeral last year and fell in love with his widow.''

''But I saw you kissing Caroline in the study.'' A frown creased her brow. ''Or was she kissing you?''

He brought his forehead down against Randy's and scowled into her eyes. ''What will it take to convince you that the only woman I want for my wife is you?''

Sidra hissed, drawing their attention to where she was curled up on the floor at their feet. She nudged Randy's leg with her nose before rubbing her head against James. A deep, purring sound emanated from the tiger's throat when James reached down and scratched her satiny ears.

''See, sweetheart, even Sidra likes me. How can you resist being married to a man who gets along with your best friend?''

Randy smiled and wrapped her arms around his neck. ''It was never a case of resisting you, James Grayson. I just didn't want to stay with a man I had trapped into marrying me.''

''You can't trap a willing victim, sweetheart. And you certainly won't find anyone more willing than I am.'' His playful grin grew into one filled with expectation as he drew her into his arms. ''How long do I have to wait before you say the words?''

''That depends,'' she countered, nibbling on his neck. ''How long will I have to wait to be married to you? Thanks to Amelia, we missed our wedding. Nana said the church was booked straight through the summer.''

James growled at her teasing. ''Then I will abduct the bishop when we reach London and have him marry us at home. One way or another, I plan on making you my wife *legally* as soon as possible. Does that answer your question?''

Randy cradled his face in her hands. There was no mocking or teasing in her clear golden eyes. ''I love you, James Grayson. With all my heart and soul, I will love you for the rest of my life. Are those the words you were waiting to hear?''

Like the keys to a prison, her response freed James from the doubts and mistrust that had become such a part of him since the duel in the meadow. "Oh, yes, Mira, those were the words."

Words were forgotten as he captured her lips in a kiss that was filled with love and unguarded emotions. Whether it was fate or Abu's explanation of karma that brought them together, or just a well-meaning grandmother trying to play matchmaker, James didn't care.

Randy loved him, and each and every day, he planned on thanking God for bringing this special woman into his life.

Chapter 22

In spite of his boast to abduct the bishop, it was three weeks before James and Randy finally were married. Between their families demanding a grand wedding befitting the occasion, and various complications brought on by Amelia, there had been no way to avoid the delay. Viscount Ryland and his bride were formally joined in matrimony on the sunny morning of May the first, with most of the *ton* in attendance.

It was only after the ceremony that Richard Wentworth, who had escorted his niece down the aisle, informed the couple that their original wedding in Calicut had been deemed valid after all. Thanks to his intercession and the aid of his peers, the magistrate's recall orders were temporarily rescinded and then reinstated, to accommodate the date of their first wedding.

Randy and James were in their cabin on board the *Diana* that night, heading toward the Ryland estate, when they discovered something else the Duke of Maidstone had done.

James placed several newspapers on the dining table. "Can you believe that your uncle did this and never mentioned a word of it to either of us? Thanks to the story he sent to all the dailies, everyone in London knows we were married in Calicut and that we were only renewing our vows for the benefit of our families who had missed the nuptials in India."

"Don't be hard on Uncle Richard," Randy said as she tied the belt to her dressing gown around her already thickening middle. "Evidently, he doesn't want anyone questioning the arrival of our child in December."

Pulling back his chair, James lifted Randy onto his lap. "I knew the duke was always concerned with society's opinion of his family, but I didn't think he would go to this much trouble to protect it."

"More than anything, I think my uncle did it to please Nana. Ever since my kidnapping, those two have become very close." She cuddled against her husband and sighed. "Nana and Richard have been acting like a real mother and son. It's regrettable that it has taken them so many years to get together.

"When Richard was a child, he resented the woman his father had replaced his mother with. Years later, when he was old enough to deal with those feelings, Amelia did her utmost to keep the two of them apart. If anyone is to blame for their continued estrangement, it was Amelia."

James shook his head. "She certainly knew how to gain Nana's sympathy with her tales of Richard's abuse."

Randy shivered. "Oh, yes, Amelia was very clever about it. One day at Mirage, she taunted Richard into striking her, knowing Nana would be watching from the window. The bruises we saw on her that morning in London she had inflicted on herself when she tore apart his library looking for her journals." A smile curved her lips. "Amelia never suspected that Uncle Richard had entrusted her diaries to your grandfather, Geoffrey Carlisle."

James hugged Randy and kissed her brow. "Poor Richard. All that work hiding journals, paying investigators, courting the favor of the *ton,* and for what? A trial that will never take place."

"They certainly can't prosecute a dead woman. I knew the

growth in Amelia's head was killing her, but I never imagined that she would die so soon. One night in that sanatorium and she passed away in her sleep.''

''Amelia's death saved your uncle from the degradation of appearing in court to testify against her. The gossips would have had a free-for-all with that kind of fodder.''

''Won't those same gossips be astounded when Uncle Richard returns from his trip to the continent next fall with a new bride?'' Randy laughed. ''And I wouldn't be surprised if Caroline is carrying a child of her own by then. After years of being alone, Uncle Richard is eager to start a family.''

James rested his hand on the slight swelling of her abdomen. ''Speaking of starting a family, how is my heir doing today? Has my son been causing you any problems today?''

''No, our son or *daughter* has behaved very well, and I am feeling wonderful,'' Randy replied with a smile. ''Jarita said that I am very fortunate that my nausea has stopped so soon. But your mother warned me that it could start up again.''

''With five children, I suppose Mama knows about such things.'' His hand began to stroke her belly. ''By chance did you discuss anything else about having babies with my mother?''

Randy could see the sensual hunger in his eyes. After weeks of sleeping apart in his mother's home for propriety's sake, she was just as ravenous for making love as he doubtlessly was. But a small part of her couldn't resist teasing him first.

''Oh, yes. Your mother was quite helpful. She reminded me to eat properly and to get plenty of rest.''

James frowned. ''Mama didn't offer you advice on—um, being active with your husband?''

Randy struck a thoughtful pose, then she nodded. ''Now that you mention it, Cat did tell me exercise is important. She even suggested that I take walks with you every day. Is that what you are talking about?''

''Well, not really.'' Obviously unsure how to proceed, James averted his eyes from her gaze and let his fingers lightly trace her breast through the velvet of her robe. "I was rather hoping Mama would tell you about some of the other things we enjoy doing together. You know, without endangering the babe."

The wistful tone of his voice caused Randy to take pity on him. Putting her lips close to his ear, she whispered, "If you are trying to ask me if I am able to make love, the answer is a resounding yes, James."

His head snapped up to look at her. "Are you sure making love won't prove harmful to you or the child, sweetheart? I love you too much to risk hurting you because of my male needs."

Smiling, Randy wrapped her arms around his neck. She shifted her hips seductively and felt the proof of his desire growing hard beneath her. "According to your mother, James, my passionate nature will require almost constant attention during the next few months. It seems breeding women can be quite insatiable. Do you think you are man enough to handle *those* needs, husband mine?"

James laughed at her challenge as he untied her belt and slipped his hand beneath her robe. He cupped the warm globe of her breast with his palm. "If I'm not, Mira, my love, then I will die trying."

"Are you saying that I could be the death of you, James?"

His mouth fell over hers then, tasting, exploring, and possessing her before he raised his eyes to meet hers. "Not likely, my love, but wouldn't that be a glorious way to go?"

Much later that night, James sprawled across the bed with Randy, happily replete from their lovemaking. He could feel contentment and satisfaction flowing through him like a potent drug. He was a changed man, and the reason for his transformation was lying in his arms.

"Who would have thought my business trip to India would give me such a treasure?" he mused to himself.

"James, what are you thinking about?"

The sound of Randy's voice in the darkness startled him. "I thought you were sleeping, my love."

"How can I sleep when I feel your emotions racing through you? What's the matter? Are you worried about something?"

James chuckled and hugged her closer. "My only worry is being a good husband to you, Randy. I never want you to regret leaving India and marrying me."

Brushing a kiss to his chest, Randy gave him a reassuring pat with her hand. "Then you have no worries at all, my lord husband. I may have strange talents, a menagerie of wild pets, and a household of servants who are more like my family, but I am also an extremely happy woman. You are my soulmate, and you make me complete. My name should be Content. Now, go to sleep, James. I need my rest."

A thought suddenly crossed his mind. "Randy, I know it's months away yet, but have you considered a name for our son?"

He felt Randy nod against him. "Yes. At first I thought about naming our son after my father, but I changed my mind."

"Jonathan Collins Grayson would be a fine name. What's wrong with it?"

"Nothing," she replied. "Jonathan Collins is a very fine name; it just wouldn't belong to our son. I was named for my grandmother. It was an honor, but I never really felt that it was appropriate for me. I want my children to have names of their own."

James rubbed her back. "All right, so we won't name our son after your father. What other names have you been thinking about for our son?"

"Something strong and masculine. Like Balin or Haidar."

James scowled at his wife in the dark. "Aren't those Hindi names? One day our son is going to be an earl. He should have a name befitting the English or Irish heritage of our family."

"But I like those names," Randy objected. "Balin means mighty soldier and Haidar is Muslim for lion. These names remind me of the life I led in Calicut and the people I came to love over the years.''

''That's all well and good, sweetheart, but I must insist on this,'' James said tersely. ''Our son will have a name like Edward Michael or William Brian. Good, strong names, depicting his proud ancestry and noble family. There will be no swaying me on this issue.''

''Well, James, I can be just as stubborn as you,'' Randy reminded him. ''Somehow we will find a compromise.''

And they did.

Their baby was born on December the first and they named her India Erin.

Epilogue

Ryland Estate
April 2, 1833

Sunlight was shining through the window, warming the chilly morning air in the nursery. From her place beside the cradle, Sidra watched her newest charge sleeping.

This cub is small and has little hair. Her roar is loud, yet she cannot move without aid. But my lady seems to cherish this cub with all her heart, so I will care for it as well.

The tiger rolled her aching shoulders and stretched out on the carpeted floor. The sun felt good on her fur. Age and old injuries had left her a bit slower, but nothing could weaken her determination to be ever vigilant of her duties.

A squeak of protest came from the cradle. Beneath the pink wool blankets, the little one awoke, her tiny hands flailing in the air. Sitting up, Sidra looked into the bed. The eyes that met hers were gold, like her lady's. A toothless smile curved the little one's small bowed mouth.

So, you are happy to see your Sidra again. That pleases me, because I plan to be with you for a very long time. Yes, my sweet little cub, a very long time. . . .

Dear Reader,

I hope you enjoyed reading *Golden Fire* and meeting James, Randy, and Sidra. Creating them was a genuine labor of love for me.

If you would like to know about the rest of the Grayson family, my next book is about James's parents. The story of Catherine and Miles shows how an angry young nobleman and an infamous lady outlaw start out as sworn enemies and fall in love. *The Hellcat* will be published in May, 2000.

If you would like to write to me or learn about my future releases, I can be reached at P.O. Box 16434, West Palm Beach, Florida 33416.

Yours always,
Susan Grace

Put a Little Romance in Your Life With
Janelle Taylor